LINDA SANDIFER

EMBRACE THE WIND

ZEBRA BOOKS
KENSINGTON PUBLISHING CORP.

ZEBRA BOOKS

are published by

Kensington Publishing Corp.
475 Park Avenue South
New York, NY 10016

First Printing: April, 1993

Printed in the United States of America

In the Dark of the Moon,
Through Silver Ghost Shadows she roams.

Chapter One

Wyoming Territory

Matt Riordan stared into the campfire, knowing it was a foolish thing to do. The flickering flames hypnotized his tired mind and made him drowsy. Careless. He'd seldom been careless, and he couldn't afford to be now.

With all his willpower he pulled his eyes from the fire, propped himself up straighter against the trunk of the big pine, and hunched down deeper inside his heavy wool coat. The clouds scudding across the moon made him think of snow. It didn't matter that it was May. Up here in the high country, snow could fall any time. It would be warmer in the lean-to, but if he went inside, it wouldn't be as easy to see movement along the outskirts of his camp.

And something had been out there . . . watching.

As if his very thoughts had summoned the mysterious visitor, he suddenly heard a faint sound from the depths of the forest. His muscles bunched the length of his body, and his sleepiness vanished. From reflex alone, his hand moved to the butt of his Colt revolver, ready for whatever—or whoever—was out there. He didn't recognize the sound that had alerted him, but he knew without a doubt that he was no longer alone. Gradually, he realized it wasn't the presence of a wild animal that he felt tonight. No. Even as the night wind blew cold across his face, he sensed the stirring warmth of the woman. He was certain it was *her* burning gaze that once again watched him from the shadows beyond the firelight.

He didn't want to frighten her so he stayed as still as death itself, hoping she would come closer. Over the heavy thudding of his anxious heart, he listened for a footfall, for the faint rustle of her black braids against her soft doeskin blouse, even for the unlikely snap of a twig beneath her moccasins.

Why did she return time and again and yet never step from the darkness? If she feared him, what kept her coming back? Did she have the insight to know that he was searching for her—this woman he hoped was Sky McClellan? And, if she did know, then did she merely mean to provoke him, to torment him, and make his search so frustrating and difficult that he would give up and leave these mountains that were her domain?

He strained his eyes but saw nothing at all in the dark forest. He shifted his gaze to the orange dance of the campfire's flames.

His heart leaped in his chest. His breath caught and held.

Across the licking tongues of the fire gleamed the

yellow eyes of a gray-white wolf. The animal was only twenty feet away, crouching on its stomach, watching him.

In an instant, his revolver was in his hand, but the wolf seemed to know his intent and bared its fangs; a deep snarl rumbled in its throat. It lifted its magnificent body to full height, and the hair on its back stood on end. It seemed unafraid of the fire, but it also seemed satisfied to keep its watchful distance. Matt was surprised at its boldness and wondered if it was rabid.

A movement in the trees swept into Matt's peripheral vision. He wanted to follow the movement but he feared taking his eyes off the wolf. The animal remained motionless and Matt's gaze was drawn from it to the darkness of the woods as if pulled there by a magnet. If the woman was out there, he wanted to see her again. And he had to speak to her . . . question her.

There was a suggestion of something white drifting through the trees almost like a filmy strand of smoke, but there was no sound save the growl in the wolf's throat and the pounding of Matt's own heart. He squinted against the night, seeking the tall, slender form of the woman whom he had seen fully but once before. Unfortunately, the moon had shrunk to a crescent this past week and offered little light through the shroud of the tall pines. He waited, but whatever had caught his eye seemed to have been only an illusion.

He jerked his attention back to the wolf.

It was gone.

His gaze darted over the shadowy perimeters of

the camp, and he wondered uneasily if the beast had circled the fire and planned to spring at him from the dark.

An unnatural silence settled over the Wind River Mountains, and the cold chill rushed over him again, chasing away that temporary warmth he had felt at what he believed to have been the woman's presence. Perhaps it had been the wolf's presence he had felt and not hers at all.

He came to his feet and peered into the pockets of darkness between the stately trunks of the mountains' sentinels. He heard only three distinct sounds; the gurgling stream nearby, the crackling fire, and the distant, eerie cry of a night bird far away in another ravine. Whatever presence had been with him only moments before was gone, along with the wolf.

It seemed a sacrilege to interrupt the stillness of the night, but he did, lifting his voice to a normal tone as if speaking to someone from across the campfire. "Stay and talk to me," he said. "I'm your friend. I need to speak to you, Sky McClellan. It's important. I won't hurt you."

His voice thudded dull and alien against the emptiness, and then vanished into the black depths as mystifyingly as everything else had.

He went to the opposite side of the fire. There was a slight indentation in the grass where the wolf had lain. At least he had not imagined *that*. Perhaps what he'd seen in the forest was the wolf's mate, or others in a pack. Had he therefore dreamed the woman because he needed to find her? Or because her elusiveness was beginning to intrigue him in a way he couldn't understand? Surely he wasn't losing his sanity because of this futile search that had gone on for much too long?

He left his position by the tree and went to his lean-to. A sixth sense assured him that he was completely alone now. He looked across the fire to where the wolf had been. He didn't expect it to come back — it had satisfied its curiosity. But his own was still very much piqued by the woman.

He considered sleep, but plans for the daylight crowded his thoughts and gave him no rest. As usual, he would search the perimeters of his camp for some sign of the woman just as soon as the sun gave its light. He would find something that verified his suspicion that she had been watching him these many nights. Soon she would leave something behind that would give him solid proof he wasn't imagining her. He would find a bead, or possibly some fringe from her doeskin blouse, maybe even a track. With patience he would find her. For only a ghost could vanish into thin air.

The old chief sat cross-legged in the center of his tipi. His hair hung long and gray past his shoulders, and his face bore the weathered lines of age. But his youthful eyes and tall physique were those of a man much younger than eighty — the age which he must surely be.

His regal posture insinuated that his words and his laws were not to be disputed either by his people, or by his visitors. From the many exploits of battle painted on the inner walls of the tipi, anyone could see he had rightfully earned his position as chief of the Wind River Shoshoni, a position he had held now for over forty years. And indeed, he still ruled his people with a strong hand, even though they had long ago been relegated to a reservation.

He held his mackinaw blanket around his shoulders. But it was from habit only, for a small fire swayed at his feet and the sun lit the cylindrical hide walls of the tipi, making its interior bright and warm.

One old hand released the corner of the mackinaw and slid across the new wool of the red blanket which Matt had brought as a gift. "Much good. *Je vous remercie,*" he said in an odd mixture of English and French, as though he considered the two languages one and the same. "But I cannot tell you what you want to hear, Matt Riordan, detective for Pinkerton."

Matt's eyes never left the open countenance of the intelligent face. "Sky McClellan may know who has been killing the settlers in Long Moon Valley, Chief Washakie. It's important that I find her."

A trace of cynicism emerged in the chief's black eyes. "But it is not important that your great white chief in Cheyenne finds out who steals our cattle?"

Washakie's English by itself wasn't fluent, but intermixed with the French and Shoshoni; following all three languages, Matt was able to understand what he said. He hadn't been briefed about the problems on the reservation, but it didn't surprise him that the Indians' cattle were being rustled right along with the settlers'. The Indians tended to treat

10

their cattle like they did the buffalo and allow them to wander at will.

"I'm sorry you're having this problem, Chief Washakie," he said. "I'll bring it to the governor's attention when I see him again. I can make no promises for his actions, though. I have no power over his decision."

Washakie measured Matt in a deep and thorough manner. At last he nodded his head and said, "Few white men have tongues not forked, Matt Riordan. Your eyes tell me you speak truth."

"I know you are an honest man, too, Chief Washakie. You're known among our people as such. Will you tell me then what you know of Sky McClellan?"

The chief's face remained in serious repose for some moments. "I know more of her mother, Chilsipee," he finally replied. "She was of our people, and of the French. Her father was a French trapper who lived with our people until he died. Chilsipee married Charles McClellan, a man who looked much as you do with yellow hair and eyes the color of the sky. They went into the valley of the Long Moon to live and raise cattle. They were all killed seven summers ago. Some say the *egenayfi*—the girl, Red Sky—escaped into the mountains. I do not know."

Matt hadn't known that the girl was also part French, not that it mattered. When Cameron Welch, the territorial governor, had hired the Pinkerton Detective Agency to find Sky McClellan, it had only been mentioned in passing that her family was all dead and that she was part Shoshoni. Matt had thought no more of it. At the time it had merely been

11

another assignment, but now anything he could learn about the elusive woman was one more piece of information he relished.

He waited for Washakie to continue, but the old chief apparently had no intention of disclosing anything further.

"If Sky's mother was of the Shoshoni," Matt prodded, "then are there any relatives here on the reservation I could talk to?"

Washakie considered it. "Many years pass. Many children are born to Chilsipee's brothers and sisters. They may remember Red Sky. I do not know. But there is Chilsipee's uncle, Many Claws—brother to Red Sky's grandmother. He was fond of Red Sky when Chilsipee brought her to visit. He may tell you what I cannot." The chief rose to his feet. *"Kim.* I will take you to him."

Matt followed the chief outside. Along the river stretched the majority of the Shoshoni dwellings. He noticed that most of the tribe still cherished their tipis, but some had accepted the small government-built houses. To the north, sagebrush flats and rolling sagebrush-covered hills reached for miles until they butted up against more mountains.

Back to the east about a mile away across the broad plain, Fort Washakie lolled in a stand of cottonwoods on the Little Wind River. Cavalry troops were presently stationed there to protect the reservation Indians from marauding bands of Indians from other tribes. Fort Washakie, named in the chief's honor, was also an important supply center.

To the south and west of the Indian encampment, more sagebrush-covered foothills gradually lifted to

12

steeper, broken heights until they became the rugged Wind River Mountains. Pine, spruce, and fir mingled with aspen and circled their middles like a brave's breechcloth. Above timber line, granite peaks rose naked and sharp into the cloudless May sky.

And up there somewhere was the woman he searched for.

Chief Washakie led him through the encampment to a large tipi that bore interesting designs in bright paint of many colors. The main object of interest was the drawing of a huge grizzly bear, the animal held in reverence by the Indians and believed to have much "medicine."

The door flap was down, which was an indication to visitors that they should ask for permission before entering. Washakie did, and a gruff voice responded, *"Yayxi."*

Washakie obeyed the command and lifted the tent flap, bending his tall frame to fit inside. The man who stood before them was shorter than both Matt or Washakie, but he was muscular and well built. The deep lines around his eyes and the creases along his nose and mouth attested to a long life, at least six decades. His broad face, high cheekbones, and dark skin, made it plain that no white blood tainted his veins. It was not, therefore, from his side of the family that Sky McClellan had gotten her French blood.

His long black braids, streaked with gray, came down over his shoulders and were tied with strips of leather. Around his neck hung a necklace made of bear claws that rattled with each movement he made. Like Washakie, he wore a combination of

White and Indian attire. His hat was a traditional white man's hat but sported an eagle's feather. He wore fringed buckskin pants and moccasins, but a red plaid cotton shirt and black vest covered his thick chest.

Unlike Washakie whose benevolent smile had put Matt at ease, Many Claws' dark, cold gaze slid over him suspiciously, but even so he stepped aside to allow their entry. They moved to the north of the omnipresent fire in the center of the tipi and once again settled themselves cross-legged.

A quick glance about the interior of Many Claws' tipi told Matt that he was a shaman, or medicine man. The inner lining of his tipi was also covered with exploits of his life, and it was interesting, but not surprising, to see that he'd killed a number of bears. There was no furniture, save some backrests constructed of limbs and hides. The earth floor was worn flat, swept clean, and partially covered with furs and skins. On the walls hung religious images and other fetishes, as well as a headdress made of buffalo horns and feathers.

Washakie made the introductions, waving a hand toward Matt while speaking the Shoshoni tongue. Matt was able to understand enough to know that Washakie was explaining to Many Claws who he was and the reason he was here.

Solemnity marked Many Claws' eyes and his weathered lips compressed into a stern line. Matt detected a guarded veil descending over the shaman's face, and he had the feeling that his visit here would be fruitless, just as his search in the mountains had been thus far.

"These killings are for many seasons." Many Claws spoke in English much clearer and with a broader understanding of the language than Washakie had. "Why do you not come sooner? It is too late now to capture Chilsipee's murderers and rapists."

"I don't know what happened seven years ago, or why the McClellan case wasn't pursued," Matt replied levelly. "I'm here because the governor is disappointed in the way the local law officials have treated the continued killings and rustling in this area. He wants the lawlessness stopped. Anything you can tell me about Sky McClellan's whereabouts could be beneficial. The governor seems to think she may know something that could help. If she escaped the killers herself, she may be able to identify them."

Many Claws sat for so long in silence that Matt began to wonder if he would speak again. His frustration mounted at the situation. He could try to talk to every relative of Sky's here on the reservation, but he sensed that if Many Claws would tell him nothing, then no one else would either, and he couldn't help but wonder if they were protecting her.

Damn it! Here he was one of the best trackers in the country. He'd spent five years tracking down outlaws from every corner of the West, and yet he could not find one small woman. He had found no solid evidence that she had ever been to his camp the night the wolf had appeared, nor had he felt the disturbing tingle of her presence since. Two weeks had passed while he had searched extensively the area where he believed she was hiding. She had not returned to conduct her strange observation of him as she had nearly every night in the beginning. As time faded, so did the belief that she even existed. If he found nothing soon, he would have to return empty-handed to Governor Welch and the Pinkerton agency.

The shaman's perusal of Matt barely concealed distrust when he spoke again. "Are you with the others who search for Red Sky?"

The question caught Matt off-guard. He had seen other riders combing the mountains, but he had thought they were merely cowboys out looking for stray cattle. So he was not alone in his search for the woman?

He shifted uneasily on the buffalo rug. "How do you know others search for her?" he asked guardedly.

"They were here, as you are. Some even believe it is she who kills the settlers . . . to avenge the deaths of her family."

This information troubled Matt. "Then these men who also search for her could mean to harm her?"

"And you do not?" One gray eyebrow rose as if the shaman was amused.

"I've come only to question her and to take her to Cheyenne under protective custody if she has any information that will help us."

The sage old chief drew the blanket tighter about his shoulders and said nothing. But while Washakie remained calm, Many Claws grew angry and spat, "*Kaig!* Not so! She would mean nothing to you after you had your information."

Matt had tried never to get personally involved in a case. He just did the job the agency sent him to do. But something had happened to make this job different. The nights in the mountains—knowing she was near, knowing she watched him, and seeing her beauty but for one second on a moon-washed night—had caused him to become highly aware of Sky McClellan. She intrigued him. Finding her had become more than a job; it had become an obsession. And now that he knew he wasn't the only one looking for her, he feared for her safety. Her only hope for survival was to stay hidden. But she couldn't stay hidden forever.

"You're wrong, Many Claws," he replied at last. "I would do everything within my ability to make sure she did not meet with harm."

A stubborn set came to Many Claws' jaw and his eyes burned black like chunks of obsidian. His personal opinion hadn't been swayed by Matt's rebuttal, and he didn't like to be told he was wrong.

He scrutinized Matt thoroughly. There was something that distinguished Riordan from other men. Perhaps it was the tailored cut of the black serge coat, vest, and white shirt; or the handsome Stetson shadowing austere lines of a face that revealed no more than what he chose it to reveal. Despite the trail dust covering his person, he seemed well-groomed and carried himself with quiet dignity and confidence, unlike so many other white men who didn't seem to care how dirty or untidy they were.

And perhaps the distinction came from eyes so blue they were almost startling. Many Claws found himself staring into their depths, into a gaze vaguely unnerving, too direct, wary, and even calculating. But the eyes held a quality of truthfulness that was rare for a white man. In the bright blueness swam

17

the sort of knowledge and wisdom that comes only with experience. But there was also a degree of intolerance.

At last, however, it was Riordan's hands and his revolver that drew the main focus of Many Claws' interest. His hands were just like the rest of him — lean and hard, even scarred in a place or two, and the long fingers were undoubtedly quick enough to draw the big gun on his hip before a man could blink. But the gun itself told the true story of Matt Riordan, for the plain wooden grip was worn smooth. It was a gun that did not sit idle in the holster.

From his perusal of the stranger, Many Claws sensed that Riordan was more than capable of his claim to be able to protect his niece. Without being told, Many Claws knew the man held no illusions about life or death, and probably harbored very few sentiments. He was a man who needed no other man. A man who would do what he set out to do.

"You are paid to kill," he said, "but I see no love of killing in your eyes as I did in the eyes of the others who came asking about Red Sky. They wanted to find her — for her own good, they said. But I will tell you what I did *not* tell them, for they were fools and they thought me one, too."

He paused, as if in that moment he might change his mind. But at last he proceeded. "Like you, I have seen the young woman who moves with the wind. A great legend she has become among our people. On some dark nights she has come to me, as she did you. She sits across the fire. There, where you sit. And she says nothing. But if I blink my eyes, she is gone, and only the smoke from the fire remains.

"Some say it is Red Sky McClellan, Chilsipee's daughter. But you must forget about the Woman of the Wind, the way the others must. She cannot help you find the men you seek." His eyes filled with regret and much sadness. "You see, *meahtivo* . . . she is not really there."

It took a moment for the shaman's words to become lucid. The night of the wolf returned in vivid detail, and with it, the same eerie chill as before. Matt was not a man to be frightened or alarmed, even to be moved by most things. A man who had seen and done as much as he had could not be surprised, and the words of others did not normally sway his thinking. But oddly enough, at this very moment, he wished that he, too, had a blanket about his shoulders like Washakie's to chase away the unexpected, haunting chill.

The woman had to be alive! My God, he had seen her with his own eyes!

Yes, but she had vanished like the smoke from the fire.

He stood up slowly, as if in a trance. What had he really seen out there in the mountains? Unlike the superstitious Indians, he did not believe in spirits who walked the earth.

"I saw someone," he said, his voice level and sure. "If it wasn't Sky McClellan, then it was someone else. And I intend to find out who."

Many Claws rose to his full height, his eyes flashing angrily as they bore into Matt. "Then beware, Matt Riordan, for just as the killers think she is a threat to their secrets, they may think the same of you. Now, I will speak no more of this." He waved a weathered hand toward the tipi's door. "You go now. It has been many seasons since Sky McClellan walked the Death Trail. No longer does she embrace the bosom of Mother Earth."

The Night Wind whispers,
And I must follow.

Chapter Two

The young woman's moccasined feet moved as soundlessly and lightly through the dark forest as an autumn leaf drifting through the sky to the ground. Following just as quietly was a gray-white wolf, stopping when the woman stopped, moving when she moved.

She paused. Her black eyes were vigilant in the midnight hour, as if it were her innate ability to see all that dwelled in the sunless realm and to know instinctively what was dangerous and what was not. The small creatures of the high country were not afraid of her as she moved along their trails. They stopped to stare after her as she passed — all except the screech owl who winged its way through the darkness, occasionally emitting its quavery, eerie wail.

The wolf moved closer to the young woman and

slid his head beneath her hand to receive her gentle stroke. In a graceful movement, she knelt on one knee and draped her arm more fully across his powerful shoulders. He sat upon his haunches and leaned his body against the fringed deerskin pants that covered her long, slender legs. His gaze was as watchful as hers, for his keen nostrils had once again picked up the scent of the man.

The woman whispered words to the beast, and in an instant, it turned from her and vanished into the night. Alone now, she crept closer to the man's camp, crouching behind the brush until she was but thirty feet from where he slept on the opposite side of the small fire. He had left the mountains for a while, but had returned, and she wondered why.

Beneath the white doeskin blouse, her heart pounded in a strange combination of fear and anticipation at the now-familiar sight of him. Her boldness was foolishness, but her curiosity was consuming. Tonight, she could not see the long, lean form of him as she had on other occasions, and she found herself vaguely disappointed. He slept deep in the shadows, deeper than he ever had before. His blankets were drawn up high on his shoulders, and his black hat concealed the hard, untamed lines of his face. It was a face that captivated her. But surely he was no different from other men, and she would be wise to remember that many of his kind were evil.

Being fully aware of this, she didn't understand then what drove her to come to his fire, time and again, or to watch like a spy from the trees in the broad daylight as he roamed the hills on his horse, a horse that gleamed like copper in the bright afternoon sun. She only knew that when she watched this man, she was fascinated, much in the same way she was on those rare occasions when she had witnessed the great mountain lion moving warily through the forest, alert to all enemies and poised to spring. She knew instinctively that, like the tawny cougar, this man with the golden hair was quietly dangerous. He had no friends — only enemies, only prey. With watchful, somber eyes, he not only moved with the same sensual stealth as that great cat of the mountains, but he seemed to have the same sixth sense that warned him whenever she was near.

His easy, graceful movements, his wild, dangerous beauty, fanned embers not just of caution, but of excitement as well. Something about him made her body tingle with an awareness of herself she had never felt before. Whenever she watched him, her heartbeat quickened and her pulse throbbed peculiarly low where the core of her womanhood lay hidden. At those moments she felt oddly restless and dissatisfied . . . and very much alone.

He was not a trapper, like her mother's father had been. She remembered that black-bearded, bushy-faced man who always sang his songs in French, and laughed and drank too much, and always had bundles of furs loaded on his horses. He had taught her much about trapping and snaring.

He had always smelled unpleasant, but he had never failed to make her laugh.

She remembered in her youth seeing men like the one on the copper horse. Men her father had called professional killers. They were men marked with a grim sort of endurance that drove them until they met success. When she was a child, they came occasionally to Long Moon Valley. Their presence seemed to put a hush over the people, even over the land. And after they had gone, there was always someone to bury.

She wondered if this man had been hired to find her and kill her. Had he somehow found out what she had done?

Even though he reeked of danger the way her grandfather had reeked of castoreum, she could not help being reminded of her father. It was probably only his physical appearance that stirred those remembrances. When she looked upon him, she felt as if she could go home and find everything as it had been in those laughing days when freedom knew no bounds and the words to her songs could be sung to the skies, not held inside in fear of being heard.

But with the pleasant memories, a horror came stealing, threatening to escape from the dark prisons of her mind if she failed to turn the key in the lock for even one moment. It erupted now with disturbing frequency ever since the golden-haired stranger had appeared in the mountains of the Sun-Father.

Suddenly a cold foreboding settled over her. Her

hair prickled and her skin crawled. The sense of unexpected danger made her decide to hasten away from the Yellow-Hair's camp. But even at the thought, a faint noise behind her warned that her decision had come too late. Adrenaline rushed throughout her body as all in one movement she whirled and reached for the knife in her waist scabbard. The Yellow-Hair lunged at her from the darkness. Together they fell backward into the brush with him on top of her. She hardly felt the branches stabbing her fragile flesh as her survival instincts took command of her actions.

She slashed at him with her knife, and he tried to grab her wrists. Oh, how he had tricked her! She should have known he was evil like all the others!

She felt herself weakening as she battled his arms, so much more powerful than her own. In the darkness she barely saw his face. Instead she saw the face of another man, another time, that image held deep and forever in her memory.

"Stop fighting me!" His husky voice boomed at her. "I won't hurt you! I want to talk to you."

She became aware only of the physical struggle in the darkness and the separate struggle being fought in her mind. Why must she relive that other time with that other man? Was she destined to have it happen again and again, not only in her memory but in reality as well?

The hopeless fear returned as the weight of the Yellow-Hair's body nearly suffocated her. His hands were like bands of iron clamping her arms up over her head. The length of his body seared into hers. She felt his strength in every steely sinew from his chest to his ankles, and especially in his thighs pressed against hers. If only she could get her hand free from his, the knife would save her. But he was so very strong, and she was simply no match.

"Esup!" She screamed suddenly. *"Paika! Paika!"*

Too late, Matt Riordan translated the girl's terrified screams. From the darkness a hairy blur of white with snarling fangs hurtled itself through the air and upon him. In an instant, he was down with the beast upon him. His hands automatically went under the wolf's throat as he tried to protect his jugular from the vicious teeth that were determined to rip it open, to kill him just as the woman had commanded. He fought with all the power he had, but seconds seemed like minutes, and every outcome seemed like sure death.

Then the woman cried out again, *"Esup! Wenr! Wenr!"*

The wolf immediately stopped the deadly attack, but stood over Matt, still snarling, intent on keeping him where he was until the woman told him otherwise.

At last she told the animal to go away. With hair still bristled on its back, it lumbered off into the shadows where it waited and watched with gleaming eyes. The woman turned on her heel and headed for the safety of the forest. Matt leaped to his feet and was after her in a second, but the wolf sprang up in his path, its teeth bared again and a low growl rumbling in its throat.

Matt could not let her get away this time. He drew his revolver and the wolf crouched, ready to spring. He knew he was taking a chance, but he called after the woman while keeping his eyes glued to the wolf. "I'll kill the wolf, Sky McClellan, unless you come back. I have something important to talk to you about."

Then he remembered she'd spoken to the wolf in Shoshoni. What if the old shaman had spoken the truth and she *wasn't* Sky McClellan after all? He didn't want to believe that, and he wouldn't, at least not yet. He called to the darkness again, this time in the native tongue.

"Wetuixa! Kaimahanite wazigade! Wait! Don't hide!"

There was no sign of her, and he cursed beneath his breath. The damned wolf would never let him near her, but still he couldn't find it in himself to kill the animal since it belonged to her. He didn't know why he cared about this strange, savage young woman who lived in these mountains all alone. But he did.

Traitorous to his objective, his male blood stirred by merely recalling the fiery, feminine softness of her body beneath his. Yes, she was very much alive, and though it was irrational, he wanted to feel her beneath him again—but not in battle. Definitely not in battle.

The wolf growled with renewed fierceness, as if he had read Matt's thoughts and hadn't liked them. Matt hoped the woman wouldn't leave the wolf, who was obviously her protector.

"I know you're out there, Sky McClellan," he said, calling her bluff. "I'll kill the wolf if you don't come out and talk to me."

He pointed the gun at the animal's head and cocked the trigger. The wolf didn't budge, but flattened its ears as its muscles bunched, preparing for another attack.

The silence stretched for long minutes and Matt was afraid she wouldn't appear, even at the risk of losing her companion. Then from behind him her voice caressed the blackness like lengths of soft velvet and made his skin quiver as if she had laid not her voice upon the night, but rather her lips upon his flesh.

"Esup . . . kim."

The wolf backed away from Matt and raced into the darkness. Matt turned in the direction of the voice but there was no one there. His heart thudded wildly. He didn't want her to go. But only God could stop the wind.

"I'm your friend, Sky. *Haynze.* Friends," he called after her gruffly, angrily. "I'm not here to hurt you. Why won't you believe me?"

There was no answer, only the sound of the wind soughing through the pines.

Matt's heart plummeted to his toes. He'd frightened her and lost her. She would never return to his camp again. He knew this as surely as he knew that the night would give way to the dawn. And suddenly he felt oddly alone for a man who had always been that way and never minded it before.

He lifted his arm and looked at his coat sleeve where blood was beginning to soak through. His arm hurt now and he felt the warm blood trickling beneath the cloth and down toward his elbow. Had wolf fangs torn his flesh, or had it been her knife? Now that it was over, he had the unnerving sensation once again that he had dreamed the entire incident. He thought he had felt her body beneath his, but that aura of mystery—that unreal quality about her—still clung like cloying perfume in the calm night air. Could it have been a dream that had simply seemed real? Was tonight's reality, tomorrow's illusion?

With the pain increasing now, he walked back to camp and shed his clothes from the waist up in order to dress the wound. He examined the wound by the firelight. It was not a knife cut but rather a fang wound. The fact that it had bled quite a bit was good; it would help cleanse it. He saturated his bandana with whiskey then opened the gash up as much as possible, laying the cloth upon the opening. He gritted his teeth so hard against the pain that it made his head throb. Finally, from his pack, he found the few medical supplies he kept on hand. He smeared black salve on the wound, bandaged it, then pulled his shirt back on. It was chilly, so he reached for his jacket.

And then he saw it—a single strand of hair as black as midnight, as shiny as the crow's wing, as straight as a great warrior's arrow. And it was captured by the button on his coat. The faint light of the stars and the moon, and the distant glow of his small campfire held it separate from the darkness.

Carefully, he closed his thumb and forefinger over it and unwound it from its captor. He held it up and watched it relax and drift down before him, swaying in the faint breeze. It was almost two feet long.

With a satisfied smile, he wound it carefully around his finger until it formed a little circle. Just as carefully, he pushed it off the end of his finger, placed it inside his vest pocket and secured the button.

He lay back on his bedroll, all doubts erased from his mind. He knew instinctively that the Woman of the Wind would never again come near him willingly. But at least he had proof that she had . . . once.

The earth belongs to me.
If I should return to it,
Who would mourn?

Chapter Three

The primroses had barely bloomed when the snow fell again. The heavy white mantle completely covered Red Sky's snares and she found them all empty. Disheartened, she reset them.

At least the snow wouldn't stay this time of year. As soon as the sky cleared, the sun would melt it away. Winter clung to the mountains for seven months of the year, but sooner or later it had to give up its hold, even here.

From her spot hidden in the deep timber, Red Sky glanced up through the snow-laden branches of the pines at the clouds rushing across the mountain peaks.

You can run faster than anything, Sky. Even the clouds before the wind.

Her brother's small voice sounded so loudly and unexpectedly in her memory that she turned, expecting to see him. But as always, there was nothing in the shadows but sun-dappled silence.

Oh, Jarod. Dear, sweet little one. Blond and slender, just like her father had been. No one would have known Jarod was one quarter Shoshoni except for his dark brown eyes and skin that looked perpetually tanned.

Yes, Jarod. I can run faster than anything. I can run so fast my feet will leave the ground and I can soar with the eagles.

No, you can't!

Yes, I can.

No, you can't!

Yes, I can.

The cold infiltrated Red Sky's moccasins. She released the memory and started back to her cave. It was painful to remember, but oftentimes when survival didn't take the foremost thoughts in her mind, there was little else to do.

She wound her way back through the dim forest, knowing that she and Esup were leaving tracks in the wet snow. But Yellow Hair—the name she'd given the man—had left the mountains. She was glad he'd gone. He'd lied to her and tricked her. She was still curious why he had wanted to talk to her, but now she would never know. At least she was safe again and the mountains were hers alone—hers and the animals'. And yet, she didn't understand why this wonderful news made her feel so dispirited.

She stopped short of a snowy clearing in the trees and scanned the surrounding area for signs of danger. Caution had become instinctive to her over the years. Like the creatures of the forest, she could almost smell danger, or anything out of the ordinary.

Very few people came to this region, but recently she had seen not only the man, but a number of cowboys roaming the high country. She thought it irregular since the cattle seldom, if ever, ventured this high up, preferring the openness of the lower ranges. There was a band of wild horses up here. It could be that the stallion had stolen some ranch mares and the cowboys were trying to get them back. Still she had to be careful. Yellow Hair knew she was alive, so somehow her secret had been discovered. Others might come—those who knew she had witnessed their murderous deeds.

She knelt next to Esup, waiting for his keen sense of smell to sniff out a presence other than their own. There was apparently none for he led the way into the clearing at a trot, getting ahead of her and circling back numerous times.

They didn't tarry and were soon in the protection of the pines again. They walked for another half mile, following a stream. When they came to the familiar lake near the cave, they veered away from the trees' protective covering and started the steep climb up the side of the mountain toward a rocky pinnacle that faced south and gave an eagle's view for miles in all directions. The trees thinned out again where a rock slide from centuries ago had thundered down the side of the mountain leaving the area strewn with boulders of all sizes. Already the snow had melted from the rocks, and

Red Sky and Esup left no tracks as they leaped from one rock to the next.

To the untrained eye, the rocky pinnacle looked like nothing more than a sheer wall of granite. But at the western end of it, the massive head wall jutted out in a thick slab and concealed an opening behind it. The narrow opening was invisible from all directions and was well concealed by brush and a few scrubby pine trees that managed to grow between large fissures in the rock. Yet behind the head wall was a cave, about twenty feet by thirty feet in size. The entrance to the cave was too narrow for bears, but it had once been inhabited by mountain lions. Now it had the human smell and the smell of the wolf, and the big cats came no more.

On top of this rocky pinnacle grew more pines and brush and wildflowers, and for many years bald eagles had made the tallest pine their home. They weren't alarmed by Red Sky or Esup, for they had all shared the lofty domain in harmony these many years.

At the entrance to the cave, Red Sky paused to finger the petal of a primrose growing with others in a cubbyhole of some rocks. But she didn't pick it. She never picked flowers unless she needed them for medicinal purposes. She supposed it was something she'd learned at a young age from her mother.

She noticed Esup's ears perk forward as he gazed at the cave entrance. Suddenly he began running around in little circles, smelling the ground. His actions alerted Red Sky to possible danger. Her first thought was that Yellow Hair had come back and had found her dwelling place. She reached automatically for the knife in her scabbard, then Esup bounded almost happily into the cave. She followed cautiously, but the fear left her when she heard the familiar deep voice speaking in Shoshoni to the wolf.

"*Haganiyane,* Esup? How are you? Have you been taking good care of Red Sky for me?"

Red Sky entered the cave. It was always dim inside even with the fire burning. The only source of light, other than that which managed to slip through the narrow entrance, came from a small hole far up in the rock ceiling. It was a place where the rocks did not quite meet overhead and the opening was so small—about the size of a man's fist—that unless light filtered through it at certain times of the day one wouldn't even notice it was there. It was the perfect smoke hole, especially since from the outside the smoke couldn't be easily detected for it had to drift through a clump of brush. The hole was sometimes a nuisance when it rained hard. Water would then penetrate the brush and run along the escarpment right into the hole. On those days, she had to catch the rainwater in a wooden bowl to keep it from splashing over onto her bed of furs.

"*Haganiyane, adah?*"

"*Tsande.*"

"I'm glad to see you," she said, smiling at the man who had made himself at home in her ab-

35

sence. "My supplies are getting low and I caught nothing in my snares today."

Many Claws wrestled playfully with Esup for a few moments, then cuffed him lightly on his furry neck and said, *"Miya.* Go. I cannot play with you all day."

The wolf obeyed the command cheerfully, lumbering to its favorite spot by the fire which crackled with fresh sticks laid there by Many Claws. Above the fire a rabbit stew simmered in a large cast-iron pot that dangled from a crude tripod of green branches.

"I could come no sooner, Red Sky," Many Claws said. "The storm was like an evil spirit lost between worlds and full of anger and desperation."

She nodded, understanding that one didn't set off into the mountains during a snowstorm, even in June. She had been confined to the cave for three days herself until it had ended.

"It looks as if it might snow again," she said. "Maybe you had better not stay long."

Many Claws seemed unconcerned. His eyes were almost somnolent as he stared at the fire and the wolf. "I will not be missed. The tribe knows I go to speak to the Great Mystery. They expect it, so I will stay with you a few days."

Red Sky studied his expressionless face. *"Huuwihyu.* Thank you. I'll enjoy your company. It gets lonely with just Esup. Are you hungry?"

"Oos. Negaidekaxande. I have not eaten, and my stomach yawns as big and empty as this cavern where you dwell."

36

She went to the corner of the cave where a large, flat rock held a washbasin carved from wood. Next to it, another rock of similar size held a clay pitcher of water. She poured a small amount into the basin to wash her hands.

"I have brought what you wanted from Lander," Many Claws said as he watched her.

From a small rack constructed of sticks and leather thongs, Red Sky removed the piece of linen she used for a towel. "Did you get the paper?"

Many Claws reached inside the large pack he'd laid on the cave's floor and one by one emptied out the supplies he'd brought. "Flour, sugar, tea, salt, bacon, beans, thread, needles, potatoes, and"—he grinned broadly and removed the last item, holding it up for her inspection—*"tevope.* Your book of paper. Now you can put the images of the mountains and the animals into the words and the pictures that bring your heart so much joy."

Red Sky's dark eyes glowed with satisfaction. She draped the towel back on the rack and glanced at the items he'd laid on the furs. He hadn't forgotten a thing she'd requested. She cared deeply for Many Claws for numerous reasons, but one reason was because he never failed her.

She lifted the lid from the rabbit stew. The aroma filled the cave, and her stomach growled with renewed vigor.

"Hand me the plates, *adah.*"

The shaman took two tin plates from the corner where Red Sky had her bowls, baskets of food,

37

and miscellaneous items neatly arranged in rows. There was everything from food to herbs to beads for her clothing. She had started with nothing when he had found her wandering in the woods seven years ago, frightened as a wounded fawn and as mute as if a wicked hunter had cut out her tongue. She had been completely unable to speak of the tragedies she'd witnessed. He had come searching for her when news reached the reservation that Chilsipee and her family had all been murdered, except that the body of Red Sky had not been found.

He found her some days later, nearly dead, her clothes almost torn from her, hanging in shreds, and covered with dried blood. Some of the blood had been hers, but most of it had been someone else's. He had feared for her life and had brought her here to keep her safe from further harm. He'd discovered this cave when he was only a boy and it had always been his secret place.

She had never told him what had happened that day. She would say nothing except, "I can't return to the valley. They will kill me if I do."

So Many Claws had watched over her until she had become self-sufficient, and he had kept her secret. She was soon trapping and giving him the furs to trade for things she wanted. But she had never wanted to leave this place. She had always become terrified when he even suggested she seek an alternative to this lonely life of hers.

For a time, the story of her death had been believed and she had been safe. But once again her life was in danger. Once again it was time to talk about moving her from this sanctuary.

Red Sky handed him a fork and tin plate loaded with stew. She also laid a helping of stew in Esup's wooden bowl on the stone floor.

"You still feed the *esup*," Many Claws said, as he did every time he came to visit. *"Ainwambe.* Foolish. He will forget how to fend for himself and become as weak and helpless as the dogs that follow the palefaces."

Red Sky filled her own plate and settled herself on a deer hide, tucking her legs to the side. "He still takes his kill, my uncle. As a matter of fact, he brings it to me and drops it at my feet as if to share it — and there have been times when I've been forced to accept his generosity, for he's a much better hunter than I. You know he's been with me since he was a pup. He watches out for me and protects me. Feeding him when I can is the least I can do to repay him."

Many Claws was adamant. "He is too smart. Too tame."

They ate in silence. When Many Claws set his plate aside his black eyes rested on Red Sky with so much seriousness that her stomach knotted, for she sensed he had something to say she wouldn't be happy about hearing.

After some consideration of his words, he said, "Men have come asking about you, Red Sky. They seem to know you are alive, and I fear for your life. But these men do not trouble me as greatly as the one called Matt Riordan, who rides alone, be-

39

cause I do not think they are smart enough to find you. But this Riordan, with eyes as sharp as the eagle's, could ferret a cunning weasel from its hole, and all because he has the patience and the time to wait. Like a warrior who must always keep food on the table, this Yellow Hair, too, is always astride his pony, weapons in hand, searching. But his elusive prey is not that which can ease the pangs in his stomach. No, his prey is man—and possibly even woman—whom he brings to stand before the paleface courts of justice. He is called a Pinkerton detective."

Red Sky shifted uneasily, remembering the name of the agency from her childhood. It explained why Riordan had that distinct aura that had warned her of danger. Many times in the past her father and other ranchers had spoken of Pinkerton. In secret meetings late at night, she had overheard the men discussing contacting his detective agency to find out who was rustling the cattle. But after her father had been killed, the action was never taken. The name *Pinkerton* itself put fear into people, for anyone employed by that agency had to be even tougher and more relentless than the criminals they set out to find.

"Did he say why he searches for me, *adah?*" she asked quietly, nervously.

Many Claws told her what Riordan had told him and Chief Washakie, then added, "He says he will give you 'protective custody' so you can speak to the white chief in Cheyenne. But I fear if you go with him, you will be cast aside like a broken spear after you have told them all you know. Then the others who search for you will find you and kill you."

"But there's no reason to go with him. I can't tell them anything."

"Those who killed your family do not know this. They believe you remember."

Red Sky wondered if Riordan had told the truth—that he meant her no harm. Maybe he had lied to Many Claws and Chief Washakie. It could be that he really didn't care what she knew about the killers. He might actually be here because he knew what *she'd* done, and was only pretending to be benevolent so he could trap her and take her to the gallows.

"I've seen this man you call Riordan," she said at last, setting her plate aside. "I'm ashamed to say he nearly captured me about a week ago. It was my own fault. I was curious and went much too close to his camp." At Many Claws' startled expression she rushed on, assuring him. "Please don't worry. He must have given up. He didn't even get close to here and now he's left the mountains."

"I do not think so. He is at Fort Washakie buying supplies. I saw him there, but he did not see me." Suddenly he leaned forward and grabbed her hands. "You must leave here, Red Sky! This man will not give up! It is in his eyes, this willpower to go on and on."

Red Sky stared down at the old brown hands encircling her own. "I won't leave, *adah*. I can't!"

"You must! It is no longer safe. Many times I have begged you to let me take you to the Flathead People. I must beg you again. My sister is there and her husband. They have children and grandchildren. She is your grandmother's sister and she will care for you as if you were her own. You could teach school on the reservation there. You could find a man and marry . . . have children."

Red Sky leaped to her feet, tearing herself free from his grasp. Her eyes grew wild with fear. "No! Never!" she cried vehemently. "Besides, the Indian agent there would learn the truth eventually."

Long moments passed between them and Red Sky could not stand the sympathy in Many Claws' eyes. She was happy here. Why didn't he believe her? She turned her back to him, folding her arms across the front of her as if to comfort a pain growing deep inside her. Esup watched their exchange, his head on his paws. At Red Sky's distress, he lifted his head toward her in concern, whimpering.

Many Claws sighed and sat back on his heels. "Can I never make you see that you cannot stay here forever? It is a waste of your life. I have not asked you to tell me what happened in the valley of the Long Moon, Red Sky. I hoped you would tell me in time—when your wounds healed. Now I fear they will never heal until you leave here.

"I know you have turned against the white men because of what they did to your family," he continued, "but do not judge all by a few. Your father was a good man. Your grandfather was a good

42

man. Listen to me and heed my wisdom. You must open your heart to someone besides Esup."

"He will never hurt me or betray me," she said stubbornly.

"No, but he listens to the call of his kind. He loves you, but some day he will go and he will not return."

Red Sky squared her shoulders. "My mother's people are here! My family's spirits roam the mountains with me. You are a medicine man and you understand this, Many Claws. You must know it brings me comfort. This man—this Riordan!— he may find me and I may die, but I refuse to leave this place where my heart is and where my family is buried."

She started from the cave but Many Claws' words delayed her departure. "I cannot live forever, Red Sky," he warned. "Once I was a brave and strong warrior. I was like the grizzly whose enemies, even the hungry wolves, scattered in fear from his path. But, that was many seasons ago and it is I now who moves aside. There will be no one to help you after I walk the Death Trail, my child. No one to keep those wolves from eating your flesh and scattering your bones to the wind. Not because you are not brave, but because they are simply more powerful than you."

Her eyes burned brightly as she looked over her shoulder at him, but Many Claws saw fear as well as defiance in the black pupils. For a moment she was that vulnerable fourteen-year-old girl who had survived the vicious murders and who had survived the wilderness, too. But then her eyes turned hard again and she was very much the woman who could survive without him, without anybody.

"Then let the wolves eat my flesh!" she declared. "What I did was cowardly and shameful, and now you want me to run again. I won't! I will stay here and fight."

"And die, Red Sky?"

She lifted her chin. "Yes, my uncle . . . *die*. If that is what my fate is to be."

The silver light of the full moon stretched the length of Long Moon Valley. Matt Riordan's copper dun, Soldier, moved through the shadows of the pines that bordered the valley on one side. From there the mountains stretched upward, growing in height until they reached the elevated slopes above timberline. The other side of the valley was protected by a long, broad, and irregular hump of hills covered with sage but freckled with pines, aspens, and rocky outcroppings.

He stopped Soldier and the packhorse in the dark shadow of the pines skirting the edge of the ranch yard. Here was where Charles McClellan had brought his French-Shoshoni wife, and here he'd had his children and begun a life that was filled with promise and dreams, but had ended in tragedy.

Governor Welch hadn't told Matt what had happened or why, and Matt hadn't asked. His job had been to come into the mountains to find a woman.

He hadn't been told she might not exist. He hadn't been told that the Indians believed it was her spirit that roamed the mountains. Looking back, if the governor *had* told him these things, he wouldn't have come. He would have laughed at the absurdity of it and asked the agency to find him another job tracking down something more substantial, something real, like killers or rustlers.

Yet here he now stood, in the narrow end of the valley, at the ranch that had been McClellan's and now belonged to a man named Rusty Glassman. From where he sat astride his horse, he wasn't very far from the two-story log house, situated with its back to a sagebrush hill where a few pines and aspens offered shade to the backyard.

The moon lit the weathered gray poles of a swing that stood off to the side of the house, and he envisioned a small, black-haired girl happily swinging there. He wondered what had happened in this peaceful place that had destroyed all those dreams of McClellan's. Many Claws had said something about wanting to bring justice to Chilsipee's murderers and rapists. Had the girl been raped, too, then somehow managed to escape death?

As he pondered these questions, voices of the ranch hands inside the bunkhouse drifted up to him through the quiet night. Two were apparently bickering over something. Then a man came out of the main house and leaned up against one of the large timbers that held up the front porch. A cigarette dangled from the man's mouth. Its burning

45

red tip glowed brightly in the darkness. The moonlight lit the man's tall, broad-shouldered form as he stood there. He, too, was listening to the hired hands. Then he pushed his hat to the back of his head and lifted his gaze to the mountains.

The action brought Matt to sudden attention. Something about the big man stirred the dormant embers of the past, of ten years ago in Texas when he'd nearly died at the hands of Bailey Loring, a man who looked amazingly like this one.

He forced himself to relax. Bailey Loring was dead. He had hung for murder and rustling because of Matt's testimony, and Matt hadn't walked away until he'd seen him swing, and until they'd thrown dirt over his coffin. Now all that remained from those days were the scars and the memories, two things Matt knew he'd carry with him to his own grave.

Yes, Bailey had faced the taut cord of justice, and his son—who couldn't be implicated—had at least been forced to bear the shame of his father's misdeeds. But what had happened to Bailey's granddaughter, Elizabeth, the lovely redhead who hadn't had the courage to tell the truth?

Matt grew cold and bitter at the memory and at the questions about Elizabeth that had often crept into his mind over the years. He'd been so young— barely eighteen—when he'd met her. In all his life, he'd had nothing. No father. No roots. Only a mother who had never wanted him, and who finally abandoned him one night in a cheap St. Louis hotel while he slept. Even though he'd only been thirteen, he'd never tried to find her. He'd just made his own way, jobbing from one town to the next, drifting and spending his nights frightened and half starved under the stars that had been his only friends. In all the years, he had only allowed himself to fall in love once, and that once had been Elizabeth.

Suddenly he turned his horse away from the ranch and headed out of Long Moon Valley, the packhorse following on lead. He'd only come to the valley to get a sense of who Sky McClellan was, thinking that by seeing where she'd lived as a child he might get some insight into the kind of person she was today. Any small clue might help him find her. It was time to wrap this case up and report back to Pinkerton's Denver office, get onto another assignment. He was getting too personally involved in this woman's life. It was making him do too much thinking. And he didn't want to think; he just wanted to work. He didn't want to care about anyone ever again.

When he was well away from the ranch, he found a place to camp. But with the memories still haunting him, he was unable to sleep. At daybreak he secured his supplies once again to the packhorse, then followed the North Fork of the Popo Agie River into the mountains to its headwaters — a lake, high and lonesome, incredibly clear, and incredibly cold. He had camped near here the night he'd encountered the woman, and he sensed this area had to be close to where she stayed.

The region was still very much wilderness. It

was, for the most part, unexplored and un-mapped. Few explorers came this way, most preferring mountaineering the higher peaks to the west. It was amazing to him that anyone had been up here to even spot the woman in the first place, but someone had, and that was apparently how word had gotten out that Sky McClellan might still be alive.

Most of the snow from the spring blizzard was melted even up here except in the granite peaks where glaciers clung to crevices that the sun seldom found. The sun had come out to warm the high mountain meadow, but not enough for a man to shed his coat. The grass hadn't been hurt by the bout of cold weather, nor had the hardy, early-blooming primroses that filled the meadow with lively pink color. Some of the flowers even grew from patches of snow.

He laid camp near the water in a spot where the trees came close to the edge. Having had no sleep the night before, he had no trouble tonight.

The sky was barely turning gray with a new day when he left camp in search of a drumming ruffed grouse, often called a pine hen, whose racket had awakened him. Following the unique, far-carrying sound that starts out slow and soft and then builds to a long, rolling crescendo, Matt easily found the grayish brown bird sitting atop a log, beating the air with its wings so rapidly that it created the unmistakable sound.

With a steady hand and careful aim, he pulled the trigger. Back in camp, he finished cleaning the bird, cut it up, and laid it in a frying pan over the flames. He was filling his coffeepot from the pristine lake when the booming report of a rifle blast sent him scrambling for cover behind a big rock. In his flight, he felt the thudding impact of something against his left thigh. A quick glance confirmed he'd been hit. Blood quickly pooled around the wound and began to saturate his pants. With a sick feeling of dread, he knew he hadn't been fortunate enough for the bullet to have gone clear through.

He shinnied down farther behind the rock, yanking his revolver from his holster and wishing he had his Winchester, but he'd left it leaning against a tree back by the fire.

In the silence that followed that first gunshot, he removed his bandana and tied it securely around his leg to stem the bleeding. Judging by the blood flow, he felt confident the bullet had missed an artery. The wound hadn't started to hurt yet, but it would soon enough.

He checked the load in his revolver, replacing the one bullet he'd used earlier on the grouse. His gaze slid over his surroundings, but he saw nothing to indicate where the sniper was hidden.

He must have waited there for nearly an hour before finally deciding to take a chance that whoever had attacked him had gone. He rolled to his stomach and began crawling back toward the fire, the protection of the pines, and the Winchester that had a longer firing range. Immediately more bullets came in rapid succession and ricochetted off the rock as he dove back behind it.

Whoever was out there wanted him dead, not just frightened, and he wondered if it was the woman. Who else could possibly want him dead?

Another shot rang out and sent his hat flying. Simultaneously he was flung back into the tall grass. Blood poured down into his eyes from his head. In those seconds he thought he would die for sure, but the thought was fleeting before everything went black.

He was surprised to open his eyes and see the sun at high noon. He lay very still for a while, not sure of where he was or what had happened. Finally, he turned his head and recognized the cirque of the mountains surrounding his campsite. The movement brought a sharp, stabbing pain and the recollection of the sniper. Gingerly he felt his throbbing head. The entire right side was matted with dried blood, as was his face and neck.

Intuition told him that whoever had tried to kill him had left the area. If they had come closer and felt his pulse, they'd have put a bullet in him to finish him off.

He rolled to his side. Not only did his head feel like it was about to explode, but his leg felt like there was a hot branding iron rammed right into the wound itself. He'd bled quite a bit, but it seemed to have slowed during his unconsciousness.

He struggled to a sitting position and from there pulled himself up against the big boulder that had been his protection. He wondered if his head had been grazed by a bullet or only by a fragment of rock. His vision blurred and he became so dizzy he could barely stand upright without support. He doubted the head wound was life-threatening, but his leg would be if he didn't get medical attention soon.

He put his weight on his good leg and hobbled toward the fire that had gone out. The pine hen was still sitting in the pan, raw on top and burned black on the bottom. He leaned against a tree for support, but the dizziness hung on. Barely able to see or stand, he took his hatchet from his gear and cut a limb he could use for a crutch. He proceeded very methodically and purposefully, forcing himself not to panic about his wounds, but only to think of what had to be done if he wanted to stay alive.

He went about repacking a few bare essentials, a task which took much longer than it normally would. His blurred vision was accompanied by more hot, sharp pains in his head that made him nauseous. It was all he could do to keep himself from lying back down and not moving an inch. He couldn't get the big packs back on the horse so they would have to remain behind.

He wasn't finished when he felt the blood seeping out of his wound again. Pervaded by weakness, he found another bandana from his pack and a spare shirt. He wadded up the shirt and made a bandage of it then tied it over the wound with the bandana.

He figured it was about twenty miles to Lander—over an arduous trail. He couldn't make it by dark even if he was well, but he at least might be able to make it out of the roughest part of the mountains by then. His horse waited patiently while he struggled into the saddle. Leading the pack animal, he headed back toward the North Fork of the Popo Agie.

It seemed the hours dragged on, but he realized the sun moved across the sky much faster than he was moving across the land. Hot and cold flashes came with more frequency and his legs began to tremble until he wondered if he could stay on the horse. He removed some jerky from his shirt pocket and chewed on it although he wasn't hungry at all and his stomach was churning. But he needed to keep his strength up. He found he needed more and more water from the canteen because he felt like he was burning up inside. All the while he gave Soldier his head as he followed the steep and rocky highline trail.

By late afternoon the blood seeping down his leg into his boot became uncomfortable. Without dismounting, he rummaged in his saddlebags and found some clean underwear. He made a new bandage and placed it under the blood-soaked one, then retied the drenched bandana.

The sun was just an hour above the mountain peaks when he fell off his horse. He watched helplessly as the pack animal ran off down the trail and disappeared into the trees.

Soldier snorted at the blood on Matt's leg but

nudged his shoulder, as if encouraging him to get up.

"Figure I'm going to die, don't you?" Matt said and watched as the horse's ears pricked forward, listening. "Well, you might be right this time, old buddy."

His eyes closed involuntarily. The pain seemed everywhere in his body now and it kept coming, rolling in like one long continuous wave. Despite the hot pain of it, he was cold. So very cold.

"I'm just going to rest for a little bit," he muttered to Soldier through dry lips, as if the animal could understand. But he said it more to assure himself that he was only going to rest for a few minutes, not forever.

Later, he had to squint against the bright light of the sun resting just off the western horizon. It would drop behind the mountains very soon.

He tried to get up but fell back down. A glance at his thigh showed he'd lost a lot of blood.

"Christ," he muttered and closed his eyes again while catching his breath. If he'd had a choice, he really would have preferred a less lonely place to die. And it was a hell of a thing to go to your grave and not know who had put you there.

Suddenly the brilliant yellow light he saw from behind his eyelids darkened as if a cloud had passed before the sun. But when he opened his eyes, it was no cloud. It was the shape of a human head with the sun's rays encircling it like a halo. He wondered if this was the person who had tried to kill him and if he would finish him off now. He fumbled for his gun, not wanting to die without a fight, but his fingers were cold like the rest of him and he couldn't make them function at all.

The person came closer and the features took the gentle form of a woman's—a woman with black eyes and black braids dangling down against a white doeskin blouse. His heart leaped. The face vanished.

He forgot about the gun and reached for her instead. "Don't go away! I need your help."

The face reappeared. She was beautiful! So beautiful she seemed almost ethereal, almost unreal. Just looking at her made his heartbeat quicken with a strange and glorious desire. But the pain remained, reminding him of the fragility of his life, and suddenly anger welled up inside him. He couldn't die! Not now. Not when she had come to him at last.

She stared down at him with fear and worry furrowing her lovely brow. Was it possible she actually cared what happened to him? Hope leaped inside him and he lifted his hand toward her again. She stepped out of his reach.

His head began to swim and the edges of his vision darkened. He knew he was going to lose consciousness again and he wondered if this time would be the last.

"Sky," he pleaded. "Don't go. Please . . . I need your help."

But she vanished and did not reappear.

He moaned and closed his eyes once again to the bright sunlight. The pain racked his body with even greater intensity; the cold seeped deep to the core of him. All hope vanished.

He was going to have to get himself to Lander. There were no miracles in these mountains, and the woman wasn't real. She never had been. He had wanted her to exist for a reason he didn't even understand, so he had imagined her those nights by the fire. And, in his fevered mind, he was imagining her now. The black strand of hair in his vest pocket could probably even be explained away.

Yes, the old Indian was right. Red Sky McClellan was a woman of the wind. A ghost. And nothing more.

Your soul my heart has seen.
But from whence?
Another time? A dream?

Chapter Four

Red Sky backed away from Riordan's bloody hand. Anxiously, she watched his eyes close and his body relax. Had he died or was he only pretending so he could trick her again, capture her, and turn her over to the law? Why was she here, tempting her fate?

She inched closer. He didn't stir. She watched his broad chest weakly rising and falling as if each breath would be the last. But at least he still lived. She felt a rush of relief and didn't know why, because he might very well be her enemy. He threatened her secret existence, and in taking her away from this place—as he wanted to do—he certainly threatened her life. Still, she had followed the trail of his blood for miles after having heard the gunshots and having found his camp up by the high, lonesome lake. All the while, she had feared for him in a way she did not understand.

Moistening her lips nervously, she gripped her knife and edged around to the top of his hatless head. Staying at arm's length, she lowered her body, balancing on the balls of her feet and keeping her leg muscles coiled like a spring so she could leap away from him if necessary.

Tentatively, she touched the vein in his throat. He didn't move, didn't stir. She could feel his desperate life's energy pulsing into her fingertips and spreading throughout her body. It consumed her with something elusive . . . a need that seemed to flow, like the warm stream of blood itself, from his soul into hers. For reasons she could not begin to understand, she felt a peculiar bonding with him. But to bond with him would mean to trust him, and she could never do that.

Frightened by the disturbing sensation, she returned her hand to her side and sat back on her heels.

The ragged gash along the side of his head, even though ugly and caked with blood, didn't concern her as much as the bullet wound in his leg. The former could cause complications, true, if he regained consciousness, but the latter appeared to be more life-threatening.

It would soon be dark and the cave was miles away. Riordan would not survive the cold mountain night unprotected, and the smell of his blood would summon wild animals; the grizzly, the wolf, the cougar.

And yet if he died, peace would return to the mountains and to her life. She shouldn't feel guilty if she turned and walked away. Here was a matter of survival, a matter of life for life. If she saved his life, he might in turn take hers.

She stood up. The turmoil of indecision clawed at her insides. She walked to his horse. It was a fine animal and she liked the way its coat gleamed copper in the sunlight. If Riordan died, this horse would run wild or be caught by the cowboys from the ranches below. Or she could keep it.

She walked toward it, holding out her hand and speaking softly. She had been a good rider in her youth and had longed for a horse many times over the past years, if for no other reason than for the companionship. But the horse shied away from her and she determined it was probably because the animal smelled the scent of the wolf on her; probably smelled the wolf itself hidden from view, watching from the woods.

Suddenly the horse bolted and ran into the trees, but luck was with her and the trailing reins caught in some underbrush. Seeing her chance, she ran forward and caught the reins. The animal whirled to face her, wild-eyed and frightened, but she pulled on the reins and made it come closer, then led it from the brush and up to Riordan. There she tied the reins securely around a tree.

As she did so, she made her decision concerning the golden-haired man. She didn't know why she had followed his trail of blood, but she knew it was not in hopes of finding him dead. Therefore, she put her knife away, removed his holster and knife sheath, and secured them to the saddle. She knelt at his side again, laying her hands to his face and feeling how feverish his skin was. She had no time nor the materials to build a travois so she had no choice but to get him back onto the horse.

"*Yets.* Get up." She tapped him lightly with her palms. "You must help me get you back on the horse. It's the only way I can help you."

After some minutes of prodding and poking and vocal encouragement, she summoned him back from the death-world he had fallen into. His eyelids fluttered open unwillingly, and his blue eyes appeared glazed and feverish, gazing at her without full comprehension. Yet, with her help, he used his willpower and the last remaining fragments of his strength to get to his feet. She wondered if he was even aware of what he did or if he did it in some dream deep in his mind.

With his arm over her shoulder, she directed him to the horse. The solid contours of his six-foot frame pressed heavily against her until she could barely stand upright. It was not the nearly overpowering force of his weight, however, that she felt most deeply, but rather the solid expanse of his chest pressing against the softness of her breast; the narrow male hip firmly rubbing the contour of her own; the lean waist held snugly in the grip of her hand; the sinewy thigh flexing against hers with each step they took. These were the things she would remember long after this night was over, regardless of its outcome.

He lifted himself into the saddle. How he managed it, she didn't know, but she knew she could never have lifted him herself. She feared that if he fell off again he might not be strong enough to help himself a second time.

He slumped over the horse's neck, holding on to the saddle horn, and looked as if he was once again sinking into the nebulous sphere that existed on the edge of death. Not allowing herself time to reconsider the dangerous decision she had made, she led the horse back up the trail to her cave.

Hours later, by moonlight, she reached the rock-faced cliff, but knew the horse would not be able to traverse it. Taking a slight detour, she led the animal around to the north side of the mountain where the slope was still steep, but grassy and covered with trees and much easier to ascend. She normally didn't use the north side because footprints could be too easily detected.

Once on the summit, she eased the horse back down the south side the few yards to the cave's entrance. Esup slipped into the cave while Red Sky tied the horse's reins to a small tree that grew right outside the cave's entrance and helped to conceal it. Riordan was leaning to the left, the side nearest the cave's entrance. In the darkness, the color of the blood blended with the black cloth of his pants. By feel alone, she knew the wound still bled, although not profusely.

Pulling him toward her, she was struck immediately with his full weight as he began to slide from the saddle. She caught him as best she could, but his weight pressed her down to her knees, nearly beneath the horse's hooves. The bulk of his body, hot and heavy, came to rest on hers. She managed to move him aside, and the horse stepped out of their way.

"You must wake up, again," she said, bending over him. "I can't carry you inside."

He apparently floated near enough to the edge of consciousness to hear her words because he stirred and made feeble attempts to obey her command. She got him to a sitting position and put her shoulder beneath his.

"Now, try to stand up," she said. "I'll help you."

He was so weak she had to do most of the work, but she was a strong woman and finally got him to his feet. Turning sideways, she pulled and dragged him through the cave's entrance. His stumbling steps helped, but mostly to keep him upright and keep the burden of his entire weight from falling onto her shoulders. By the time she lowered him to the bed of furs, her body was wet with perspiration. In the pitch blackness of the cave, she felt for the robes and pulled them over his shivering body.

She set about rebuilding the fire and was fortunate to find live coals buried beneath the ashes. With some dry twigs and leaves she kept in a basket nearby, she soon had a flame lifting the veil of darkness and casting wavery red shadows over the soot-covered rock walls.

Once, when she was twelve, she had been asked to assist her father in removing a bullet from a cowboy's leg. It was with this faded memory called to mind that she proceeded now.

She recalled her father having said that new

61

knowledge had taught men that it was important to use clean instruments, *sterilized* instruments, when working with open wounds to prevent dirt from spreading germs throughout the body.

When the fire was hot, she set a pot of water over it. As soon as the water boiled she positioned the blade of her smallest knife in the steaming liquid, leaving the handle latched on the edge so it wouldn't become too hot. She had a small can of kerosene, a precious commodity, but she placed it next to Riordan's side to be used as a cleaning agent.

Several years ago she had asked Many Claws to trade a bundle of furs for a bolt of bleached muslin. She had wanted to make a blouse for summer, like those she had worn as a girl. But she had never cut into the cloth, for it had unfortunately provoked images of another time, and of another blouse of bleached muslin covered with blood. Even now, as she looked at the bolt of unused cloth, the memories of hurtful, wicked hands returned.

She shuddered, took a deep breath, and forced herself to think of Riordan. Kneeling by his side, she saw that he had fallen into a feverish sleep. Lifting the robes away from his injured leg, she sliced open his pants' outer seam with her skinning knife and slid the cloth out of the way. The firelight flickered over his leg, lighting the curly brown hairs that covered it, and giving her the first glimpse of the ugly wound.

With gentle strokes and a basin of warm water

she cleaned the blood away and daubed the wound with kerosene. The fiery solution suddenly pulled Riordan from his feverish slumber. He rose up, crying out in pain and reaching for her shoulders to steady himself. Her first instinct was to pull away. The wild look in his eyes frightened her, but she forced herself to remain where she was and allow him to turn to her in his time of need.

At last he fell back onto the furs, but the imprint of his fingers seemed to remain behind on her flesh, leaving heat where he had touched her. How alien to her the emotion that stirred inside her at that moment; the yearning to seek out — rather than to turn away from — the touch of another human being.

Could it be possible that his hands would not hurt a woman, but would touch her with the same tenderness one would use to stroke the petals of a rose? Monty Glassman had been gentle, and so had Gray Bear — her two beaus when she was just a girl of fourteen. But Monty and Gray Bear hadn't been hardened men of the law — ruthless men. How many men had Riordan killed? How many times had he pulled the trigger and ended another's life? Had he killed with regret or with relish? And would he kill her before it was all over?

"Help me, Sky. Please. Don't go." He tossed his head back and forth upon the fur pillows and finally seemed to focus on her although his eyes remained glazed.

"I'll help you," she said. "But you must lie still."

Apparently comprehending, he closed his eyes. His hands relaxed at his sides.

The fire didn't give enough light for removing the bullet. She had several torches positioned about the cave and she lit each one by touching it to the fire. The full extent of what she was about to do made her hands shake all the while she washed them with strong lye soap. She knelt at Riordan's side, taking a deep breath to calm her nerves.

The area around the bullet's entrance was puffy and red, the skin torn and ugly. She had no way of knowing how deep the bullet was or the direction it had entered. She only knew it hadn't exited. She would have no choice but to probe for it.

For lack of something better, she started the probe with her finger, fearing that using the knife before she located the bullet would only do more damage to his leg. His eyes flared open again. He stifled a moan of pain between clenched teeth and passed out almost instantly. She would have to work swiftly before he regained consciousness.

Her probing caused the wound to bleed worse, but at last she felt the bullet with the tip of her finger. It hadn't gone as deep as she'd feared, and it had apparently been at such an angle not to touch the bone or any main arteries.

It was much later, after considerable maneuvering, and some use of a pair of tweezers, before she finally managed to dislodge the bullet. She dropped it into the basin of water, cleansed the area again gently, and doused it with more kerosene. He had already lost a lot of blood, but she allowed the wound to drain for a few minutes more because she knew this would help to cleanse the wound. She then attended to the gash on his head. He would have a scar, but his hair was thick and should cover it.

From the baskets in the corner of the cave, she found the yarrow she had collected last season. She snapped off the leaves and flower tops and put them in a bowl. These, she would use to make a tea for Riordan's fever to give him when he regained consciousness. Next, on a clean flat stone she placed several whole plants, and with another smooth, elongated rock, quickly ground them into a powder for a poultice. It would stanch the bleeding as well as serve as an astringent and keep the inflammation down on both wounds.

After spreading the poultice on the wounds and bandaging them with the clean muslin, she sat back on her heels. She had done all she could, and all she knew to do. All that was left now was to wait.

Her muscles ached and her hands still shook, maybe worse than before, now that the tension in her was easing and the weariness was taking over. With longing, she eyed the pallet of warm furs upon which he rested—her pallet. But wearily she gathered a couple of small robes for herself, put out all the torches, and turned to her rawhide backrest. Esup rose from his spot and came to curl up next to her.

Tiredness swept over her like a harsh wind, but

sleep was long in chasing away the images of this day and the unpleasant flashbacks from days gone by. Riordan had brought the memories, and with them a dark, evil foreboding. He could easily take it all with him when he left. But something told her he would not leave her life as suddenly as he had entered it.

By noon the next day, Riordan's fever had risen until his skin felt as if it burned from the inside out. Red Sky lifted his head and tried to get him to drink the yarrow tea, but he seemed mostly unaware of anything going on around him. He mumbled in his fitful sleep, talking gibberish. Only occasionally had he spoken intelligible words. He had spoken her name several times and with it the words, "Don't go. Come back. Help me." Twice he had spoken the name Elizabeth, but no other words had accompanied that woman's name; only deep, long silences followed the utterance of it, as if the recollection of this mystery woman plunged him into a deep abyss of yesterday too painful for words.

Red Sky tried to keep the robes on him, but his restless tossing continually managed to work them off. She feared that if the fever did not break soon, he would die. She had to do more to help him.

Her gaze centered on his shirt for the hundredth time. Apprehension held her back from removing it. She was uneasy at disrobing him, even part of him. It was enough that she had exposed his leg. It would not be *she* who was left naked and vulnerable, so why did she feel as if she would be?

Seeing no choice, she set her fingers to work down the row of buttons until the last one was undone. She parted the shirt and spread it wide. Golden brown hair sprouted from his bronzed, muscular chest. It served as a bold reminder of his virility. Inexplicably it increased both her fear of him and her modesty.

In the process of working his shirt off, her fingers brushed across a ridge of raised skin on his back, on the upper right-hand shoulder. The odd texture, and the size and shape of it, stopped her in midprogress. Curiously, she ran her fingertips over the peculiar array of ridges marring his otherwise smooth skin.

He stirred again, mumbling incoherently. She rolled him to his side so his back faced the flickering light of the fire. The scar of a symbol, not unlike those used to brand cattle, leaped out at her. And from all appearances it had been burned onto his flesh in the same manner — with a red hot iron. It was a quiet, ugly reminder of something terrible that had happened once upon a time in his life. A chill ran through her at the thought of the excruciating pain he must have endured, and she wondered what he had done to warrant such torture.

She returned him to his back very carefully as if the brand were still fresh and painful. Just who was he? A Pinkerton detective, yes. But what else? What were the dark secrets of his past? Was he really as dangerous as Many Claws believed? Or was there goodness in him? Goodness that she'd heard in the tone of his voice and seen in his eyes, encouraging her to help him?

These questions and more rolled through her mind in a stream as steady as the creek that flowed at the base of the cave. While she deliberated about his character, she sponged his fevered body with the icy mountain water. Twice she went to the stream to refill her container. Her hands ached from constantly wringing out the cloth in the icy water, but still the fever raged inside him.

She checked his wounds and applied fresh poultices often to draw out the poison. Finally, she sat back on her heels, exhausted from her vigil. She wondered if she should have taken him down the mountain to the doctor in Lander. But she had been afraid to appear in town. Afraid for herself. She had allowed her fear to overshadow her better judgment, and now he might very well die because of it. Again, someone would die because she had been a coward.

Suddenly the narrow shaft of afternoon light that slid through the cave's entrance was blocked by a shadow. She leaped to her feet, grabbing the knife from its sheath at her belt. She relaxed when she recognized Many Claws standing before her.

"You frightened me, *adah*," she said, walking toward him. They embraced in an affectionate manner. "I didn't hear your approach, and Esup went into the forest to hunt. You've returned soon from your spiritual sojourn. I thought you would be gone for days. Is something wrong?"

Many Claws held his position until his eyes had adjusted to the darker interior of the cave. He usually greeted her with a smile, but this time he didn't. His gaze slid to the bed of furs and the man lying beneath them. His leathered face drew up in tight disapproval.

"Masin? What is this? What have you done?" he demanded gruffly. "Why have you brought your enemy here?"

"I don't know that he is my enemy," she responded defensively. "And besides . . . I couldn't find it in myself to let him die."

Many Claws glared at her for long moments then finally said, "You have saved him, but you have killed yourself! You are a foolish woman. *Ainwambe.*"

"It's a chance I've chosen to take." She turned back to Matt. "And I'm not so sure I *have* saved him. His fever is very high and I fear he might still die." She turned pleading eyes to Many Claws. "Will you tell me what I can do to break his fever? Will you help me?"

"Aiee! Help him kill you, you mean!"

Her eyes were bright but black in the semidark interior, the pupils dilated to their fullest as she waited, begging for his assistance, uncompromising in her decision to save Riordan, even though she didn't understand her driving need to do so.

"You should let him die," Many Claws said flatly.

"So you have said, my uncle."

"I only fear for your life, Red Sky. For years,

this is so. Now you bring death not only to your door, but to your bed. *Haganionde?* Why?"

Red Sky was moved by the concern of the old man. She laid a hand to his cheek. "I appreciate your many years of caring for me and worrying about me, *adah,* but something tells me I must do this. Would you help me? You have the medicine to save his life."

"I have the medicine to take it as well."

She conceded. "Yes, but please do not use it this time."

His gaze narrowed on her contemplatively. "This man . . . why are you so concerned about him? How do you know he will not harm you? Betray you? Why does he stir your blood and your compassion so?"

She turned her back to Many Claws and began sponging Matt's feverish body again with the cold water. The questions troubled her, too. "I don't know." She touched a hand to his feverish face. "Whatever it is, I can't let him die."

Many Claws shook his head. "I am sorry, Red Sky, but I will not call upon the Great Mystery to help me with this thing that can only bring you harm. Even if I chose to help him, my powers are weakened here; my medicine is not with me. All I have is this." He circled his hand around a small leather bag that hung from his neck by a rawhide string.

Red Sky knew the bag held much of his medicine; small articles that might mean nothing to someone else, but held significant meaning, and therefore power, for him. She didn't know what was in the bag. No one saw that but himself, but it might be any number of things, from an animal's tooth to a bear's claw, hair, or a piece of hide, a special rock, even special leaves or herbs. Yes, it was his amulet, but it wasn't everything he considered necessary to conduct a healing ceremony.

She had seen his healing ritual before. He painted his face and body with garish colors, adorned himself with fetishes that supposedly gave him his great power, and he always wore the decorated buffalo skull on his head. He then spent days dancing and chanting, lost deep inside himself as he called upon the Great Mystery to lend supernatural assistance.

He stalked back to the door. "I go."

"Yes. *Go!*" she said, lifting her head defiantly. "You're right. Your medicine is *not* strong enough to save the Yellow Hair. I will continue to use the white man's medicine. It has allowed him to live thus far."

Many Claws halted in the cave's narrow doorway. Red Sky saw his shoulders straighten perceptibly and she smiled inwardly at having successfully found his weakest point—his pride. Many Claws scorned the white man's medicine, feeling it was of the evil spirits, not of the beneficent ones.

He whirled on his heel, glaring at her. "White man's medicine! And what have you done with it?"

"I have removed the bullet," she said rather

smugly despite herself. "It's something you would not have attempted."

"You are a foolish woman to think you can cure with nothing but a knife. You cannot cut out the poisons coursing through his body. You need the power of the Great Mystery to draw them out."

"But only a medicine man can summon the Great Mystery for something so important," she countered.

Many Claws walked to her side. She ignored him as if he weren't there. "If you are determined to do this, *pahah*," he said, "then I will help. But remember. He is weak now and will be grateful for what you have done. But later, when he is well, you may regret your generosity."

The Death Trail fades.
What have you brought to me,
Oh, Spirit of the Wind?

Chapter Five

The monotonous, dull chanting edged its way into Matt's mind. It came from far away at first, like something in a dream, then grew increasingly louder until it no longer remained confined to his mind, but lay beyond him, surrounding him, echoing as if in a huge cavern. Awareness encompassed him. Clarity of life—smell, touch, sound . . . remembrance. It all came back. With difficulty he lifted eyelids that felt burdened by a weight almost greater than he had the strength to remove.

Only a fire's glow broke the grip of blackness, casting wavering shadows upon walls of solid granite. The fire's movement was accompanied by the shadow of a bird, or was it a man?—rising then stooping, moving in a strange dance of shadows.

Sluggishly, Matt turned his head toward the fire, swaying to its own song in the center of the room.

The shadow that had danced upon the rock wall *did* belong to a man, his near-naked body and face painted ghoulishly with peculiar lines and symbols in garish colors. A shawl of buckskin with jagged edges hung from his shoulders, and he occasionally held it away from his body, creating the illusion of wings. His feet moved up and down in time to the drone of his indecipherable chant, accompanied by rattles and the continual clacking of the bear claw necklace around his neck. Long grayish black hair hung down over his shoulders. Pieces of hair, separated from the rest, were entwined with fur and tied with leather thongs, then decorated with the colorful feathers of flickers and eagles. Something else was attached to his hair, something that looked a lot like the yellow-bellied skin of a weasel.

In Matt's delirious dreams and dim recollections, the woman's face had been the one he had seen. It had been she who had helped him onto his horse, not this strange man in hideous paint.

He looked away from the Indian, unalarmed, and unafraid of his peculiar ritual. Matt knew subconsciously that the painted man was a shaman and he performed his magic in hopes of saving life. In this case, Matt's own.

It was difficult to see in the semidarkness, but Matt slowly came to realize he was in a cave. Beyond the fire in the dark corner lay a jumble of objects that he couldn't quite make clear; baskets of some sort and leather parfleches commonly used by Indians. But darkness kept him from seeing clearly what the baskets contained. Beneath his hands he felt the softness of fur, and he noticed he lay upon a pallet, made comfortable by grass and covered with smooth hides and more furs.

He couldn't remember coming here. He remembered only the gentle, cool touch of the woman's hands on his flesh ablaze with fire while he screamed in pain. Or was that the other time when his flesh had indeed felt the searing agony of fire? When he had cried out for another woman who never came?

He had clung to life because of the black-haired woman, in hopes of seeing her again, finding her, for she held a power over him that was incomprehensible. She had been with him and she had been so real. He was disappointed now to realize that it had all been a dream. Always a dream.

A roar grew in Matt's ears, a roar of silence. The chanting had stopped and the clacking of the bear claw necklace had ceased. His reflexes were numb and slow, but his gaze shifted once again to the shaman. The Indian stood near the fire, motionless, staring at Matt with piercing eyes that gleamed brightly from behind the streaks of paint slashed on his broad face. For a man who had summoned the powers of the supernatural to save a life, the coals glowing in the black eyes surprisingly conveyed not gratitude and joy, but anger and contempt.

He stepped around the fire and stood over the pallet, towering over Matt, looking tall and ominous from Matt's lowly and vulnerable position.

The eyes cut him to the quick as effectively as any knife.

"So you live, Riordan. I will only say it is not my wish, but the wish of the Great Mystery."

Before Matt could speak, the Indian made a sharp about-face as precise as any army general could have, and vanished into the wall of the cave itself, or so it seemed. If there was an opening there, the night kept it cloaked.

Matt's eyes closed involuntarily. His heart was made heavy by the knowledge that he had only dreamed the woman. For a moment, he pondered the Indian's comment, spoken in very good English. The voice had a familiar ring to it, but he couldn't remember where he'd heard it before, or if it only jarred a distant memory. And the bear claws. They reminded him of something, of someone. But consciousness slipped away from him again as easily and elusively as darkness slips into dawn. For another space of time, Matt Riordan pulled all his awareness inward.

Many Claws strode out of the cave and into the moonlight, removing the deerskin cape from his shoulders. Red Sky jumped up from the small cove of rocks where she had hunkered down against the night chill. They had held the heat of the day for some time, and with her fur over her, she had been warm. She looked at Many Claws anxiously, but it was he who spoke first.

"The Yellow Hair lives. The fever is gone."

The breath she had been unconsciously holding came out in a rush of relief, but she was quick to see the disapproval in Many Claws' eyes.

"Your medicine is strong, *adah*," she said.

"I only asked the Great Mystery to spare the Yellow Hair's life if he desired, and because you asked this thing of me."

"And I thank you."

"Hold your thanks until the sun has journeyed across the sky a few more times, until this Yellow Hair proves he will not betray you. Now, I must return to the reservation. As you know, we are prisoners in this land now, and we must have permission to come and go beyond the invisible boundaries they have granted us for existence." His lips curled derisively. "The time I was granted is gone."

Red Sky laid a hand to Many Claws' arm. "Must you leave in the darkness?"

"It will be light soon, and it is safer if no one sees me go from this secret place."

Red Sky glanced toward the cave, and Many Claws felt her apprehension and her fear, but he could do no more for her now. She would be alone with Riordan. He could not protect her, and that was what caused him so much anger and grief. But she had made the decision to help Riordan and now she must live with the consequences of that decision.

"It is very dangerous here now, Red Sky," he said. "You have hidden the copper-colored horse well, but if the men who roam the mountains see the horse, they could find this place. I fear for you, my child. It is not too late to let me take you to my sister's people."

She gave him an understanding smile, but one that said she would not be swayed. "I have chosen this course, *adah*."

"You are a brave woman, Red Sky. I know of no other woman who could have survived as you have, or who would help this man who threatens your life."

"There is no bravery here, only cowardice and foolishness."

Many Claws touched her tenderly on the cheek. "I have been angry with you, Red Sky, but maybe I am wrong about the Yellow Hair. I only ask that you be very cautious with him. He will be weak for many suns, but do not trust him in any way. I will return as the face of the moon vanishes, and then we will decide what to do with him."

Red Sky watched Many Claws depart into the darkness to his horse hidden in the woods some distance away. She sat on the rocks long after he was gone, but finally she gathered her fur around her shoulders, and, with knife in hand, slipped back into the cave.

She had lived here for seven years. She had been safe and alone. People seldom came to this high country, even the Indians, for they preferred the plains for hunting. They traversed these mountains less frequently, and usually only when they wanted to get to the other side for hunting expeditions. Some people might fear the wild animal, and she had at first. She had feared the night sounds, the darkness, and the creatures, but she had learned to coexist with them. The enemies she feared most now were hunger and man. And now, as Many Claws had said, she had brought one of those enemies into her life in an irreversible way.

Riordan hadn't moved from the last time she had seen him. Her grip loosened on the knife. Had she expected him to rise up so soon, full of strength to strike her down?

She added more wood to the fire and leaned against her backrest, pulling the robe over her. She hadn't slept while Many Claws had conducted his healing ceremony, but had waited nervously, listening to the chant that had gone on for hours and hours. Now she would be safe to doze for a while, knowing she might not dare when Riordan's condition improved. Her eyelids drooped. Yes, she would rest now, and when the sun rose, she would check her snares.

Matt couldn't determine if the thirst woke him, or the smell of food cooking. A shaft of sunlight slid through a tall and narrow gash in the cave wall and stretched across the rock floor. The golden light fell upon a woman, kneeling at the fire, stirring something in a large black pot. That something smelled very much like chicken soup, and the woman was either a dream again or he was at last looking upon the visage of the mysterious Woman of the Wind.

He feasted his eyes on her, afraid to blink for fear she would vanish again or suddenly become the painted medicine man he recalled from a previous dark moment that seemed now more like a nightmare than reality. From his dim corner he stared at her with as much awe as a penniless country boy would stare at a pile of gold bullion.

She sat back on her heels with rigidly proud posture and lifted a large wooden spoon, filled with soup, to her full lips. Unaware of the sensuality of the action, she sipped the hot liquid, testing it for flavor.

It would have been plain to anyone that she wasn't a full-blooded Shoshoni, which assured him even more that she *was* Sky McClellan, the woman he'd come here to find. Everything about her features was softened, diluted if you will, by blood other than Indian. But the outcome of the mixture had not resulted in nondescriptive weakness, but rather a certain mesmerizing wildness.

Her skin glowed golden in the light of the fire, tanned but not nearly as dark as that of a full-blood. Like her Shoshoni ancestors, her face was square, although it wasn't as full or wide as most he had seen, and her cheekbones weren't extremely high. Black brows arched gracefully over dark eyes that weren't black, merely brown, and she had a perfectly straight, rather small nose. Her hair—neatly braided and falling over her shoulders onto her breasts—gave the purest indication of her Indian heritage. No blond or red highlights mingled with the strands that gleamed as pure and black as a smooth cut of obsidian gleaming in the sunlight.

Words formed in Matt's mind and waited to be said, but he couldn't seem to make his dry tongue function properly. During his delirium he'd had images of this woman giving him water, as well as a bitter-tasting tea he had choked on. Now it seemed part of a perplexing dream, but apparently it had been real. She had come to him in his illness. Would she come to him now in friendship?

Unexpectedly, the wolf rose from its spot behind the woman, its teeth slightly bared and a growl rumbling in its throat. The animal had keenly sensed Matt's consciousness. Its yellow eyes focused on him, and the woman dropped the spoon back into the pot as if she'd been burned. In the same swift movement, her hand was on her knife. She came from her kneeling position in one graceful movement and backed away from him. Caution leaped into her eyes. How ironic that she had brought him here to save his life and yet she was ready to take it if necessary.

She stood tall for a woman. Another recollection flashed in his mind. A recollection of her body, lean and strong, next to his, her arm around him, supporting him, helping him onto the horse and then somewhere else—into darkness darker than night . . . yes, into this cave.

"I—" he tried to speak but his tongue stuck to the roof of his mouth. He made a concentrated effort to swallow a few times and get the saliva flowing. All the while the woman stared at him wide-eyed as if expecting him to attack her. He tried again. "I'm thirsty. Could I have . . . some water? Please."

She pointed to a small water vessel within arm's reach of the pallet. It was fashioned from an animal bladder. A hollowed bone in one end, stuffed with a wooden cork, served as the spout.

She was obviously not going to come near him if she could help it, so he lifted himself to his elbows. Immediately his head swam, but he fought the sensation of dizziness, knowing it would pass when his body adjusted to the new position.

The water was good and cold, and he drank his fill. When he was done, he recorked the bag and fell back against the furs, his heart racing from the exertion. He turned his head and looked at the woman again. "Thank you," he said. "I would have died if you hadn't helped me. But who was the medicine man I saw the first time I woke up?"

Wariness mounted in her eyes. She was reluctant to speak to him, as if communicating would somehow weaken the barrier she seemed determined to place between them. Her hand clenched and unclenched on the knife handle, but he wondered if she was aware of this nervous action.

"The shaman is my uncle, Many Claws," she said at last. "He lives on the reservation, but he saved your life."

Ah, yes, Many Claws. Matt hadn't recognized him with all the paint, but he should have recognized the bear claw necklace. The sage old man had tried very hard to convince him that Sky McClellan was dead, but as Matt had suspected, he had done it only to frighten him away and to protect her.

He felt the pain in his leg now. It was bad, but not as bad as it had been earlier. During his delirium it had felt like a firebrand. He lifted the robes and looked at the bandaged leg. "Did he get the bullet out?"

"No," she said. "I took the bullet out."

"Then it is you I should thank for saving my life."

"No. Not entirely. Fever threatened your life when I asked my uncle to help. He's a Bear Man and his medicine is very powerful. Soon you'll be strong enough to leave the land of the Sun-Father."

Her dark eyes were filled with wisdom and age beyond her years, but he wondered why she seemed to embrace the Indian's beliefs instead of the white man's. Had she, when she had abandoned the white man's world, even refused to claim the part of it that existed inside herself?

"The soup smells good," he said. "Is it pine hen? I feel like I haven't eaten for a week. I'd like to have some . . . that is, if you don't mind."

Red Sky's heart thudded in her bosom. Riordan appeared harmless, but he was weak. She wanted to trust him as she trusted Many Claws, but it wouldn't be wise. She didn't like talking to him. She was afraid his apparent friendliness would lull her into a false sense of security. She remembered too well the night he had tricked her, and even now she felt the strength of his dangerously hard body pressing the breath out of her. She had come

83

awake nights remembering it, and had shivered from the disturbing memory that was both frightening and peculiarly stirring.

"It has been a few days," she conceded. "You've had only water and tea."

His lips twisted wryly. "Yes, I remember the tea."

She filled a small wooden bowl with the grouse soup. Keeping one hand on the knife, she set the bowl on the rock floor next to the pallet as cautiously as if he were a snarling, rabid dog. She was ashamed that her courage had vanished as suddenly as the stars before the rising sun. She backed away and watched while he struggled to his elbows again. He turned to his side, propped himself up on one elbow, and took the bowl in hand. She realized she hadn't given him a spoon and he didn't ask for one. He lifted the bowl to his lips and sipped, but it was hot and he finally set it back down.

He collapsed on the pillow. "Do you think you could help me? I'm as weak as a newborn colt."

She didn't move.

"Don't be afraid of me, Sky. I can't hurt you, even if I wanted to, which I don't."

Now just lie still, you little hell-cat! This ain't gonna hurt. You might even like it. And I'm sure going to. . . .

She brushed the memory aside and met Matt's waiting, enigmatic gaze. She saw no evil, but he could be a practiced deceiver of the likes she had never known.

"You give me no reason to trust you, Yellow Hair. I've heard the lies of your kind before."

"Yellow Hair? Is that what you call me?"

"It suits you."

"My name is Matt Riordan, but then I expect Many Claws already told you that, didn't he?"

"Yes, and he told me why you are here. Know now, Matt Riordan, I won't leave this place and go with you. When you're well, you'll leave here alone. I can tell the governor nothing about the men who killed my family. I don't remember their faces and I never knew their names. I'll help you get well, but remember . . . I'll kill you with less reservation than I had in saving your life."

She approached the pallet with a wooden spoon, setting it aside while she guardedly rolled up some more furs, fashioning a larger pillow than the one presently beneath his head. With extreme caution she slid her arm beneath his head to help lift him, then propped the new pillow behind him. Each time she had touched him during his convalescence the contact had sent a strange current of heat and shock through her body, and it was more intense now that he was conscious and watching her. In fact, his eyes followed her every move, making her feel vulnerable and uneasy.

She handed him the bowl of soup with the spoon in it. He lifted the first spoonful to his lips. She noticed his hand shaking and the soup balancing precariously on the spoon. Just as it came to his mouth, he misjudged and hit his lip, spilling the hot contents on his bare chest.

85

He swore. She grabbed the bowl in one hand and brushed the hot liquid from his chest with the other, doing so purely from reflex. He sighed and laid his head back against the fur pillow, closing his eyes.

"I'm sorry. I don't have any strength."

She sat back on her heels on the hard floor next to him, still holding the soup. Despite her fear, she watched with a degree of fascination the rise and fall of his hairy chest, the ragged and weary breaths. She recalled how his skin and the coarse hair had felt on her palm. Peculiarly exciting to the touch.

"I'll help," she said quietly. "Please, open your mouth."

She filled the spoon with soup, but her hand trembled nearly as much as his had. She managed to get it to his mouth, however, without mishap. He swallowed it with a little difficulty but seemed to savor the taste.

"I'm sorry to intrude on your privacy," he said in a gruff but tired voice. "But I won't for any longer than I have to."

She saw in his eyes a trace of shame and anger, and she sensed his weakness threatened the image he held of himself as a man. Having seen him before his injury, she knew he was a proud loner used to doing for himself, who expected and wanted nothing from anyone. In these respects the two of them were very much alike, even if she hated to admit to having any kind of kinship with him.

He said no more and neither did she. She had

become accustomed to the silence of her dwelling, of her life. As she spooned the soup into Riordan's mouth the small noises sounded very loud and accentuated the uneasiness that straddled the space between them: the clicking of the spoon in the bowl and against his teeth; the fire crackling; a bird calling outside. The silence made her more aware of him, of his breathing, of his eyes following her movements, delving into her thoughts and trying to read them. And, just as a horse can sense its rider's fear, Red Sky knew Riordan sensed hers. Would he use that fear against her when she helped him regain his strength?

At last he weakly held up a hand. "Thank you. I've had enough for now. The soup was very good."

She said nothing, and just gratefully and quickly moved away from him, back to the safe side of the fire.

My pulse stirs to an unfamiliar beat,
In the Morning of Memories and Dreams.

Chapter Six

It was going to hurt worse than nine kinds of hell, but Matt didn't see that he had a choice. He propped himself up on his elbows and managed to sit up, bringing his legs off the edge of the pallet despite the searing pain in his thigh. The movement drew Sky McClellan's attention immediately, pulling her away from the bowls and spoons she was washing and sending her hand to her knife.

He struggled to his feet, using the rock wall to support himself. Leaning heavily on his good leg helped to take the weight off the other one, but still the pain pulsed with each rapid beat of his heart, making him grit his teeth until it passed. But it didn't pass. Coldness and then heat struck him; his heart's tempo came harder and faster; beads of perspiration sprang to his face; dizziness stole his clarity of vision and threatened his balance. At last he collapsed back to the bed of furs.

"What are you doing, Yellow Hair?"

He opened his eyes and found Red Sky's darkly suspicious gaze intently fixed upon him. But she remained where she sat, not coming to his aid.

"I was going outside."

"Why must you do that?"

He had assumed she would know why, but her chariness told him she suspected his every move and action to be motivated by evil intent. She must not consider him a human being with feelings and needs similar to her own. Or did her fear of him — the fear so blatant in her eyes — keep her from having compassion?

"I need to go out, Sky," he said, then paused to catch his breath. "To attend to . . . business."

Realization seemed to approach her slowly then swallow her in one gulp. She flushed and looked away in embarrassment. "Oh, yes. Of course."

"I could use your help."

He heard her intake of air and saw the horror-stricken look on her face. He nearly smiled through the pain, amused by her misunderstanding of his request. "Just help me get outside. I can do the rest. I'll make myself a crutch as soon as I can, but right now I need some help."

He doubted she would be any more enthusiastic about touching him than she would be to face down a grizzly bear with nothing more than a club made of sagebrush. But she finally resigned herself to her task and approached him warily.

She slid her arm around his waist and put her shoulder beneath his. When her warm hand closed around his to help steady him, he felt a jolt, like a bolt of lightning, shoot through his body. It nearly made him forget the pain in his leg and the reason he'd asked for her assistance. Instead, his thoughts flashed back to the bed of furs and to imagined images of her lying there beneath him, warm and soft and willing.

She began to move him swiftly toward the cave's entrance. He saw the vein pumping erratically in her neck and knew she wanted to relieve herself of the duty and burden he imposed quickly.

"Wait, Sky. Give my head a chance to clear and let me catch my breath."

In those moments she suffered her fate of having to hold his body against hers, and she refused to look at him, keeping her eyes averted.

"Okay," he finally nodded. "I'll try it now."

Hobbling and hopping, he made it to the cave's door and out into the bright sunlight of the late afternoon. The towering position of the cave almost set his head to reeling again. The land sloped away in one direction, but nearly fell to a precipice in the other. The view was incredible, but to a weak and dizzy man, it was also damned scary. There was no level ground and he found it difficult to stand.

She navigated him to a large rock and he gladly sat down.

"I'll leave you now," she said, obviously relieved to have finally deposited him away from her helping shoulder.

"Come back, okay?"

She gave his weak smile and attempt at friendliness nothing but a concentrated look, then hurried back into the cave and out of sight. He watched her retreat with escalating anger. Why in the hell wouldn't she open up a little? Why was she so determined to believe he meant to do her harm? Why did she act as if touching him was even more distasteful than handling rotting flesh?

He tried to calm his crazy anger over her behavior, but like a spirited stallion that chooses to run from the rope and the saddle, she had become a wild thing with only memories of a domesticated life. And, like the wild stallion, it would take time and patience to gain her trust. Perhaps he never would. For once the wild one has tasted freedom and the wind, you might tame it to the touch but you will never fully tame its heart or win its absolute devotion.

When he felt relatively strong, he completed his business and returned to his seat on the rock, enjoying the coolness of it against his bare, feverish leg. She had cut his pant leg along the seam almost to his hip, but she'd apparently done it in a hurry because the opening was uneven, a little ragged, and he wondered if it could be fixed. Luckily he had another pair in his saddlebags.

He searched the area surrounding the cave dwelling with a wide, sweeping glance, wondering for the first time where his horse was. But he doubted she would keep it anywhere nearby, or even in sight, because to do so would jeopardize the security of her sanctuary.

He had no idea where he was, only that it seemed to be at the top of the world. From here a person could see to all horizons until the mountains and the sky faded into one blue haze in the far distance. It was a clear, brisk day but the cool breeze was refreshing after being in the dark of the cave. Over his head was a tall but weathered pine, missing a lot of branches except those draped at the top like a head of shaggy hair. Its few boughs held a large eagle's nest. One of the eagles circled over him, eyeing him speculatively.

"Are you ready to go back?"

Her voice startled him. As usual she moved with less sound than the wind. Seeing her standing there, as tall and slender as a young aspen sapling, her dark, fathomless eyes watching him warily from beneath thick black lashes, brought a knot of need and desire to his stomach and loins that was hard to ignore. She was more beautiful in broad daylight than in the glow of the firelight. She was very real now, whole and solid, but still she held that aura of mystery insinuating that she must not be touched or she would vanish once again into a dream.

He had known many beautiful women, but it remained a puzzle to him why this one's presence and beauty affected him so intensely. On the one hand, she seemed to know every thought that passed through his mind, both good and evil, and on the other hand, she seemed utterly innocent.

"The fresh air feels good," he said, scrutinizing her as the eagle had him.

"You can stay out then. I have things I must do inside." She started back to the cave, obviously wanting to be away from him as quickly as possible.

"No need to run off."

Her steps faltered and she seemed to give second thought to her haste. Finally she turned back around, waiting expectantly for him to say more, to say why he wanted her to stay.

He wondered if he was crazy to be feeling the way he did about her. She wasn't some mythical goddess. She was a woman with a woman's heart. And he had learned long ago that a woman's heart was not to be trusted, was not the foundation on which a man could lay dreams.

"It's a nice day," he finally said. "I just wanted you to stay and talk. There's a lot we need to discuss."

"I have nothing to discuss with you, Yellow Hair."

Did she never smile? Did she have to be so damned difficult and stoic? He'd never been much of a conversationalist. He'd never had to do much talking that wasn't related to business. He'd never even had to talk to Elizabeth very much. No, Elizabeth had only been interested in one thing. And he'd been so naive. He had misconstrued her desire for sex as love. He'd had such stupid notions back then. Notions of settling down with her on a ranch somewhere and raising a family. But he hadn't been good enough for Elizabeth—at least not for husband material.

He looked up at the eagle overhead, floating effortlessly on the breeze. "You must like it here, sharing the top of the world with the eagles."

Her gaze followed his. She clearly enjoyed the graceful flight of the huge bird. *"Piagwinyaq,"* she said. "The eagle. He is Lord of the air. Symbol of the wind and sun. My guardian spirit. And yes, there are worse places to be than here with the eagles."

Matt studied her solemn face as she watched the great bird circle and dip against the blue sky. "What do you mean, your guardian spirit?"

She drew her attention from the bird rather suddenly, seemingly reminded by his question that she had actually spoken words to him that hadn't been necessary. He thought she might not answer him so he encouraged her.

"How exactly does one go about getting a guardian spirit? I could use one in my line of work," he said lightly, hoping to loosen her up a bit. But still she didn't smile.

"You wouldn't be interested."

"If I wasn't interested, I wouldn't have asked."

Her perusal of him was thorough and revealed very little tolerance. She seemed to know exactly how he was trying to work her around to trusting him, and he sensed it made her more determined than ever not to. But what she didn't know, or believe, was that he really was interested. He wanted to know everything about her.

"All right," she said at last, conceding but with an edge of defiance. "I'll tell you what you want to

94

know, what I have been told. In many Indian tribes it's believed a person should have a guardian spirit to lead him safely through the hardships in life. Customarily, boys in their early teens are expected to seek their guardian spirit by going on a vision quest. Sometimes girls do this, too, but it isn't expected of them.

"A vision quest is much like the confirmation in the Christian religion, and is the high point in the life of a youth. It is his first solitary communion with the Great Mystery. But it is only the first of many times a person will seek guidance or help from the power that rules all the earth.

"The person seeking the vision must go some place where he can be alone and where he feels closer to God, so he will usually choose a mountaintop or some other isolated summit. He gives offerings, not materialistic offerings, but sacrifices of a symbolic nature such as tobacco or sacred cornmeal. He prays and fasts for two—maybe three—days and nights. It's at the end of this time that he will oftentimes be overcome with a 'dream.' If he has a vision, then the things he sees in the vision will be interpreted as having a special meaning in his life. They might even be interpreted as being prophetic. A youth, seeking his vision for the first time, will change his name according to what he saw and felt in the vision. For example, if he saw a bear, then his name might have something to do with that animal and that animal will be forever his guardian spirit."

"Have you ever gone on a vision quest, Sky?"

"No. But my guardian spirit came to me at a time when I truly suffered, when I lay near death. And then after I came here, so came the eagles."

"So you live by the Shoshoni's religious customs and beliefs rather than the white man's? Is that the way it was when you were growing up on the ranch in Long Moon Valley?"

She grew impatient with his questions and responded sharply. "I do not wish to share my personal life with you, Yellow Hair."

She started back to the cave, but again he stopped her.

"I'll be here awhile, Sky. What else can we do but get to know each other?"

"I see no need to get to know you. You'll be leaving soon."

"Perhaps, but you can't blame me for having some curiosity about you, can you? For that matter, I'm sure you have questions about me."

"You flatter yourself. I have no questions about you. Only the desire that you leave me in peace as soon as you can travel. If it will make your departure come quicker then I'll tell you what you want to know so you will have no more questions and no more reason to stay.

"I learned both religions from my mother and father. Since then I've chosen the path that suits me. But the power of God, the Great Mystery — whichever you prefer to call Him — seems closer to me now than when I was a child. Perhaps age and wisdom give a person more respect for God." She looked at the great panorama before her with obvious love and respect. "God is here, Yellow Hair," she continued with conviction. "The universe is His cathedral. Perhaps He can hear a worthy man who speaks to Him from the benches of a wooden or stone temple amid a mass of people—this I do not know—but my own personal belief, and that of the Indian, is that religion is a personal thing between man and God. I believe that when you seek God, you must go alone. The Indian's religion is a silent and solitary thing. Here, in the wilderness, I've come to know that better than any words could have told me."

"I've never spent much time philosophizing," Matt admitted.

"Indians are a deeply religious people, Yellow Hair. They take no credit for anything themselves. They believe that everything they are given was granted to them by God. I feel closer to their simple beliefs than I did years ago. Living here as I do has made me understand the nature of their lives. You must be clever to survive in these mountains, but you must never forget the power of God to give and to take away."

Matt had never been a very religious person himself. He'd never had any religious background or education. He hadn't even read the Bible. He couldn't recall his mother having had one. He had made his way alone and he just always figured that was the way it was supposed to be. A man had to be smart enough and strong enough to survive; he couldn't expect divine intervention to keep him alive.

"Does the name Red Sky have something to do with your vision of the eagles?"

She kept her eyes on the huge bird; Matt was sure it was a safe way for her to avoid looking at him. "No," she replied. "My father gave me the name Red Sky when I was born. I chose not to change it because it held a special meaning to me. I don't believe my mother and father would have wanted me to change it."

"What was the special meaning?"

"What does it matter to you, Yellow Hair?" she asked derisively. "The meaning is only special to me and my father."

He shrugged. "I'm a man of many questions."

"And you torment people until you have your answers?"

"Generally."

She made absolutely no response to his attempted lightheartedness. Her gaze shifted to the mountains and valleys while her thoughts drifted back in time. Amazingly, she proceeded. "When I was about four or five my father lifted me out of bed, blankets and all. I was so sleepy I could barely keep my eyes open. He carried me outside into the frosty winter morning, and he pointed to the southeast. 'Look there,' he said, 'see that sunrise?' The sun hadn't risen, but it would very soon. And the sky was swathed with thin bands of clouds painted in brilliant shades of red. Even the snow had a reddish tint. It was the most beautiful thing my young eyes had ever seen. I remember it so vividly, and my father said, 'You were born on just such a morning. That's why I named you Red Sky.' He made me feel so special, and I thought I was the luckiest child alive to have been so privileged."

The animation with which she had told the story suddenly faded. She drew inside herself again, closing him off from her secrets. The evasiveness in her eyes suggested that she had shared more than she had intended and now regretted it.

"Are you ready to go back inside?" she asked.

"No," he said, smiling, "but my body doesn't agree with me."

This time she willingly offered her shoulder, and he slid his arm across it. The hot, inner strength of her and the warm, soft outer shell combined to flood him with awareness of her femininity and of how it could take him to a height of ecstasy he longed to know with her and her alone. For a moment he nearly forgot the pain in his leg again. But quickly he reminded himself he was here to do a job. Just a job. Nothing more.

Red Sky watched Matt Riordan fall asleep almost as soon as he laid his head back against the pillow of soft white rabbit fur. She sat on her heels by the fire and studied him in this moment of calm when his blue eyes could not meet with hers in that indiscernible, disturbing way and when his lips could not ask all their probing questions. He hadn't tried to hurt her. He had wanted to speak of eagles and visions and God. Was this kindness of his merely more tricks to delude her, to gain her trust so that when he regained his strength he could easily make her his prisoner?

She didn't know the answers to these questions, but she knew she must not lower her guard. She found it increasingly hard not to do this, though, because the sight of him stirred memories and feelings she had almost forgotten during her daily struggle for survival in the mountains.

You'll be my wife some day, Sky McClellan, and we'll rule Long Moon Valley together, like a king and his queen.

Don't be silly, Monty. Who wants to be a queen? They just sit around and do nothing. They can't even dress themselves. Besides, I'm only fourteen and I have no intention of getting married until I'm at least *twenty.*

Twenty! Well, don't expect me to wait six years for you.

Suit yourself. Another man will come along who I'll like better than you anyway.

Don't be so sure, Sky McClellan. It's not every day handsome strangers ride into Long Moon Valley.

The memory faded and she focused once again on Matt Riordan. Her shoulder still felt the masculine heat and weight of his body. She wondered if she would ever sleep in her bed again without thinking that he had lain there. Would the furs retain his particular musky, male smell that inexplicably titillated her senses?

You run away from your red-haired Monty Glassman, Red Sky. You run away from me. Why can't you make up your mind which of us you want?

I run because I enjoy running, Gray Bear. I'm not running from anyone.

But you run from his arms into mine.

How can that be? I didn't even know you were here in the woods waiting for me.

Tell Glassman that it is I you will belong to.

I belong to no one but myself, Gray Bear! I haven't yet met the man I'll marry. But when I do, he won't try to possess me the way both you and Monty do. He'll let me remain free.

What is this riddle you speak? How can you remain free and still marry?

The man I marry will understand. He'll know what I mean.

She turned away from Matt Riordan, and from the memories of her two beaus of long ago. Monty Glassman was dead now, killed the same day and by the same people who killed her family. Gray Bear was probably still on the reservation. Red Sky had never asked Many Claws about him. She had felt it better if she didn't know the direction his life had taken. He had only been a friend and could never be more. It was best to let him continue to believe she was dead.

Disturbed and saddened by the memory of those childish dreams that would never be, she rose abruptly and moved away from Riordan. He was the only man who had come into her life for seven years. And she must get him back out of it as quickly as possible.

She went outside into the coming darkness. Esup appeared from the forest and followed her. As always, she listened and looked to make sure there was no sign of anyone about but herself and Esup. Then she stepped lightly down the rocky slope and into the pines. There she searched until she found a good dead limb that would serve as a crutch. Darkness had taken the land by the time she returned to the cave.

She scraped the dry bark from the limb, fashioned the arm piece, and measured the stick against Riordan's sleeping figure to make it the right length. She found some small rabbit hides, grayish brown in color, and secured a pad to the arm piece so the limb wouldn't gouge his skin as he pressed his weight into it. While she worked, Esup kept his place by the fire. At last she completed the crutch and laid it aside.

But her work was not finished. Next she washed Riordan's shirt. When she was done with that, she went to the pond at the base of the cliff and bathed herself in the icy water by moonlight as she did every day during the warmer weather. In the winter she heated water over the fire and bathed inside.

Shivering, but dried and reclothed, she made the climb back up to the cave. After the first night Riordan had been with her, she had made herself another smaller pallet of dried grass and leaves, covered with hides, and had placed it on the opposite side of the fire. Now she stretched wearily upon it. But her thoughts were troubled, anxious.

Despite her long day of work, time had stepped into the next day before she finally found sleep.

Even though Red Sky had only a few hours of sleep, she awoke with the dawn as usual. Something was different. A certain smell extrinsic to the cave. Suddenly an image appeared in her mind of her father sitting at the breakfast table, with his old sweaty cowboy hat pushed to the back of his head and a chipped cup cradled in his hands, hovering just near his lips.

Coffee!

She bolted upright. Riordan was not on his pallet. He was not even in the cave. The crutch she'd made last night was gone. The flames in the fire were high, and next to them, just off to the side, was one of her small cast-iron pots with the coffee she had smelled simmering inside. For a moment she thought he'd gone, and for a moment she'd been very upset at that possibility.

But she shouldn't have been. She should welcome his leaving her life as unexpectedly as he had entered it.

Now, however, she became shaken that she'd slept while he'd risen, made coffee, and hobbled right past her on his crutch out of the cave. He could have easily taken her prisoner. He could have even killed her! But he had done neither. He had allowed her to sleep. Was he waiting until he was stronger to capture her? Trick her?

He would probably return soon to drink the coffee. Quickly she began rebraiding her hair before he saw its untidiness. During the night many of the strands had fallen from their confinement and poked out every which way in complete disarray. It was foolishness that she should care how she looked in front of him—a man who might be the death of her—but for some reason, that little flight of vanity sprang to the fore.

Her fingers worked rapidly, a bit nervously, unwinding the hair. She went to the basket that held her hairbrush and leather strips she used to bind her hair with. But luck was not with her this morning, for she had only pulled the brush the length of her hair a few times when his shadow blocked the light from the entrance. With heart pounding, her gaze shot to his.

"You're up early," she said nervously, forcing herself to keep her eyes from his bare chest, even though they seemed to be pulled there by a magnet. "I didn't hear you. Why didn't you wake me?"

Matt barely heard her words and no reply was forthcoming. His breath caught in his throat. He stood transfixed by the black cloud of hair falling over her shoulders like a shimmering yard of pure silk, tantalizing him to feel its softness beneath his lips.

He took a step toward her, then stopped, wobbling a little on the crutch. He could not pursue these desires that tormented him. This woman would never let him touch her. And perhaps it was just as well, because she held such a mysterious power over his emotions that if he did touch her, he might be a prisoner to her charms forever.

Finally the few words she had spoken filtered into his mind. "You were sleeping so soundly I didn't want to disturb you," he said at last. "I hope you don't mind me using one of your pans for coffee, but the packhorse I had all my gear on got away from me. Luckily I had a small pouch of coffee in my saddlebags."

She turned away from him, as if looking at him too long would poison her mind in some way. It made him angry that she thought he was so completely without honor, but could he blame her? Perhaps she knew him better than he knew himself. Knew this very minute that he'd like to lay her back upon the pallet and take her body to his.

He watched her fingers working, rapidly rebraiding the length of hair. She didn't use a mirror, but worked from feel alone. She twisted the lengths of rawhide around the ends in a clever fashion both attractive and secure. Then she came lithely to her feet.

"I've washed your shirt." She pointed a slender finger to it hanging on a wooden rack. "It's probably already dry. And over there in that small bowl is more poultice for your leg. You can heat some water from those clay pots if you care to wash. Now, I must go check my snares and move your horse to new grass. When I return, I'll fix something to eat. While I'm gone you should change your bandage."

She hesitated, and he saw in her eyes that she didn't favor walking past him in order to leave the cave. Her hand drifted to the knife at her waist and she moved forward, her long legs bringing her to within feet of him in just a few easy strides.

He considered forcing her to slide past him, forcing her bosom to brush against his chest. Even as the thought came to mind, he moved aside. Still, it was not enough that she could totally escape contact. As she bolted for freedom and safety beyond him, her hand brushed his. The pleasant, electrifying charge surged through his body, and it was all he could do to keep himself from pulling her back into his arms.

"Red Sky."

She halted in the shaft of sunlight that streamed through the doorway. Wariness was still embedded hard and deep in her eyes.

"Thank you for making the crutch."

An emotion he couldn't discern flickered across her face but was swiftly gone. "It was nothing," she said. "You needed to get around and I have many things to do. I can't spend all my time helping you."

Before he could say more, she was gone. She pretended to be indifferent to helping him, but the simple fact that she had was testimony to her hidden inner compassion.

With her gone, the stillness of the cave settled in, as well as a certain emptiness despite the cozy warmth of the fire. Even her belongings, silent marks of her existence, seemed to lose meaning and substance without the sustaining breath of her presence.

He wondered how she had managed to stay here all the years that she had with only the wolf as her companion. Being alone was second nature to him. He preferred it. But a woman . . . well, there weren't many who could tolerate it, and only a handful who could have survived in these mountains. But she didn't seem to resent being here. If anything, she seemed to have chosen it and preferred it.

He limped to one of the large rocks posing as chairs and sat down, stretching his injured leg out in front of him. It still hurt like bloody hell, but he knew from past experience that wounds of any kind healed quicker if a body got up and got around, regardless of the initial pain. The longer a man stayed in bed, the weaker he became.

He heated water to wash and shave in. When it was warm, he removed the torn pants. He had soap, razor, and a toothbrush in his saddlebags, but the towel needed a good scrubbing. He found a clean, soft chamois-type skin lying near the basin and decided it would serve as a towel until he could wash his.

In thirty minutes he felt much better. With a fresh poultice and bandage on his leg, and dressed in his clean pants and shirt, he felt almost whole again—except for his hips. They felt damned naked without the weight of his revolver and bowie knife.

He began searching the cave to see what she had done with his weapons. He went through her things timidly, feeling uneasy about snooping. In his line of work he had to do a lot of snooping, but this was different because she wasn't a criminal and he wasn't here to find incriminating evidence against her.

She had both personal items and food items that she could have only gotten from town. She was obviously in touch with someone from the outside world—probably Many Claws—but possibly someone else as well.

He forgot what he was looking for as his interest shifted to these things that belonged to her. The baskets and wooden bowls held everything imaginable: herbs, sewing material, beads, porcupine quills, knives, plates, utensils, food. The leather parfleches, constructed like envelopes, ranged in size from that of a small reticule to a large bag. Some were empty: In one parfleche he saw a fine white buckskin dress and leggings decorated with an intricate design of dyed porcupine quills in colors of blue, red, and yellow, and beadwork that must have taken scores of hours to design and attach.

Furs of small game animals such as rabbit, beaver, squirrel, ermine, marten, and mink had been sewn together to make warm blankets. The bed held a buffalo robe with painted designs on the inside, and he wondered if Many Claws had given it to her. Skins that hadn't been used for clothing and other purposes, skins of a lesser quality, had been laid beneath the bed or scattered about like rugs as protection against the coldness of the cave's floor.

Leather pouches held arrows and he saw several finely crafted bows, metal traps, wooden traps, and materials for snares. He saw no guns, no ammunition. But it would only make sense that she wouldn't fire a gun and draw attention to herself.

He even found a small wooden bowl and a bullet inside. Intuition told him it was the one she'd taken from his leg and he immediately picked it up to examine it. He guessed it to be about a .52 caliber. Unfortunately, the slug by itself wasn't much of a clue to who shot him, but he tucked it into his vest pocket anyway. Something might turn up.

His gaze finally fell upon a notebook, tucked sideways in between a couple of parfleches. Something warned him that this might be a personal thing; a diary perhaps. But for that very reason, he couldn't refrain from picking it up.

He debated whether to look inside but finally lifted the cover. What he saw were detailed charcoal drawings of trees, mountains, animals, even people. He was surprised to recognize one of the people: Many Claws. The drawing was more finely detailed than the others with every line drawn in his old face and every detail of his clothing. It was apparent that the shaman had sat to have his portrait drawn.

The other people—a man, Indian woman, two boys, a girl of about ten or twelve—he guessed to be Sky's family. There were also drawings of a cowboy in his late teens and an Indian brave of about the same age. But there were mostly animals and scenes from the mountains.

Suddenly the notebook was jerked from his hands with such force that it threw him off balance. The crutch beneath his arm fell and tumbled onto the fire, scattering sticks of burning wood onto the rock floor. Matt lost his balance and put too much weight on his wounded leg, crying out in pain as the leg gave out from under him. Red Sky automatically reached for him, even in her anger, but his weight was too much for her and they fell onto the sleeping robes.

She was pressed beneath him, but not for long. She struck his head and shoulders with her fists. He barely felt the blows, so great was the pain in his leg. Moaning, he rolled away from her and onto his back, gripping his leg. She leaped clear of him and backed well out of his reach. When the waves of pain gradually subsided, he managed to open his eyes.

"Damn it, woman . . . why did you do that?"

Anger gushed from her like the ongoing rush of a mighty waterfall. "You have no right going through my things! What did you hope to find? What! Tell me!"

Her bosom heaved beneath the buckskin blouse and her brown eyes shot poison arrows at him. He struggled to his elbows and then to a sitting position, clenching his teeth against another onslaught of pain as he readjusted the position of his injured leg.

"I was looking for my weapons, damn it! Then I came upon that notebook and I thought there might be information in it about the killers."

110

"You should have known I would have personal things in here!" She shook the notebook at him.

He didn't like being chastised—even if he did have it coming—and he retaliated. "Yes, I guess I suspected that you might, and I wanted to find out something about you since you refuse to talk to me if you aren't forced to!"

"I have nothing to say to you! I want you to leave here as soon as you can ride!"

"And you can bet every damned hide you have in this place that that's exactly what I'll do! But I'm not going anywhere until you give me my gun and my knife."

She pulled the notebook up to her breast, holding it there with both arms folded protectively across it. "Do you think I would be so foolish as to let you have them so you can kill me or capture me?"

"And how do I know you won't use that pigsticker of yours on me?"

"You don't."

"Exactly. I have to hope that since you saved my life, you won't turn around and kill me. You're just going to have to trust me, too, Sky McClellan. I have no intention of hurting you—I've never laid a malicious hand on a woman yet, and I don't intend to start now. And I definitely don't want you dead. You're the prime eyewitness in this murder case. I won't take you prisoner, but I would like you to go back to Cheyenne with me willingly."

"I have nothing to tell you. I don't remember the faces of the men who killed my family. It was all a blur, and I don't know any names!"

"It sounds to me like you just recited a speech you've had memorized, and I recall hearing it before! You got away from them, Sky, so you must not have been blindfolded. I don't know what happened to you, and I'm not asking you to tell me, but I'd bet money there *is* something — or somebody — you remember."

She remained silent, but her brown gaze pierced him with extreme resentfulness. Then she turned on her heel and started from the cave.

"I want my gun!" he hollered after her. "And my knife!"

She pretended not to hear.

Listen closely,
The Song of the Wolf is deceiving.

Chapter Seven

For a week they prowled around each other like warring mountain lions licking wounds from a previous fight. Sky spoke no words to Matt that weren't required. She wouldn't give him back his gun and knife. He searched the cave every time she left, but he finally decided she had the weapons hidden outside somewhere. He only hoped she hadn't destroyed them. When he left here he was going to need them, whether he went with her or without her. And the way it looked, it would probably be the latter.

She had placed her notebook beneath her sleeping robes while she thought he was asleep, but he hadn't been. He would have liked to have read more of what she'd written, if for no other reason than to get inside her head, and maybe because she might have written something that would give him a clue to who the murderers were. But he didn't for the sake of her privacy. He would have to find his answers another way.

She was gone this morning early, as usual, checking her snares and hunting for fresh game with her bow and arrow. He had gotten up every day and walked outside to strengthen his leg, taking the back side of the mountain's face since the going was easier. But today when he left the cave, he eased his way down over the path of rocks that led to the lake and the creek that it fed. It would be logical for her to have his horse staked near water, and possibly she had his weapons there with the tack.

He found Sky at the lake, diligently cleaning a pine hen. It amazed him, but she brought one home almost every day, killed from a well-aimed toss of a rock. Today it looked as though she had two of the birds. Of course she heard him clumsily making his way along the rock slide, but didn't offer to help. He sensed that much of the reason she didn't help him was not because she didn't possess compassion, but because she didn't want to be too close to him. She seemed to cringe from physical contact of any kind.

By the time he reached level ground, his leg was hurting mightily, but it was healing quite well. It was still red and tender, but Sky continued to make poultices for him and gradually the fiery soreness was being drawn out.

He positioned himself on a large boulder by the small lake and watched her. She didn't like being watched. But he sat there anyway, hoping to annoy her enough that she'd say something. He was getting tired of her refusal to acknowledge him, or to speak to him.

She placed one of the birds inside a clean bag made from an animal stomach, sealed it tightly with a rawhide thong at the top, and then encircled it with sand-filled intestine that had also been made from some previous kill and was apparently kept exclusively for this purpose. The weight of the sand held the meat on a rock shelf beneath the water. He couldn't resist asking her why she did this. Besides, direct questions could not easily be ignored and she was forced to acknowledge his presence.

"I've done this for many years," she replied. "It keeps the meat fresh until I can use it. In the winter, the meat freezes, but when it's thawed it's as good as fresh. After the snows come there are many days when game is scarce. Most animals move to the lower parks to feed. By doing this in the fall, and freezing all the game I can kill, I've been able to keep from going hungry."

While he watched her lovely skilled hands at work, he considered the lonely life she had led in these mountains. But she didn't seem to feel sorry for herself, nor did she seem unhappy. She gave no indication that she would want anything else. Survival seemed to be her only purpose and she seemed content with that. But surely the loneliness affected her. Didn't it?

"Who knows that you're alive besides me and Many Claws?" he asked. "Are there others from the Shoshoni people who come here to see you and help you?"

"It's been best for everyone to believe that I'm dead," she answered simply and without looking up. "No one knows I'm here except you and Many Claws."

She finished cleaning the other pine hen, then gathered up every trace of her presence here by the stream. It amazed him that she left no tracks, as if it had become second nature to her to step where a track, or even an imprint of a foot, could not be seen. Her dwelling place was a very good one because there were many rocks about and she always traveled over them when possible.

After washing her hands in the stream, she rose to her feet. "I'll cook this for breakfast."

She started up the rock slide again, but Matt didn't follow. He remained where he was, committing to memory the sensual way her slender hips swung when she walked, and the way her braids fell forward to rest on the perfect uplift of her young, full bosom.

She stopped and looked back at him. "Aren't you coming?"

"I believe I'll just stay here for a while," he said in explanation. "Soak up the sun and rest before I start the climb back up. I'll go check my horse if you'll tell me where he is."

He saw her mind working as she considered what might happen if she gave him the information. "Will you be leaving here now, going back to your work?"

116

She kept her face very passive, so he had no way of knowing if she hoped he would go, or if she would regret his leaving. He had to assume she looked forward to his departure.

"I don't believe I'm quite ready to go yet, Sky. The distance isn't far for someone with two good legs, but it's considerable for a man in my condition."

Again, she gave no outward sign how she felt about his having to stay longer. But at last she said, "Your horse is about a hundred yards from here in a thick grove of young pine, staked about thirty yards south of the creek. I've already taken him to water this morning, so you wouldn't have to unless you want to."

She said no more and started her climb to the cave again. As soon as she disappeared inside the mountain, he placed his crutch beneath his arm and started down the creek to find Soldier, irritated that she hadn't offered to come with him. He seriously wondered if he'd even be able to find the horse without any better directions to its whereabouts. But maybe he was merely irritated that she seemed to detest being around him. Was it more than just fear that made her keep her distance?

Following the winding creek, he didn't hear anything but his own thoughts and his clumsy progress through the brush. But suddenly she was by his side again, grabbing his arm and dragging him toward some thick undergrowth. As wide-eyed and fearful as a hunted doe, her gaze was trained up ahead, in the direction he had been going.

"They're coming," she whispered frantically. "The men on horses. I saw them from the cliff. We must hide or they'll kill you for certain this time."

She pulled him into the brush, dropping to her hands and knees and crawling beneath the thick, tangled foliage. "Come on," she motioned, and he followed as best he could, towing the crutch behind him. She crawled farther and farther from the creek. For Matt it was painful going, and it was all he could do to bear it in silence. He felt warm wetness beneath his bandage and knew the wound was bleeding again.

At last she stopped and lay down flat on her stomach beneath the buckbrush that offered a secure haven. It was impossible to see outside the brush at all, so they lay side by side in the dim silence, listening as the riders drew nearer. It was some minutes later before Matt heard the snap of twigs and the clink of horseshoes against rock.

The riders followed close to the creek. He could only hope they wouldn't see Soldier hidden in the pines, and that Soldier in turn wouldn't see or smell them and whinny, giving away the fact that Matt was alive and nearby.

The cirque of mountains concealing the cliff cave was a virtual deadend. The lake was continually fed by runoff from the mountains and from glaciers farther up that never completely melted. To go beyond this area would be difficult and there was no easy pass over the mountains at this point.

Matt and Sky waited in their hiding place for at least an hour. The riders moved toward the rock slide and the cliff. Shortly they returned, apparently having seen nothing of interest. Matt felt frustration at them being so close and yet not being able to see who they were, or even hear what they were saying.

It was a considerable time after they passed, and after Matt and Sky could no longer hear the creaking saddles and the murmur of voices. They both released the breath they'd been unconsciously holding.

Sky rolled to her back. The tension visibly drained from her body and she momentarily closed her eyes in relief. "They're gone and didn't find anything. They won't return."

"I wouldn't be so sure of that."

"There's no reason for them to come back," she insisted, glancing over at him. "To cover every mile of these mountains would be an endless task, and they won't come to the same place twice if they found nothing unusual the first time."

"That may be, but you never know about men like that bunch." Matt still lay on his stomach, holding his upper body up off the ground with his elbows. His gaze slid over Sky's face as lovely as a primrose in spring, just inches away and for once in complete repose. She didn't seem aware of their close proximity.

"You said earlier that they'd kill me for certain this time," he continued. "But it's you they really want, Sky. I'm just an obstacle, an unwanted witness they can do without. And how do we know they're the ones who shot me? Personally, I'm not

119

so sure. There's five of them. When I was shot, the bullets came from only one direction, and from only one gun. These boys might just be out searching for that wild stallion who's probably stealing ranch mares."

She considered his words, but gave no response.

Matt's gaze slid over the smooth but strong angles of her face, the velvet softness of her lips, and down to her breasts jutting enticingly upward beneath the loose doeskin blouse. He felt the stirring in his loins so powerful that if he had ever determined to put her from his mind, the thought was forgotten now.

They had lain side by side, hips touching, beneath the cover of the thick brush for nearly an hour, and still she didn't seem to notice. He wondered if she might be losing her fear of him after all the days in his presence.

Then, as if suddenly reading his thoughts and sensing a new form of danger in them, she made a move to put distance between them. But in that instant of retreat, Matt second-guessed her, caught her shoulders, and pressed her back to the cool, rich earth. As erratic as the frightened thrumming of a caged bluebird's heart, her breasts rose and fell against his chest in rhythm to her racing pulse. But even as she began to struggle in those seconds, his lips closed over hers.

Her sweetness flowed into him like the sweet nectar so favored by the hummingbird. He had waited so long to sample her, to see that she was indeed real, but the drugging petal softness of her lips beneath his lasted only a brief second. She lashed out at him with her knee kicking him squarely and soundly on his wound. He rolled away from her, yelping in pain, and quicker than lightning she was over him with her knife to his throat. Her eyes glinted with the fearful but deadly glow of a cornered animal that will fight for its life if necessary.

"Damn it! Put that thing away, Sky!" He grimaced, holding on to his leg and trying to ride out the excruciating pain that brought a stifled moan to his throat. The blood now seeped freely through the bandage and onto his pants leg. "I only wanted to kiss you, for Christ's sake! But I guess I should have expected that kissing a mountain lioness wasn't exactly going to be like licking on a spoonful of sugar."

His words fell on deaf ears. "If you ever touch me again — you . . . you *pigih!* — I'll kill you!"

"Don't go throwing that Shoshoni crap on me, Sky. I can understand some of it, remember? And if I'm a pig then you're nothing but a *taiped.*" Her eyes narrowed to slits. For a minute he thought he'd insulted her enough to make her use the knife for sure, but he continued. "It would be wise for you to remember something else, too. Killing a man is a lot different than killing an animal."

The mask of hatred and contempt faded and altered upon her face until her top lip curled derisively. "You're so very right, Yellow Hair. You just *kill* a man. You don't have to gut him and skin him and haul him a mile or two back home! You just leave him out in the woods and let the animals eat him. You don't have to—"

She stopped suddenly and he saw her lower lip tremble before she bit down on it—hard.

"Put the knife away Sky," he said more gently, wishing he could do something to take away the strains of bitterness and cynicism he had heard in her words and in the speech that had almost sounded like a pathetic plea for understanding. He realized in that moment just how hard it had been for her to kill to survive.

"You fear me for no reason," he continued, all the while slowly sliding his hand up her trembling arm to her hand that held the knife. If she felt his touch, she made no indication. "Tell me, did you have a sweetheart before you came here? Possibly that young cowboy I saw in your sketch book, and the one you wrote the poem about. Did he ever kiss you? Or am I the first?"

Her fingers clenched and unclenched their hold on the knife, unwilling to give up the battle. "Don't pride yourself, Yellow Hair. I've been kissed before you."

"Did you enjoy it?"

"That's none of your business!" Her temper flared anew.

"No. Maybe it's not. I was just trying to make a point."

"I don't want to hear your points."

He wanted to ask her what happened that day seven years ago. Had another man, or men, scorned the fragile innocence of her youth, an innocence which could be so easily crushed, so easily destroyed?

But he couldn't bring himself to ask her these questions. He wasn't really sure he wanted to know the answers, and he didn't know what it would do to her to tell him. Sometimes when something bad happened to a person, that person often felt as if he had done something to deserve it. And telling someone else about it only made it worse, more ugly and vile. He knew this, because of the brand on his back. When people had seen the brand, he'd been shunned or pitied, but it had made people suspicious of him, too, because even if they wouldn't admit it, they secretly wondered if he had deserved it.

Well, he didn't want anybody's pity. He would prefer to be shunned. All he really wanted was to be left alone about his past. He sensed Sky McClellan wanted the same. And she deserved the same.

"Help me up," he said. "I think it's safe to go back now."

Red Sky remained unsure of Matt Riordan and of what to do. Her lips still felt the pressure of his, leaving hers with a swollen feeling, and she decided the memory wasn't entirely unpleasant. She remembered kisses from both Monty and Gray Bear, and while they had been sweet and fun they had been tentative and unsure. There was something infinitely confident and reassuring about Riordan's hot, firm mouth upon hers; there was something infinitely reassuring about Riordan himself. Even though he had nearly walked the Ghost Trail, and was still physically weak, his personality was one that emanated strength and self-possession.

She had never felt this peculiar yearning with Monty or Gray Bear, this yearning to linger in an unfamiliar embrace that nevertheless promised tender sustenance to her wounded heart. But she wasn't at all sure Riordan would be content merely to hold her and replenish her lonely soul with a gentle and loving embrace. He had the dangerous look of a man whose thoughts tapped into a deeper and stronger desire than the simple consolation of friendship. She sensed he had needs that would ask too much of her, and it frightened her. All she was really certain of was that she hadn't liked being called a *taiped,* a child!

He waited there on his back for her to make up her mind whether she was going to help him, watching her with his knowledgeable blue eyes — as if he knew precisely what the thoughts were that wheeled through her mind like tiny thrushes being helplessly tossed about in crazy circles by the wind.

She refused to let her eyes travel the length of his muscled body, but she saw his lean form in her peripheral vision and in her memory from the hours and hours she'd spent washing him with cold water to cool his fever. His hat lay beneath the bush where it had fallen when he'd rolled to his back, and a lock of his golden hair had fallen onto his forehead. She had pushed that tendril back so many times during his fever that she had to catch herself from doing it again.

She had grown accustomed to touching him during his illness, but she was not accustomed to him touching her now. When he took command, it frightened her. She wanted to believe him, to trust him; she would even like to experience his kiss again. But above even the fear of death, she feared lies and betrayal. Riordan was a man of the law and he had a job to do. If he knew what she'd done, he would easily cast aside his romantic inclinations, put her in jail, and ride away. Then all her years of struggle for survival would be for naught.

But then, wouldn't they be someday anyway when the cold north wind blew over her bones and the hungry wolves scattered her remains to the four winds?

"It's safe to go now," she said. "Lead the way."

He glanced at the knife in her hand. At least it wasn't pressed against his throat now. "You don't plan on putting that thing in my back just to get even with me for kissing you, do you?"

"Not unless you try it again."

A flash of irritation crossed his face. She waited while he got to his hands and knees again, knowing she ought to help him, but feeling it would be better if she didn't touch him again.

"You know, Sky," he said, assessing the blood on his pants leg, "we could try trusting each other. It would sure make things a sight easier."

"I learned long ago that words are usually lies, Yellow Hair. Besides, don't lay all the blame on me. You're not an overly trusting man yourself. I see it in your eyes, your actions. If you trusted people, you wouldn't have had yourself armed like an entire battalion of the U. S. Cavalry when you came here."

"In my line of work, a man can trust very few people, Sky," he conceded, "and he can depend on even fewer to get him out of a bind. But at what point do two people, like you and me, decide to trust each other?"

Sky's lips tightened into a thin line. "For you and me, Yellow Hair? There may never be a time."

That night Sky left the cave. In a few minutes she returned carrying Matt's holstered pistol, rifle, and knife. With trembling hands, but a determined jut to her jaw, she handed the weapons to him.

"You'll need them if those men return," she said, evading his piercing blue gaze. "And you'll need them if you are to leave soon."

She moved back to her pallet, as straight and proud as if she were going into battle fully prepared to die. The wolf rose from his place by the fire and lay down beside her. She turned to her side, placing her back to Matt. He thought she must be testing him to see if he had spoken honorably of his intentions toward her. From the words she had spoken this afternoon, he would have never thought she would change her mind about trusting him, especially so soon.

"Thank you, Sky." His whisper revealed the surprise he felt at her change of heart.

She didn't turn around, nor did she reply. He watched her for a long time and she pretended to sleep, but her body was rigid beneath the sleeping robes and her breathing too shallow to deceive him. The firelight flickered lightly over the undulate shape of her body beneath the furs, and cast a blue sheen to the stormy disarray of her black hair. But the firelight was not the only thing that touched her; his eyes lingered, too, caressing her in the only way he could, in the way the sun warms the earth and yet never touches it.

Everything inside him urged him to leave his pallet join her beneath her robes, to pull her into his arms and mold her curves to his hardness, to protect her and let her know that he would never harm her. He ached for her! God, how he ached. It seemed he had from the first moment he'd caught a glimpse of her ethereal beauty in the moonlight. She'd been an enigma, a ghost, a wonderful figment of his imagination. And because she hadn't been completely real he had been able to make of her what he wanted her to be. He had envisioned her coming to him with open arms. Ah, such was the stuff of a lonely man's fantasies!

Now he must face reality, and if he was to continue to gain her confidence he must move slowly. If he didn't, every step of progress he had made thus far would be lost. And just as snow vanishes in the river, she would be lost to him, too. Forever.

Many Claws didn't come until the moon began its new cycle. From Matt's position by the lake, hidden in the pines, he saw the old Indian following a game trail that paralleled the stream. Having just sharpened his hunting knife, he slid it into the scabbard on his belt and reached for his rifle leaning against a rock. Quietly as possible he checked the load. The Indian gave no sign that he'd heard, but he moved directly to the spot where Matt was hidden in the shadows. It didn't surprise Matt that the sage old shaman knew his position.

"Even in the shadows your gun and your knife flash like lightning in a night sky, Riordan," the old man said mockingly. "You should be more careful to stay away from the long reach of Father Sun's fingers."

"I saw you coming. I wasn't trying to hide."

"I am sorry to see you are still here, Riordan. This is not good for Red Sky."

"And why is that, Many Claws?"

"Because you put more burden on her small shoulders. You are one more mouth to feed, and she barely has enough food now."

"She seems to do quite well. A day seldom passes that she doesn't bring home fresh game."

"From which you fill your plate and your belly."

Matt wouldn't let the piercing black eyes or the harsh words intimidate him, although he did feel guilty enough as it was for not being able to go out and help her hunt. He was still dependent on the crutch and made too much noise moving through the forest. He would be more of a hindrance to her than a help.

"It won't be for long, Many Claws. I'll be leaving soon."

"Then you are satisfied that Red Sky knows nothing about the people who killed her family?"

"No. I'm not satisfied at all."

"It would be wise to accept the truth. Red Sky can tell you nothing because she remembers nothing. Sometimes when a bad thing has happened to a person, he or she will push it far back in his mind. Sometimes that is the only way to live with it. She does not allow herself to see what happened that day."

Matt thought of the horror of his own past, of Bailey Loring and his son Red and the hired hands. All of them standing over him, sneering and laughing and enjoying their sadistic game. He could even remember the faces of the hired hands, although he admitted they had faded a little over the years, and maybe if he hadn't seen them before the incident, he might *not* remember them. He had relegated much of it to the far corners of his mind, as Many Claws had said Red Sky had done, but he hadn't forgotten it. No, not at all. And especially not the ridicule, or the pleasure his tormentors had had at seeing him suffer. That humiliation, that helplessness, was a pain worse than the brand. It was the one thing that had taught him how to hate.

"Perhaps you're right," he said noncommittally,

hiding the upsurge of emotion that the memory brought.

"You do not believe a person can put things from his mind that he does not wish to remember?" Many Claws' rough voice rose in a tone that suggested he wished to argue.

"Yes, I believe he can, but I also believe it's time for Sky to remember and to face what happened. I think she could tell me something if she would, but she refuses to speak of it. And so do you."

"I can tell you nothing, for she has told *me* nothing."

"That's what you said before and I found your tongue was forked."

Many Claws' black eyes sparked with anger, glittering like sunlight touching the smooth surface of two chunks of obsidian. "I was protecting her." He lifted his jaw defiantly even though he had no choice but to concede the truth of the matter.

"Yes, I know that now, and I can't say that I blame you. That reminds me" — with thumb and forefinger Matt dug around in his vest pocket and finally pulled out that which he sought — "Here, I have something for you."

Many Claws hesitantly reached for the unseen object, his eyes glowing with suspicion as Matt dropped it in his outstretched palm.

Many Claws stared at it. "What is this, Riordan?"

"Don't you recognize it, Many Claws? That's the bullet Sky dug out of my leg. I thought you might want it back . . . since it belongs to you."

Many Claws' long fingers curled around the slug as his narrowed gaze lifted to Matt again. "How did you know, Riordan?"

"I didn't . . . until now."

Knowing how easily he had allowed himself to be tricked, Many Claws' face darkened with fury and his jaws clenched even tighter, but he said nothing.

"I played a hunch and set a trap," Matt continued. "Can I help it if you walked right into it? There aren't many of those old Spencer rifles around like the one you have there, Many Claws. I'd say it was a war issue — a 56-56. But technically it uses a .52 caliber cartridge. Most cowboys nowadays are using Winchesters and Colts — .44.40's. It's kind of a favorite with the ranch crowd. Besides, only one man shot at me. If those cowboys had ambushed me, I would have been dead. I got to thinking who would have the most to gain by killing me. I considered Sky, but she doesn't own a gun. And of course I doubt she'd have had a change of heart and have saved my life if she'd been the one to shoot me. Then I thought of you. But there's just one question I don't yet have the answer for."

"And what is that, Riordan?" Many Claws asked irritably, his big weathered fingers still curled tightly around the slug.

"Why did you help Sky save my life when you wanted me dead?"

Again the defiant lift to the shaman's head and the proud straightening of his shoulders. "Because

131

she asked me to, Riordan. And I could not refuse her."

"Why would she want to save my life?"

He shrugged. "Who can read the mind of a woman?"

Even though the shaman had been the sniper, Matt didn't fear him. He sensed he wouldn't try to kill him again unless he was provoked. "Sky means a lot to you, doesn't she, Many Claws?"

"She is like a daughter."

Suddenly from the trees across the meadow, a streak of white caught their attention. Esup bounded happily toward them and ran immediately to Many Claws, waiting for his friendly roughing, then nosed around the burlap sack that held provisions.

Both men saw Sky come from the trees and they watched her walk across the meadow toward them in movements all feminine grace, like a lovely goddess from a mythological world. Matt's heart began a rapid thumping and his body came alive as it always did in her presence. By the time she had joined them, he had temporarily forgotten the matter with Many Claws. She gave Matt a glance that made his heart lurch, but she went directly to Many Claws and greeted him with an embrace.

"Let's go to the cave," she suggested. "I'll fix us something to eat and we can talk."

She led the way over the rock slide to the cave. Matt struggled to his feet and propped the crutch beneath his arm, disappointed that she had given him only a cursory glance. Many Claws' gaze followed her retreating figure as he gathered up the burlap sack and flung it over his shoulder. The lines in his aged face deepened, taking on the appearance of deep scores in the earth left behind by millions of years of water, wind, and sun.

"You worry needlessly, Many Claws," Matt said. "I won't tell her it was you who shot me."

Many Claws' black eyes, cradling suspicion and a degree of contempt, shifted to Matt. "This is generous of you, Riordan. But be warned . . . if you hurt her in any way, I *will* kill you. And next time I will not walk away until the buzzards pluck out your eyes."

"I never doubted it, Many Claws. But if I was the sort of man to hurt her, then you would be well within your rights to kill me."

It is the gentle whisper of the rain
Whose touch opens the primrose.

Chapter Eight

Red Sky gauged the passing of time by the blooming of the wildflowers and the transformation of buds to blossoms on the berry bushes. The days on a calendar were of no use to her. She only knew that summer had officially arrived, and Matt Riordan was still with her.

It had been nearly a month since she'd removed the bullet from his leg. The wound was still very sore but healing had progressed remarkably well and he was able to get around much better now. He had said nothing about leaving, though, nor had she mentioned it again, because in all honesty she was reluctant to face the loneliness that she knew would settle over the high country once he was gone, loneliness like the cold silent blanket of winter's snow. Only one thing disturbed her—that she had not dreaded the loneliness before his arrival, but merely accepted it with quiet resignation.

The riders that had nearly stumbled upon them had left the area and had not been seen in the nearby vicinity since. She knew they searched for her, but she pondered over Matt's words that they were not the ones who shot him. If not them, then who?

It had become Matt's habit to go outside every day and take the walk down to where Soldier was at, then back. He tried to help her with the things that he could, insisting upon "earning his keep," but he wasn't up to going hunting with her. With his crutch, he made too much noise and frightened all the game away.

He had at first asked her to go with him on his walks to restake Soldier, but she had always refused, saying she had too much to do. And it was true. Summer would only be in the high country for a short time and then she would once again face winter. If she was to survive those long, cold months, she had jerky to make, herbs and plants to gather, hides to tan for clothing, and roots to dig and store.

Matt was gone for many hours when tending to his horse, but even though the walk was long, he could have returned hours sooner. Red Sky sensed he stayed away from her on purpose. At first she was grateful for this, but as time went on, it began to annoy her.

On this day, she made her way back along the creek with fresh game. She had caught two rabbits in her snares, and they had fine coats that would, when sewn together with others, make warm clothing.

As always, she and Esup hesitated at the clearing to check for danger, but they saw none and hastened across to the trees on the other side. Then, as they neared the lake at the base of the cave, she heard peculiar noises, and a voice. Cautiously she advanced. The trees thinned out around the water and she was able to see clearly. Before her, stark naked, Matt stood in the icy lake, apparently bathing, but obviously not enjoying it.

She crouched back in the trees, watching, even though she knew she shouldn't. But the forbidden sight of his sinewy back, firm buttocks, and muscular legs had a hypnotizing effect on her and she was held to the spot. He must have just gotten into the water, she decided, because he kept lifting his legs up and down, as if he were walking on hot coals instead of cold rocks.

"Damn it! Shit! Sonofabitch!" He suddenly proclaimed. "Damned water isn't any warmer than it was yesterday!"

Red Sky bathed in the lake every day herself after Matt had gone to sleep at night, and she knew it was cold, but such behavior by this big, strong man made her smile. A chuckle even escaped her throat, surprising her, and she quickly put a hand over her mouth to stifle it. Esup looked up at her quizzically, then continued to eye Riordan with indifferent laziness. He had grown fairly tolerant of their visitor, even going so far as to lick the man's hands on occasion and allow his head to

136

be patted. He had warily accepted Riordan into the cave, but he hadn't accepted him into his heart. Red Sky knew it was because she had remained distrustful and the wolf sensed it. But seeing Matt naked made him less the dangerous predator and more the vulnerable human being.

"Friggin' cold water! Damn it!"

Riordan turned around and Red Sky was startled by a front view of him. She nearly turned away in embarrassment as well as respect for his privacy, but her gaze held at the last instant, sliding from the golden brown curls on his chest to his flaccid manhood nestled in a mound of similarly colored hair. The apparatus hardly looked threatening at the moment; it was drawn up tightly to his loins as if trying to get as far away from the cold lake water as possible.

Riordan finally found the courage to sit down in the pool on the flat rock she had placed there herself for the purpose of bathing. The water wasn't deep and only circled up past his waist. His knees jutted up, uncovered, and his wound was visible, raw and red.

She turned away then, feeling guilty at watching him perform such a private function. She would just remain hidden until he had completed his task and gone back to the cave. She could hear the water splashing, though, and the occasional expletive. Finally, she heard the rustle of clothing. She glanced over her shoulder and saw he had his pants back on. He then proceeded to shave. This she watched with a certain fascination, just as she had watched her father when she was a young girl.

Why do men have whiskers and women don't, Daddy?

Well . . . I reckon so men can tickle the women with 'em and make 'em all mad. Ouch!

Oh, no. Did you cut yourself again? Does it hurt?

Yes . . . and yes. But that's what I get for talking when I'm trying to shave.

You know, Daddy, when I grow up, I'm going to marry somebody just like you! I wanted to marry you, but Mama says I can't because you're already married to her.

Well, that's right, pumpkin. Besides, I'd be all old and shriveled up and you'd want somebody young and handsome.

I'll bet I won't ever find anybody as handsome as you.

Maybe not. I guess God did sorta break the mold when he made me.

Oh, how he'd humored her! And how silly she'd been to think she could marry him. But then, when she was five, she hadn't understood what marriage was all about. Her dad had just been her hero. Her idol. She could still see that day so clearly, even the shaving soap floating in little globs on the water and the pieces of whiskers stuck to it. The tinges of blood from his cut.

The blood—

Suddenly Riordan bellowed. She jumped from her reverie and Esup sprang to his feet, fur ruffling around his neck and a growl rumbling deep in his throat. That fool Riordan was singing! Red Sky completely forgot herself. Without thinking, she pushed her way through the foliage and rushed toward him.

"Hush!" she commanded in a low frightened tone. "Be quiet or you'll have those men back."

He rinsed his razor off and felt his face for more stubble. She noticed how smooth his face was now, knowing it would be as soft as her dad's had been when he had just finished scraping off the whiskers. Her eyes strayed to the bit of soap still clinging to one corner of his lip and she saw the wry smile that suddenly appeared there.

"I had a feeling you were over there spying," he said blithely. "I hope you saw something to make it worth your time."

A flush leaped onto her cheeks. "I wasn't spying!"

He arched a brow, disbelievingly.

"I came up the creek with these rabbits and heard you bellowing loud enough to wake the dead," she continued defensively.

"I wasn't bellerin'. I was singing."

"Singing? You sounded more like a frantic cow trying to find her lost calf."

"You cut me to the quick, woman. For your information, I used to sing to the cattle on the drives from Texas when I worked as a cowboy. My voice was so pure and clear it put those animals into the most restful state of mind you can imagine."

"More likely a stampede. And if you're going to continue to make so much noise, I'm going to have to ask you to leave. Besides, you're well enough to ride and you're jeopardizing the location of this place the longer you stay here."

He sobered. The cheerfulness left his eyes, and once again he became the man with the dark secrets and thoughts she couldn't fathom or trust. "Aren't you afraid I might tell someone where you are?"

She looked away from his disconcerting, waiting gaze. Once again his presence was forcing her to make choices. "I don't see how I can prevent it from happening if that's what you choose to do. It was a chance I took when I brought you here."

"Yes," he said solemnly. "You did take a big chance, and I'm grateful for that. So don't worry. I don't choose to tell anyone where you are. I'm here to take you safely back to civilization, if you will go and testify. Then, if you choose, I'll let you come back here. I'll even bring you back."

She felt betrayed by the trust she'd put in him. "I thought you said you'd leave as soon as you could ride."

"I've changed my mind."

"You mean you lied! Well, I've told you, I won't go! I can see now I should have let you die! Many Claws was right."

She turned sharply on her heel and started away, but he caught her arm. She reached for her knife, but he was too quick for her this time and anticipated her move. He caught her other arm and drew her up closer to him. The wolf growled but

140

Matt told it to shut up, and amazingly enough it listened to him.

Red Sky felt intimidated by the expanse of Matt's bare chest and the muscles bulging in his arms. Her breathing quickened and she began to feel light-headed. He could snap her wrists easily, if he chose to. He could break her, make her go with him. She had let her guard down, been captured, and now he could do anything he chose.

She could call upon Esup to protect her. He would obey even though he knew Riordan. And she would, yes, if she had to.

"Let me go, Yellow Hair," she demanded.

"I'm not Yellow Hair! My name is Matt Riordan and I wish you would call me that!" She saw his patience thinning.

"You're raising your voice. Voices carry." She tried to squirm away from him, but he had regained enough of his strength to be the master of her.

"I'm not worried because no one is within miles of this place."

The words alone, coupled with the sudden sultry look in his eyes, made the fear continue to rise inside her, but it wasn't the same fear she had felt for those men seven years ago, or even the fear she'd felt toward Matt in the beginning. No, this was a different kind of fear. She feared her own weakness, and the strange desire his nearness caused inside her. The feeling made her want to give in to her own surging weakness and his strength. To turn herself over to his protection. But would he protect her, or would he leave her used and torn like those other men had left her family?

Surely he had been kind only to get what he wanted. She must never surrender to his kindness. How could she be sure if he was truly the benevolent man he appeared to be, or if he was like so many others who were masters of deception?

"How do you know no one is about?" She forced herself to look into his hypnotizing blue eyes and to steel herself against the unsettling emotions thundering through her mind and body. "You didn't hear my approach."

"Maybe not, but I've always sensed your presence, Sky. I've always known when you were watching me — always."

It was true. He *had* always known when she was near. And she was embarrassed now that he knew she had followed him and had watched him many times in the beginning, long before she had brought him here. But she'd never watched him do anything as private as taking a bath. She had always just watched him riding the copper horse, fascinated by the way he sat upon it as if he were part of it; intrigued by the maleness of him and that mysterious quality she did not possess and did not understand, but that her own body seemed to need in some inexplicable way.

The darkening of his eyes sent danger signals throughout her body. Once again he seemed poised to spring.

"Let me go," she demanded, struggling against his iron grip.

142

"Take a walk with me, Sky." His voice softened persuasively. "It's a lovely day. Your work will wait."

Surprised by the peculiar invitation, her gaze locked with his. A walk? A walk had nothing to do with survival, with his injury, or why he was here. A walk had nothing to do with leaving here and going to Cheyenne. What was his motive for taking a walk?

Her gaze slid uncontrollably to his lips. She had thought many times, even in her dreams, of the way his mouth had felt on hers. He had not tried to touch her since she had threatened him with her knife. But as the days stretched one into another, she had come to realize that she missed the physical contact and had even begun to yearn for it. Even despite the fear of this moment, she didn't want him to release her. She felt truly alive. With a strange ambivalence she debated whether she would want to feel his lips again. If she went on a walk with him, might he kiss her again? If he tried, would she let him?

"I don't want to take a walk with you, Yellow Hair," she said belligerently so he wouldn't be able to read her true thoughts.

"My *name* is Matt Riordan."

"All right—Matt Riordan!"

"That's better," he said. His tone deepened, lowering to a gruff and seductive whisper that sent chills down her spine. "Now, we're going to take those rabbits you just caught and we're going to go into the woods and cook them up and have a little picnic. I'll bet you haven't had a picnic for a long time, have you, Sky? Well, we're going to have one because I'm tired of being in that damn cave. It's dark in there and I don't much like being penned in. I like to be outdoors where I can see what's coming. You might disagree with me, but that cave reminds me a lot of a trap."

Red Sky found her constitution weakening to a dangerous point of no return. His eyes, his words, even his hands on her arms — firmly but caressingly — sent a tingle through her body, persuading her to give in to him. She felt an old spark of frivolity. A picnic! How wonderful. It had been so long since she'd had a moment of unguarded pleasure. But even as she had the thought, she retaliated.

"You're a fool to be darting off on a picnic of all things! You were nearly killed just a month ago. Do you know no caution?"

He remained unmoved by her heated argument. "Not much. But life isn't worth a damn if a man can't take a few risks now and then. Isn't that right? Or wouldn't you know about taking risks?"

Her top lip lifted in a sardonic curl; her eyes glowed with contempt. "Every day of my life is a risk, Riordan. You know that, so don't insult me."

"The name is Matt."

"All right — *Matt!*"

His stern countenance softened; the edge of his mouth loosened but not enough to be called a smile. "Now, where do you want this picnic to be?"

"I don't *want* a picnic," she snapped. "But as

long as you insist, there's a spot about a quarter of a mile from here."

They frequently had picnics after that, when Matt could coerce her to leave her work. She had numerous excuses but they were poor ones and were always met with a quick rebuttal from Matt.

"But winter will be upon me soon," she'd argue, "and I won't be ready for it."

He would reply, "If you'll come, I'll help you tan that hide when we get back." Or, "I'll gather all the kindling you'll need for *two* winters!"

On this particular day, he said, "I gave up my crutch two days ago, Sky. Let's take a walk and let me try out my leg."

She wasn't behind in her work, thanks to his help. But as each day passed, she felt the bond between them tightening. She didn't know if he felt it, too, but it troubled her. She didn't want to start depending on him for everything, especially companionship. He had a life beyond these mountains. A job to return to. Possibly a woman. Once she'd wanted him away from here as quickly as possible. Now, she found herself capitulating to his every whim and for no good reason. She couldn't keep her mind on her work anymore for it was always wandering off, lost in images of him and wondering what he was doing when they were apart. She had nearly stepped in one of her own traps one day because she'd been lost in thought about Riordan. His presence was weakening the alertness necessary for survival in these mountains. He should leave, but how could she make him go?

And each time they walked, she secretly hoped he would make a move toward her. That he would try to kiss her again. She wondered with increasing anxiety why he seemed no longer to want to kiss her as he had wanted to do in the beginning. Did it mean he did not find her attractive? That, perhaps to him, she was indeed a child?

"All right," she replied, feigning exasperation. "But we must not be gone for long."

"Bring your sketch book this time," he said. "You could draw something." She hesitated, but he always seemed to read her mind. "Don't worry, I won't look at anything if you don't want me to."

She led the way along the game trail through the trees. As always they paused at the meadow to doublecheck for any sign of interlopers. When they saw none they proceeded on to the other band of trees. There was one spot Red Sky particularly liked, and sensed that Matt did, too, although he never said so. It was a clearing in the middle of some thick pines. The reason no trees grew there was because it was rocky ground. An outcropping of slab granite, warmed by the sun, provided the perfect place to sit.

"I guess this will do," she said, not wanting to soften toward him even though inwardly she knew she was.

"This is fine," he responded.

He found a position behind her and slightly above her on one of the long, flat rocks. The heat emanating from the rocks, and the sun warm overhead, made him drowsy. He lay back, shielding his eyes with his hat. But he didn't pull the brim down too snugly over his face, and he could see out from under it. Sky sat just a few feet away with her back to him, her pitch black hair, neatly braided as always, gleaming in the sunlight.

Matt supposed that if they'd been children he would have been set upon by mischievousness, and have wanted to give those braids a good tug, then run away laughing. Even now, as a full-grown man, he had the urge to feel their silky thickness in his hands, to caress it, and draw the tresses to his lips. Sometimes, like now, the urge was almost more than he could resist. His hand was only inches away from the braid when he drew it back. Things were going smoothly between them. He would be foolish to destroy the growing bond. But never had he treaded so carefully with a woman. It was nearly driving him insane.

She opened her sketch book and, with charcoal in hand, began drawing a meadow. As the picture took shape, he recognized the craggy cliff that concealed her cave, the lake, and the meadow at the base of it. She added a woman in buckskins with long, flowing hair whom he recognized as herself. In the picture, she looked toward the cliff dwelling with a solemn, almost wistful expression. Behind her, she drew a man, watching her, seemingly waiting. By the time she had added a gun to his hips and a hat to his head, there was no doubt

147

in Matt's mind that he was looking at an image of himself.

There was an awfully hard edge to the man's jaw, and a hooded look in his eyes. Matt had never pictured himself as being so hardened, but he knew now that she saw him that way. No wonder she seemed to cringe at his touch and had been so slow in trusting him. Even now, for all appearances, she didn't trust him fully. He saw in her eyes the fear that at any second he would turn on her or prove to be a liar. And then she would be satisfied that she had judged him correctly.

He needed no interpretation of the picture, or at least he didn't think so. Sky was obviously troubled by the decision to leave this place or to stay; a decision that could mean death no matter which course she chose. And suddenly he wasn't so sure that taking her away from here was the right thing to do.

Having completed the sketch, she turned the page to a clean sheet. The image of a pair of chipmunks playing on a stump fell onto the paper with alacrity, ease, and perfection. She drew a couple more sketches then closed the notebook, looking as pensive as she had in the picture she'd drawn of herself.

"You're an excellent artist, Sky," he said, pushing his hat to the back of his head and sitting up. "I recognized Many Claws in your sketch book that day I was snooping around. Who were the other people? Your family?"

148

She shifted uneasily on the rocks. "I thought you were asleep."

"No, just dozing."

She didn't speak for a long time, but finally said, "Yes, they were my family."

"Even the young man—the cowboy? And what about the young Indian brave?"

She sighed, fidgeting with the corner of the closed sketch book. She looked straight ahead, giving him only her profile. Her response seemed forced. "The cowboy was Monty Glassman. A friend of mine. He was there at the house, visiting me the day . . ." There was a long pause but finally she concluded abruptly. "He was killed, too."

Matt stored the name and information away. These were things that might help him solve this case. True, he had only been sent here to collect Sky as a witness, but now he knew he would never be content to walk away until he found the men who had destroyed her former life.

"And the Indian? Is he some relation to Many Claws?" he continued to probe.

"No. His name is Gray Bear. He, too, was a friend of mine."

"Were they your boyfriends?"

The memories obviously troubled and saddened her. She was a moment in answering. "Yes, they both were. So different they were, too. Gray Bear still lives, but of course I haven't seen him for seven years. And now—" she twisted on the rock and finally lifted her eyes to his. A certain defiance replaced her melancholy. "And now—your turn. Who is the woman Elizabeth that you spoke of during your fever? Your wife perhaps?"

It was Matt's turn to squirm. In a nervous gesture, he removed his hat then pulled it back on, tugging it down tightly onto his forehead. "I'm not married."

"Then Elizabeth is a girlfriend, waiting somewhere for you when you complete your business here with me?"

"No. She's not a girlfriend either."

"Then she *was* a girlfriend?" she persisted unmercifully.

"No! She . . . she was . . ."

Sky smiled—a flash of beauty unlike anything Matt had seen before—and he completely forgot what he was about to say. He had never seen her smile, and this was a full, wide impish grin. His heart lifted, his pulse quickened. She was teasing him, making him pay for interrogating her and snooping into her things, for looking over her shoulder while she drew. But he didn't care. He fought the most powerful urge to scoop her into his arms, to feel her sun-heated body pressed against his, to lay her back into the warm grass where they could slowly and passionately meld into one.

"So," she said, that smile still curving her lovely mouth, "you like to ask questions, but you don't like to answer them?"

He felt the ease with which she sat in his company today. It had increased with each day since she'd given him back his weapons and nothing had happened.

"Elizabeth was a pretty redhead I was in love with once upon a time," he managed.

An indiscernible shift in her expression made him hope she might be as jealous of Elizabeth as he was of her Monty Glassman and Gray Bear. It didn't matter that it was years ago. They had held a place in her heart once upon a time and he sensed they always would.

"That's a coincidence," she said, looking away into the past. "Monty Glassman also had red hair. His was a light, coppery color, not much darker than your horse. It gleamed in the sunlight so incredibly, but he seldom removed his hat because he hated being called Red."

Her casual reference to "Red" seemed to hit Matt like a blow below the belt. Bailey Loring had been called Red, and his son had been called Red Jr.

"Elizabeth's hair was that color, too," he said quietly, inexplicably disturbed by the coincidence of it. "It gleamed with blond highlights."

She nodded, as if she envisioned the exact color he spoke of.

"How old were you when you and Elizabeth were in love?"

"I was eighteen. But that was ten years ago, Sky."

"What happened between you and Elizabeth? Why didn't you make her your wife?"

Matt didn't want to talk about Elizabeth to anybody, and especially not to Sky McClellan. If he told her what had happened and why, she might choose to believe the accusations and not the truth, as so many others had. Then he would lose their newly formed bond of trust and friendship. She would reject him as others had.

"Elizabeth Loring simply didn't love me enough, Sky," he said. "That was what happened."

Red Sky sensed that just as she had her ghosts, so did Matt Riordan. There was much more he wasn't telling her, and maybe never would. But in the quiet moments they shared she found herself dreaming again. Dreaming of the handsome stranger who came riding toward her to carry her away to a life of love and fulfillment and of happiness. But Matt Riordan would never carry her away to dreams and songs. When he found out what she'd done, he would have no choice but to carry her away to prison and to the gallows.

"Why were you branded, Matt?" she asked quietly. "Who did such a terrible thing to you?"

He stood up suddenly, wincing from a sharp pain in his leg. "It's not worth talking about. Now, I believe we'd better go back and finish up your work."

Red Sky moved in front of him, blocking his retreat. She almost laid a hand on his arm, but caught herself at the last moment. The wind grabbed her hair and pulled some of the shorter strands from her braids and into her face. He lifted one from her cheek. The rough texture of his hands, hot and tender on her flesh, made her

152

heartbeat quicken with that strange yearning she was coming to know with increased frequency. She didn't move; she didn't even reach for her knife. And she wondered why she was becoming so complacent and so reckless with this stranger who had intruded upon her life so unexpectedly.

She fell into the mesmerizing pool of his blue gaze. She saw understanding in his eyes. If only the two of them could comfort each other in some way — allow their bodies and minds to absorb the pain of one into the other, diluting it until it vanished.

"We're two people with pasts that we'd both like to forget," she said. "Have you found, in your travels, that it is like that with many people, Matt?"

"Yes, I think so," he replied. "But without those pasts, we wouldn't be here right now . . . with each other. So possibly, even some good comes out of tragedy."

She nodded with understanding, then said, "Let's go home. *Kim, nehaynzeh.*"

Come, my friend. Her words had stayed with Matt for days. He'd even heard them in his sleep, and he'd fought an ongoing battle to stay on his pallet and away from her. But each night the desire grew worse and the erotic, warm glow of the firelight dancing and swaying over the cave's rock walls seemed to only enhance and arouse further the urge within him to sample her sweet innocence.

153

But if she had been violated, as he suspected, it would not be easy for her to give herself to a man. She might never. For her to enjoy such a union would take patience and understanding from her partner. He didn't know if he could be the lover she needed to erase the tragedies of her past, and it troubled him. As much as he wanted to make love to her and show her that not all men were motivated by evil and selfish intent, he was also afraid he wouldn't be able to draw out the beauty of the act and show her the pleasures a man and woman could experience together. For the first time in his life he seriously considered the future. What would become of her, and of him, in the days to come? This was one woman he could not simply bed and then walk away from.

So he stayed where he was, in physical and mental anguish and in uncharacteristic fear. Like the night wind, her presence brushed over him, but she remained an intangible substance he could not hold. She possessed his mind, his every waking moment, even his dreams.

And so it was one early morning when he stepped out of the cave, lost deep in thought and desire, that he came face to face with an Indian brave. The man she called Gray Bear.

My youth has faded on a Dream Song,
The tune is remembered but not the words.

Chapter Nine

Both men automatically leaped apart and into a battle stance, reaching for their weapons. Circling wide of the other, each waited to see if the surprise encounter would escalate into a fight.

Then a startled voice sounded from the cave's entrance. "Gray Bear? Is that really you?"

The brave couldn't keep his eyes from straying to Red Sky. She released a little cry of joy and ran forward, flinging her arms around his neck and giving him no choice but to dismiss the pretense of battle. His arms closed around her, holding her tightly. Matt straightened, stung by a searing hot flash of jealousy. All this while he had treated her with kid gloves only to see her melt into the arms of another man like warm honey onto hot bread.

But the thought had no sooner surfaced than she set the young man away from her, a frown of worry creasing her brow and replacing her momentary joy.

155

She gazed at him anxiously, and he at her, with a thirst that seemed almost incapable of being quenched. He took another step toward her, but she retreated, holding up her hand to keep him at arm's length. Sorrow and pain filled her eyes. And regret.

"Oh, Gray Bear, my old friend, I never thought we would meet again. It's so wonderful, but . . . it isn't good that you're here. How did you find me?"

Gray Bear seemed reluctant to respond to her question and to her sad, pleading eyes. Finally he glanced beyond her. For the first time both she and Matt saw Many Claws standing beneath the pine tree where the eagles had their nest.

Many Claws left his position and came forward. "He followed me, Red Sky. I did not know until it was too late."

"My dreams were haunted with your image," Gray Bear said fervently, taking her hand in earnest. This time she did not retreat. "Even when Father Sun comes to lift the veil of night, my heart has yearned for the impossible — to see you once again!"

His black eyes consumed every detail of her face as if even now he could not believe she was real. He picked up one of the decorations that hung around his neck and lifted it for her eyes. "See, I still wear the strand of your hair that you gave me on that last day I saw you."

Sky had forgotten about the lock of hair, and was mildly surprised that he had held it so dear. He had braided it, bound it tightly, and attached it to a piece of rawhide.

His grip on her hand tightened. "For my dream to become real must surely be a gift of the Great Mystery Himself! The Shoshoni believe you long ago walked the Death Trail, for they saw no way you could have survived alone the cold and hunger of the Winter Moons. But, somewhere along the Death Trail, they believed that your spirit sorrowed of joining the Sky People alone, and, having been separated from your family, your spirit drifted over Mother Earth, searching for their souls. We laughed at the White Eyes for thinking you were alive, when we knew it was only your spirit that roamed, lost, in the high country.

"Your uncle made many journeys to the mountains for spiritual guidance," Gray Bear continued. "He told the People it was to ask for things that would help our tribe overcome its hunger. But I began to think that he made too many journeys, and then palefaces came asking about you. When this man came, this Pinkerton, I listened at the tipi, and I heard the things he said to Many Claws and Chief Washakie. He seemed certain you were alive, and my heart leaped with joy and hope of its own.

"Many Claws has forgiven me for following him. I told him how I had long ago chosen you to be my wife, to share my blanket and be the mother of my sons. My heart has not changed in this matter, my beloved Red Sky."

Many Claws stepped forward. "I allowed him to come here, Red Sky, because some day I will die, and you will need someone else to help you."

Red Sky managed to remove her hands from Gray Bear's. The tightness in her chest made it difficult to draw a breath. A cold fear settled over her. What had happened to the peace of her world? She could blame only her own carelessness for destroying it. At some point she had accidentally allowed someone to see her, and they in turn had told others. The riders had come and then Matt Riordan. Now Gray Bear, complicating things even worse.

"This is most kind of you, *adah*," she said respectfully. "But I've survived, and even with you gone I can continue to do so because you've taught me what to do. As happy as I am to see Gray Bear again, I'm afraid it wasn't wise to bring him here. Now the knowledge of this place is known by yet another. The secrecy of my dwelling has been truly jeopardized."

"If I am wrong to bring Gray Bear here," Many Claws said, "then were you not wrong to bring Riordan? Your secret is safe with Gray Bear, with the Shoshoni, where you have become a legend. It is *not* safe with this paleface stranger. Once he is gone from here, he will tell all."

Red Sky glanced from one man to the other. The warmth she had felt at seeing her old friend turned into a confusing emotion when her gaze caught Matt's. Many Claws had called Matt a stranger, but at this moment, he felt less a stranger to her than Gray Bear did. In his eyes, she saw understanding, and something more that made a warm fire stir within her, but it was not something she necessarily feared the way she had in the beginning.

"I had no choice but to bring him here," she replied. "He would have died. There's no point in arguing this further."

Gray Bear's lips curled derisively, but Many Claws cut off any possible retort the young brave might have had planned. "Since you and Gray Bear have not seen each other for many seasons," he said, "it would be wise for you to talk in private. Gray Bear is willing to take you from here to a safer place. Since he has long wanted you to be his wife, it is good that you are together again."

Red Sky's eyes flashed. "I've told you many times I won't take a husband! Gray Bear shouldn't be led to believe I'll marry him. I will marry no one."

Matt came forward and stood next to her, almost protectively. "Don't any of you understand that if she goes with me to Cheyenne, testifies and names the killers, or at least gives us information as to who they are, then we can capture them and prosecute them? After that she would be free to live the rest of her life as she pleases — *anywhere* she pleases, and with any*one*. Or even alone if she so chooses. She won't have to hide anymore." He looked down into her eyes and she felt her heartbeat quicken at the tenderness on his face. "Don't let them talk you into something you don't want to do, Sky."

"You are one to speak such words, Riordan," Many Claws replied. "Have you not stayed here two moons and tried to bend her to your will? You are well, I see. You should be gone from here. Why do you stay? *Haganionde?*"

Matt couldn't deny the shaman's accusations, but he saw his way as the better one for Sky. He wanted her free, not like a coon trying to outrun the foxes, only to be killed in the end when she finally grew too tired and too weak to run.

He saw another threat in Gray Bear. He didn't want to lose her to this man from her past. What

159

were they to each other? Friends? Former lovers? But something told him no to the latter question. Sky would have only been fourteen then, and Gray Bear about the same age. Indian society held strong beliefs against sexual intercourse before marriage, just as the white society did. It was not likely that two fourteen-year-old adolescents would have done more than hold hands and steal a few kisses. The thought gave him some peace of mind. But now they were both grown, and Gray Bear was a man with lusty desires, confidence, and arrogance. And Sky was a woman awakening at last to her own femininity. She would be very vulnerable now, and if anyone were to tap her desires, Matt wanted to be the one.

"Come with me, Red Sky," Gray Bear said. "We will talk of the seasons we have been separated."

Red Sky's gaze darted over the three men. She felt caught in a tug-of-war. Didn't Many Claws and Gray Bear know that seven years couldn't be erased? That they couldn't change what had happened by simply making her go to another place? Even if a person longed for the past, there was no going back to it. Time changed people, and circumstances changed people. Red Sky wasn't sure who she was anymore, but she knew she had long ago ceased being the girl Sky McClellan who Gray Bear fancied himself to be in love with.

Their possessive and authoritative attitudes angered her. "You may all go back to where you came! Leave me to my own peace and my own world. If the killers come, I'll stand and fight, the way I should have done before!"

160

She ran away from them, down the rock slide with the ease of a lynx, and then disappeared into the trees. But soon she saw Gray Bear following. Matt stood at the top of the cliff with Many Claws. Even from the distance, and from his stance alone, she sensed Matt's disapproval of the entire incident, but he didn't try to follow.

She would have preferred seeing Gray Bear again under different circumstances, but perhaps she should give him a chance to speak his piece. She stopped her flight, sat down on a fallen log, and waited for him to catch up to her.

He wound his way quickly through the woods and halted suddenly when he saw her, not expecting her to be waiting. He joined her on the log, sitting so near she felt the heat of his body emanating to her. Some familiarities returned, like the distinctly musky smell of him, not unpleasant, just uniquely his own and different from Matt's, which she had grown accustomed to. She wondered if she, too, smelled of the outdoors, of leather, and of wood smoke.

It was odd being with him again. She waited for the old feelings of attraction to return. After all, he hadn't changed. He had only become more handsome. But like everything of her youth, the feelings, too, were gone and could only remain as bittersweet memories.

"You're still slow, Gray Bear," she said, unable to keep from teasing him. At least that part of their former relationship returned with ease.

He smiled. *"Kaidivise.* Not true. I am not slow, Red Sky. You were just born with wings on your heels."

She chuckled, remembering having heard those words before. "Yes. My brothers and my sister used to tell me that. I could outrun all of you."

For a moment she was lost in the pleasant memory of childish games they used to play in the warm, grassy meadows of Long Moon Valley. But only for a moment. Gray Bear picked up her hand, which she immediately withdrew. Tensing, she stood up and moved away from him, unable to look at him. "Please understand, Gray Bear, this is all so sudden and . . . and things have changed!"

He came to stand behind her, laying his hands on her shoulders. Again she moved beyond his reach and he became visibly perturbed. "Have you not longed for my touch as I have yours?"

How could she tell the truth and hurt his manly pride? Over the years she had longed for no man's touch, only for the comforting arms of her mother and father. And now, the only touch she seemed to want was Matt's. She knew that to allow Gray Bear any privileges, even small ones, would be dangerous. He would take too much liberty and assume she felt things she didn't, simply because he felt them. That was the way Gray Bear was. Suddenly she remembered how stifled he could make her feel, like a caged animal — doted over and cared for but not free to do its own bidding.

"I've thought of the good times, Gray Bear, but it isn't of much use to dwell on things that can't be."

"But they can be — now!"

"No. As I said, things have changed. I've changed."

He stared at her, his black eyes twin points of confusion and frustration. "Explain this to me."

"There's nothing to explain. I won't run away to another place as Many Claws wants me to. I'm accustomed to the life I have here. You know we've always been friends, Gray Bear, and we always will be, but don't ask more from me than that."

"You have lain with the White Eyes, haven't you?" he asked accusingly. "You are *his* woman now. Before, it was that other White Eyes, Monty Glassman, and now it is Riordan — this lawman who wishes to fool you into going to Cheyenne with him. He does not care for you, Red Sky! He has a job to do. He is a man who takes the White Eyes' money to kill other men. He does not do it to protect his People, or even himself! He will walk away from you when he has done this thing he calls a 'job.' "

"He isn't my man, and he tries in vain, as you do, to make me leave here."

"He shares your cave for many suns, Red Sky. How can he not touch you? I think he is not a man at all, but a woman."

"Enough of this, Gray Bear," she tried to hold on to her temper. "I'm happy to see you, but I won't go anywhere with anybody until I'm ready. Can't anyone understand that to leave here would make me a stranger in a strange land? That frightens me! I don't feel as if I belong anywhere but here. I have no people. *My* people are gone."

"The Shoshoni are your people. They will help you if you will let them."

"I'm not safe on the reservation and you know it. If the Indian agent didn't turn me in, someone else would. Not all of the Shoshoni have benevolent feel-

163

ings for a breed. They scorn us the same as the white people do."

Gray Bear came to his feet, his frustration mounting. *"Tivise.* True. But your excuses are lame. You pretend to be one of the People, but your heart deceives you. I think you are afraid to share the suffering and the shame of the Shoshoni."

"Ha! You have become a fool, *nehaynzeh.* You know nothing of what I've suffered, and you would be wise to hold your tongue until you do."

They said nothing for a time, both silently regretting the harsh words spoken after so many years apart. She turned to him, sorrow filling her eyes again. "Are things really that bad on the reservation, Gray Bear? I thought the government gave you cattle to raise. And you have farms now to grow food. Many Claws gives me the impression the People are doing all right now."

"There is much Many Claws does not tell you," he replied bitterly. "The government supplies us with food, yes, but I think it is only when they feel like it. They do not seem to know we must eat every day. We are not allowed to leave the reservation without a permit, although many of us do leave so we can go into the forest and kill game. We are only allowed to hunt once a year. The palefaces can hunt all year— even on our land, the reservation. Our cattle dwindle away with each passing season like the wild game. The cattle are stolen by palefaces and even other Indian tribes, and by traders who bring firewater to the reservations and abuse our women. Did you know that some of the men in our tribe are so poor they sell their daughters to the palefaces so they can feed the rest of their families?"

She felt so completely helpless and angered by the situation. "Can't the rustling be stopped?"

"The government does not care that our cattle are stolen," he answered vehemently. "It is only when a big rancher is murdered that they seem to care. And many palefaces have been murdered since your family was killed, Red Sky, but the law can not seem to catch the killers. Or maybe they do not want to."

"But why not?"

"I do not know." He shrugged his broad shoulders, and his eyes, too, were filled with helplessness. "But fewer people come to start ranches and settlements. They fear for their lives. I do not care that they stay away — it is better for us — but it is strange that some of the ranchers are not touched by the problems that the others are."

"What do you mean?"

"Glassman, for one, has had no trouble. He says he has lost cattle, but his herd grows, spreading across the plains like the great herds of buffalo that once roamed there."

"You only hate Rusty Glassman because he's Monty's father," she said. "You've singled him out."

"My heart holds no kindness toward him for that reason, but what I say is true."

"All right, but what about the crops on the reservation? Have they been failures, too?"

"We try to grow potatoes, wheat, and other foods, just as the Indian agent teaches us. But we are not farmers! We are warriors and hunters! And they keep us on leashes like dogs and goats!"

She heard the frustration he felt with his life, but

165

she could offer him no solution. There was nothing she could do about the situation, although she would like to. One person was no match for the government or the careless attitude of the law, unless . . . unless that one person could tell them who was rustling and killing.

"I'm sorry to hear that nothing has changed on the reservation in these years. Now, tell me why you have not taken a wife. I'm sure there are many lovely girls who would want to share your blanket."

Gray Bear leaned back against a tree, resting his hands on his narrow hips in the arrogant stance she remembered so well. He wasn't as tall as Matt Riordan or as solidly built, but he was younger and his body had not reached its full maturity. He had always refused to wear the garb of the white man and she saw that his pride still remained intact. His bronzed torso, naked and hairless, sported only an array of necklaces and pendants made of every sort of thing from animal's teeth, to claws, shells, and beads. Leather breeches covered his legs and they in turn were draped with a leather breechcloth. Moccasins protected his feet. His black hair was well combed, hanging long, with front portions braided, tied with rawhide thongs and adorned with feathers. He moved with the same regal dignity befitting a chief, and if he had lived a generation or two sooner, she was sure he would have been a great Shoshoni leader.

"I took a wife, Red Sky, but she was untrue. I put her away from me. Scorned mightily by our people, she married a man of the Arapaho."

"But they have long been the Shoshoni's enemies!"

He shrugged. "We are forced to share the reservation with them. They on one side, and we on the other. But you know this. She is gone now and it matters little to me."

"Had she no children for you?"

"No. But that is past, Red Sky. And now I see that it was not meant to be because the Great Mystery knew I would someday find you again. Oh, Red Sky!" He dropped to one knee before her and took her hands in his, holding them tightly. "When I heard you still lived, my heart lifted and sang! It sang with the songs you once gave to the forest, and to me. In my dreams, many times, I have heard your voice lifting to the heavens, sweeter than even the trilling songs of the bluebirds. Sing to me again, Red Sky. Then I will know this moment is not a dream."

Red Sky stood up, politely pulling her hands free of his and moving a safer distance away. She wished she could be responsive, but she couldn't. She looked away, pain piercing her heart like a thousand arrows. "I don't sing anymore, Gray Bear."

His handsome face darkened with concern. "Why has this happened?"

"I couldn't let anyone know I was here. To the world, I'm dead, Gray Bear, and I have been for seven years. Do you know what it's like to be dead?" When his only response was a bemused expression, she sighed and proceeded. "Besides, there's no song in my heart."

He came to his feet but refrained from touching

her again, something she realized was very difficult for him to do. She also saw the pain of her rejection clearly on his handsome face.

"I'm sorry, Gray Bear," she said. "I can no longer be the girl you once knew."

He was still confused. "But you *will* sing again, Red Sky, when I take you from here. I know this. We can go to the mountains away from here and live. We need belong to no tribe, no people. And you would be safe. I would protect you."

An oppressive weight settled upon her. Her peaceful world was falling apart and decisions had to be made. Lives might even depend on her. But could she tell the authorities anything important enough to help? Or would she just be giving away her position and placing herself in jeopardy for nothing? She had put so much of that horrible day from her mind, purposefully trying to forget it. Now Matt Riordan wanted her to remember. And Gray Bear and Many Claws wanted her to keep running.

"I must have time to think, Gray Bear. To decide what is the best course to take."

"If this White Eyes had not come into your life, you would not have this decision to make," he declared hotly. "You would let me take you away from here!"

"Riordan is only a consequence of what happened many years ago," she replied. "I don't want to leave here, and I don't think you want to either. You say it now, but in time you would yearn to return to your people and you'd resent me for taking you away."

She started up a forest path away from him. He

hurried after her. "That is not so! Remember the way it was, Red Sky. It can be that way again, only better, if you come away with me and be my wife. If you go with the White Eyes, I fear you will die!"

She stopped. Even now, asking her to run away with him and be his wife, he hadn't said he loved her. She saw more clearly than before that Gray Bear was possessive, and to him a woman would be another possession to show off to his fellow braves as one would a fine string of horses or a new Winchester rifle. Oh, she should not doubt the sincerity of his heart, but she knew Gray Bear was a dreamer, and she couldn't help but wonder if he was more in love with the dream than with her.

She faced him. "You must try to understand the way I feel, *nehaynzeh*. I'm confused about these developments and I don't know what to do. But my heart speaks loudly on one matter. And even though it fears death, it tells me it no longer wants to be a fugitive."

"This I do understand, Red Sky. But understand my heart as well. I do not want to lose you again now that I have found you. And know that I would never hurt you or betray you if you came away with me. Can you be so sure of the White Eyes you have called back from the Death Trail?"

"Yes, I know I can trust you, Gray Bear, and that is a great comfort. But I don't want to put your life in jeopardy."

"But I would die for you, Red Sky!"

"No one should die for me. It's a foolish sacrifice and I couldn't live with myself if anything happened to you or Many Claws because of me."

"It is your talk that is foolish! I do not like to listen to it! I think that maybe you *want* to die. That you think, somehow, you deserve it."

"Maybe I do," she said levelly, meeting his gaze. "I don't know the answer to that. I only know that death frightens me more when it stalks someone else. As for myself, I face it everyday. In its whispering silence, my knife has brought death many times. Like the animals, I know my time will come, just as theirs will. Many times I've thought that I should return to the valley and face the killers. I was a coward to come here, and I'm a coward to stay. If I run away with you, I'll be a coward again."

"Then you *are* thinking of going with Riordan?" His black eyes snapped disapproval. "Now I know you wish to die!"

"I'm only thinking of the choices that lie before me, Gray Bear. But consider this — if I did go with him, I might be able to save the lives of others. I might be able to help end the hunger of the Shoshoni."

Before Gray Bear could say more, Red Sky sprinted across the meadow, out of the protective cover of the trees. He immediately set out after her, calling her name. But she kept running, and as usual, he couldn't catch her. She quickly vanished into the thicker trees some distance away.

He followed, but at last had to stop and catch his breath. She was nowhere to be seen. It was no wonder she had eluded the paleface murderers seven years ago. He heard only the thumping of his own heart, not even the snap of a twig. The birds hidden in the pines gave their sweet melodies to his ears as if all was peaceful with Mother Earth below them.

Suddenly he had the strange sensation that the last few minutes had not happened except in his mind and that the moments he'd spent with Red Sky had been imagined. Had he wanted to see his heart's desire so desperately that somehow his imagination had tricked him into believing she had been real and by his side? He stood alone, feeling as foolish as if he had been chasing a spirit.

But no! He wasn't in a dream state. Red Sky was alive and it was the White Eyes that had brought these undesirable and rebellious changes to her. It was the White Eyes who had clouded her mind until she couldn't see who her friends were.

Angrily, he stalked back toward the cave. He would not lose her again. If the paleface was what stood in his way, then he would get rid of him. And soon.

Long is the shadow
Cast by the Black Wings of Fear.

Chapter Ten

The horse's hooves barely sounded on the game trail. Sunlight filtered down through the trees, falling in a golden slant across Matt Riordan's back and heating the flesh that was already hot and hard against Red Sky's breasts. She rode behind him on the horse with her arms around him and her body conformed to his. She hadn't wanted to ride with him, so close, so vulnerable to these new emotions and desires that he instilled in her, but he had insisted she would not walk the distance to the fishing hole on the North Popo Agie if he had to ride. His leg was getting better, but it still had far to go before complete recovery.

But with the rocking gait of the horse, shifting her body constantly against his, came the disturbing but not unpleasant flutter of butterflies in her stomach, a throbbing sensation in the apex of her legs, and a powerful urge to rest her head on his shoulder and snuggle her bosom against the hard wall of his back.

He was not relaxed. She felt his tension, saw the way his head moved from one side to the other in constant vigil of their surroundings and possible danger. Even in her arms as he was, she still saw and felt the predator she'd recognized in him from the very beginning. But she saw another side, too. A man of sensitivity and vulnerability. A man who could be kind, or deadly, depending on what the situation required.

They'd seen no more of the cowboys roaming the mountains, but even if they didn't return, Gray Bear and Many Claws would. For the past week this had troubled Matt although he'd spoken very little about it. She had seen it only in his eyes as he watched and waited for them to return and take her away.

"I have no intention of leaving here," she had said, but he only looked at her contemplatively, and she knew he wondered if she spoke the truth, or if she would be weak enough to succumb to the wishes of the two Shoshoni men who were determined to make her leave the mountains for her own safety. She wondered, too, if he might not be jealous of Gray Bear, for he had aimed a few caustic remarks at the brave.

For the most part, and consuming the majority of their time, he had helped her with her chores, preparing a hide for tanning and staking it out in a secluded spot in the trees. He had helped her make lye soap, and assisted in her search for plants that would provide medicine and food for the upcoming winter. Then, today, he'd insisted they go fishing.

She had questioned him only once more as to why

he stayed on when she had made it clear she wouldn't leave here for, or with, anyone.

"Maybe because I'm tired of tracking down outlaws, Sky," he had said. "And maybe, too, because I don't have anything to go back to but the agency and another job. If you get tired of sharing your cave, I'll leave, but I'll still be around."

His words were only half truths and she knew it. In actuality, he was waiting for her. Waiting for the day she would say, "All right, I'll go to Cheyenne with you." But she couldn't say it. She couldn't seem to dispel her fear of leaving here, of facing the secrets and the pain and all the ghosts that still made their nightly walks through Long Moon Valley. She couldn't do it for him, or for Gray Bear and Many Claws.

At last the game trail opened to a clearing through which the North Popo Agie placidly ran. The pines were much thicker here, skirting the large meadow, and rising above their green pointed heads stood the granite mountains in their perpetual, protective and watchful stance. Leaves of the quaking aspen trees quivered in the warm summer breeze, making a fluttering noise. Wildflowers of red, yellow, blue, and white added color to the tall, swaying grass. The humming of bees seeking the sweetness of nectar filled the air.

Matt swung his right leg over the horse's neck and slid off the saddle to the ground. Not asking permission or waiting for any, he encircled Sky's waist with his hands and helped her from the horse. For a moment when her feet touched the ground and his hands lingered on her waist, only mere inches separated them. His eyes drew hers to his as surely as a magnet summons shards of metal. She found herself falling into the incredible azure depths. There was a tenderness there she recognized now, but there was also a deeper glow that reminded her of a hard piece of unyielding steel. Then suddenly he released her and stepped away, as if mentally shaking aside an unwanted thought.

They had been cautious in their gradual descent from the high country to this place and had seen no sign of anyone. Nevertheless, Matt staked Soldier in the cover of the trees. With the saddlebags flung over his shoulder filled with their day's supplies, he led the way to a heavy band of tall bushes that lined the river.

They wound their way through the bushes until they reached the bank of the river. Here the breeze didn't touch them, and it was hot. Crickets chirped in the grass, and birds twittered in the trees. There were a few mosquitoes about, but not many this time of day. The evening would find them in numbers, but Matt and Sky would be gone by then.

Red Sky found a large boulder near the water and positioned herself on it, watching Matt deftly cut willow poles and attach line and hooks. Esup settled down in some shade, as if preparing himself for a long, boring day. He immediately put his head on his paws and closed his eyes, apparently deciding a nap was a viable alternative.

"I'm not a good fisherman, you know," she said, a smile touching her lips. "I seldom try because I just don't have any luck."

He glanced askance at her, lifting an eyebrow in

disbelief. "I find that hard to believe, Sky. From what I've seen, there's nothing you can't do."

His solemn mood gave way to a lighter one as if suddenly he was determined to have some fun. She realized that a man like Riordan probably never saw many good times. It was one more thing she supposed they had in common. They were two people so caught up in just surviving that their lips barely remembered how to smile, their hearts had lost all songs, and there was no such thing as a moment when caution could be cast to the wind.

She knew Matt had brought her here in hopes of finding at least temporary pleasure before they had to face Gray Bear and Many Claws and the decision that would come with that meeting. How wonderful it would be to put aside the cares of the world for a few hours and let her heart behave like that of a child's again. It had been such a long time since she had felt true joy and relaxation.

With the feeling growing inside her, she laughed lightly, but not loudly, so conditioned was she to silence. "I am honestly no good at fishing," she insisted.

"Maybe you just haven't had the proper equipment and know-how. Personally, I've always been pretty good at it."

"Then maybe you can teach me what you know."

His gaze snared hers again. She felt, as she had frequently of late, that he was searching her eyes for answers; that he was watching their depths intently so he would be able to see the precise moment when she finally capitulated to his desires and his wishes.

"All right. Watch closely," he said, "and I'll share with you what I know."

With his knife, he opened up the moist soil near the bank and found some worms. After baiting the hooks, he handed her one of the poles. She looked with chagrin at the worm dangling on the hook. "This is all you do?"

He nodded.

"But this is exactly the way I do it and it never works."

He shrugged. "Well, then maybe you've just never found a good fishing hole, or maybe you didn't have the patience to wait for results."

He dropped his line into a deep pool that skirted under a bank. Looking content, he lay back on the grass and pulled his hat down over his face, shifting his body around on the grassy bank until he found a comfortable position. "Now, we wait."

Her heart sank. *Wait*. Of course that was the secret of being a good fisherman and the reason she wasn't. She absolutely hated anything that involved waiting. When she set out to do something she wanted results right away. With the snares she didn't get results immediately, but she could set them and then do something else.

Wait.

She slapped at a mosquito and glanced at Esup, his ears involuntarily twitching in his sleep to ward off the bugs and flies trying to nestle in the sensitive cavities. She sighed, and resigning herself the way Esup had, she lay back on the grass and put her arm over her eyes to shield them from the sun.

But she couldn't sleep. It was too hot. She turned

her head and allowed her gaze to travel the length of Matt's body. His hands lay idle, resting on his chest in the position which one would place a dead man's hands. But his chest rose and fell with regularity, and occasionally he swatted at a fly that tried to burrow in his ear after having previously, unsuccessfully attempted entrance into Esup's ear. She smiled, thinking she would rather move over next to Matt and fan the flies off him than sit and wait for a hungry fish to find her worm.

Wait.

She was sure five minutes hadn't even passed and yet it already felt like an hour. She lifted her line and dropped it again absently into the water several times, wondering if by moving it a little the dangling worm might catch the eye of some unsuspecting fish.

"You've never said where you're from, Matt," she said, suddenly feeling conversational. "Where were you born?"

His body tensed visibly, and Red Sky realized that he might have already dozed off; perhaps she had woken him up. But, after an interminable silence, he finally replied in a flat-sounding voice that was also muffled by the hat over his face.

"I recall my mother saying once that I was born in Texas."

"Oh? Where at in Texas? Did you spend your childhood there?" She hoped she wasn't annoying him, but it was simply too boring to sit and stare at the end of her fishing pole.

He cleared his throat and she watched his Adam's apple bob as he swallowed. The hat remained over his face. "Why don't we just fish, Sky. I don't feel much like talking."

Red Sky studied him, growing angry that he'd cut her off. Were they only supposed to talk when he felt like it? What about the times he'd interrogated her as if she were a criminal on trial?

"There you go, again," she said hotly. "You think that questions should only come from your mouth. You've been living with me for over two months, Matt Riordan. I have a right to know something about you."

There was a long silence beneath the hat. She had nearly come to the conclusion that he was not going to respond, when finally he did, but it was still from beneath the hat. "You'll have to forgive me, Sky. I haven't met many people who wanted to know about me or my past. But you saved my life, you've kept me alive for weeks now. You *do* have a right to ask me anything you want to. And I have an obligation to answer.

"Apparently my mother never thought it was worth mentioning exactly where I was born," he said, going into a recitation of his past. "But for some reason Austin sticks in my mind. I know we spent more time there than anywhere else. My ma never dwelled on things like that, and I guess I was too young to care really — or to think about it. So I didn't ask. It didn't seem important at the time."

"But surely you grew up in a town, or at least near one? You went to a school. Even *I* went to school."

"Yeah, I went to school, but my mother moved around a lot and we didn't stay in any place too long. So I didn't necessarily go to school in the same town where I was born. After I started working ranches, I met a guy who was pretty educated and he taught me a lot of what I'd missed from all the moving about. He loaned me books he had."

"You speak only of your mother. Did your father die?"

If Red Sky thought his earlier silence was lengthy, this one was even more so. At last, he sat up, shoving his hat to the back of his head in an agitated gesture. Blond curls of hair fell out onto his forehead boyishly. But the strain around his eyes deepened the lines there and, in contrast, added years to his face. Crouching forward, he encircled his knees loosely with his arms. He kept his back to her and his eyes on the river. She noted a sudden sagging in his posture; a certain deflation of . . . what? . . . pride?

"I never knew my father," he said quietly. Then his tone changed to one of bitterness and contempt. "I don't know what he looked like or who he was. I don't even know his name. Riordan is my mother's maiden name. My mother was a prostitute, Sky." He gave her a cold, defiant look. "She had so many men I doubt even she knew who my father was. And, of course, he never knew he had a son. I was just somebody's wild seed, tossed to the wind to take root wherever I could."

Red Sky felt the pain he felt, and if she could have taken it from him, she would have. He waited for her reaction. What did he think he would see in her eyes? Shock? Pity? Disgust? He was obviously ashamed of being a bastard, as if it was somehow his own fault. She supposed she should stop asking questions, but she suddenly wanted to know everything about him. The dam of restraint had finally broken and all her curiosity about him came gushing forth.

"Where is your mother now?" She expected him to get angry and tell her to be quiet, but he just sat there in the same position with his back to her.

He sighed, a weary sound of resignation, and then picked up the pole and fidgeted with it. "I don't know. I haven't seen her for fifteen years. She was sick — she'd been sick a lot. She had a lot of trouble with headaches and she took a lot of morphine that some doctor in a cow town in Kansas prescribed. She got to where she couldn't live without the morphine, and it got expensive.

"I remember the last time I saw her," he continued. "We were in St. Louis. She was working at some brothel. She left me every night in our one-room apartment so she could work. That night she didn't come back. I went to the place where she worked the next day and asked about her. I thought she'd been killed or something, but they said she'd packed her bag and taken the stage out of town with some gambler. Nobody knew which direction she'd gone or where her destination was.

"I figured that if she'd have wanted me to go with her, she'd have come and got me. So from that time on I looked out after myself. I lived on the streets mostly, and I found some odd jobs. Then after about a year, I headed to Texas and found work as a cowboy. It didn't matter that I was only fourteen when they hired me. They took 'em young. I could ride, and I learned the rest. I made twelve dollars a month."

He stopped his story so abruptly that Red Sky

sensed something else edging into his memory that he didn't care to speak about any more than he'd cared to speak about his mother and his childhood. Was it Elizabeth, maybe? But she decided right now might not be the time to ask.

"Maybe your mother—"

"No, don't try to give her honorable motives for what she did, Sky," he said gruffly. His eyes turned cold, looking, Red Sky thought, like what frost would look like if it were blue. "The truth is simple," he continued. "My mother just wanted to be what she was, and a kid got in the way of that. She never talked about finding other work, hoping for something different, like a home. The only time she was happy was when she was working. When it was just me and her, she was sullen and cross. I think she really resented me crowding into her fun. I made her old and she wanted to remain perpetually young and beautiful and desirable."

Red Sky asked no more questions, but couldn't help but draw parallels between her life and his. Raised entirely differently, they each had been forced to live on their own from their first years as adolescents. But regardless of how hard her life in the mountains had been, she wondered if her life had been easy compared to his. After all, she at least had the warm memory of a family who had loved her. A father. A mother. Brothers and a sister. She had been loved and cherished once. She sensed Matt Riordan never had been. And the one woman he *had* loved, hadn't loved him enough, or so he had said. Yet, she decided he must have a well of love inside him because he had been kind and gentle to her, understanding and patient. His bitterness toward his mother hadn't bled onto the rest of his life and his relationships.

"Your line's caught on a bush over there," he said, coming to his feet. He tugged at it for a while but it wouldn't come free. Balancing on one foot, he started to remove a boot.

"What are you doing?" she asked.

"Taking my boots off. I'll have to go in after it. I don't want to cut the line since I don't have much more."

He didn't bother to roll up his pant legs, just waded right into the water up to his thighs, stepping carefully to keep his footing. "Damn," he grumbled. "This water's as cold as that lonesome lake of yours."

Red Sky chuckled, remembering all too well how he had looked that day she had caught him bathing. He glanced over her shoulder, seeming to read her thoughts. His dark mood lifted, so she smiled more broadly. She saw the warmth return to his eyes as he once again put the past behind him.

"Don't laugh at me, Sky McClellan, or I'll drag you in here and make you help me."

She giggled even louder.

He switched directions and came back toward her, pure devilment written on his face.

Her eyes rounded with alarm. "Don't you dare," she warned jokingly, scooting herself back away from the bank but very happy to see his depression lift almost as quickly as it had descended.

He made a couple of playful swipes at her leg before she got her feet beneath her and scrambled beyond his reach. "Don't tease me, woman." His blue

183

eyes twinkled. "I can still come up there and get you."

She waved a hand toward the water. "Just get the line free." But he ignored her, now determined to haul her in with him. He started up out of the water wearing a grin of mischievousness she had never seen on him before. He reminded her of a youngster about to stuff frogs in his teacher's lunch pail.

Suddenly his pole, lying forgotten on the bank, leaped upward and darted toward the river. "Matt!" she shrieked and pointed. "Your pole!"

Dismay replacing his playfulness, Matt abandoned his pursuit of her and watched with momentary surprise as the pole hit the water and started downstream. He raced after it, sloshing through the water with extreme effort.

"We've got a big one, Sky!" He yelled gleefully. "We'll have trout for supper now!"

He lunged for the pole but suddenly fell out of sight; the water closed in over the top of him. Red Sky shrieked again and raced to the water's edge, preparing to leap in after him. At that moment he resurfaced, pole in hand, hair dripping wet and down in his eyes.

Moving his arms to keep himself afloat, he tossed his head to the side and flung the wet hair from his face. "There's a damn hole in here deep enough to take us to China!"

He looked so comical, Red Sky couldn't refrain from another burst of laughter.

He struggled up out of the hole, half swimming and half crawling, and finally got back to the bank. He sat there, soaked to the gills. As for the fish, it was still on the hook, and he dragged it away from the water so it couldn't get back in. He looked at it proudly. "Why, I'll bet that's at least a three-pounder. What do you think?"

She stared at it dubiously. "It's pretty big."

Matt took it off the hook but it immediately started flipping and flopping its way back toward the water. They both leaped onto it, bumped heads, and watched it flop away.

"Get it, Sky! We can't lose it!"

Forgetting the temporary pain to their heads they took after it again like two children. Matt finally tackled it like a cowboy would wrestle a steer to the ground, getting it under him and holding it there with his body. His face was pressed into the river-bank and covered with bits of grass and dirt. He twisted his head enough so he could see Sky kneeling next to him, waiting expectantly.

"I've got it," he said. "It's under me. Reach under there and get a good hold of it. And whatever you do — don't let it get away."

He lifted one side of his body, keeping the side of himself next to the river pressed down firmly to the ground to prevent any gaps for the fish to slide through. Red Sky rubbed her hands on her buck-skins, drying them from the previous attempt. She slid her hands under him about where his waist was, feeling uncomfortable at the close, intimate contact with him. But he seemed only concerned with the fish, which was flip-flopping and smacking him in the stomach repeatedly with its tail and head.

"He's quite a fighter, Matt," she said, suddenly feeling guilty for trying to capture such a determined creature. "Maybe we ought to let him go."

"Not on your life, woman! I can taste him already. Fried up in a pan with a little flour and a lot of salt. Come on, Sky, don't go and get sentimental on me now."

She encircled the big fish with her hands but it was so slippery she couldn't get a good grip. She was actually more concerned with touching Matt in his private place than she was about capturing the fish. "I don't think I can hold it, Matt."

"Too bad we can't rope it."

She laughed again and continued to grope around beneath him, forever having the slippery fish elude her grasp. Suddenly her eyes lit up. "Oh! I think I've got it!"

"Don't take any chances, Sky," Matt warned. "Toss it up there away from the water."

She nodded. He raised up a little more and she carefully pulled the fish out from under him, and just as carefully got to her feet. With eyes as round as saucers, and peeled on the fish, she started to move backward, holding it up in the air in front of her.

And then it started to squirm.

"Oh, oh . . . it's . . . oh no! . . . Matt! . . . Help, I'm losing it!"

He grabbed for it. The fish spurted from her hands, soared through the air, and hit the water with a splash. It swam a distance and vanished.

Matt sank to the ground and ran his hand through his wet hair. "Well, damn."

Red Sky stared at the water for a minute, feeling completely deflated and guilty for losing the fish and letting Matt down. Then she looked at him. Slowly, laughter began to build inside her until it could no longer be restrained. It finally burst from her lips and continued until tears streamed down her face, and still she couldn't stop.

His lips quirked irritably. "What's so funny?"

"You. You look so . . . so . . . pathetic. It's only a fish, Matt."

"Well, I wanted to eat that fish, dang it!"

She wiped the tears from her eyes and finally managed to suppress her laughter until it had subsided to giggles. "Come on." She held out both hands to him. "We'll catch another. There's got to be more than one fish in that river."

He placed his palms in hers. Embers sparked and fire leaped from his fingertips to hers. Their hands tightened around each other as she helped him to his feet. Only inches away from him, her gaze locked with his, Sky clearly saw the dangerous and sultry glow of desire enter his eyes. She wanted to feel the heat of his passion, but she feared the ultimate burn. She tried to withdraw her hands from his, sensing it was the only safe thing to do, but his grip held her fast.

"Don't run away from me, Sky," he said in a husky tone. "You know by now I'm not going to hurt you."

His mental and physical persuasion was like a magic potion she didn't understand, leaving her powerless to disobey, powerless to do anything but trust his word. Forgetting caution, she found herself mesmerized by his brilliant cerulean gaze and firm lips coming down to meet hers.

His mouth closed over hers, hot and tender, drawing a response she couldn't hold back. Her mind whirled away from all things sensible, while the feelings rushing through her body took command. He released her hands and drew her into a compelling embrace that she had no will or desire to break. His hands moved over her back, caressing her provocatively through the soft buckskin blouse. At his touch, the blood in her veins tingled and coursed with a new purpose and a new life that she had thought impossible just a few months ago.

The pressure of his lips deepened and her mouth parted, seemingly of its own volition. She felt the tip of his tongue on her lips, wet and fiery. His warm breath mingled with hers and set off a whole new series of sensations and emotions rushing through her, plummeting her heart to the core of her womanhood, where it remained, pounding out its own insistent, urgent beat.

Her legs began to tremble until she thought they might crumble beneath her. Apparently sensing her debility, his arms tightened, molding her body the entire length of his. His hand splayed across her lower back and he pressed her closer to the hardness in his loins.

Suddenly something flashed in her mind like a tremendous explosion of light. With it came images and sensations of touch, sound, and fear. A stifled moan of denial rose in her throat, escaping her lips to fall upon his. She pushed against his chest and wrenched herself free of his embrace. She stumbled backward, gasping for air. She couldn't seem to breathe. The memory of hands around her throat brought vivid flashbacks which she just as quickly blocked from her mind. She put a hand out toward

Matt as if to keep him away, but through a blur she saw he wasn't moving toward her at all. He was just standing there, breathing almost as erratically as she was, and studying her with a hard set to his jaw and blue sparks of fire leaping in his eyes.

"Don't ever kiss me again," she managed in a near whisper.

The masculine line of his lips, their impression still burning against her own, tightened and thinned. What thoughts raced through his head? Whatever they were, he voiced none of them and finally turned back to the fishing poles, acting vaguely disgusted. But that was all.

Red Sky stared at him, surprised that he was obeying her wishes and not his own volatile male desires. He truly wasn't like those other men seven years ago who had simply taken what they wanted with no regard to their victims.

The frightening and yet pleasant sensations Matt's nearness had induced faded. Gradually the world found its way back into her brain. Once again she heard the birds singing, the river flowing, the insects buzzing about their heads. Her breathing began to slow and her head cleared, but she felt so confused. A yawning emptiness suddenly engulfed her. A pit in her stomach made her feel as if she'd gone hungry for days and had finally sat down to a meal, only to discover it consisted of one grain of rice and nothing more. She'd wanted his kiss. Why then had she reacted so violently?

Matt tossed the line out into the water and she stared at his broad back. "Get your pole, Sky," he said without turning around to look at her. "We'd better get fishing. We're running out of time before we have to head home."

Her mouth had gone so dry it took an extreme effort to swallow. She moved hesitantly to the second pole, picked it up, then settled herself in the grass about six feet away from him.

She had never felt more miserable in her life. Embarrassment and shame washed over her, rising up her neck to her cheeks like the mercury in the thermometer that her daddy had attached to the outside of their cabin's wall. She knew her skin was surely as crimson as the sky had been on the day of her birth. But Matt didn't look her way again, and she wasn't sure if she was grateful or disappointed. The only thing she *was* positive of was that she still wanted him to like her. Desperately she wanted him to like her. She still wanted him to be her friend, too. And, despite her words, she *did* want him to kiss her again. If only she could keep the horrible, fearful memories from returning.

She watched him covertly from the corner of her eye. After a few moments, he leaned back in the grass once again, stretching out full length and pulling his hat down over his eyes. Chased away by the momentary flash of fear, the feelings his kiss had ignited inside her began anew and radiated out from deep within her as fiery as the rays of an August sun beating down, surrounding her and encompassing her in warmth and a very tangible sense of security. She would have liked to touch him, to ease the anger in him somehow, and comfort the pain inside herself. To say, "I'm sorry. I'm afraid. I don't know what to do or what to think."

But she didn't say the words.

Over the years she had resolved never to need or want another human being for any reason for as long as she lived. She'd allowed only Many Claws to help her, to care for her, and she in turn to open her heart to him. She had convinced herself she would never miss the company of others. It had seemed so much safer and simpler in this life she'd chosen to live, and it had been easy until now. But the sureness of that decision was crumbling apart like mountains falling beneath the force of a mighty earthquake.

There was a solution to it all, though. A very simple solution. All that would be required was for Matt Riordan to leave the mountains of the Sun Father, and then her life would once again be her own.

Swift is the warrior's blade,
Brief is the triumph of his thunder.

Chapter Eleven

Matt left Red Sky at the clearing so he could return Soldier to the trees and stake him for the night. First, though, he watched as she ran, graceful as a doe, across the meadow with Esup at her heels.

Gray Bear would return soon. Would this woman who had drifted into his heart as subtly as smoke drifts into the clouds, choose to go with the other? Matt didn't care so much anymore if she testified; the case was no longer foremost in his mind. *She* was. If she left with Gray Bear, she would be lost to him forever. With each passing day in her company, his spirits lifted. The obligation and the burden of duty, so required for his line of work, felt as if it had shrunk like a loosely staked hide left out in the sun too long. He wasn't so sure he even wanted to leave this mountain paradise and return to the agency. It would be entirely too easy to stay here with Red Sky until the eagles no longer flew and the sun no longer shone. And yet, as his feelings for her deepened, his fear for her safety increased.

At last he turned Soldier back to the shadows and to a spot he hadn't yet grazed, knowing even as he did so, that with each day he remained here, the horse would leave more sign, and it would be easier for searchers to realize the presence of people. He was truly jeopardizing Sky's security. Time was running out. He either had to convince her to go with him, force her to go with Many Claws, or leave her to her peace and pray no harm would come to her.

He unsaddled Soldier and replaced the bridle with a halter. Carefully he hid the tack next to a large fallen log where the grass grew high and easily concealed it.

Suddenly a faint noise alerted him. His hand went automatically to the gun on his hip and he slid back as quietly as a shadow against the trunk of a big pine. He eased the Colt from its holster and held it up, ready. The noise came again. A whisper of movement, the rustle of grass, the faint crunch of last winter's dead leaves beneath careful feet. And then silence. Complete silence. Not even a bird winged its way through the woods.

He felt the presence of something . . . of someone. He turned his head to the left. Not twenty feet away, with arms folded arrogantly across his bronze chest, stood Gray Bear. He had arrived early of the promised date, and Many Claws was not with him. Matt's gaze took in the large hunting knife sheathed in the scabbard on Gray Bear's hips. The knife had been there before, but this time Matt sensed it would be drawn in battle. Surliness in his black eyes told Matt he had come for more than Red Sky.

When Matt said nothing, Gray Bear spoke. "Do you not wonder why I am here, White Eyes?"

Matt's reflexes, honed for response to sudden danger, were coiled and ready to spring into action. He watched Gray Bear closely, reading him with years of experience that would tell him the second before the Shoshoni brave would attack.

"I know why you're here, Gray Bear. You've come for Sky."

"Yes, White Eyes, that is true. But first I will spill your life's blood into the hand of Mother Earth because I do not think you intend to release my woman."

Matt leveled his gun on the brave's heart. "You're right, Gray Bear. I don't intend to let you take her."

"You will not kill me in cold blood." Gray Bear sneered boldly at the Colt. "You palefaces have a 'code of honor.' That is, the foolish among you. And I believe you are one of them."

"Unfortunately for you, your estimation of me is totally inaccurate. I have nothing to lose and everything to gain from your being out of Sky's life — and mine."

"So it is true that you want her for your woman, and not just your captive?"

Matt said nothing and Gray Bear's mock smile deepened. "Let us fight for her then, White Eyes. Put your gun away and face me like a man. Unless you are not a man, but an old woman." He slid his knife slowly from his scabbard. Once clear of leather, he twisted it purposefully one way and then the other so the remaining sunlight caught on the gleaming, razor-sharp edge.

Matt forced a calmness even as the adrenaline pumped. His level of reflex became fine-tuned. "You are the old woman, Gray Bear," he replied, matching the brave's derision. "You're afraid Sky will choose me, not you. You fear her choice so much that you know your only chance with her is to kill me so she'll have no one to turn to but you. I can tell you that she doesn't want you."

Gray Bear didn't like to hear such things; it was obvious in the disquieting light that came into his soot-colored eyes, in the nerve twitching alongside his jaw, and in the way his brown hand clenched and unclenched its grip on his knife.

"But I'll fight you, Gray Bear," Matt continued, "if you think that will ensure Sky's confidence in your manhood. If you think it will make her want to share your blanket."

Not trusting Gray Bear's own code of ethics, Matt never took his eyes off his opponent while he removed his gun belt, stripped to the waist, and flung his shirt, vest, and hat into the tall grass. He pulled his knife from its scabbard.

Crouching, they circled each other slowly, each watching for the perfect moment to strike with the first assault. The blades of their knives gleamed with cold deadliness as the last rays of sunlight filtered through the trees and then vanished, leaving them in the first shadows of twilight.

Closer and closer they advanced toward each other, their knives slashing back and forth and sounding like the wings of a great horned owl, lifting and falling against the still evening air. Continually they danced out of range of the wide, slicing arcs of the other's weapon. Then Gray Bear's knife found not air but Matt's upper arm. Blood sprang to the surface, but Matt barely flinched, feeling only the sharp sting and the warmth of the blood as it trickled like war paint down his arm to his wrist.

The fight commenced again. Their knives clashed and the resonant ring of steel against steel echoed time and again through the forest. Matt's knife found Gray Bear's chest. The brave leaped back, but only for a second. When he saw his own blood it seemed to send him into a rage. The *whoosh* of the knives increased, the clangs grew louder and more frequent. Vicious gashes sprang with alarming frequency until each man's torso dripped beads of crimson.

They taunted each other, feigned and struck, danced beyond each other's reach with the agility of wolves experienced in the kill. With each passing minute their breathing became shallower and more labored, their steps more clumsy. The perspiration began to roll down their faces into their eyes, trickling onto their chests, stinging their open wounds, mingling with the blood and diluting it until it ran in watery red rivulets to the waistbands of their breeches.

Apparently tired of the game, Gray Bear suddenly released a blood-curdling scream and lunged. Matt leaped easily aside and the young man tumbled into the grass, rolling, then quickly righted himself. It was the break Matt had been waiting for. In an instant he was upon Gray Bear, flinging him to the ground. He grabbed Gray Bear's hand that held the knife and slammed it back against the trunk of a fallen pine tree time and again. Gray Bear, fighting the pain, at last yelled out in agony and released the knife. It flew through the air and disappeared in the grass.

Gray Bear tried to hold Matt's hand back as the knife came closer and closer to his throat, but at last its cold deadliness lay against his brown flesh. With eyes large with fear, he inhaled, awaiting the end. The knife moved and blood sprang up beneath its blade.

Matt's chest heaved from exertion. "Beg me, you bastard," he growled hoarsely. "Beg me and maybe . . . *maybe* . . . I'll let you live."

"Never, *tivo*. Never."

"Then you will die."

"Matt! No! Stop!"

Red Sky's scream startled both the men, but Matt didn't move from his position on Gray Bear's chest, nor did he allow himself to be distracted from the brave's watchful, ready eyes. The Indian would not miss the opportunity to retaliate, even now with Red Sky present. Matt pressed the knife deeper against his flesh, drawing another trickle of blood.

"Stop this!" Red Sky screamed again, standing over them with fists clenched at her sides.

"Stay out of it," Matt ordered. "This is our fight. Not yours."

"I don't care. You can't kill him. My God, Matt, he's my friend. Think of what you're doing."

The moment to kill had been lost to hesitation. Her pleading found its place in Matt's heart and he knew he was lost. He should have killed the Indian when he had had the chance, but Gray Bear had sensed he would not take a life in cold blood and the brave was right. He would take it in battle, in self-defense, but the battle was past and his opponent now lay beneath him, a helpless victim.

Angrily he stood up, leaving Gray Bear sprawled on the ground. "Get out of my sight, Gray Bear, and don't come back. Next time there may be no woman to save you."

Gray Bear scrambled up, touching fingers to the trickles of blood creeping down his throat. Slowly the fear that had made him look too much a boy and a coward, changed into a victorious, sneering smile.

"I was right. You are foolish, White Eyes. I would have killed you and not hesitated. There *will* be a next time. I will return and you will die, and I will take that yellow hair of yours to adorn my belt."

He ran away into the coming darkness, leaving Matt no recourse or opportunity for retaliation of any kind.

Matt went to the spot in the grass where Gray Bear's knife had fallen. He picked it up and held it out to Red Sky, handle first. "Keep it," he said, "or return it to your *friend*."

She hesitated in taking it, seeing the blood — Matt's blood — smeared upon it. At last she curled her hand around its handle and watched in silence while Matt cleaned the blade of his own knife in the grass. He gathered his shirt and vest and returned his hat to his head. He left the battle site and she followed, suddenly very aware of his anger with her for intervening. She noticed his limp was more pronounced. The battle had taken its toll on his leg.

They walked in silence to the cave. Matt filled a basin with cool water and began to bathe his wounds. Red Sky stood in the shadows of the firelight, feeling helpless but angry that Matt had come so close to killing Gray Bear. Yet, she was greatly upset, too, because it could have just as easily been Matt who'd had the knife to his throat. She wasn't at all certain Gray Bear would have hesitated the way Matt had. He had the warrior blood that had taught him there was no place for conscience or hesitation of any kind in battle. It translated to him as weakness.

Matt lowered himself to the only chair, a block of wood, and Sky saw the weariness etched in his handsome face, burdening a body that was still weak from the bullet wound. He must be very strong indeed to have gotten the upper hand of Gray Bear so soon after nearly facing death himself. Either that or his experience had won him the battle.

She stepped in front of him and dropped to her knees. She feared any reaction to her might be hostile after the fight, so gently, cautiously, she rested her hand on his. "Let me help you, Matt."

His gaze lifted and held hers. Indeed, anger still paced through his mind, but she saw that he tried to get control of it. At last he handed the cloth to her and she began dabbing at one of the ugly cuts on his chest. Inwardly she cringed at the way Gray Bear's knife had so neatly laid open the golden flesh and added more scars to the body of this man she had come to care a great deal for.

While she worked, Matt's eyes followed her every move. There was no discerning the cause of the fires that burned so deeply in those blue pools of emotion. But she felt something powerful building inside him, something beyond anger, something even more volatile. It was so tangible that she began to have a feeling that if that emotion exploded from him, it was going to be aimed at her.

Perhaps if he spoke of the incident it would help calm him. And yet, speaking of it might also be the catalyst that would set it off. Still, she had to take the chance.

Licking her lips nervously, she said, "Why were you and Gray Bear fighting?"

He didn't respond immediately. When he did, he snapped at her. "Don't play the innocent. You know the reason."

She couldn't look at him. Couldn't bear to face the intense force of fury she would see in his eyes. She dipped the cloth back into the basin, watching as the red ran out of it and into the cool water. Blood. Always more blood. God, would she never quit seeing human blood?

"It was because of me, wasn't it?" She felt her own anger rising at the utter primitive foolishness of it.

"Yes," he said coldly. "You were to be the prize for the winner."

"And the loser?"

"The loser would die."

She flung the rag into the pan, splashing water everywhere. "I've never heard anything so stupid! You both could have been killed."

She started to rise but he caught her shoulders and held her. As she'd suspected, speaking of it had at last released his fury, and it was indeed aimed at her.

200

She shivered at the dark and frightening glow in his eyes, then realized another emotion was chasing away the anger, the weariness, the weakness. She was powerless as he pulled her toward him. She could do nothing but grip his thighs to balance herself.

His voice was raw, but deadly calm. "But we weren't killed, Sky, and I was the victor. And now . . . I want what I fought for."

Before she could react he crushed her to him and took her lips in a hungry, searing kiss. She tried to fight him, but he grabbed her wrists and held them. Seemingly not satisfied with the kiss, he hauled her up into his arms and in two strides was at his pallet, lowering her to the furs and pressing her back with the weight of his body. She tried to fight him but to no avail. She opened her mouth to protest, but her words were swallowed by his kiss, halted by his tongue upon hers, demanding her response while invading with blatant possessiveness the softness of her mouth.

He was wild with passion, with lust. It terrified her and confused her. She had feared this from the beginning, and when she had finally let her guard down, he had sprung. She began to whimper, begging him to stop, but he seemed not to hear. Fear crowded upward and threatened to consume her. She pushed against his naked arms and chest and felt hot tears slide from her eyes, scalding the tender flesh surrounding them.

"Damn you. I trusted you," she cried.

He lifted his head. Their gazes locked. The fury of battle still raged in his eyes; the pain of betrayal swam in hers. But gradually, she felt the rigid set of his body relax, saw the light in his eyes soften, felt his gentle fingertips wiping away her tears. His kiss found her lips again, this time soothing them while he whispered, "I'm sorry, Sky. Please forgive me."

The change in him brought a change in her. She no longer fought him. Deep inside, she was dimly aware of something other than fear developing. His body's length still felt hard and strong, but it was no longer frightening, threatening. His touch had turned tender and alarmingly sensual.

For weeks she'd lived here with him in this cave. She had grown familiar with every line and angle of his face and body. She had dreamed of his hands and his lips touching her in erotic ways she would never have openly admitted to. Her body responded to his now, answering the latent call of desire. A quiet, lambent flame leaped to life.

He gathered her braids in his hands and in seconds had them free of the rawhide thongs. With hunger and awe in his eyes, he sank his hands into the black mass of it. She was reminded of a man scooping up gold—gold that belonged to no one but him.

"Your hair smells like wildflowers," he moaned against her ear. "And your skin of the sun and the wind."

She gripped his shoulders, thinking she would hold him just a moment longer and then let him go. But not yet. No, not yet.

While his lips rained kisses on every spot of exposed flesh, his hands slid downward from her hair, to her shoulders, and then to her waist. One hand found the curve of her hip. The other slid beneath her doeskin blouse, leaving a molten path of fire as it moved toward her breast. His fingertips swirled around a nipple, jolting her with a sensation that caused her to inhale sharply in surprise. She should have pushed him away then, but the unexpected sunburst flowed out to every part of her body. She arched against him, wanting to prolong the pleasure. His lips pressed gently against the sensitive length of her neck. Flames roared through her entire body with the force and swiftness of a prairie fire. She felt a prisoner of her own desire, as if she might do anything — even beg — to make the fires continue.

New needs surfaced of a sort that left her in anticipation of something she didn't understand, but something she wanted to experience just the same. It wasn't until she felt him tugging at the cord that held her trousers around her waist that the thrill and excitement was doused in the wake of fear. The latter grew at an alarming pace once again, engulfing her in panic. The little bits of ecstasy she had felt were extinguished and she knew she had to run, to flee before he touched that most private part of her. That part she would never let a man touch again.

"Matt. Please . . . don't. . . ."

He cursed and rolled away from her and to the far side of the pallet, lying flat on his back with his chest heaving. His eyes stared upward at the cave's dark ceiling.

Red Sky quickly departed the pallet and backed away from him, vaguely aware that much of the blood that had been on his chest now stained her doeskin blouse.

He came off the pallet so suddenly, and had such a wild look in his eye, that she gasped and stumbled away from him. But to her surprise he strode past her, out of the cave and into the early darkness.

When she had first come here, she had felt with painful intensity the silence and the loneliness of the cave. As time had passed, she had come to accept it and to feel comfortable with it. Now, as her gaze slid over her domain, over the crackling fire, over the pallet of furs where the two of them had just lain, she felt that awful loneliness again.

And something more. Something worse. Shame and sorrow all rolled into one. The shame stemmed from her allowing him to touch her so intimately in the first place. What must he think of her? How could she have, even for a moment, wanted to have a man touch her again after the ugly things that haunted her memories? And the sorrow. It played ambivalently against the shame. She had turned him away, and in so doing she had hurt him and made him angry with her. She didn't want him to be angry with her. His touch had been exciting, not debasing, but she didn't understand the tumultuous feelings she had when he touched her. Nor did she understand his volatile reaction to it all.

She sat on her furs and mechanically began making a poultice for his wounds. She didn't cry, although tears hovered nearby. It seemed hours passed before he returned, but when he did he paused in the cave's entrance, glaring at her.

"I thought you'd be asleep," he snapped, almost as if he wished she were.

"Your wounds need to be taken care of."

"They'll be all right," he said tightly. "I washed them in the lake. Nothing like ice cold water to

204

stop the bleeding and cure whatever else ails you."

"Matt . . . I . . ."

"You don't need to say anything, Sky. It's I who should apologize. I'm sorry for forcing myself on you. The fight with Gray Bear had me keyed up. It won't happen again."

He started toward his pallet, but then stopped suddenly and turned back to face her. Anguish and pain tore at his handsome features, and the fury in him she'd felt earlier broke loose again. "Damn that Shoshoni bastard!" he declared in a voice like the growling of an angry grizzly. "These cuts hurt like hell."

The harsh words, even though not directed at her, made her feel as if she, too, had been wounded, somewhere deep inside where medicines and bandages couldn't reach. She longed to put her arms around him and comfort him, and in the process comfort herself. But to do so would only rekindle the dangerous passions she could not deal with.

"Then let me help you," she said softly.

He moved guardedly toward her. Was he fighting the rekindling of feelings just as she was? He settled himself by the fire again. She lifted a small amount of the poultice to the wound that looked the worst. He flinched, taking in air through his clenched teeth. His eyes closed as if to help ride out the pain.

"I'm sorry it hurts," she said. "I'm trying to be careful."

"No need to apologize," he said with a clenched jaw. "I've discovered nothing good in this life comes without pain."

She lowered her gaze to the bowl of poultice again and brought out another portion with her fingertips.

She sensed his words held a deeper meaning, possibly something aimed directly at her. She continued calmly, but it was with a great effort, for frustration was building inside of her. Everything in her life that had been settled, peaceful, and calm a few months ago was now colliding and coming to a catastrophic climax: the riders out in the mountains searching for her, wanting to kill her; the past haunting her; Gray Bear's promise to return and kill Matt; and finally Matt himself, who made her feel as if she was on a see-saw with no way to jump off.

To top it off, guilt enveloped her. She knew she should try to do whatever she could to bring her family's and Monty's killers to justice. She should do what she could to help the situation on the reservation. But could one ever walk boldly into the face of his own death if he were first given the choice not to?

Matt made her uneasy with his steady perusal, as if he saw the many things troubling her and waited to see if she would be cowardly and remain hidden and uninvolved.

She applied poultice to the last wound, then bound his chest tightly with the white linen to help hold the poultice in place. The moments so close to him were tense ones for them both. When she was done, she busied herself by cleaning the wooden bowl. After a time she spoke, if for no other reason than because the silence was driving her mad.

"Gray Bear will return, Matt," she said with her back to him. "His warrior pride rules, even over good judgment. If he makes a promise, I know he'll keep it."

"I'm not afraid of him."

She whirled about to face him. "But he'll kill you! Or you, him! I can't let that happen. I care for you both."

She immediately wished to retract the statement, especially when his eyes seemed to bore into her even deeper. Was he just wearing a facade of caring to deceive her? Or was there true jealousy and hurt in his eyes?

"Then come away with me, Sky," his tone softened. "It wouldn't be running. It would just be leaving. Because you can be certain that if Gray Bear and I fight again, one of us *will* die."

She looked at the cave's floor and then at the poultice bowl, anything but Matt's waiting gaze. "I can't." She nearly choked on the words. "There's something I've . . . something I've done. I can't go to Cheyenne. I can never return to the valley."

She lifted her head defiantly and Matt thought how lovely she was even with fear in her eyes — the fear of an animal, trapped. She seemed helpless and vulnerable in those moments and he felt an overpowering need to protect her. He saw the way she looked at him, trying to decide if she could trust him or if he would betray her in some way. Surely she couldn't think she'd done something wrong because an evil man, or men, had physically abused her? But who could possibly know how a young girl's mind might twist things in an instance like that. Could she possibly think that what had happened was her own fault? He was so ashamed of himself for letting his lust get the best of him. He would never have raped her, but he had surely made her think it had been his

207

intention. Now, she might never fully trust him again.

He picked up his shirt and pulled it on carefully over his bandaged chest. "What could you possibly have done that would have been so terrible, Sky? What is this secret of yours?" He stepped around the fire and took her hands in his. Her eyes softened with agony and indecision. "Tell me," he whispered. "We're friends, remember? *Haynze.*"

The use of the Shoshoni word seemed to crumble the wall she had constructed around her and helped to erase the tension of their earlier battle. He saw her will weakening. She started to turn away, but he caught her arm and pulled her against him.

"Tell me, Sky. How can I help you if I don't know?"

Suddenly her eyes flashed fire, but it was almost immediately quenched by helpless, angry tears. "All right, damn it! I'll tell you! I killed two men! *Two* men, Matt! You're a Pinkerton detective, and now you'll have no choice but to turn me in so I can hang!" She thrust her wrists at him. "Here, put your cuffs on me! Get it over with!"

He took her wrists, but gently in his hands. "What is this all about? I wasn't told that you killed anyone. If I'm to help you, you must tell me what happened that day. You can't keep it inside yourself any longer."

Her body relaxed; she gave up the struggle with a sigh of defeat. He pulled her against his chest. It hurt his wounds badly, but he didn't complain. After a time, she gently extricated herself from him and went to her pallet where she settled herself cross-legged.

"Sit down, Matt. Here." She patted the furs next to her.

He obeyed and moved to her side so that his thigh touched hers in a solid, reassuring way for them both. Her gaze drifted to the fire and to its soothing flames sensually lifting and licking the darkness. All was peace again, finally.

"Once upon a time there was a young girl named Red Sky McClellan," she began. "Sky could run very fast. She loved to sing. And in her complete innocence, there was nothing in life she couldn't have. There was nothing in life she feared. . . ."

I was the Grizzly,
awesome and brave,
But the Moon is gone,
and footsteps I hear.

Chapter Twelve

Sky McClellan thrilled to the power in her long, lean legs as they covered the grassy meadow in consuming strides. With her skirt and petticoats hiked up past her knees, she ran faster and faster. Faster than the clouds before the wind. Faster than the swift little pronghorns darting through the sagebrush eluding their predators. She imagined herself a fleet-footed deer. A wild mustang. A golden eagle.

Yes, an eagle, soaring upward to the heights of the mountains, dipping on the breeze, flirting with the sun.

"You've won, Sky! Come back!"

She recognized the voice of her boyfriend, Monty Glassman. He sounded irritated with her, probably because he hadn't been able to keep up with her, but she ran on just the same, laughing with exhilaration. Monty had insisted on wearing those high-heeled cowboy boots even though she had personally made him a fine pair of moccasins. He had his pride, he said, and no self-respecting cowboy would wear moccasins.

Well, she could outrun him any day, with or without moccasins. As a matter of fact, she was sure she could even outrun the braves on the reservation.

Yes, Sky McClellan could outrun anybody.

"Sky!" Her little brother Jarod shouted, sounding as if he was about to cry. "Come back, dang it! You've won! The race is over! And it's dinnertime! Pa's gonna be madder than a wet hen if you don't get — "

But she didn't hear the rest of his words. She was simply too far away, and the wind, created by her own movement, roared in her ears. With head flung back she drank of it and surged on.

She left the meadow, still running, but when she reached the path that led into the aspen trees, she slowed down to dodge the low limbs and the brush that grew near the path, and the occasional tree that had toppled over to block the way. She took the fallen trees with delight, pretending she was a wild mustang leaping over them, easily outracing the ranchers' lariats. Life on her father's ranch had made her strong and fit. She not only helped with many of the outdoor chores and rode horses, but she spent much time in the woods, running and singing, gathering herbs and firewood for her mother. Her father said she was really just collecting daydreams.

Finally, she stopped to catch her breath. Her run had taken her out of the valley and into the first lift of the hills that eventually lost their gentle curves to the thrusting steepness of the Wind River Mountains. She went to a little sagebrush knoll nestled in the middle of the aspen trees. It was a favorite spot of hers. From her slight vantage point she could look back over the broad expanse of Long Moon Valley, green with high grass and dotted with the motley colors of the Longhorns. And in the pasture, the new red-and-white Hereford breeding stock.

She couldn't see the ranch house or the outbuildings for they were around a bend in the hills, but she could see the tiny figures of her two brothers, Jarod and Nathan, as they climbed back onto their paint pony, riding double. Next to them was Monty, eighteen and handsome, four years her senior. He was a top hand on his dad's ranch across the valley, ten miles away, and he wanted to marry her. Of course, Daddy wouldn't let her marry until she was sixteen. And she wasn't pressing the issue. She was having too much fun to settle down and take on the tasks of being a wife and mother, which to her, looked to be rather mundane and boring.

Besides, she had this fantasy of a handsome stranger on horseback — a man, not a boy. She couldn't see this stranger's face in her daydream, but her heart never failed to skip a beat as he rode toward her, all broad-shouldered, big and silent, and even a little dangerous-looking, but a man who was actually as gentle as a kitten when at last he touched her. Smitten by her beauty, he would gather her up and they would ride away together on his horse into the mountains where they would live happily ever after.

She sighed at the sheer romance of it. So, needless to say, she wasn't quite ready to give up the dream.

She wanted to wait a little while to see if that stranger really would come riding into Long Moon Valley and sweep her off her feet.

Even from the distance she saw Monty remove his hat in frustration. For a second his red hair glistened in the sunlight, then he yanked his hat back down over it. He looked up into the trees, searching for her. When he didn't see her he cupped his hands around his mouth and shouted, "If you don't want to walk home you'd better come back! I ain't waitin'!"

She'd ridden out with him on his horse, but she didn't want to return just yet. She wanted to be alone, even if it meant walking home. After all, it was only about a mile.

She sat down in the grass and gazed at the perfect blue of the sky. She wished Monty would come back and talk to her, but he was apparently more interested in dinner than pursuing her — either that or his pride had been wounded because she'd won the race. Maybe he just needed to sulk for a while. Boys were like that when a girl beat them at something.

She lay back in the grass, hands beneath her head. The sun was getting closer to the western horizon but was still hot on her face. There were about two hours of daylight left. She really should go back for dinner. Her father thought it inconsiderate when the dinner bell wasn't answered on time. Her mother didn't mind, though. Her mother seemed to understand her need to run wild and free, and therefore she never tried to curb her. But that was the Indian way. As for her father's acts of discipline — they were always evenly tempered with acts of love. And she loved him dearly.

She closed her eyes against the hot July sun, deciding to enjoy it just a little longer before going back to the ranch for supper. Her younger sister, Bliss, who had just turned twelve, would be mad at her anyway for shirking her duties and she'd have to go through a squabble with her. But she had a good excuse — Monty had come courting. And chances were her mother would stand up for her this time.

As she often did, she lifted her voice in song, the sweet strains filtering into the aspens. She liked to sing in the evening when the color went from the land and stillness settled over the forest, and when her voice echoed, coming back to her so she could hear how she sounded.

Unexpectedly a youthful male voice joined hers. She stopped singing, but the male voice continued. It was not a voice particularly on key, and it cracked occasionally as young men's changing voices often did. She smiled at it anyway, stood up, and shook the grass and twigs from her skirt.

There in the shadows of the trees, sitting astride his Medicine Hat horse, was Gray Bear, her Indian friend from the reservation. He'd been a playmate of hers all her life, but the last few years he, too, had begun to look at her with the desire she recognized in men's eyes when they were attracted to a woman. She liked Gray Bear and was flattered by the way his black eyes touched her and lingered. He was really much more handsome than Monty, and there was something sultry and mysterious about him. She knew he desired her, maybe even more than Monty did. In truth, she had more in common with Gray Bear. He was of the earth and the sky and the sun,

214

just as she was. He understood her feelings for these things better than anyone except her mother.

"You've come a long way, Gray Bear," she said. "Have your cattle wandered all the way from the reservation to Long Moon Valley?"

He slid to the ground, unfettered by a saddle. He was such a good rider he didn't need one. It was something that had always impressed Sky. She was a good rider, too, but she had never been able to top Gray Bear's ability on horseback. She could run faster than him, though. She could run faster than anybody.

"Cattle know no bounds," he replied. "I came to see you, but I see the White Eyes got here first. Why do you run from him?"

He caressed her chin with a brown hand, but made no attempt to kiss her as Monty would have done. He fingered her loose, flowing hair, held back from her face by a ribbon as yellow and silky as a Glacier Lily.

"Your hair reminds me of the crow's wing, Red Sky," he said, "but why do you wear it loose for Glassman and then braid it when you plan to meet me?"

"I thought that's the way Indians liked it," she teased.

"No. I like it loose. My hands find it a pleasant nesting place."

His smoldering eyes and his suggestive words sent little chills down her spine. But his advances also made her mildly uncomfortable for she sensed he wanted what she wasn't ready to give. Sometimes she longed for the yesterdays when they were children

215

and life was uncomplicated. Back then they ran and played together, laughed, even fought, but they had been equals and the differences in their sexes had had little meaning. Back then the future stretched out endlessly in days of sun and play. She stood on the threshold of maturity now, but there was still so much of the little girl in her she was reluctant to let it go. How could she tell him that she just wanted them to be the children they had always been?

Gray Bear pulled his knife from his scabbard that hugged his slim hip. They often took turns throwing it at a stump, a tree, or a fallen log. The one who came closest to the center of the target was the winner. But this time he pushed her hair back and pulled out a strand from underneath.

She laughed and tried to pull away. "What are you doing?"

"I'd like a strand of your hair so that when I'm not with you, I can still have you near. No one will even notice it's gone."

She tried to toss her head, but his grip on the strand of hair kept her from getting away. Still, he didn't hold her tight enough to hurt her. "If every man who liked me took a piece of my hair, I wouldn't have any left," she said saucily.

He grinned. "Come on, Red Sky. I won't take much and it'll grow back."

She tilted her head forward a little. "All right. Take a strand—a *small* strand. But don't you dare tell Monty because I don't want to lose any more of my hair."

He laughed and with a downward stroke, a long black strand of hair lay in his hand. He pulled a leather fringe off his buckskin shirt and twisted it around the hair in such a fashion that the ebony lock would not be lost. He then tied it to his shirtfront so it dangled there like a decoration.

Sky suddenly laughed. "Your coup, I presume."

He laughed along with her, a rather high-pitched boyish sound. He flicked his wrist and his knife flew toward a big aspen that had dwelled in the forest for many decades. The knife stuck in the center of one of the black "eyes" on the aspen's white bark, vibrating for several seconds before it stood motionless.

"Can you beat that, Red Sky?"

She walked to retrieve the knife and pulled it free after some effort. She touched an even smaller eye on the tree. "What you've done is nothing. I can put the knife in the center of this one."

He laughed. "Your boasts will put you to shame, *nehaynzeh*."

"Oh, I think not."

She walked back to his side. She barely glanced at her target before sending the knife through the air again. It found its mark, dead center.

He turned to her and took her by the shoulders. "I am the tree, Red Sky, and your knife has plunged into my heart. I will die if you marry Monty Glassman. Tell me you will not."

He was always so full of poetic words, but his eyes still gleamed lightly, as if it was all part of the game they played.

"I have no intention of marrying him — or anyone — for a long, long time."

Suddenly his eyes narrowed with anger and disappointment. As unexpectedly as he had arrived,

217

he stalked away and swung back onto his pony.

"Gray Bear," she said, irritated by his sulkiness. "Come back, for heaven's sake. I didn't mean to upset you. I'm simply too young to marry — and so are you!"

He gave her one last, long disapproving glance then rode away, soon vanishing in the cover of the trees.

She turned back to the aspen tree. He was so sensitive these days. It seemed she was always walking on eggshells when in his company. She pulled the knife out, realizing she'd have to give it to him when he came back — *if* he came back. She slipped it through her belt.

With feet not quite as light as they had been, and the songs gone from her heart, she headed back to the ranch and to dinner. She didn't run home, but merely trotted. She had probably missed supper and her father wouldn't be happy.

Her feet slowed when the two-story log house came into view. Right away she saw five horses, besides Monty's, tied out front at the hitching rail. A quick scrutiny of the horses told her that they weren't from the McClellan Ranch, which didn't surprise her because the hired hands were out checking the herds for sickness and monitoring water supplies. This time of year, creeks could go dry overnight.

She liked company and they didn't get it often. But their visitors were usually only other cattlemen who had come to talk to her father about the perpetual rustling problem and what they were going to do about it. It seemed her father was always designated the head of the meetings. From the looks of the horses, she figured this was another meeting of that sort so she didn't get too excited about hurrying to join them.

With her mind once again on Gray Bear and his anger with her, she entered the back door, being careful not to let the screen door bang as she frequently did. The kitchen was empty, and she thought she might just get a bite to eat and avoid walking in late into the dining room. She didn't want to be chastised and subsequently embarrassed in front of company. Of course, it would serve her right. She really should start being more responsible.

She hesitated at the door, but it was a moment before she realized that there was no noise on the other side. No rattle of dishes or clinking of silverware. No discussion. Perhaps they were all done eating and had gone into the sitting room to discuss business. But as soon as the thought came to her, she shook her head. No, that couldn't be, because her mother and sister would be clearing the table and would more than likely be in here doing dishes.

With her curiosity piqued, she quietly pushed the door open that led to the dining room. The room was indeed vacant, and it appeared as if everyone had left the table before they were done with their meal. Growing concerned at such an irregularity, she walked toward the sitting room where her father usually talked to the cattlemen in front of the fireplace with their cigars and liquor. The serenity of the large, homey room encompassed her as it always did. Even with no fire dancing in the fireplace on this hot summer day, there was peacefulness here. This room embodied the spirit of her life in Long Moon

Valley, a life she never wanted to change. But like the dining room, this room was also unoccupied. Empty leather and horsehair chairs sat on the big oval rug that had been placed in front of the fireplace. The clock ticked away over the mantel with the family's smaller knickknacks and odds and ends on either side of it. The paintings of mountain and ranch scenes from her father's budding collection stared back at her from the dark walls, suggesting nothing out of the ordinary.

Then she heard noises from upstairs, noises that weren't exactly people engaged in conversation but sounds made by people just the same. Her gaze shifted to the curving wooden stairs that led to the second floor. Perhaps someone was sick or hurt and they had all gone upstairs. She lifted her skirt past her ankles again, and moved soundlessly on her moccasins up the stairs, anxious now to find out what was going on.

Down the hall she saw doors open to the bedrooms with the day's last light spilling out into the hall. It seemed everyone was congregated there, but the sounds she heard sounded more like grunts than conversation. There was an occasional deep-throated chuckle. Why in the world would all the company be congregated in the bedroom?

At first, the last rays of the sunlight from her parents' bedroom window blinded her. Nothing registered in her mind but hazy images scattered about the room in the gleaming golden light. But finally her mind cleared the sun from the images and she saw it. Blood. On the floor at her feet, on the walls. On her father, her brothers. Monty. All dead on the floor. Mama on the bed. Bliss on the floor. Naked. Men holding them. Laughing, sneering. Brown, spread-eagled legs. Men on their knees. Bare buttocks. Thrusting against the brown legs. Like machines. Laughing and sneering. Mama's tears. Bliss's eyes. Blank.

The roar in her head became so loud it seemed to block her thinking. But the knife came into her hand as did the thought to kill. With no hesitation she flung it, and it *whooshed* through the air. The roar in her head blocked the sound of the knife's flight. Nor did she hear the dull thud as it settled deep in the center of the man's back. The man hurting Mama.

He fell forward. The sneering and laughing stopped. In the strange, throbbing silence that followed, all the eyes turned to her, but her feet remained rooted to the floor. She saw Mama lift her head off the pillow, crying, struggling against the men who held her. The man with the knife in his back fell over on top of her.

Mama's scream suddenly shattered the stillness.

"Run, Sky! Run! They'll kill you! RUN!"

She moved then. She didn't know how. But she was out of the room and down the stairs as if her feet had indeed grown wings. From behind her she heard cursing and running feet. "She's mine. I'll get her!"

But she shouldn't be running. She didn't know if Bliss was dead, but she should help Mama. She had to go back. She had to!

"Run, Sky!"

Her mother's hysterical screams followed her down the stairs, reverberating through her, right along with the blood coursing through her brain.

"Run! Run!"

She ran out the back door and into the yard. She stumbled and fell. Heavy footsteps were right behind her. She couldn't seem to breathe. Fear and shock consumed her. She struggled up and fled to the hill behind the house. Tears blurred the trail, but if she could get into the timber she might find a place to hide. Maybe she could find Gray Bear. He could help her. They could help Mama.

She heard a thundering noise, and looked over her shoulder to see a man coming from around the house on one of the horses.

You can run faster than the clouds before the wind, Sky. Faster than the pronghorn. Faster than anyone or anything.

She topped the ridge. The deep timber was close. There was a trail that went into the underbrush. She could get in there and lose him. Oh God, how her lungs burned. Spasms of pain gripped her legs.

The ground shook beneath the horse's galloping hooves. Another glance confirmed it lunging up the hill behind her. She ran harder, feeling as if her heart would burst. She felt the heat of the animal's body nearly on top of her. A hand closed around her streaming hair and yanked her back. Incredible pain shot through her head. She went down but got up and began to run again.

The man leaped off the horse, and dragged her down. He threw her hard against the ground, nearly knocking the wind from her. He straddled her and pinned her with his weight. She tried to fight him, but almost instantly she felt the cold metal of a knife blade thrust against her throat, and she froze in terror.

"That's it. Now, just lie still, you little hellcat! This ain't gonna hurt. You might even like it. And *I'm* sure going to." His voice was like someone scraping sand over a chalkboard. She doubted she would ever forget that voice.

Leering, he ripped her blouse open and she screamed. With another downward stroke, he ripped her cotton chemise and her breasts spilled free. He laughed and began groping at her with his one free hand. She whimpered as hot tears stung her eyes. She tried in vain to cover herself with her hands, but he just knocked them aside while he continued to squeeze and paw until she was crying uncontrollably.

"We're just beginning, little gal. You don't know the half of it, do you?"

He leaned down to her and suckled and nipped at her breasts hard and cruelly. She sensed he enjoyed knowing he was hurting her, but she couldn't stifle the cries that escaped her lips. She felt herself losing control, giving in to panic and pain.

She struck his face with her fist. His hat flew off. He slapped her in retaliation with so much force it threw her head to the side and momentarily stunned her. Through the blur of increasing tears and fear she saw his hair, nearly solid gray, framing his nondescript face. She was surprised because he couldn't have been more than thirty-five. But she knew she'd never seen him before.

He leaned over her again and covered her mouth with his. His tongue forced her lips apart and thrust inside her mouth time and again until her stomach turned and she gagged, nearly vomiting.

"You little bitch," he hissed and his fist came

down on the side of her head. The fight went out of her. Everything began to fade. She saw the sky whirling overhead as gray as the hair framing his face. She saw him remove his gun belt and toss it aside, out of his way. She felt her skirt being hiked up. Another jerk by his big hand and her pantalets were ripped apart. He rose above her and undid his pants. His huge, threatening male member spilled out. She tried to move, to fight, but the blow to her head had left her stunned and unable to respond. She hovered on the edge of consciousness, angry and frightened because she couldn't move.

He wrenched her legs farther apart. His hands closed over her most intimate part. She cried out in pain and shock as he thrust his fingers inside her again and again, laughing as he hurt her.

"Like that, do you? Well, I've got something even better. It'll teach you to run. And then the boys will give you a few more lessons."

The tears suddenly stopped. Burning rage surged through her. The bastard would not get away with it. She would kill him or die trying. The blow to the side of her head had stunned her, but her anger seemed to renew her and she felt the haze lifting from her mind. Adrenaline began to stream through her again.

"Now, comes the good part, you half-breed bitch," he said hatefully.

She lifted her hands to the knife he held against her throat. She was prepared to feel its sharp slicing motion take her life in a second, but better to die now than suffer what he and the others would do to her before they finally killed her.

And then she saw it! Not far away lay the butt

of his gun protruding from the forgotten holster.

"Let go of my hand or I'll slice your throat here and now," he warned. The blade pressed into her skin and she felt a stinging sensation followed by a warm trickle of blood on her neck.

She dropped her hand to the ground as he'd commanded, but in so doing she reached toward the gun belt almost hidden in the sagebrush. A gurgle of victory rumbled in her tormentor's throat and he lowered his mouth to her breasts again. She blocked his nauseating, painful touch from her mind. She stretched her arm out more — two inches, three. Her fingers closed around the wooden gun handle and she slid it from the holster.

With lust consuming his thoughts and glazing his mind, he pulled away from her breasts and pushed his hips down between her thighs. His white hot flesh thrust against her, hit her thigh, and thrust again seeking her virgin territory. But before it found its destination she rammed the gun to his side and pulled the trigger.

He screamed, falling to the ground and grasping his bleeding side. With shocked pale blue eyes, he stared at her for a moment, then his eyes closed and he fell forward on top of her.

She didn't remember pushing his body away. She didn't remember getting up. She only remembered running. Running like the clouds before the wind. Running until darkness and exhaustion overtook her.

Your lips are as the Morning Sun,
Awakening me from slumber.

Chapter Thirteen

Matt's arms closed around Sky and she rested her head against the solid security of his chest. With the story told, silence settled over them. Sky drifted deeply into her memories and shared no more with him.

Matt stared over the top of her head at the flames and at the wolf on the edge of the firelight. The animal had been droned to sleep some time ago by the murmur of Sky's voice and by the warmth of the fire. Outside, thunder rolled ominously, the first indication of a summer rainstorm moving over the mountains. A blue flash of sheet lightning lit the cave's narrow entrance and briefly its interior. It was soon followed by the hard fall of rain on the rocky ground.

Sky's words still echoed in Matt's head. Even though she hadn't told him exactly how she had felt and what she had thought during that harrowing incident, leaving her descriptions vague, he had been able to read between the lines. He could imagine how an innocent fourteen-year-old girl — one sheltered away from the harsh realities of life in the idyllic world of Long Moon Valley — would view the things she had seen and experienced. Those things had left scars on her young, impressionable mind. Over the weeks, she had put her trust in him, but it would not be so with everyone, and it could very well be that she would harbor a fear and an aversion toward men for the rest of her life.

At least she hadn't been raped, something he had feared from the beginning. But her innocence had been shattered just the same, and the things she'd seen, and the things her assailant had done to her were bad enough for an inexperienced girl who had never shared a bed with a lover, never known the gentle hands and tender kisses of a man who cherished her.

The top of her head was just beneath his chin, and he laid a comforting kiss on the gleaming strands of hair. She didn't stir from the deep state of thought she'd sunk into, the remorseful remembrance of all she'd had and lost.

He eased back on the pallet, drawing her with him, until they lay full length on their sides. She seemed not even to notice the change in their position, but rested her head next to his on the fur pillows and continued to stare at the fire. He tightened his embrace, drawing her against him until he felt the soft curve of her buttocks against his loins and the backs of her thighs against the front of his.

The rain continued outside and soon was dripping through the smoke hole in the top of the cave, plopping incessantly onto the rock floor. After some time Matt noticed Sky's eyes had closed and her body had relaxed. She had fallen asleep and he didn't want to disturb her by getting up and putting a pan beneath the drip. Luckily the storm was short-lived and soon rumbled away. Only a small puddle was left behind on the rock floor.

A chilly intrusion of a night breeze finally forced Matt to pull up a fur robe, and at the action, Sky rolled to her back. He settled back down next to her, facing her, and laid an arm across her. Still, she didn't stir, having fallen into an exhausted sleep caused not from physical exertion, but mental.

Her face was in the shadows, but lit by the fire's backwash. Without her keen brown eyes watching him, he studied and memorized the length and thickness of her black lashes and how they lay like black butterfly wings on her tanned face. He wanted to trace the sensuous, petal-soft curves of her mouth with his finger, but instead merely traced to memory the way her full lips parted slightly in sleep, the upper lip arching into the hint of a Cupid's bow. His gaze traveled along the length of her aquiline nose and to the arched eyebrows, black and perfect, plucked by tweezers to make them that way. It was something he hadn't paid any attention to before. He smiled suddenly. This lovely young woman claimed not to be the girl Sky McClellan anymore, but rather the quarter-breed Red Sky, living like a savage in the wild. And she would make you think she wanted it no other way. But it was plain to see that the civilized world was still a very integral part of her life. There were things she could not or would not give up. Like

228

a simple pair of tweezers, or the bolt of muslin cloth she hadn't used until he'd needed bandages.

He picked up a black strand of hair, spreading its glossy length over her shoulder and breast. It was the one thing he could kiss without disturbing her, and he lifted the silky strands to his lips, inhaling the scent of her hair and of her; the mixture of wind and sun, of furs and flowers and fire.

He laid his head down close to hers, the strand of hair still coiled around his hand. He wondered what it would be like to share a bed with her for the rest of his life. He didn't quite understand it, but her nearness eased his loneliness and intensified it all at once. He'd never had anyone love him. Would it be too much to ask that this woman whom he had loved almost from first sight might grow to return his feelings of need and desire? He would gladly stay here with her forever if that stroke of luck should happen. He felt no need to return to the world, for there was nothing and no one in the world for him to return to. He wanted to take her to him as a man does a woman, but for now he would simply take what pleasure he could from her nearness. After all, this might — in the end — be all he would ever have to remember of Red Sky McClellan.

Coolness invaded the spot where the heat of the male body had been pressed the length of hers. Red Sky awoke with a start. Matt was there by the fire, on one knee. His blue eyes watched her in a troubled way, but when her gaze met his, he looked away, putting a few more sticks on the fire where a pot of coffee had not yet reached the boiling point.

She glanced at his pallet and saw no rumpled furs, no indentations on the top of the furs. She allowed her hand to slip to the spot next to her on her own pallet. It was still warm. He had slept with her all night then.

"I'm sorry. I must have been very tired to . . . to have . . ."

"Yes, you were very tired," he replied softly, politely saving her from her own clumsy attempt at explanation. But the hooded, appraising look in his eyes made her uneasy. She wondered at first if she had been wrong to tell him what had happened to her. Did he now think she was dirty or soiled because of the vile man who had touched her and her family?

She found her brush and smoothed her hair so she could begin braiding it. All the while she wound the strands into plaits, he continued to study her in that same shuttered manner. No matter what she did, his eyes remained fixed on her.

And then suddenly she thought perhaps she knew why.

As if bracing herself for combat, she sat up stiff-backed on the pallet, jutting her chin out defiantly. "I suppose you have no choice now but to turn me over to the law for killing those two men."

His pensive expression changed to one of surprise. "You killed them in self-defense, Sky. No jury could possibly hold that against you."

She looked down at her lap. "I didn't know. I thought . . . you might not see it as something necessary. I thought you might not believe me."

"You're worrying needlessly, Sky." He spoke so low and soft, bordering on a whisper, that his deep,

230

masculine voice sounded almost hoarse in the morning quiet of the cave. "But something has been bothering me."

She shifted uneasily as if she expected a degree of interrogation. "And what is that?"

"I've been sitting here wondering why the governor didn't tell me about the two men you killed."

She gave his question a measure of consideration. "Is it possible the killers took the two bodies with them, and the authorities didn't know I killed them?"

"Either that or no one considered it something I needed to know. After all, I wasn't put on the murder case itself. I was only sent to find you and bring you back for your testimony. But Many Claws said there are people who believe *you're* the one killing the settlers and small ranchers in revenge for what happened to your family."

He wasn't surprised by her appalled gasp; he thought the suggestion absurd, too.

"But why would they think I was killing settlers and small ranchers for revenge?" she asked, thoroughly stunned. Worry lines creased her brow over this new development. "Unless settlers and ranchers were the ones who killed my family. But I have no idea who was behind the murders or even why."

"It almost makes me wonder if the people in the area know more about the killers than the authorities do."

"It doesn't make sense anyway because settlers and small ranchers were — and apparently still are — the ones being targeted. They wouldn't be killing their own. But my father was in neither category. He was not a sodbuster, nor a small rancher. He was one of the first ranchers to settle Long Moon Valley. He was here even before the big rush of men and cattle that came up from Texas looking for more open range back in the seventies."

"Is it possible he could have found out who *was* behind it? Could the settlers and small ranchers have been in somebody's way? Possibly a big rancher or two who didn't want to lose the range to them? Range wars are everywhere in the territory. Do you recall any friction of this sort? Did someone specifically resent the settlers coming into Long Moon Valley?"

"Oh yes. There was always talk of it. Many of the ranchers who had come here first greatly resented the dwindling range. They all got together at meetings and complained about it, but as far as I know that's all it was — just complaining. The ranchers around here aren't killers. They're just men trying to make a living the only way they know how.

"My dad never said much in their presence, though, because he had a philosophy that didn't agree with theirs. He said there was no stopping the influx of people. It had never been done anywhere in the world in the past and it never would be done now as long as things were desirable for them to keep coming. He said that from the first opening of the West, ranchers have always been the first to settle a place. And then when things were relatively safe, the sodbusters came, then the city people. He said one can't expect things to remain the same because they never do, and we all just have to adjust to changing times. So, he tried to protect his interests by buying as much land as he could so he could graze his cattle without relying on public domain as so many of the ranchers did."

"Then your father was, so to speak, the odd man out in his beliefs. That alone would be enough for somebody to turn against him."

Red Sky nodded, realizing that what he said very likely could have been the situation, but she'd been a young girl. She had gone her own way and not paid much attention to the "politics" of the cattle industry. She lived in her own idyllic world, a world her father supplied for her, but she'd never questioned any of it, or doubted that it wouldn't go on forever. And while she roamed the mountains and sang her songs and flirted with Gray Bear and Monty Glassman, little did she guess that her father might have found out something that had targeted him and his entire family for death. Just as she was targeted now — once again.

"Do you think you could identify any of the other men that day — besides the gray-haired one you killed?" Matt asked, bringing her back to the present.

"I'm not sure, Matt. Their faces aren't clear in my memory. It all happened so fast, and the sun was in my eyes as I stepped into the room. The impressions hit me all at once, piling one on the other. I never really saw faces. It must have only been a few seconds before I reacted and ran."

"What about the horses? Did you happen to notice a brand, or any particular marks on any of them? Some of the animals might still be in use by their owners."

She searched her memory. "One of the horses was a young black gelding, probably only a three-year-old. I remember him because he stood apart from the others and his conformation was wonderful. The other animals were various shades of brown — nondescript actually. I glanced at the brands because I always do when visitors come. It's a way of knowing who's inside. But I didn't recognize any of them as being from outfits I knew. And I honestly don't remember what any of them were. It's one of those things when a person doesn't know the information will be important later on, so he makes no special effort to retain it."

Matt stared at the coffeepot, trying to put the bits and pieces together, wishing they would have told him more about the case when they'd sent him out to find Sky. He was no longer interested in just bringing her back. He wanted to get to the bottom of the mess.

"Then you will go now?" she asked softly, scattering his musings.

He lifted his gaze again, trying to read her expression but having very little success. She seemed to be very careful about keeping her feelings from surfacing in her eyes. Did she want him to go? Or did she want him to stay? Had the kisses they'd shared, the weeks spent together, the hours in each other's arms last night, meant as much to her as they had to him? Was she safer here than in the valley? Safer here than in Cheyenne? Safer with Gray Bear and Many Claws than with him?

He ran his fingers through hair that needed cutting. He couldn't delay his parting any longer.

Whether she came or not, he had to report back with something.

"Yes, I suppose it's time to go. But how can I do that and leave you here alone? Those men are still out there, Sky, determined to find you. And Gray Bear and Many Claws will be returning soon to take you away from here if they possibly can. I can't stop them, short of killing them, but they don't know what they could be leading you into if they take you away from here. They'll be no match for the killers if they catch up with you. I know the sort, Sky—and so do you. They'll stop at nothing. No, I don't really see how my conscience can allow me to leave you here alone."

Red Sky herself was torn between her desire to stay here and her desire to stay with Matt. Yes, it had come to this, but there were reasons he should go, whether she went with him or not.

"You can't stay here," she said. "Gray Bear is going to return. And the first thing on his mind will be to fight you to the death—just as he promised he would do."

She watched him come slowly to his feet, in an uncoiling fashion. He took her hand and drew her up next to him. She tried to control a little shiver of pleasure as his hands slid up the sleeves of her doeskin blouse, across her shoulders, and gently up her neck until her face was held in his tender palms and her heart was beating wildly in her bosom. She was surprised to feel the hard sinews of his back beneath her hands, surprised that her arms had gone around him voluntarily. She watched with fascinated anticipation as his lips parted and his head lowered to hers.

She met the kiss, rising on her tiptoes into his embrace.

His lips sampled hers with slow, decisive relish. She felt the passion in his body, coursing through him and into her. Little shivers of excitement pulsed in her veins when his tongue made a tentative exploration of her lips then slipped between to create a heady new fire that made her heart race even faster.

He lifted his mouth from hers, but only enough to end the kiss, not the contact. "If Gray Bear and I fight, Sky, is it for my life that you fear?" His warm breath brushed the words softly against her lips, sending more tantalizing tingles throughout her body. "Or is it Gray Bear who holds your heart?"

Oh, how could she think when he was touching her so? When his kisses lay a scalding yet wonderful trail of fire along her neck? She didn't understand all she felt for Matt Riordan, but she knew she liked this closeness with him, needed it, wanted it. She wondered how she could go on living in these mountains without him.

His presence always scattered her thoughts like an October wind scatters autumn leaves. She couldn't focus on anything but him. How could he expect her to answer questions? She finally removed his arms from around her, which he allowed reluctantly and with a puzzled expression. She turned away from him and began pacing restlessly around the cave. After a few seconds, he took her arm and halted her.

"Why can't you tell me, Sky?"

She sank into those fascinating eyes of his again, and wondered at the thoughts behind them. He did not speak of love, but he treated her with affection.

"Because I care for both of you," she said softly. "I don't want either of you to die."

She could tell by a vague look of disappointment on his face that it wasn't exactly the answer he'd hoped to hear.

"It appears to me that if you want to prevent Gray Bear and me from killing each other," he said, "then you have no choice but to go with me."

"But I can tell the governor nothing, Matt. The only man I remember is dead!"

"I'm sorry my being here is bringing some changes you may not like, Sky, but I have a job to do. I'll either take you back to Cheyenne to testify to the governor, or I'll stay here and track down those riders until I get to the bottom of this case. It's not my habit to leave a case defeated, or empty-handed. And if I stay, Gray Bear and I will most certainly come to blows. Not because I necessarily want to, but because his foolish and proud warrior blood tells him he must.

"It's no longer a question of your testimony, Sky. But the decision must still be yours." He picked up his hat and put it on, pulling it down snugly onto his forehead. "I'll give you some time alone to think about it."

Before she could think of a response, he had left the cave.

Extreme silence settled over the dwelling place. A deep pain began in Red Sky's heart, and it grew until she wondered if she could bear it. Soon the silence was interrupted by the burping of the coffee in the pot, finally boiling. She removed it from the heat then sat back on her heels. Esup came to silently request his morning portion of attention, which she gave to him by absently stroking his gray-white head.

She had come at last to the crossroads, or perhaps the crossroads had come to her. But whichever it was, there was no turning back. She knew — *had* known from the moment she had brought Matt Riordan into her life — that the day would come when she would have to make a decision and take one of the roads that now lay before her. But which one, when possible death waited at the end of each, if not for her, then for Matt or Gray Bear?

The decision would seem to be a hard one, but actually there was no decision, no alternative. Lives hung in the balance and she carried the weight of them all on her shoulders alone. Above all else, it was time to settle the matter so peace could return to the mountains and to Long Moon Valley. It was time to avenge the deaths of her family. She couldn't do that alone, but she could with the help of Matt Riordan.

The decision, in part, was made not from practicalities, but from the heart. She didn't understand it fully, and wanted to deny it, but she knew if Matt left the mountains this time, there was very little possibility he would return. If that happened she would never again feel his lips on hers, or his strong, comforting arms around her, his hard male body next to hers on the furs making her feel safe and not so alone. And if that happened, she would never again experience that strange but desirous feeling deep inside her body that urged her to turn to him, to touch him intimately, to confide her secrets to him, and to learn his in turn. Sooner or later they would have no choice but to part. But not yet. Let her savor the sweet companionship a little longer.

She rose, moving to the corner that held her personal belongings. She selected one large parfleche that was made like saddlebags, designed to fit over a horse's flanks. She began placing some of her belongings inside. It wouldn't take her long to be ready to go.

"You must stay here, Esup," Red Sky knelt next to the wolf. *"Nangakande."*

The wolf stretched out upon the cave's floor and laid its head on its paws as if planning to do exactly as told. Red Sky rose, but her gaze remained on the wolf in a troubled way. "He understands," she said to Matt who stood by silently watching the exchange. "But I've never been gone for more than a day, and I'm afraid he might give up on me and go back to the wild."

"Then let him come with us."

Her brow furrowed. "I'm afraid it wouldn't be wise to take him from the mountains. This is all he knows, and I don't know how he'll react to towns and people. Not to mention, someone might mistake him for a wild wolf and kill him. No, I will have to make this journey without him."

She looked over her dwelling place with a rise of sentiment, wondering if she would ever see it again. She didn't want to take this journey. She would much prefer not facing the past again, not speaking of it again, especially to strangers who might judge her as a coward or a killer. But now that she had made the decision, she was very anxious to get on with it. So, with parfleche in hand, she stepped from the cave and into the sunlight.

Matt flung his saddlebags over his shoulders and palmed his Winchester. Like Sky, he took one last look at the cave. It had been a comfortable, safe haven, and he, too, felt some reluctance in leaving the peace of it. As his gaze slid to the furs on the two pallets — his and Sky's — his memory drew on last night when she had allowed him to hold her.

Uneasiness built inside him. He had finally gotten his wish and she had consented to go with him. But would he someday rue this moment? What if something happened to her? What if all his well-laid plans and those of the governor went awry, and the men who wanted her dead somehow succeeded? Might it not have been better to stay and fight Gray Bear? He wasn't afraid to. He'd fought many men in his life and he had always known he would die by the hand of an adversary some day. In the past, he hadn't cared about death; now the thought of it unsettled him. He didn't want to leave this world and leave Sky alone, possibly to go into the arms of Gray Bear.

Foolish selfishness it was, and nothing more, but he couldn't change or deny the feelings.

He paused next to the wolf. Impulsively he patted the animal's head. "I'll bring her back, Esup," he whispered. But the cave's walls echoed the words back to him, giving them a hollow and meaningless sound, just as it did the departing click of his boot heels on the rock floor.

A distant yesterday she leaves behind.

Chapter Fourteen

They departed from the mountains with caution, watching for the riders, but they saw no one. They rode double when the terrain allowed it, and when it didn't they both walked. Matt's leg began to ache but he refused to ride if Red Sky had to walk, although she suggested it time and again and thought him foolish for being so chivalrous at such a time and under such conditions.

It was midafternoon of the second day when they saw, from their position on the foothills, the tipis of the reservation spread out before them along the river. Red Sky wanted to tell Many Claws what they were doing, but she knew it wouldn't be wise. He might try to interfere, and Gray Bear would most certainly.

They waited until dark, then made their way into the valley and to Fort Washakie. Matt left Red Sky in some thick brush by the river and approached the fort with the intention of buying a second horse. Red

Sky had only to wait about an hour before Matt returned with a brown gelding in tow.

"Do you think they knew who you were?" she asked.

"The army officer I talked to didn't ask and didn't seem to know or care. I paid him more than the horse was worth and that's apparently all that concerned him. I was lucky enough to catch him functioning on about a half bottle of whiskey so he was in a complacent mood. Since I didn't try to get a saddle, I don't think he thought anything of me trying to replace the packhorse I'd lost. There was no way for him to know or even suspect I had a companion. But we'd better get away from here to make camp. We don't want to be where they can see us in the morning. I'm not worried about the army getting involved in this, but if they see you they could innocently supply answers to the wrong people.

Red Sky swung bareback onto the gelding with no difficulty. Like ghosts in the light of the gibbous moon, they faded into the shadows along the river. From here until they were past Lander, Matt had decided they would travel at night because much of the terrain was open and they could too easily be seen in daylight by anyone who might be following them. Once past Lander, they could travel by day. At that point, if they had eluded the riders who haunted the southern reaches of the Wind River Range, they should be relatively safe. It was very unlikely that people away from the Wind River Range would know anything about Sky McClellan or the legend she had become to her mother's people.

They skirted the Oregon Trail and the Sweetwater

River, preferring to stay off the main thoroughfare and away from its frequent travelers. Between Split Rock and Devil's Gate, they headed south to Whiskey Gap through the Green Mountains in the west and the Seminoe Mountains in the east. Matt had watched their back trail these last couple of days in the binoculars and had seen nothing unusual. Fifty more miles behind them and they'd be to Rawlins and the railroad.

It was shortly after that comforting thought that he noticed three men following them. They were a rough-looking, scruffy, trio that had been camped at Whiskey Gap. They were keeping their distance, staying always about a mile behind. For some reason, Matt didn't feel they had anything to do with the group from the Winds who had been trying to find Sky, but he didn't like the way they had looked at her nonetheless. He knew their sort. They'd seen easy prey, and, like a pack of wolves, they were following and waiting for their chance to attack. They were the kind of renegades who wouldn't hesitate to kill him so they could get to her.

Sky drew men's attention, and it wasn't just the fact that she was dressed like an Indian. She was the sort of woman men would talk about over whiskey and poker in the saloon. She had a face and a figure a man wouldn't forget.

If those three were going to make a move for her, they would make it before Rawlins. Probably tonight.

He had to think of a way to lose them and he didn't want to say anything to Sky because he didn't want to frighten her. She naturally questioned him when he continued to ride well past the time they usually set up camp. He rode until dusk sat on the edge of darkness. He couldn't see the men any longer, so he knew that if they were still following, they wouldn't be able to see him either.

He searched the coming darkness for a place to camp where they wouldn't be seen or heard. They watered their horses at a creek and Matt saw through the fading light that farther up the creek were the high banks of a dry gulch. Naturally Sky questioned the intelligence of his decision to camp in the gulch, but he told her it was for security reasons. She accepted the explanation because they'd stayed to themselves as much as possible on the entire trip, not mingling or talking to other travelers any more than they'd absolutely had to.

The banks of the gulch were steep, gouged out by deep flood waters over the centuries, but they finally found a piece of the bank that had broken off and provided an easy descent into the bottom for the horses. There was very little grass in the gulch, but it would be enough to allow the horses a meal. After stripping them of their tack and the other supplies, Matt tethered them on long ropes so they could graze. It was completely dark now and only the light of the stars enabled them to see what they were doing.

Sky had wanted a fire since they'd left the mountains, but Matt had considered it too dangerous. He still didn't feel it would be wise. Even if no one saw it, those three men following them might smell the smoke. So they shared a cold camp in weary silence and ate jerky and hardtack and washed it down with water. Neither was very talkative. Matt was used to the grueling travel, sleeping on the ground, subsisting on next to nothing, but it was taking its toll on Sky. She hadn't ridden a horse for years and he saw in her eyes how exhausted she was.

"Get some sleep, Sky," he said. He was not going to let her know how edgy he was about those renegades. He hoped they couldn't track him and Sky into the gulch in the dark. But when the two of them disappeared and the men couldn't find a fire, they might put two and two together.

He doubted he'd get very much sleep tonight.

As on the other nights since their journey had begun, Matt helped Sky clear a spot on the ground for her bedroll. She slid beneath her blankets, fully clothed, and put her back to him. She always did, though he wished just once they could lay the blankets together and share them.

He watched her for a long time. She was asleep in seconds. He wondered what her true feelings for him were. She'd accepted him, and he thought she trusted him much more than she had in the beginning, but did she long to hold him in her arms the way he did her? And with increasing frequency, and a certain dread, he wondered what the future held beyond Cheyenne. He didn't want to think that far ahead, but he found himself doing so just the same.

It was pure torture being so close to her. He was beginning to think that if he had to spend many more days and nights in this physical agony that he would not be able to keep his promise and take her back to the mountains. He would have to send her back alone or find some other Pinkerton to escort her.

245

At last he released a weary sigh and put his bedroll a few feet from hers. With a willpower he hadn't known he was capable of, he forced his mind away from her enticing body. Morning would be here soon enough, and he had those men to deal with. He couldn't afford the luxury of idle musing.

Matt heard the voices just seconds before the crack of thunder. He came up from his bed with his revolver in hand. Lightning struck, and he saw the slinking movement of three figures on the perimeters of their camp rushing toward him and Sky. He fired two shots in rapid succession and two of the outlaws fell. Sky came awake with a stifled scream. Darkness closed over them again and the third renegade disappeared.

"Matt, what is it?" she whispered fearfully.

"Three men. They've been following us. I got two of them, I think. The third one's still out there." He handed her the Winchester. "Be ready."

"What do they want?" She levered a bullet into the rifle chamber.

He didn't answer, but looked grimly through the darkness waiting for another bolt of lightning. If the last man's two partners were hit badly, or possibly even dead, he might leave.

"Matt, damn it, I asked a question."

He still didn't look at her, but kept his vigil on the darkness surrounding them. The thunder rolled and another flash of lightning lit the night. He saw nothing and everything was dark again.

"They want you."

She was silent for long moments. When she spoke he heard the new fear in her voice. "You mean, they followed us all the way from the mountains? Why didn't you tell me?"

"We picked them up at Whiskey Gap. I didn't say anything because I wasn't sure of their intent and I didn't want to frighten you needlessly."

"So you think they know who I am?"

"No," he said. "I don't think they know who you are. You're a pretty woman and they want you. It's that simple."

Matt glanced at her then, his gaze lingering longer than it should, but the sad realization of the greedy, animal lusts of some men hurt him as badly as it hurt her. "There are just men like that, Sky," he tried to explain. "Some, when given a clear opportunity, will take advantage of it. You mustn't believe that the majority of men are like that."

"They seem to be."

"No, that isn't true. Think of the ones we've passed on the road who have been good people. Remember them, Sky. Remember. If you think otherwise, paranoia and hatred will destroy you."

She said nothing, but he sensed she didn't believe him. After all, she'd barely left the mountains and already she had more men who wanted to hurt her. What else was she to think?

Another ferocious crack of thunder seemed to shake the very earth they sat upon, and simultaneously another bolt of lightning struck. In seconds the summer storm that had boiled up unexpectedly behind them finally reached them, unleashing a torrent of rain. In another second, it seemed as if a floodgate overhead had been opened. They were drenched almost immediately and could barely see each other for the downpour. Twenty yards away the frightened horses danced nervously at the end of their tether ropes.

When the lightning struck again, it lingered, shuddering across the sky as if moving in a chain reaction. It lit the night for several frightening seconds and Matt saw that the two men he'd hit were still on the ground where they'd fallen, farther out in the middle of the wash. They were dead or hurt too badly to move. The third man, apparently having seen himself left alone, had taken to higher ground and cleared out. At least, Matt could hope the man would have the sense to get out while the getting was good.

"Get your bed rolled up and let's get out of this gulch," Matt said, exuding haste. "I have a feeling this storm's dumped a lot of rain before it reached us. We could get hit with a flash flood."

The thunderhead had completely obliterated the moon and stars. They were only able to see what they were doing by the continual stabs of lightning as well as the sheet lightning that undulated across large pieces of the sky.

Though they worked quickly, their bedrolls were soaked before they had them securely wrapped in the tarpaulin liners. A strange roar behind her drew Sky's attention, and even as she turned to see what the noise was, the lightning struck again, illuminating a growing stream of water seething through the gulch directly toward them and toward the two dead men.

248

Matt saw it, too. "Get to higher ground!" he shouted through the downpour. "Carry what you can back up the bank. I'll get the horses out of here before they break and run."

Sky gave no argument and started by hauling the bedrolls out of the gulch. Before she could complete one trip, the furious force of the rain channeled down the steep banks carrying water in swiftly increasing volumes, stripping away topsoil and turning the footing into an impossible quagmire. The bodies of the two outlaws disappeared as the water swept them away. The gentle slope they'd used to bring the horses down was rapidly disintegrating. It was now nearly perpendicular and so slimy that footing could be dangerous if trying to climb it and lead horses, too.

Still, they had no choice. She started back down the bank on her fanny for another load of their gear and supplies. The lightning opened the night again, turning a large portion of the sky white for the length of several seconds. She saw Matt at the base of the slope with the horses, water lapping now around his ankles. Her heart leaped to her throat. The water in the gulch was rising at an incredible speed and churning wildly. In mere minutes it would reach their remaining gear and sweep it all away.

"Go back up!" Matt yelled up at her, squinting against the deluge from the sky. "I'll toss you the ropes. The horses will be able to get up easier if we give them their heads."

She nodded and scrambled up the bank as quickly as she could, losing her footing and falling on her stomach in the mud several times. Finally she

249

reached the top and Matt tossed the tether ropes up.

When she had as much slack in hand possible to give her some control over them, she called back down, "Send them up!"

Matt slapped the frenzied animals on the rumps with his hat. Sky tugged on their tether ropes and they lunged upward, stumbling and falling up the rapidly deteriorating bank. At the top, Sky pulled their tether ropes up short and had them under control in seconds.

"Come on!" she called down to Matt. "Hurry."

"I need to get my rifle and saddle!"

The water was swirling almost to his midcalf now. Sky had heard of cloudbursts and flash floods, but never in her life had she seen so much rain come so fast. Another crack of thunder and a sizzling bolt of lightning came so close that the horses squealed and nearly broke away from her.

"Matt, no! It's too dangerous. The water's rising too fast."

But he was already gone. She yelled after him, furious and frightened. How could he be so stupid as to take such a chance? As the lightning lit the night, she watched him stumbling along the edge of the water. It was rising at an unbelievable pace. The power of it frightened her more than even the lightning. It was forcing Matt up higher and higher on the steep bank.

Suddenly, just as she had feared, she saw the land move. In one sickening movement, an entire portion of the bank slid into the water, carrying Matt with it. She screamed as he vanished in the muddy maelstrom, but she could do nothing to save him. The mighty force of the water swept him away and around a bend, out of her sight.

She tossed the tether over her horse's neck and swung up onto its wet back. She didn't dare turn Matt's horse loose for fear they'd never find it again, so clutching its lead rope, she raced her horse along the edge of the gulch as quickly as possible, leading Soldier. She tried to spot Matt in the water through the downpour and occasionally caught a glimpse of him bobbing on the fomenting waves before he was sucked under again.

She followed the raging current for at least a mile, trying to keep sight of him, but she didn't see him again. At last she stopped the horses and stared helplessly at the raging river that had only minutes before been a dry gulch.

My God, this couldn't be happening. It had to be a nightmare. He had come into her life and helped her see joy again, helped her walk away from the past. He had shown her kindness, maybe even love. He had made her dream dreams again of a future. He'd given her hope. Now, she'd lost him. He was gone. And for what? For a stupid saddle and a 30-30 Winchester!

The rage crept over her slowly, but when it finally consumed her, she suddenly screamed her frustration and her pain to the sky and to the empty land, and perhaps to God, if he happened to be listening. In the end, she frantically rode back and forth along the bank, looking down into the darkness for any glimpse that the lightning might afford her.

It was some time before she realized that the moisture on her face wasn't rain but tears. And the light that was guiding her was not the lightning but the moon and the stars.

The storm had passed.

Drenched to the bone, water dripping from the ends of her moccasins and from the fringes of her buckskins, she finally slid to the ground on shaky legs and began searching for Matt's body. She hoped the water had not carried him on too far, but had relinquished him to a bank or a shallow eddy so she could bury him.

It was amazing to her, that as quickly as the torrent had risen, it began to recede. The water had raced on to another place where it would disperse and eventually sink into the ground.

She saw a scrawny tree clinging to the edge of the gulch and tied the horses to it. Feeling time working against her, she hurried along the edge of the bank on foot, retracing the distance back to the camp.

In her search she found the gruesome bodies of not only the two renegades that Matt had shot, but the drowned corpse of the other one, as well. Fearing for Matt's fate, she finally returned to the horses. She would have to remount and head south. But she had no sooner swung onto her horse's back when she saw movement below and to the right. It was Matt, and he was alive!

She was off the horse in a second and skidding down the bank on her heels. She slipped and slid to where he was sprawled, covered with mud and clinging to the base of a sturdy bush.

Gasping for breath she dropped down next to him and turned him over. She collapsed on his muddy chest. All the fear and love poured out of her in a mixture of crying and cursing. "Damn you, Matt Riordan, why did you do such a stupid thing? You nearly got yourself killed!"

He weakly lifted his arms and put them around her. He was still trying to draw an even breath and his chest rose and fell erratically beneath her bosom. "My rifle . . . Sky . . . I couldn't . . . lose it."

She sat back on her knees, angrily swiping tears from her muddy face now that she knew he was going to live. All her anger at the risk he had taken poured forth. "No, you'd rather lose your life! You brought me out here, damn you, and then you nearly got yourself killed. I don't know where the hell I am. What was I supposed to do with a dead guide?"

He struggled up to his elbows. His blue eyes, showing through a muddy face, suddenly crackled with fire. "Oh, so all you care about is whether I stay alive so I can get you back home! And here I thought your concern was for my *life*. I went into that damned wash in the first place to try and lose those bastards that had been following us so they wouldn't hurt you, and this is the gratitude I get!"

He pushed her aside roughly and she landed on her fanny in the mud. He wobbled to his feet, stumbling around in circles to try and get his bearings. He started clawing his way up the muddy bank, but he was so weak, he slid back down on his belly repeatedly.

Sky grabbed him by the arm and tried to help him. "I do care about your life, and I don't fault you for making the decision to camp in the wash. Under the circumstances it was understandable, but I thought a man like you — with all your experience and all the

253

caution you *continually* exercise—would have had better sense than to go back for a rifle and a saddle in the face of a flash flood!"

"What I did, I did, and it can't be undone—stupid or not," he snapped. "And that rifle—if I could have reached it—might have just saved your life tomorrow, Sky McClellan! All I'm interested in now is seeing if there's anything left of our gear and supplies. Otherwise your *Indian* training might become necessary to get us across the next fifty miles of this godforsaken territory."

"My *Indian* training? How dare you . . . I'm beginning to think that coming with you was the biggest mistake I could have possibly made! I should have gone with Gray Bear. He wouldn't have been so stupid as to—"

Matt whirled on her and went to grab her shoulders, but slipped in the mud. She automatically reached out to catch him but only succeeded in being pulled down with him, landing hard on his chest. In their anger with each other, she struggled to get away from him and he struggled to get away from her. They became a muddy tangle of flailing arms and legs before they finally extricated themselves and fell back onto the ground, side by side, glaring at each other and gasping for breath.

In a lighter moment, Sky might have been able to laugh at the silly way Matt's blond hair stuck up, matted with mud, and how his clothes were not even a discernible color and clung to his body like a coat of plaster of paris. But his eyes shot heat—the equivalent of lightning—and effectively nipped the notion in the bud.

"All right," he managed between ragged breaths. "I'm tired of begging and pleading and coercing. This damn case can just go to hell for all I care. I'll take you back to your old flame. You can go with him to some distant place, live in peace and harmony with the land, and start your own little tribe of Shoshonis. He's such a brave and handsome warrior so fully capable of protecting you. And I'm just a stupid paleface who had a lapse of good judgment in his attempt to keep you alive. But who, save God, could have guessed it was going to rain!"

He grabbed her muddy wrist and started hauling her toward the horses.

"Let go of me, damn you!"

"Quit swearing at me."

"Let me go."

"I'm taking you back to your lover. Hopefully without getting waylaid by those renegades again — if any of them are still alive."

"They're all dead, and Gray Bear isn't my lover and you know it!"

"But you'd like him to be, wouldn't you, Sky? I wonder why in the hell you even came with me. Are you sure they're dead?"

"Yes. I found their bodies. Damn it, Matt, stop. I'll go to Cheyenne. This argument is completely out of hand."

"You started it, if I recall."

"You misunderstood everything."

"Hardly. You're making yourself very clear for a change. You wouldn't have said those things if you didn't mean them."

He didn't stop until he'd reached the horses. After

remounting, they started back to find what was left of their camp. Matt said nothing else to her except for asking her to hold the horses when they arrived at the spot. He slid down the gulch again and returned ten minutes later with his saddle, rifle, horse blanket, and the bridles. A couple more trips and he had the remainder of their supplies, all intact, wet but otherwise undamaged.

"None of it was lost," he said unnecessarily. "The water stopped just inches from it. It would have been fine if I'd just left it alone, so now I guess you can say, 'I told you so.' "

"Stop it, Matt!"

Still refusing to look at her he collapsed on the ground with his gear. "We've got to get dried out before we go anywhere. We have no choice but to wait till daylight. Then we'll see if we can find a stream clear enough to wash off in. Then we'll head back to the mountains and Gray Bear. As for those three renegades, I'm not burying them so don't ask me to. They can just rot in the sun!"

"We'll go to Cheyenne," she said testily. "I'll tell the authorities what I know, and I'll find my own way back home so it won't inconvenience you any further. I've come this far and there's no sense in turning back now. And I wasn't going to ask you to bury those outlaws. I don't care if they rot in the sun. They've caused us nothing but trouble!"

"Well, at least we agree on something." His eyes flashed fire and then he looked away from her. A muscle tensed and untensed in his jaw. "God, I should never have brought you out here. I nearly got us both killed by camping in that wash."

256

"It will hardly do any good to blame yourself," she snapped, getting annoyed at his continual self-reproach. "How could you have foreseen that storm? There wasn't a cloud in the sky when we went to sleep."

"There's no excuse for carelessness."

"And you're the mighty Pinkerton who's never supposed to make a mistake, is that right?"

He glared at her. "Yes! That *is* right! I can't afford to make mistakes! You're in my custody. It's my job to get you to Cheyenne!"

That said, he ended the argument by stretching out on the wet ground with his back to her, diligently attempting to sleep.

She had the overwhelming urge to pound on him and to cry all over again. She was just another job to him! All along he'd made her think she meant more, but in the end she was just another unpleasant assignment. She had been a fool to think his kindness, his kisses, had been anything more than a ploy to get her to leave the mountains. And to think she'd actually begun to dream again of love and happiness, of that handsome stranger of yesterday who had galloped through her childhood daydreams. She'd even been foolish enough to think that it might be him.

She had allowed herself to be deceived by his charms, and all because of her loneliness and the strange and wonderful feeling his presence aroused. But she was nothing to him and never had been.

My God, she really should have listened to Many Claws. His wisdom far exceeded her own.

Follow soon,
The Phantom Path of Heart's desire.

Chapter Fifteen

Nearly two days later, they reached the little cow town of Rawlins stirring under the first crows of a distant rooster. Matt and Sky sat astride their horses in the charcoal-colored dawn, on the bare hills that sprouted to the west and north of town. They had purposefully camped outside of town and waited until now to ride in, hoping to draw minimal attention to themselves.

They had gone on to Rawlins and not back to the mountains because eventually they'd cooled off and Matt had allowed Sky to convince him that they should continue the journey. They'd also cooled off enough to bury the renegades who had tried to kill them.

They'd spent the ride in virtual silence, however. They'd taken turns bathing in a stream, washing away the mud from their ordeal, each waiting with his back turned for the other to finish. Even though they had still been angry from their fight, Sky had had the strange desire to ask Matt to join her, to hold her naked in his arms and make up after their harsh words. And she wondered if he'd felt the same emotions, but his stoic expression had given her no clue to his inner thoughts.

Now, tired and dusty once again, they both wanted nothing more than a warm bath in a bona fide tub and a hot meal that someone else had cooked. Especially Sky, who had been deprived of such luxuries for so long.

This time Matt led the way down off the knoll, for at the sight of the town, Sky was no longer eager to take the lead. They covered the distance on a trot, but Matt slowed his horse to a shuffling walk through the sleeping town, moving almost soundlessly down the dusty street that now showed no signs of the rain.

Doors were closed, shutters drawn. The blacksmith seemed the only one awake as he clanked about in his smithy stoking a fire in the forge. From one of the homes, or possibly one of the restaurants, the aroma of bacon and eggs and fresh-baked biscuits met their nostrils, reminding them of just how hungry they were.

Red Sky's attention, however, was drawn from the delicious smell of the food to the pretty sight of an emerald silk gown in the window of a dress shop. The shop was dark inside, but the dress, covering a body form, was positioned next to the window. The rich color reminded her of the high mountain meadow of her dwelling place and it shimmered much the same way as the tall grass when the warm winds of summer rustled through it. A ruffle of the same silky fabric adorned the low, round neckline, and the puffy, elbow-length sleeves sported a wide, elongated ruffle that draped down halfway to the wrist and was decorated further with three-inch white lace and green ribbons. It fit the body form snugly at bodice and waist, and the bodice piece came to a point below the waistline where the gathered skirt then flared out with more drapes of cloth, flounces, ribbons, and lace.

Feminine frippery was something Red Sky had nearly forgotten living in the mountains, but she felt a yearning to see herself in the dress, if just for a little while.

Matt drew Soldier to a halt in front of the cattle town's most prominent hotel. He stepped to the ground and wrapped the reins around the hitching rail while surveying his surroundings. His chiseled features and eyes were as tightly shuttered as the buildings surrounding them, told Red Sky nothing of his thoughts, except that he had once again become the silent stranger expecting trouble. He looked the dangerous man of the law, not to be crossed for any reason.

She saw clearly now the man he was inside and the man he presented to the world. Two different men, and yet one. She saw the existence he had led on the edge of life, anticipating opposition or even death at every turn. It made her feel considerably safer knowing he was deadly with a gun and was taking every precaution, but she wondered if there could ever be peace and security for either of them. Or would they spend their lives being hunted — and haunted — each in his own way.

She slid from the horse's back, feeling the objection from muscles that hadn't been accustomed to riding and now ached so badly she had to stifle a moan. Matt was by her side almost immediately with a hand on her elbow to assist her. Still watching the sleeping town with vigilance, he pulled the parfleche from off her horse's flanks and removed his saddlebags and Winchester from his own mount. He walked so lightly that his booted feet barely made a noise — and her moccasins made none at all — on the wooden steps leading to the hotel door.

The clerk wasn't behind the desk registry. As a matter of fact, there was no sign of him anywhere. Receiving customers at such an early hour was not anticipated and he was probably still in bed.

Matt set their gear on the floor and leaned the Winchester against the high counter. He slapped the bell with the palm of his hand, not once but several times. He then turned the registry book around and was signing a name — not his own — when they heard the clatter of feet on the second floor. The clerk rushed down the stairs, pulling his suspenders over his shoulders, disregarding the flapping tails of a collarless shirt that had been hastily buttoned askew.

"Oh, good morning," he panted to a halt at his position, swaying a bit as if his head was still filled with sleep. "What can I help you with this morning? Breakfast? If so, the dining room will be open within the hour."

"Actually, we've been riding all night and would like a room," Matt said. It wasn't the truth, but it was close enough.

"Oh —" the clerk said, surprised. "Oh, well. Let's

see. . . ." he fumbled in his pants pocket and finally removed a pair of gold-rimmed spectacles. Vision seemed to help clear the haze from his head, but for the first time he saw Sky clearly, and the smile that had perched on the corners of his thin lips suddenly plummeted like a sparrow being shot off a fence post.

"A room for you . . . *and* your companion?" he asked, nonplussed.

"Yes," Matt replied, his blue eyes suddenly as cold as Sky's high mountain lake. "A room for my wife and me."

Sky came to attention with a start, but she said nothing, going along with the charade. The clerk cleared his throat as if the annoying cotton that had collected there in the night was fighting to be dispelled at this precise moment. He glanced at her again, rather nervously, but then suddenly elevated his chin in an arrogant manner.

"I'm sorry, sir. But this establishment does not rent rooms to . . . Indians." He pointed to a sign behind the desk. "See it's right there. We reserve the right to refuse service to — "

In a movement almost too quick to follow, Matt had the clerk by the shirtfront with his left hand and the muzzle of his .45 rammed against the man's Adam's apple with his right hand.

"Now, *sir*," he said in a deadly whisper. "I'm not real sure I heard what you said. Would you care to repeat it?"

The clerk tried to clear his throat again but the gun's muzzle seemed to present a restriction. Finally the man lifted his hands in a degree of surrender, tried to speak but couldn't. Matt lowered the gun to a position just under his ear, allowing mobilization of the larynx. The man finally croaked, "Yes, sir. We have a room for you and your wife on the second floor. Last door on the left. Overlooks the street. Best view in the house."

Matt smiled without humor. "Now, I *thought* that's what you said."

He lowered the Colt's hammer with a decisive click that made the clerk jump, then he dropped the Colt back into its holster with such practiced ease that it barely seemed to skim leather. "Later this afternoon," he added, "after we've had some sleep, we'd like a tub and plenty of hot water brought up. We'd also like dinner brought to our room. We'll pay extra for the bath and room service."

"Oh, certainly, certainly. That will be fine, sir. Just let us know if there's anything else we can get for you."

"As a matter of fact there is. Do you know of a young boy who wouldn't mind picking up a little pocket change? I'd like someone to take our horses to the livery, brush them down, see that they get water and grain."

The clerk's eyes darted nervously. "I'm sure my son would do it for you, sir. He's twelve and is always eager to earn a little extra. I'll get him up and have him tend to it right away."

"Good. Thank you."

Matt reached in his vest pocket for the proper coins while the desk clerk removed a key from the hooks behind him with a pale, shaking hand. When the exchange was made, Matt once again took Sky by the arm, gathered up the bags, and led her upstairs to the room.

The double bed, with massive headboard and footboard, yellow-and-green flowered quilt, green bedskirt, and fluffy yellow pillows, monopolized most of the small room. A five-drawer dresser stood against one wall and a small armoire faced it from the other wall. The only other furnishings were a chair upholstered in green velvet, and a nightstand with a kerosene lamp sitting atop it on an intricately crocheted doily. Another doily covered the center of the dresser and protected it from the base of a white porcelain washbasin and matching pitcher. All the furniture was cherry wood, complimented by flowered wallpaper, also in the tones of yellow and pale green. A large rug in the same color scheme, only with more browns and beiges, covered the floor.

"God Almighty!" Matt declared in a low tone, dropping the dusty bags on the floor next to the door. "This is worse than a field of sunflowers buzzin' with honey bees."

Sky smiled, amused by his male opinion of the busy, feminine decor. "Oh, it isn't so bad."

Matt walked directly to the window, glancing over his shoulder at her with half a smile. "You're not serious."

"It's different from the cave."

"That's an understatement."

His smile made her heart lurch, and brought the return of those peculiar little butterfly wings to her stomach. He pulled the blind and lifted an edge of the curtain as if to verify that the desk clerk hadn't lied about the view. He still seemed vigilant, but had relaxed somewhat now that they were in the room.

Red Sky watched him, studying with a certain fascination the play of the sun's first golden rays across his broad shoulders. He removed his hat and tossed it on the bed, then absently ran a hand through his hair. The sun's rays touched the golden strands, making them shine like spun gold. She forced herself to refrain from an overpowering urge to walk across the room and run her fingers through the gold. It troubled her that her heart was getting so close to him. It would be a foolish thing to do in the end.

"Don't tell me you prefer the cave?" she asked. "You said once it made you feel like you were in a trap."

Still staring at the street below, he said, "I didn't like not being able to see out, but I liked the fire burning in the center of the room and I liked the furs." He dropped the curtain and turned to face her. His gaze caught and locked with hers in a penetrating way. "There was something special about the cave. Something exciting."

Red Sky turned away, disconcerted by his huskily spoken words. It seemed safer than to meet those enigmatic blue eyes whose mere touch caused her body to flood with heat.

"I miss it already," she said wistfully, sitting on the edge of the bed. "I miss Esup, too. It frightens me to be here in this town with all these people. When I was a young girl I used to enjoy going to Lander and looking in all the shop windows and going with Mama and Daddy to the mercantile. All the smells at the mercantile were wonderful! Everything from peppermint candy to oiled harness leather. But now,

I . . . I don't know exactly what it is, but it's as if I no longer belong to the world that . . . that people belong to."

The mattress dipped next to her from Matt's weight. The action tilted her right into his embrace and against his chest. "Don't be afraid," he murmured, his finger tracing the shape of her ear, his warm breath tickling her neck. "I'll take you back there safe and sound when this is over."

His gaze shifted in a sultry way from her eyes to her lips.

But will you stay with me? she wondered.

As suddenly as his interest in her seemed to peak, he left her side, almost as if he'd heard her silent question and chose to avoid answering it. In motions that were too brusque to be natural, he shook out his bedroll beneath the window.

"Let's get some sleep," he said. "We're both exhausted. We'll rest up and catch tomorrow's train to Cheyenne."

He opened the window and the morning breeze eagerly rushed in, lifting the curtains away from the wall and making them flutter. It would be noisy in the street before the day was over, but it would become unbearably hot in the room otherwise.

He removed his gun belt, boots, hat, and vest, and laid down on the bedroll with his back to her. Red Sky watched him, wondering again why he had turned away from her so suddenly. She was positive he had thought of kissing her, and she had wanted him to. She was starting to want him in the way she never thought she would want any man. But would

266

things change—would he change—now that they were away from the mountains?

"Thank you for defending me to that clerk," she said, "but it really wasn't necessary to tell him I was your wife."

Matt didn't turn over but replied with distinct conviction. "It *was* necessary. It wouldn't be safe for you to be in a separate room. I did it to protect you, just as I promised."

Duty. He stays with me out of duty.

After a few moments of staring at his back, she saw the heavy and steady breathing that indicated he'd fallen asleep.

She glanced at the yellow quilt, and even though the bed looked inviting, she didn't want to sleep in it until she had the chance to take a bath and wash the dust away. So, like Matt, she unrolled her bedroll on the floor, on the opposite side of the room and on the opposite side of the bed. From her position, she couldn't see him at all. The floor was harder than her pallet, and thoughts of fear and worry entered her mind, but weariness was a powerful antidote. Soon, she, too, had fallen asleep.

A knock sounded at the door, snapping both Matt and Red Sky from their slumber. Matt swore softly as he dragged himself from the bedroll and into a state of forced alertness. Almost automatically, as if it were second nature to him, he palmed his revolver. Barefooted, he moved cautiously to the door.

"Who's there?" he asked gruffly.

A youthful voice replied, "The desk clerk sent us up with a tub for your wife."

Matt glanced at Sky who had come awake into a sitting position on her bedroll. He wondered why she hadn't taken the bed. "My God, is it three o'clock already?"

She pushed the long strands of black hair away from her shoulders, mussing it sensually without realizing it. As always when he was with her, he began to feel the threads of desire tighten throughout his body. He was, he thought, like a guitar string strung too tightly, ready to snap at the slightest provocation.

"It must be," she mumbled sleepily.

With one hand still on the Colt, he opened the door, glanced over the two young men holding the round tub, then stepped back out of the way. "Put it over there," he said, pointing with his gun to the only spot in the small room where a tub could possibly fit.

The young men eyed the big gun nervously but did as ordered. They left and returned shortly carrying buckets of hot water, followed by buckets of cold water until they had the water the temperature Sky wanted it.

"It's a little cold, ma'am," the oldest one objected dubiously. "You sure you don't want us to bring more hot water? It won't be any trouble." He glanced at Matt again, noticing he had now holstered the gun, but it still hung threateningly off his hip.

"No, but I would appreciate one bucket of warm water if you have it so I can rinse my hair."

They hurried off and returned in record time — with two buckets of warm water. "An extra one, just in case," the oldest boy said with a nervous smile.

When they finally left, Matt gathered up his saddlebags and sauntered to the door. His brow furrowed with concern when he turned to her one last time. "I guess I'd better go find a bathhouse and check the train schedule."

He was nervous about leaving her, but even if he remained on guard outside the door, as protocol would demand, he wasn't sure he could make himself stay there, knowing that on the other side of the door her lovely nakedness invited his touch and his kiss.

His desire to make love to her was increasing as her acceptance of him was improving. On the journey here, they had laid their bedrolls out side by side every night. They had been so close for weeks now that it was getting almost impossible to sleep next to her and not touch her. He didn't know how much longer he could go on keeping his passion in check. It was becoming a very natural thing to touch her. Claiming her as his own had nearly become an obsession, but so fragile was her trust, he must wait until she was ready to take him to her bed. But could he wait that long? Could he wait until *she* came to *him?* What if it never happened and she remained content simply to keep treating him as friend and protector?

"Will you be all right here alone?"

"Yes, I'll be fine," she replied, but he detected uncertainty in her eyes.

She was an incredibly brave woman, but she had stepped back into a world where civilization brought complacency and destroyed caution. In the mountains she had had the ability and the surroundings to elude her hunters because she had constantly been

269

on guard. Would she make the mistake of lowering her guard now? And here she had only four walls and a flimsy door, the room itself a virtual trap. She had the Winchester, but an attack could come too suddenly for her to use it.

"Lock the door," he finally said, knowing he had no choice but to leave for a while. He had to check the train schedule one way or the other and he would have to do it alone. The less the people in the town saw of her the better.

She nodded.

He hesitated on the threshold. His glance drifted to the Winchester in the corner and her gaze followed his. "Use it if you have to, Sky."

She smiled bravely. "I'll be fine, Matt. Go on now before my water gets cold."

"I thought you liked it cold."

She managed a smile, and his heart and his constitution weakened even more. "Yes, but I'll try it this way. It's been a while."

Finally he ducked out of the room, but Red Sky didn't hear his footsteps fade away down the hall until she had turned the key in the lock.

I shall touch your soul,
And you shall bring my morning.

Chapter Sixteen

Matt Riordan was not a man to hurry through things. It had always been his way, and the way of his job, to take things slowly. For when one took his time he didn't blunder, he didn't overlook danger. He didn't get himself killed by an unseen enemy.

But this time, Matt Riordan hurried. He went to the general store across the street and bought a new suit of clothes for himself. At the bathhouse he scrubbed down in record time and dressed in the new clothes. It seemed the wait at the barbershop was three hours instead of one. The barber was talkative and in no particular hurry as he cut Matt's hair and shaved his face. Matt squirmed in the black leather barber chair as restlessly as a six-year-old boy would have done. And all the while he worried about Sky alone in the room. What if someone had followed them from Lander? Found her?

Possibly an even greater fear was that Red Sky

would have second thoughts and head back to the Wind River country alone. He'd seen her glance longingly over her shoulder many times during their journey here, long after the wild, ragged peaks had diminished to nothing more than hazy, blue obtusions in the far distance.

He hurried down the boardwalk back to the hotel. But he found his pace slowing as he approached the dress shop they had ridden past at dawn. He'd seen Sky looking at the green dress in the window, not with the same longing he'd seen in her eyes to return home, but with longing just the same, and a certain unmistakable fascination.

He didn't know what it was that took hold of him, but he opened the dress shop door. Overhead, a tinkling bell announced his arrival. Inside, the smell of yard goods and faint perfume stirred a dormant memory in his mind of a time when as a very small boy he had tagged along behind his mother into a dress shop very similar to this one. She'd told him, rather harshly, to go back outside and play. But he'd started to cry because when she was out of his sight — as she so often was — he feared he would never see her again. Those many hours spent away from her were long, agonizing ones. The time with her was brief and seldom satisfying, but at least when she had been with him he hadn't felt so frightened.

Finally she had relented and allowed him to come into the dress shop, but she had done it only to "shut him up," and then she'd jerked him roughly along behind her, scolding him with profanity, calling him a nuisance and a little bastard.

He couldn't remember what she'd bought. He

could only remember the images, the sights, the smells, the sounds, the colors. All of it female. Like his mother. Alien and strangely interesting. Untouchable.

Now, don't you touch anything, Matthew.

I won't, Mama. I promise.

You do and I'll leave you out in the street next time, you hear?

Yes, Mama. I hear.

"Can I help you, sir?"

He started at the sound of the soft female voice, so different from the harsh tone his mother had always used. Quickly he regained his composure. The proprietress was a woman in her early fifties, quite lovely and shapely, and extremely neat. She was pinning a threaded needle to a ruffle on the bodice of her dress while waiting for his response.

Her friendly behavior relaxed him, but it didn't completely obliterate his nervousness because he knew nothing of women's clothing and had never bought anything for a woman in his life. The only money he'd ever spent on women was to pay them for giving him a night of their time.

With thumbs looped in his gun belt, and leaning on one hip, he nodded to the dress in the window, hoping his total ignorance wasn't obvious. "Yes, ma'am," he said. "I'm interested in that green dress in the window. I'd like to buy it for my wife—that is, if it's for sale."

Red Sky eyed the tub dubiously. She felt uneasy with the noise outside in the street, and the footsteps constantly traversing the hall outside her door. Even though she had four walls around her, and a locked door separating her from the world, she still felt as if she were standing naked in the middle of the street. She didn't trust the lock and was afraid somebody — those boys or that nasty little beady-eyed clerk — would come barging in for some reason. And what if the people who wanted her dead had somehow followed her and Matt here?

"This entire situation is just going to require your tolerance," she muttered to herself, testing the water with a toe, then a foot, then a calf. "And soon, very soon, you'll be back with Esup and things will be back to normal."

Finally, she stood in the tub with both feet. She folded her lithe body into it and immediately felt the soothing effects of the warm water on all the muscles that had rebelled from the days of horseback riding.

She smiled as she sank down into the warm water. Soon the outside world was forgotten.

Matt shifted all the boxes he was carrying to one arm. Juggling them to keep from dropping them, he groped in his pants pocket for the room key. He had tapped lightly on the door upon first arrival and received no response. He'd become immediately alarmed, his first thought being of Sky's safety, but the door was still locked from the inside so he told himself she was probably sleeping again. He had pushed them hard to get here and it might take more than a few hours of daytime sleep for her to feel completely rested again. If that was the case, he didn't want to wake her.

He finally managed to turn the key in the lock, and swinging the door wide to allow for the packages, stepped quietly inside. There he saw her asleep, just as he'd suspected, but she was still in the tub. She had a large white towel wrapped around her freshly washed hair and another towel beneath her neck, cushioning it from the hard edge of the tub.

Carefully, he set the boxes on the floor next to the door. At first there wasn't anything he could do but allow himself the pleasure of seeing her full young breasts partially covered by the water. He was held captivated, too, by her long legs, knees up, poking through the calm surface of the water. Her creamy smooth skin tempted his touch, having the flawless and delicious appearance of golden honey.

Regardless of how lovely she was, he realized he shouldn't be caught staring at her like a lascivious derelict or a slack-mouthed teen who had never seen a naked woman before. Getting control of himself and his emotions, he pulled the quilt from the bed and loosened the top sheet from beneath it.

With the sheet in hand, he went to her side and placed a hand on her shoulder. She came awake with a start, gasping at the sight of him and immediately trying to cover herself.

"Here," he laid the sheet over her. "Better get dressed. I stopped at the desk and they'll be bringing dinner up pretty soon."

"Why didn't you knock?" she demanded. But there was no anger in her eyes or in her voice, only embarrassment.

He turned his back so she could get out of the water. "I did, but you didn't hear me. I figured you were asleep so I used the key, I just didn't think you'd be asleep in the tub. I'm sorry to have walked in on you."

What a lie, Riordan, he thought. *You've been wanting to see her naked for weeks.*

She stood up and wrapped the sheet around herself, sloshing water onto the large, oval rug as she stepped out of the tub. "Just give me a minute and I'll get dressed. Don't turn around."

"Before you put your buckskins on," he said, obediently keeping his back to her, "there are some things in those boxes over there that might interest you."

He could imagine her inquisitive gaze shifting to the stack of boxes by the door: four square ones and one round.

He continued. "I was passing a dress shop and I decided that it might be best if you had a traveling suit to wear on the train tomorrow. It would draw less attention to you and make my job of protecting you a little easier. People wouldn't pay us any mind. They'd just think we were a married couple going on a trip."

There was silence behind him for what seemed an ungodly long time, and he wondered what was running through her mind. Had he offended her by suggesting she wear something other than buckskins? Did she object to posing as his wife?

Finally he heard her move around the bed and to the boxes. The temptation to turn her into his arms and lay her down on the bed was becoming overwhelming. If she'd been some other woman, one less innocent, he would have followed his instincts without hesitation. But he could not force himself on her if he wanted to maintain the trust it had taken him so long to gain.

"I'll just step out in the hall so you can have your privacy," he said. "You can call me if you need help."

He left the room without waiting for her response.

Red Sky made sure the door was firmly closed behind him before she let the sheet drop to the floor. The towel holding her wet hair soon followed, and she pushed the damp locks over her shoulder and out of her way. Tentatively, she removed the lid to the round box. Lifting some tissue paper out of the way, she smiled delightedly at the hat inside. She was surprised by it at first. It was the sort of hat a mature woman would wear. But she realized she truly was a woman now. In the mountains, time had a way of standing still, and it was easy to forget she was no longer the fourteen-year-old girl who had fled there looking for refuge. She was now twenty-one. Most women were married and had children by her age.

She lifted the hat out very carefully. Dainty and fragile-looking, it was enhanced by small, colorful green feathers and bows. After admiring it for a few moments, she set it aside as carefully as she'd picked it up. Getting into the spirit of things, she opened the next box with less hesitation than the first. It was the traveling suit Matt had spoken of. Matching the hat, it was made of black cloth but lightweight enough for summer. A short, removable cloak was attached at the shoulders and back. Dark green braid enhanced the tight-fitting basque jacket at the neck, wrists, and lower edge. The skirt was simple, falling to the ankle in soft folds but with no ornamentation.

In the bottom of the box, she found a pair of black traveling boots made of leather and cloth—leather on the lower portion and sturdy black canvas cloth on the uppers.

Now, like a child at Christmas, she tore into the third box and found various undergarments, hair ornaments, pins, even a lacy cotton nightgown.

Fully into the mood, she tossed aside the lid of the fourth box but was totally unprepared when the green dress she'd admired in the store window tumbled out into her hands. In awe, she lifted it the rest of the way out, drawing it automatically against her naked flesh. Made of the finest silk, it was amazingly soft and alluring. Even as a girl she'd dreamed of owning a dress like this.

"Oh, Matt!" She couldn't help the squeal of delight and ran to the door, still holding the dress. Her hand was on the knob, ready to pull the door open, when she remembered she was nude. Laughing, she called through the door to him. "Oh, Matt, it's the most beautiful thing in the world! Thank you! How can I ever repay you?"

"Just put it on," came his pleased tone from the other side of the door.

"Oh, I will!"

Without delay she put on the basic undergarments and carefully pulled the silk stockings onto her legs. Without reservation, she tossed the boned corset aside. Maybe it was a customary foundation for white women, but her mother, being Shoshoni, had never worn one, and even though she had dressed in white women's clothing she had never encouraged Red Sky to conform to that particular item of dress.

Red Sky saw no purpose for the contraption except to put undue stress on one's body and contort it into ill and unnatural proportions. And she hardly needed it to make herself look thinner. She had not one ounce of excess flesh anywhere on her body.

She pulled the dress on over her head, allowing it to glide down over her body without tugging. She then saw the matching green slippers in the bottom of the box and happily pulled them on. They were about a half size too large, but she was amazed that Matt had been able to guess her size as well as he had. As for the dress, it fit as if it had been made for her.

She went to the mirror, surprised by the shapely woman staring back at her. Her hair was a mess and immediately she grabbed up her hairbrush to smooth it. It was still slightly wet so she dried it more with the towel, not wanting to have water spots ruin the dress. She then coiled it atop her head as best she could and pinned it up with the hairpins and ornaments Matt had bought.

"How's it coming in there?" Matt asked from behind the door, sounding impatient.

She hadn't buttoned the dress yet, and now at his inquiry she hastily struggled to do so, twisting into all sorts of contortions, but finding she could only reach a few of the tiny buttons that marched up the back of the dress out of her reach.

"Can I come in?"

"Oh . . . no . . . I mean, I . . . can't seem to get it buttoned."

"Need some help?"

"I guess so, but — "

He was inside without delay, but stopped suddenly

in the doorway. She whirled to face him to prevent him from seeing her exposed back. She felt nervous, skittish as a colt under his admiring eyes. She clutched the dress to her bosom, trying to keep the low neck from falling down off her shoulders.

In those peculiarly quiet moments they just stood and stared at each other. She noticed how attractive he was, dressed in new black pants, white shirt, and black vest. Even without a suit coat, his shoulders looked wonderfully wide, his chest enticingly broad and hard. His freshly cut golden hair glistened; the shorter length accentuated the chiseled features of his tanned face and even made his eyes appear bluer.

"That color is good on you, Sky."

She glanced down at the dress, away from the alluring glow in his eyes. "Thank you."

He came toward her. "Let me do it up for you."

She nodded, feeling painfully self-conscious.

He moved behind her, so near that the heat from his body warmed hers. The alluring scent of bay rum aftershave tantalized her nostrils. With each button he picked up, his fingers brushed her naked flesh and sent a hot current of physical pleasure coursing through every part of her.

"I should have bought you a necklace," he said, tracing his finger lightly along her bare neck and partially exposed shoulder. "You need one with this dress."

Their eyes met in the mirror. He seemed to be looking clear through to the soul of her.

"Why did you buy the dress, Matt?" she asked shyly. "I mean, it's beautiful—the most beautiful dress I've ever had—but I have no place to wear it."

"Oh, but you do. You can wear it tonight to dinner."

"But we won t be leaving the room."

"I wish we could. I'd like nothing better than to have everyone see me escort you into the dining room and envy me such a beautiful woman on my arm. But I'm afraid the more exposure you have, the more likely your safety will be jeopardized."

His reflection in the mirror mesmerized her. She couldn't have moved if she'd wanted to.

"When this is over," he continued, "and those men are found and prosecuted, we'll find the fanciest place in Cheyenne and have dinner. Maybe we'll even find a dance going on somewhere. Do you like to dance?"

The glow in his eyes told her he liked the way she looked in the green dress. His fingers slid from the neckline, touching her shoulders again. She felt distracted by his questions, wanting only to focus on his touch.

"I . . . really don't know how to dance, Matt. Except maybe the square dance or the Virginia reel."

He laughed, a pleasingly robust sound to her ears. "Then we'll be a pair, Sky, because I'm not so good at dancing either. I had to take lessons once when I was posing as a government official for a case I was on in California. Maybe what I learned will come back to me, with a little practice."

She loved his strong face, his manly laughter, his sparkling, sensual eyes. It would be wonderful if she would be able to see these things every day for the rest of her life. He spoke of the immediate future.

But was there anything beyond that? Anything beyond their journey to Cheyenne?

She saw no deception in his eyes, no hint of it in his expression or in the nuance of his voice. And then all her thoughts were forgotten as in one sudden movement he dropped his hat on the bedpost nearest him and bent his head to hers. His lips went directly to the curve of her neck, then to her bare shoulder. Riveted by the thrill of his magical touch, her eyes closed automatically and she leaned back into him, almost groaning from the pleasure of the long-awaited contact. She didn't understand the way his touch weakened her ability to move away from him. His closeness was a drug she craved.

Another knock sounded at the door, and a voice quickly explained the intrusion. "We're here to remove the bath water and tub. And we've brought the table for your dinner."

Matt released a softly muttered expletive against her flesh. Having no choice, he let them in.

They worked swiftly and soon had the water emptied and the tub removed. They set up the table and laid a white tablecloth over it. The oldest boy took every opportunity to glance covertly in Sky's direction. Matt was not even able to get the door closed behind them before two young girls, around fifteen, brought dinner.

But finally they were alone again. Matt wanted to return to what they'd been sharing, but the mood had been destroyed and would have to be built again. He pulled out a chair for her at the table. Carefully gathering her dress and smoothing the bulk of it, she sat down. He settled himself in the chair opposite her and removed the cloth that covered the plates. It was a simple but delicious-smelling meal of veal, potatoes and brown gravy, dinner rolls with fresh butter and currant jelly, green peas with sugar, and an ample slice of hot apple pie.

He poured the dinner wine. Red Sky shook out her napkin over her lap, feeling as if she were in a dream, sitting here at a small table alone in a hotel room with a handsome man, drinking wine from crystal-stemmed glassware, and wearing a dress of green silk. It was a world apart from the life in the mountains. And because it was, she felt very much the imposter, but didn't quite understand why. She realized, with a certain nostalgia, that her mother and father would never have allowed — and certainly not approved of — her being alone in a hotel room with a man before marriage. But she was a woman now, not a child of fourteen. And she had no family. No one to censure her actions.

She and Matt engaged in idle conversation during the meal and occasionally lapsed to silence, but they had been together for so long, day in and day out, that their silence wasn't an uncomfortable one.

When they were done with the meal, Matt wiped his lips with his napkin and leaned back in his chair. "Have you ever played poker?"

The question surprised her, having no connection with anything they'd been discussing. "Why, yes — when I was little. Daddy used to let us kids play poker with him. We used matchsticks for money. Mama said he was corrupting us, but Daddy always got his way when it suited him."

Matt slid his chair back and went to his saddlebags on the other side of the bed. While he rummaged around in them, Red Sky watched him with a growing curiosity. When he straightened he held out one calloused palm filled with matches. A worn deck of playing cards was in the other.

He grinned. "How about a little game of five-card stud?"

Delighted, she came to her feet. The idea sounded wonderfully fun. And what else were they to do until bedtime? They couldn't go out. Immediately she began transferring the dishes from the small table to the top of the dresser.

Matt caught her hand. "Let's just sit on the bed," he suggested in a low tone, the grin on his face having faded to only a slight curve of his lips, but a curve shamelessly seductive by Red Sky's interpretation. "The maid service will be back pretty soon for the table and the plates anyway."

She consented, not sure if it was such a good idea to be on the bed with him, but maybe only her own thoughts dwelled on possible intimacy. Perhaps his were focused on cards.

She settled herself against the headboard, finding some difficulty in positioning herself gracefully. Matt propped himself against the bedpost at the foot of the bed, his booted feet crossed at the ankle and hanging slightly over the side of the bed in an attempt to keep the bright yellow quilt clean.

Seeing her constantly squirming about in search of a more comfortable position, he said, "Take your shoes off, Sky. Sit Indian style. Unless you don't know how."

284

Her lips pursed sardonically. "Oh, I think I can figure it out."

In seconds, her slippers were over the side of the bed on the rug. Using the headboard as a backrest, she sat cross-legged with the yards of green dress more than amply covering her legs. She gave him a smug smile and waited for him to shuffle and deal, which he did with fascinating expertise.

"Ante up," he said.

She grinned and tossed one match into the center of the bed, thinking to herself that this was the most fun she'd had in a long time. For a fleeting moment, she could almost imagine herself a child again at the kitchen table with her family on a cold winter night when the wind howled outside and the snow lashed at the windowpanes, and they had all been safe and warm inside.

Matt laid a card facedown in front of her. She peeked at it, then tried to conceal the look of excitement on her face. It was an ace.

He dealt himself a card, facedown, looked at it with an expression that told her nothing, then gave her another card face up. This time, a king.

"Want to place a bet?" he asked. "You're high."

She puzzled over it for a minute, glancing at his cards. She could only see his face card which was a deuce. "U-m-m-m . . . I'll bet two matches."

"All right. I'll meet your two matches and raise you three."

Red Sky wondered if he had another deuce in the hole. She considered her cards again. They were both high but amounted to nothing. Finally she capitulated. After all, it was only matches she was gambling with. Recklessly, she tossed three more into the pot and looked up at him expectantly.

Matt had only given the game a fraction of his attention, for it had been the beauty of Sky that had captured the bulk of it. He had been thoroughly enjoying the different expressions flitting across her face, like little starlings dipping and soaring in a windy sky, playing tag with one another, constantly changing position. The expression he enjoyed the most however, was happiness. It made his heart flip-flop, his loins ache, and he wondered if he could continue this charade much longer when all he wanted to do was lay her back against the pillows and make love to her.

"Ready for the rest of the cards?" he asked. "Or would you like to put some more money in the pot?"

Red Sky was thoroughly enjoying his light mood and her own. "Let's see the rest of the cards."

She watched while he gave them three each, alternating back and forth. Red Sky studied her hand, having ended up with nothing but two aces. She knew Matt had at least one pair — two fours — and possibly a card in the hole which would match one of the face cards. If all he had were the fours, she could beat him. She had no choice but to take the chance that he didn't have anything of consequence in the hole.

"Place your bet," he said.

"I'll bet you" — she counted her matches — "three more."

A small grin lifted his top lip, barely enough to allow her a glimpse of his straight, white teeth. He dug into his match pile. "All right. I'll meet your three and raise you two."

Again she considered whether he might be bluffing. "All right. I'll meet your two and raise *you* two."

He dropped two more matches without reservation.

"Okay, let's see what you have," she said animatedly, quite positive she was going to win.

Matt turned his hole card up. He hadn't been bluffing. He had two deuces and two fours. Her smile plummeted. She turned her hole card up. "I've just got the two aces. You win."

"Don't look so glum. You might win the next one." He chuckled and gathered up all the matchsticks, poking them down into his palm so that when he released them they rolled back out onto the quilt in a neat little pile.

He handed her the cards. "Your turn to shuffle."

She'd never been good at shuffling, even when she used to play cards with her family. And she'd been out of practice for seven years. Her sister had always been able to make the cards meet perfectly, and had even been able to bend them upward while shuffling in such a manner that when she released them they riffled back down together perfectly in her small hands.

Sky tried to shuffle but the cards hadn't been mixed well. She tried again. She had better success and decided to do it several times, the way Matt had, to make sure they were mixed up really well. On the fourth try, her confidence was increasing and she tried the little trick her sister used to do. The cards flew in every direction, all over the bed and floor. She stared at them, with chagrin and Matt's laughter boomed in the small room. Soon they were both up on their knees in the center of the bed, laughing and reaching to all four corners, even over the side, gathering the fifty-two wayward cards.

When the cards were all back in the center of the bed, some upside down, some right side up, they leaned away from each other, still laughing.

"You deal," she said. "I'm no good at it."

Matt reached for the cards, to collect them and straighten them, but as the sun drifted slowly behind the horizon, his smile soon drifted from his face. He came to his knees again, this time in a slow, sensual way that set Sky's heart to pounding. The cards fell from his hands, forgotten. He moved toward her and his knees came down on the skirt of the green dress, capturing her. Her strength dissipated when his hands found the bare flesh of her shoulders and traveled along them to the curve of her neck.

"You're beautiful, Sky," he whispered. "So very beautiful."

He took her face in tender but rough palms, and then he lowered himself to his side and drew her down into his arms. Her head found the pillows and his hard length stretched over her, one leg across hers, pinning her.

She craved his dangerously unfamiliar but exciting embrace. The magical touch of his hands roaming her body created feelings she had never known existed. His lips, moving with possessive ardency, fed the growing flame, and she clung to his powerfully muscled back, feeling suspended on his kiss, dangling, waiting expectantly for more.

His tongue moved against hers, hot and rough and increasingly more urgent. Her sensitive flesh reacted in a glorious way devoid of fear. She made no objection when he slid the green dress off one shoulder and traced her bare skin with his lips and tongue.

The dress slipped farther and farther beneath the gentle tug of his hand until his lips found the swell of her bosom. Breath caught in her throat. She sank her fingernails into his back.

Then he was on his knees again and drew her to a sitting position. Beneath his nimble fingers, the buttons down the back of her dress came free of the buttonholes seemingly much easier than they had been fastened. The dress fell away from her bosom completely and he pushed it down off her arms all the way until it lay in a green puddle at her waist. Seconds later, it was completely off and draped over a chair. Nothing covered her but her chemise, pantalets, and silk stockings.

She didn't know what drove her on in such wantonness. She only knew she wanted his touch to continue. She knew she should think of tomorrow, of love, of what would happen after Cheyenne, but all her mind could focus on was the glorious wonder of his lovemaking.

She lay back against the pillows and drew him down to her. She felt the hard shaft of his manhood against her thigh, saw its shape through his black pants. Why didn't he remove his own clothes? Why was he holding back? Was he afraid he would frighten her with the sight of his naked body? She'd seen him naked, and the memory only made her blood pump harder and faster. She ran her hands over his chest, felt the taut muscles, visualized the golden mat of hair concealed beneath.

His hands lifted the veil of fear that had encased her these many years. Like the moon spilling over a black and empty land, his lips cast a silver and wondrous glow over a heart and soul whose memory had forgotten light. She had not been aware of the sad darkness inside her. She had grown accustomed to it. She had never expected anything else. But the strength of his body defined the fragile femininity of her own. She came alive beneath his tutoring. She saw it all differently now. At last she knew the pleasures of the flesh.

His hands, tantalizingly rough, were too weatherworn to glide smoothly over the fine cotton and lace as they undid the ribbon on her chemise and laid the cloth aside, baring her bosom. Her first reaction was to cover herself, suddenly self-conscious of her nakedness. But he locked his fingers through hers and spread her arms back over the pillow.

"Let me touch you, Sky," he whispered. "I won't hurt you."

Within his eyes burned something other than desire, something soft and gentle and loving. Her body ached for his. She lifted toward him, moving not from her mind's commands, but from some mysterious force within her.

He cupped her breasts with gentleness and lowered his head, taking first one nipple into his mouth and then the other. A searing sensation flashed through her like a bolt of lightning. She lifted her hips toward him, toward the hardness in his loins, searching for a way to ease and satisfy the need rampaging through her.

Suddenly a tortured moan escaped his throat. He

came away from her, at the same time roughly pulling the chemise back over her naked breasts. Ashamed and confused by his change in attitude, she sat up, groping for something to cover herself with. Her fingers closed over the green dress.

"I'm sorry, Sky," he said, running an agitated hand through his hair. "I'd better leave while I still can. Lock the door behind me."

He grabbed his hat from off the bedpost and pulled it low over his eyes. In another second he was gone.

Red Sky stared at the closed door, still confused and still clutching the dress to her bosom. She had felt pain and loss before, but never this particular kind. What had she done to make him so angry? Had it been the dress? Had he bought it for her in the hope that she could somehow take the place of his mysterious Elizabeth? Had he been disappointed when she had failed?

She got up and through misty eyes searched for her buckskins. She would put them back on because they gave her security and reminded her of who she was and who she couldn't be, and where she would be returning to when this was all over.

But what about Matt? What was going to happen to him when this was over? Would he leave her life and never return to it? He had promised to take her back to the Wind River country, but would he? Or would he just get on his horse and ride away . . . the way she had once wanted him to do?

To the Power of Passion surrender.
Quench thy thirst with the
Nectar of my Song.

Chapter Seventeen

Matt left the hotel and went directly to the noisiest saloon he could find. Even though his emotions ran high, his natural instincts took over when he entered the dimly lit, smoky room. A person in his occupation could never be too careful. Who could, with all confidence, say whether he and Red Sky had or had not been followed down out of the mountains, or whether he had an enemy from the past who would recognize him and decide to shoot him on sight?

As he expected, nearly every head in the crowded room turned toward him when he pushed his way through the swinging doors. Men and barmaids alike stared at him without friendliness, but after brief appraisals they all went back to their business.

At the bar he ordered whiskey and asked the bartender to leave the bottle. The barkeep mopped the bar and glanced at him occasionally, no doubt gauging his receptiveness to talk. Sensing that he wasn't receptive, the man finally turned his attention to another customer. Matt drank in brooding silence, and didn't mind it because he wasn't one to share his problems.

He was three shots into the bottle before the pain in his loins began to subside. But the pain in his chest, centered in his heart, lingered on.

He didn't know what to do where Sky was concerned. All he knew for certain was that if he had stayed in their room a moment longer, he might have forced himself on her, reducing himself to the sort of animal Bailey Loring had once claimed he was. She had seemed willing; she had acted as if she wanted his lovemaking, but did she fully understand a man's needs and how very close to the edge he stood? Did she understand that while she craved kisses and caresses, he wanted it all?

In the beginning he had wanted to show her that not all men were like those who had wanted to harm her, but he hadn't known then that he would completely lose his heart to her. He had thought she was only a beautiful, mysterious woman who intrigued him, and once the mystery surrounding her was abolished, so would die the interest. After the pain and humiliation he'd suffered from loving Elizabeth, he would have never thought he could love again, but love he did, and with an intensity and need he never thought himself capable of.

He should be up in their room right now, protecting her as he had sworn to do. But first he had to cool off and hope the whiskey would dull his senses and his desires.

A hand touched his hip in a feather-light way just as a female body leaned brazenly against him. The smell of perfume was cloying. He looked into the painted face of a blond-haired whore who couldn't have been much more than sixteen.

"Hey, handsome," she crooned, her hand sliding suggestively away from his hip to the curve of his buttocks. "You look like you just lost your best friend."

He poured himself another whiskey. "Sorry to disappoint you."

She was undeterred by his cool indifference to her. If anything, it was merely a challenge to try harder. He considered letting her ease the ache in his loins. If he were to go upstairs with her, then maybe he wouldn't go back to the hotel room still wanting to make love to Sky.

Yeah, maybe.

But not likely.

He bought her a drink and handed it to her, then put his arm over her bare shoulder. Her low dress revealed most of her bosom, but he still felt no overpowering urge to see the rest of it, or any other part of her. He was all too familiar with the hollow moments her kind offered. And tonight he'd rather have nothing if that was the only choice he had. In the past, he'd spent all his lust and all his seed between the legs of women just like her because he'd had a need. A *need*. God only knew how many bastards he'd fathered, more unloved children like himself. If he thought about it too long it made him sick, so he didn't.

"We could go upstairs," she suggested demurely, sipping at her drink.

He glanced at a card game going on a couple of tables away. "Actually I was thinking about sitting in on that card game over there. How about you being my good luck charm for a couple of hours?"

She caressed his buttocks again and slid her hand around to the front of him. "Why sure, doll. I can't think of anything I'd like better, but a girl can't make a living that way." She looked up at him, her lips forming a pout.

"I guess you're right," he said, pushing away from both her and the bar, taking his bottle in hand. "Don't let me keep you from your work."

Red Sky moved to the window and watched Matt exit the hotel and go directly across the street to one of the saloons. Tears puddled in her eyes and slid quietly onto her cheeks. She hastily wiped them off and willed no more to come. She had to accept that his kindness and apparent interest in her had just been a ruse to get her here. She'd been foolish to fall in love with the first man she'd seen in seven years. But there had been those dreams of a handsome stranger . . . and he had so perfectly pleased her heart.

A knock sounded on the door, startling her. She whirled. Her heart began to race. Why hadn't she locked the door as soon as Matt had left? She debated whether to keep silent or speak, but a youthful male voice said, "We're here to pick up the table and dinner plates, Mrs. Riordan, if you're done."

She released the breath she'd been holding, but she couldn't relax her guard completely. She recalled the oldest of the young men, and the way he had looked at her earlier, his eyes lingering on her breasts as if he could see through the cloth that covered them. She didn't want to let them in, but she felt she had no choice. They might try the door, find it unlocked and come inside anyway.

"One moment, please."

She wiped the tears from her eyes and rapidly pulled the green dress back on. She could never manage the buttons up the back in a speedy fashion, so she merely pulled it onto her shoulders and draped the black shawl over it. She removed her knife from her belongings and hid it in the folds of the dress. With her other hand she held the shawl together in the front.

Trying not to show her fear, she called, "Come in." The door opened and she backed next to the Winchester in the corner. God, would she forever be afraid of men and suspicious of their motives?

The boy glanced her way several times. Could it be he just thought she was attractive? Matt had said that when men stared at women it was often for that reason. Or was he making mental note of the fact that Matt was gone? He did nothing but ask questions, however, and those pertaining only to the job he'd been hired to do: How was the meal? The wine? Was the service adequate? Could he get her anything else?

296

She answered as politely as possible. To her relief they completed their job promptly and moved to the door. The oldest boy, probably just a few years younger than herself, ran his eyes over her one last time. "Have a good evening, Mrs. Riordan," he said, then closed the door behind him.

She hastily reached over and locked it.

Alone in the room again, she breathed a sigh of relief and sat back on the edge of the bed. From her position, her reflection in the mirror summoned her like a voice she couldn't hear, but could only sense. She stood up in front of the glass, automatically releasing the shawl and smoothing the silk folds of the dress. As she studied her image, her hands were drawn to her own breasts, still sensitive from Matt's touch.

Outside the hotel room people bustled back and forth on the boardwalks; drank and danced in the saloons and dance halls; talked and laughed with family and friends. But she was alone. Alone in body. Alone in mind. Separate in thought and in her philosophy of life. Her Indian heritage as well as her struggle to survive in the mountains had made her separate, different, and suddenly she wondered if she could ever truly fit into society again.

Had Matt sensed it, too? Is that why he had bought the dress, perhaps hoping at least to make her *look* like she belonged? And is that why he left so abruptly, when he realized she never would?

She stared at the dress, wondering just who the woman was beneath the silk ruffles and folds. Was she Sky McClellan, daughter of white rancher Charles McClellan, young lady in lace and silk and slippers? Or was she—deep down inside—the savage quarter-breed who many considered her to be, living off the land in a cave, content in her buckskins, braids, and moccasins? Was she one, or both? Was she like a circus freak with two heads and two sides to her personality? Could she successfully return to society? Did she even want to try?

She moved away from the mirror, for the image of herself seemed only to confuse her. She was not sophisticated. She was not educated past the eighth grade. She had never been to a finishing school for girls. Men like Matt Riordan would surely want wives who had those qualities. Not wives who could kill and skin a deer, but wives who could prepare fancy meals for guests and gracefully pour tea into dainty blue-and-white china cups. All one could really say about Red Sky McClellan was that she was a survivor.

She removed the dress once again and this time hung it carefully and lovingly in the armoire, running a hand one last time over the fine cloth. She was very tired and decided to dress for bed. This time she took the bed rather than her bedroll on the hard floor.

Beneath the soft, cool sheets that were so different from her sleeping furs, the questions continued to rage through her mind, but there seemed no satisfactory or final answers. She must sleep. Yes, sleep was the only way to find a temporary peace.

The two eagles hung motionless against the sun, momentarily blocking its blazing light. Beyond the jagged tips of their gigantic wings, a golden halo fanned out into the perfectly blue sky. Suddenly one eagle dipped and dove toward the earth, and soon the other followed. Their high-pitched screeches echoed over the mountaintops, rising to the heavens, plummeting to the shadowy, pine-filled canyons. In a patient game of their own making, they soared again, circled each other, then drifted on a breeze that pulled them closer and closer together.

High above them, ever changing gray clouds rushed before a tumultuous wind. But the wind never touched the eagles. They continued as before, seemingly oblivious to the restless clouds and the powerful force that raced too high above to disturb their languid flight.

At last their wing tips met and they hung in motionless suspension. But slowly, slowly, the smaller eagle began to fade inside the larger eagle.

In the twinkling of an eye, it was gone.

"No!"

Red Sky came awake with a start; her heart thudding wildly and fearfully. She was covered with cold sweat and yet she was so hot she had to throw the covers back. She knew instinctively that she had been the eagle that had vanished, and she didn't understand it, except that it frightened her.

"Sky? What's wrong?"

She heard faint rustling on the floor as Matt came out of his bedroll. She was surprised because

299

she hadn't heard him return to the room. She wondered what time it was. Midnight? Predawn?

Her head cleared. "I'm fine. It was just a dream."

She heard him groping around in the dark, then the bed dipped beneath his weight. His hand moved over the covers until it found hers. "Are you going to be all right?"

She nodded, feeling foolish, but the dream had left her very troubled and inexplicably frightened.

He put his arms around her, providing her with the security she needed. She welcomed the embrace, melting into it with great need. Oh, how wonderful it felt to be in the safe haven of his embrace. Nothing could hurt her when she was there.

"Are you worried about meeting the governor?" he asked. "There's no need to be."

She wondered if the dream might have been indicative of that particular fear, and, if so, she marveled at his uncanny perception.

"I suppose I am just a little afraid."

"Everything is going to be all right, Sky. He seems like an understanding man who just wants this all cleared up."

He held her in the darkness for a time that was immeasurable. Then she did something very bold. She ran her hand along his naked thigh, and pressed a kiss to the curve of his neck. "Thank you for understanding, Matt."

Darkness allowed the sense of touch to come alive in a way it couldn't in the sunlight. If any sleep remained in Matt Riordan's head, it was gone now. He felt the hot blood of desire in his body dart to his loins like a flash of fire, demanding to be quenched. He felt with increased awareness the solid strength of her lithe body, and yet the incredible softness of it, too.

She touched her lips to his throat and his grip immediately tightened on her hip.

"Good God, Sky," he moaned. In the darkness the words sounded like a tortured plea. "You'd better stop, girl. You're setting me on fire."

Her kisses stopped as requested, but he could still feel the warm little puffs of her breath against his neck and the heat of her breasts barely brushing his chest.

"But I want to kiss you, Matt," she whispered. "You left the room before. Why did you go?"

He pushed her away from him until the only part of their bodies touching was one of her feet pressed against one of his. Even that was amazingly erotic.

"Don't you understand a man's needs, Sky?" he whispered hoarsely. "Sometimes those needs become powerful, especially when triggered by a beautiful woman. I couldn't stay earlier. I wanted to make love to you too much. Do you understand that? I didn't want just to keep on kissing you. I wanted to lay with you and be your man in every sense of the word. I left because I was afraid I couldn't control myself, and then I'd hurt you in a way you'd never forgive me for."

"Nehaynzeh." He heard her smile in the dark. He didn't have to see it to recognize the tenderness and understanding surging forth in just that one word. "You could never hurt me the way those men hurt

Mama and Bliss. You're not that sort of man, and this is different. I know this is different. I'm frightened, yes, but I want to know about this thing between men and women. I never did . . . until you came to the cave. Then I began to feel a . . . a . . . yearning. And now I want you to be the one to teach me about this thing."

Matt Riordan suddenly had heaven laid out before him. For all his eagerness to seize the moment, he was probably as frightened as Red Sky, only in a different way. Her expectations were great, and he didn't want to disappoint her. Since the first moment he had seen this mysterious woman he had wanted to make love to her with an intensity that had bordered on obsession. Now he couldn't allow himself to question the right or wrong of it, or question what would happen when daylight changed the appearance of things. He had never found true love, and this might not be it either. But if he couldn't win her love forever, he was not above taking it for a few hours in the night.

"I'll teach you, Sky, and I'll try to do so without bringing you dissatisfaction. But I don't want the darkness to cloak this moment or keep your beauty hidden from me."

She touched a hand to his face. "I want to see you, too, Matt. You may light the lamp. Please."

While Matt groped in the darkness for the matches, Red Sky knelt on the bed behind him. To her it seemed forever before he found the matches on the nightstand and opened the night with the tiny, flickering flame. He lit the wick and turned it down low. The faint light pushed the darkness to the corners of the room and laid their shadows upon it.

Sky's heart thumped unmercifully with both excitement and apprehension. Was he the lover she'd dreamed of so many years ago? The man who would cherish her above all others? Or would he be one to pass beyond, like everyone in her life so far, leaving her once again alone? She didn't know, but it was a chance she had to take. Their eyes met in questioning need, but there was no turning back now.

He drew her into the competent fold of his arms. He was fully naked and she saw his male flesh rise hard from its nest of golden brown hair. It looked so different from how it had the day she'd witnessed him bathing in the lake. She found to her amazement that the sight of it didn't frighten her at all, but instead intensified the need growing inside her. He was not the man with the silver hair who had tried to hurt her that fateful day years ago — that man whose flesh had been ugly and repulsive and frightening because of the evil inside him.

She felt the cool softness of the sheets and pillows beneath her, and the hot strength of Matt's muscled nakedness above her. The lamplight shone off his golden hair and bronzed skin. She slid her fingers through the golden brown curls on his chest, caressed his arms and shoulders, gripped his back that offered pure male strength and a primal counterpart of femininity.

But it was not enough.

Boldly her hands took in the slender contours of his buttocks and thighs, also tight with muscle and lightly sprinkled with more blond, curly hair. She touched the flat of his stomach and the velvety hardness of all that made him a man. He inhaled sharply at her touch of his male member, and she thought at first that she'd hurt him, but his closed eyes and his expression indicated utter pleasure.

"Oh, darling," he managed, "not yet. I need you too much. Wait . . . to touch me."

She obeyed, and moved her caresses to other parts of his body. While her hands transmitted to her brain the full picture of his brawny contours, he conducted his own exploration of her. Soon his hands drew out exquisite sensations that made her focus selfishly on her own pleasure. She could do nothing but cling to his solidness and silently beg for him to continue, but her silent pleas were miraculously heard.

He lifted the length of her hair and spread the black tresses out over the white pillowcase, clearing an invisible path along her neck and shoulders for his lips to make a lengthy sojourn upon. There was a spot at the base of her throat that, when touched by his mouth, drove her to curl her fingernails deeper into his back.

Tremors built inside her, a quivering need that made her want to whimper for more. Over the thin cotton of her gown, his experienced hands moved with confidence but tenderness, bringing her alive. Never had she been so aware of her body, or the body of another human being. The burning proficiency of his hands found her stomach, drawn taut, and her breasts that seemed suddenly fuller and throbbing beneath his gentle kneading with a need of their own. She found herself short of breath when those same hands went to her knees and pushed the length of her gown up to her waist, then edged their way slowly, almost torturously, upward along the inside of her thighs. His touch made her feel like silk, soft and fragile and beautiful, and she never wanted the feeling to end. She didn't know where he was taking her. All she knew was that the journey was one she would want to take time and again.

She wondered if he saw the erratic pounding of her heart, the anticipation, as he removed her gown. She wondered what he thought of her naked body. Did he find it attractive? But she closed her eyes and did not even try to read his expressions, for the sensations flowing through her allowed her to do nothing else but sink into them as one does a deliciously warm tub of water.

His lips on her naked stomach, his hands on her breasts, told her that he must find her attractive. Hadn't he said earlier he wanted to make love to her? She relaxed. Yes. Yes, they were meant to do this. Their minds were together on this.

Her thoughts scattered. She inhaled sharply at the exquisite sensation of his moist lips closing over first one nipple and then the other. He seemed to know exactly what she needed. As the sensations mounted, his hand glided over her to the mound of hair between her legs and found beneath it a slumbering desire easily awakened by the touch of his gentle fingers moving in just the right manner to bring her even more excitement and pleasure.

She gripped his shoulders even harder, finding it more and more difficult to bear what he did, and yet all the while she knew it was impossible to ask him to stop.

Lights began to dance inside her head. She sank into a realm where sensation was all that mattered. Her stomach burned with his lips as they moved from her breasts downward. His hands took the place of his lips on her breasts. His fingers rolled gently over the taut and responsive nipples.

A sudden apprehension, mild fear, and great embarrassment shocked her momentarily when his lips found her most secret part. She made a move away from him, but through the dim light she saw his blond head lift. His eyes met hers.

"Let me do this for you, Sky."

"Matt . . . no . . ." It was a feeble attempt to deny herself what might be pleasurable. He sensed it and persisted.

"Let me, Sky. Open yourself to me. Don't hold back your feelings, honey. I want to be a part of you."

If she was to learn, she must listen to the instructor. She was weak and wanton and had no willpower. The need pounded inside her, waiting, waiting for him to continue.

She lifted her legs, widened them for his easier access. His blond head lowered and she gasped as his lips found that which was so privately her own,

306

but now strangely his.

Cries of mixed agony and pleasure rose inside her. She clutched his shoulders as the sensations built quickly inside her, rushing over her with the intensity of the thunderstorm they had nearly perished in. But she would not perish in this. She might drown, but she would not perish.

The reward came quickly. A tormenting and yet glorious wave of heat began to roll through her like sheet lightning rolling through the clouds. She had never felt anything so fiercely electrifying. She found herself in a place between body and mind where she had never been before. The wave built and built, and she was helpless to stop her cries of pleasure just as she was helpless to stop Matt.

She lifted her hips toward him, wanting more and more of this exquisite pleasure he offered so unselfishly. A need drove her on. The sensations piled one on the other. It seemed she was climbing to an invisible height like the eagle that soars toward the sun and the clouds, toward the peaks of the tallest mountain. The tension mounted and she was pushed to a higher and higher sphere where a definite destination awaited her. The sensation seemed to pause, as if balanced on the edge of a precipice, and with it she, too, hung suspended, waiting to fly higher, or fall.

Suddenly the brilliant sensation exploded inside her, pouring liquid flames out to all parts of her body, rocking her in waves of heat and ecstasy she could never have imagined possible. With her head tossed back against the pillows, she cried out with stunning relief. She felt bathed in a golden sunlit realm between heaven and earth. Only gradually was she set back to the solidness of earth.

Matt stretched out next to her again and drew her into his embrace. The kisses he continued to shower over her made her feel very close to him, loved. Cherished. He touched her body in a different way now than before, a way that was more soothing than erotic. He knew he had taken her to the ultimate peak of passion, and just as he had guided her there, he brought her back safe and sated.

She nestled in his arms, almost exhausted, as if indeed she had traveled a long journey from earth to heaven and back again. They lay that way for an indeterminate length of time, until the thudding of her heart had slowed to normal. Finally she whispered in a voice like that of a child who has just discovered a fantastic new wonder of the world. "Matt, when men and women join . . . is the feeling like that?"

"Yes, Sky," he murmured, smiling down at her. "It can be. It was intended to be."

"Then I want us to feel this thing together."

Brown eyes locked with blue. Hers waited. His questioned. He voiced his concerns. "Are you sure, Sky? Once I make love to you in that full and complete way, there's no going back."

She didn't know exactly what he meant by that. Did it mean he would be committed to her? Or did he mean he would expect her to be his woman forever and ever? She didn't want to ask the questions because she didn't want to hear the answers. They might destroy the magic of the moment. There was no place for tomorrows and realities in this moment.

The need began anew inside her, hot and demanding, aching for fulfillment. Now that she had opened herself to him, entrusted him with this most intimate act of pleasure, she wanted to give him what he had given her.

Timidly, she circled his extended manhood with her hand. A sharp breath caught in his throat, his eyes closed, his embrace tightened.

"God, Sky," he moaned. "I need you. I've wanted you like this from the beginning."

"Then come to me, Matt," she whispered against his throat. "Come to me, now."

She spread her legs to either side of him, lifting her knees. She grasped his hips and drew him down to her, feeling his hard flesh against the soft folds of her own, and finding the contact alone stimulating, new, and wonderful.

He took her tenderly in his arms. It was easy for his lips to bring her to full desire again. She allowed the feelings to flow freely through her and from her. She was not afraid of him in any way now. There was beauty in their nakedness and in their intimacy. For the first time she not only kissed his lips, but kissed the heated, excited flesh of his body, knowing him in the way he now knew her.

When his entry came she did not fear it because a part of her instinctively sought their union. She felt only a minor, short burst of pain, and then she was filled with the hot hardness of him. Relief and pleasure rushed through her. At last she was whole, realizing just how empty she had been. As he started moving inside her, any discomfort was replaced by a powerful ecstasy that gripped her and held her. Soon she was moving with him in a dance of fire, of need; of passion, of love.

As his thrusts became stronger and more urgent, so did hers, and she lost all awareness of the outside world. Her mind was focused only on their joining. He lifted her to a height even greater than he had before, and even more ultimately satisfying. Together they cried out their fulfillment, clinging to each other in rapturous desperation. The waves of pleasure rocked them again and again before slowly subsiding and leaving them exhausted in each other's arms.

She nestled against Matt's chest, wondering how she could ever have feared him and could ever have wanted him out of her life. Now, she merely wondered how she could keep him in it.

Matt rolled to his side, taking his weight from Sky, but keeping her close against his length. He had never experienced such passion, such satisfaction, and he knew she never had either. He had waited so long to make her his, and he had not been disappointed in the outcome of their union. And yet, having her at last had done nothing to quench his thirst for her. He knew it had only made him want her again and again. Forever.

He kissed the sweet, tangled mass of her black hair, knowing that what they had shared had been right. Never had he felt more complete, more of a man, than he had with this woman. He knew he was lost to her in mind just as he was lost to her in body.

Words crouched on the tip of his tongue, waiting to be said. Words of love. Words of marriage. Words that would make this moment go on and on. But they remained there. He was too afraid to let them go forth, because it was so much safer to go on taking pieces of love and harboring hopes than it was to speak and risk losing all.

So he held her, and he made love to her again. And it was the small hours of the morning before they slept.

What is this Ghost Shadow
that brushes my shoulder?

Chapter Eighteen

The train picked up speed outside of Rawlins. To Red Sky it seemed to be flying for she had never ridden one before. It slowed down going through the Medicine Bow Mountains but then once again seemed to shoot like an arrow toward Laramie, taking her to her destination much quicker than she wanted to go.

Matt sat next to her, staring out the window at the fast-moving landscape, apparently lost in thought. He had said nothing for miles. Was he thinking about last night and having reservations about what had transpired between them? Or was he thinking of Elizabeth? And if not her, possibly another woman who Red Sky knew nothing about?

When they had finally slept last night, the dream had returned, and the disturbing connotation had been the same as it had been the first time. The circling of the eagles had had a calming, peaceful effect initially, but the feeling associated with the rushing clouds the second time was stronger and seemed to be a definite portent of a power greater than herself that would deceive and destroy her, swallow her as the one eagle had done to the other.

She glanced at Matt. No smile eased the brooding quality of his face. He definitely looked troubled. He must have felt her gaze then for he turned his attention to her. He lifted her hand to his lips and placed a kiss to the back of it. In those quiet seconds, all they had shared last night was revived. His eyes remained on her for a moment, still contemplative, but finally he turned back to the window and once again to his private musings.

Are you the one who will destroy me, Matt Riordan?

A shiver ran through her. The mere thought unsettled her as badly as the dream itself had. She didn't want to even think such a thing. But was it possible that he was so adept at his job that he had fooled her in the worst way? And now, perhaps he was regretting it, or thinking he could give up the charade very soon.

She glanced down at his strong hand twined with hers. She made a move to pull free, but his fingers tightened and kept her from slipping away. It was a difficult and daring decision, but in those disquieting moments she chose to consider it the grip of a lover, not the chain of her captor. She chose to think he would stand by her in this, and that he wouldn't turn her over to the law to be tried for dual murders.

She leaned her head back against the cushioned seat and closed her eyes. Her hat fit high enough on her head that it didn't cause her undue discomfort. Beneath it, her black hair was coiled and braided and pinned. She'd done it with the help of a hair-dresser who had been willing to come to the hotel.

When she and Matt had finished dressing this morning, she had looked very much like a lady on the arm of a gentleman. They had received scores of stares on their walk to the train, and she had been nervous about that, but Matt had assured her they were only looking because she was such a striking woman.

Although she had been extremely flattered, she'd asked, rather nervously, "But what if someone puts two and two together and realizes who we are?"

His lips had thinned to a solemn line. "It's a chance we'll have to take unless you want to ride horseback the rest of the way to Cheyenne."

"Yes, let's do," she replied with hope in her eyes. "I prefer horseback."

He'd been amused, but in the end wouldn't allow it. "Come on, Sky. Let's put the horses in the live-stock car and ourselves in the passenger car. We can be in Cheyenne in a matter of hours and then this will all be over. By horseback, it'll take days to get there. We could even be more vulnerable on horse-back if for some reason the killers have found out I've taken you from the mountains."

She had consented, feeling once again like an im-postor in the black traveling suit. The image of her-self in the mirror had both pleased and unsettled her. It was as if she had become a woman overnight. And perhaps she had. But it was also as if she had become someone else not of her own making, but of Matt's. She wasn't sure she wanted to be the person staring back at her from the mirror. Maybe it would just take time to assume the role and to accept it as genuine.

"Tired?"

Her eyelids fluttered open. Matt was watching her. "I didn't get much sleep last night," she said, a faint suggestive smile lifting the clouds of doubt and reminding them both of what they'd shared.

He squeezed her hand and they exchanged an intimate look that started stirrings deep inside her again. She willingly cast aside her earlier doubts about him. She might be an Indian in white woman's clothing, but Matt Riordan was who he said he was and she should not question his sincerity without deeper provocation.

"Get some rest," he said gently. "I believe I will, too."

Red Sky closed her eyes again, but Matt Riordan didn't. Instead he studied her lovely profile for a time, wondering—as he had done for days—if he was making a mistake by taking her to Cheyenne. It was a peculiar feeling, but he felt he was destroying the mysterious woman of the mountains whom he had fallen in love with from first sight. With a tremendous yearning, he wished they could go back to the cave and continue on, just the two of them, wrapped in each other's arms forever in a world that involved no one but themselves. It seemed the

315

only lasting way to hold on to the idyllic impressions he had of her and of love.

He still toyed with the idea of asking her to marry him, but then this morning something had happened that had been troubling him the entire trip. It had made him realize that while they had finally come together in a sort of magical dream, reality could easily destroy both idealism and feelings of the heart.

While he dressed for the trip, he had watched her put on the traveling suit. During a covert glance he had seen her look longingly at the doeskins in the parfleche and had seen her run a hand over them lovingly as if she were giving up a deeply cherished part of herself. Was she, in her heart, more Indian than white? Could she ever leave the freedom she loved for the confines of civilization? It was much the way she'd looked over her shoulder at the Wind River Mountains, and he not only felt guilty for tearing her from her home, but he wondered with increasing concern if she could ever be a part of any world but that which she'd left behind. If she couldn't, then could he truly spend his life with her in the mountains? It sounded fanciful and wonderful, but realistically they could not isolate themselves from the world, or raise their children that way either. Even Indians sought the companionship and safety of the tribe.

He stared out the window again, watching the landscape rush by. For years he'd been wandering, searching for fulfillment, doing jobs to make a living and to stay alive, to keep himself so busy that he had no time for thoughts and emotions like those tormenting him today. Long ago he had wanted a ranch and a good woman who would love him and comfort him at the end of a hard day. The dream was returning and he wanted Sky McClellan to be that woman. Now that he had known her in the most intimate of ways, his life would be even more aimless and pointless than it had been before if he had to go on without her. If that happened, he might as well keep moving and keep living by the gun. And some day undoubtedly die by it as well.

His gaze rested on her. She appeared to be sleeping; her hand had relaxed inside his. Yes, he wanted her to be his wife, but he didn't want to push their relationship along too quickly and risk losing her. She was troubled by many things right now. It wouldn't be wise to burden her with a decision like marriage.

And there was always the problem of Gray Bear. The Shoshoni loved her, too, and he could offer her the freedom that had become such an integral part of her. If she had the chance, which of them would she choose?

He loosened the white bandana knotted at his collar and undid the top button on his shirt. It was hot in the train and hotter outside. At least a breeze came in through the open window. But it was a hot breeze, and because it was hot, it reminded him a godawful lot of Texas. . . .

"I'd better leave, Elizabeth." He sat on the edge

of her ruffly bed and reached for his pants. "Your pa's bound to be home pretty soon from that cattleman's meeting."

She only smiled seductively and pulled him back down into her arms, pressing her full bosom against him. "Oh, quit worrying, Matt. If he comes, you can just go out the window."

"He'll see my horse."

"Then you can tell him you've just come to visit. Come on, make love to me again. I won't see you for a while and I need lots to dream about on lonely, *sultry* nights."

Elizabeth Loring was as sultry as the weather she spoke of. Sex was all she thought about. But maybe that was because her daddy took care of everything else for her.

He ran a finger along her shoulder and tried to be serious because he wanted her to be serious. "You're sixteen, Elizabeth. That's old enough to marry. I don't like all this sneaking around. What do you say I ask your pa for your hand? We can tie the knot. Settle down in a little place somewhere."

She sighed and rolled her blue eyes in exasperation, pushing her red hair away from her naked shoulders and breasts. "We've been through this before, Matt. I don't want to get married, at least not yet. Besides, you don't have a ranch and it could take you a long time to build it as big as my daddy's spread. And my daddy wouldn't let me marry a man who didn't have anything but a job as a cowboy."

"I wouldn't make you live in a shack, for God's

sake, Elizabeth. You know I'm a good worker and I've got a lot of plans. I'd provide for you. You'd never be wanting."

"Oh, Matt," she said impatiently. "Why can't we just enjoy each other and have a little fun? We're young and there's still so much out there to do. Marriage would only tie us down and make us old in a hurry. There would be kids and all. We can wait a couple of years."

Matt couldn't really see her point. He had never been young, he supposed, and he'd had to work all his life. Things weren't going to change in that respect, at least not for him. But he had to remember that she *was* young—and more than a little spoiled. It struck him then that he didn't know whether or not he really did want to marry her. She would probably be very hard to keep satisfied. But he'd taken her to bed—although he had never been truly sure if he'd taken her virginity—and she was a decent woman, not a prostitute, so wasn't marrying her the proper thing to do?

"And what if you get pregnant?" he asked cautiously, finally broaching a subject that had bothered him for weeks now but that had seemed of no concern to her.

She shrugged indifferently, as always. "Oh, I know of a woman who handles that sort of thing. She's done it for some other girls I know." She snuggled closer to him. "Enough of this talk. Come on and give me what you know I like."

He didn't like what she was saying about destroying a child that might be his, but when she moved

319

against him like that, he was lost. She took his hard flesh in her hand, making him forget everything but satisfying his lust. He couldn't refuse her or deny her. Her hair spilled out over the pillow as red as a vixen's, glistening and wavy in the afternoon sun. Her curvaceous body lifted to his, enticing him on.

He didn't hear the footsteps coming down the hall. He only heard the pounding of his heart and his blood racing through his body like wildfire as they came together in a heat of passion. She gripped his shoulders, her fingernails digging in viciously into his back as they sometimes did, but he said nothing because she was whispering against his ear, "Yes, Matt, yes. More, Matt. Oh . . . *yes.* More . . . more . . ."

Then suddenly she was hitting him in the head and screaming at him in a tone that was filled with anguish but loud enough to carry clear out to the yard. "No! Stop! Don't do this to me! No!"

The door to the room burst open with the sound of splintering wood. Matt leaped away from her, stunned by the sight of Big Bailey Loring and his son, Red, halted in the doorway, their eyes blazing murderously. Before he could get out of bed and reach for his pants, Bailey was on him. The big brute of a man jerked him off the bed and smashed a fist to his stomach and one to his face. He fell, sprawling across the floor. Bailey came at him again, kicking him with the pointed toes of his boots. He curled up to protect his stomach and his genitals, but he couldn't get away. Then Red had him by the arms and was holding him while Bailey landed his big, meaty fists into him. He could taste the warm blood spurting from his nose and his mouth. He heard bone break: his nose, his jaw, a rib. The blows made him nearly senseless and he couldn't defend himself in any way.

Through blurred vision he saw Elizabeth on the bed, clutching the bedding to her bosom, shrieking and crying all at the same time, "He . . . made me . . . Daddy! He dragged me up here . . . everybody was gone . . . and he dragged me up here! He raped me, Daddy! He raped me! He said he'd kill me if I didn't do what he wanted!"

Still functioning on blind fury, Bailey yanked his gun from his holster and laid it against Matt's temple. The hammer clicked back into firing position.

Elizabeth shrieked. "No, Grandpa! Don't kill him! They'll . . . ask questions . . . people will know what he did. They'll know I was . . . raped. I'll be humiliated. I won't be able to show my face ever again. Please, don't kill him. Just send him away."

"She's right, Dad." It was Red speaking. "I don't want my daughter's reputation tarnished because of this. We can keep it between the two of us."

"All right. We won't kill him here. Let him get his clothes on."

"Grandpa, don't kill him," Elizabeth pleaded. "You'll get sent to prison if you do. I'll . . . be all right."

"You keep out of this, girl. His kind will just try it again. We'll decide the proper justice for this bastard Riordan. Should never have hired a stinking drifter like him, that's for sure."

"Tell them the truth, Elizabeth," Matt gasped, trying to breathe through the pain. "Tell them the truth."

But she only sat there in the middle of the bed, the sheet pulled over her breasts and a scared look on her face.

Red Loring gave Matt a shove and he fell onto the floor. He crawled to his clothes and fumbled with them, feeling vulnerable and humiliated in his nakedness. At last he got his pants on, and they dragged him from the house, leaving the rest of his clothes behind.

They took him outside and were forced to drag him between them because he couldn't walk. They put him on a horse and started off, but the pain in his ribs was so excruciating he passed out. He woke up with them throwing him over the horse like a sack of grain. The pain streaked through his head and his body again. Blood dripped from his nose and down onto his bare arms and hands. He couldn't see very well and knew his eyelids were cut and nearly swollen shut.

They rode for miles into the blazing hot Texas sun, and all the while he faded in and out of consciousness. His nose finally quit bleeding, but the blood on his face attracted the flies and they wouldn't leave him alone, and he couldn't even swat them away. He remembered them stopping once and hearing Bailey and Red talking to some other men. Through swollen eyes he recognized the foreman of the ranch and two of the top hands. They were just coming back from town and must have been highly trusted to remain silent because Bailey told them he'd raped Elizabeth and they were going to teach him a lesson. Then they rode on, taking the hired men with them.

At last they stopped and Red pulled him off the horse. He hit the ground hard and lay there for a long time. At first he thought they were just going to leave him there to let the sun kill him. At the moment he didn't care, but soon he smelled the smoke of a fire. He managed to get his eyes open enough to see Bailey take a branding iron from off his saddle. He couldn't remember him having picked it up before they left the ranch. But maybe he had.

It was then he knew what the lesson was going to be, and he wished he'd died en route, wished they'd just shot him in the head and been done with him—innocent or not. With some inner strength he got to his knees, knowing he had to escape, but they saw him and knocked him down again. The next thing he knew he was flat on his face, spread-eagled and they were staking him out like an animal. He couldn't move anything but his head. He saw Bailey twisting the branding iron in the fire, making sure it was good and hot.

"I didn't rape her," he said, but realized it was only a mangled whisper. He said it again, as loud as he could. *"I didn't rape her!"*

"Shut your mouth, you bastard." It was Red Loring who answered him. "My daughter wouldn't lie to me. You're nothing but scum and you'll pay for violating her."

The hired hands stared at him without emotion. The branding iron got redder and redder and finally the end of it turned white.

Bailey Loring wrapped his gloved hand around the iron's handle and pulled it from the fire. He turned to Matt with hatred in his eyes. Matt screamed once, but the pain lasted only a second before he lost consciousness.

Matt leaned his head back against the seat and closed his eyes. There was much about that day that had dimmed and blurred, but he still remembered the pain. The goddamned pain. They'd left him there beneath the blazing sun, staked out to die. He would have, too, if a drifter hadn't come along and cut him free and taken him to a doctor.

When he had recuperated he'd set out to ruin Bailey Loring, and it had been easy enough to do. While working for Loring, Matt had had his suspicions about the man's involvement in rustling, but he hadn't looked very hard for answers because of Elizabeth. He started investigating, though, having nothing to lose, and found out that Loring *hadn't* been at a cattleman's meeting that day. He had been branding stolen cattle in a canyon ten miles from the ranch. That's why he'd had the branding iron on his horse.

Matt had gone to the law and become involved with some Pinkerton agents hired for the case. Together they set a trap and caught Loring in the act. Matt was just sorry he hadn't been able to implicate Red, too, because he knew he was involved. But Bailey had insisted Red wasn't part of it, and since Red had been at the ranch the night of the raid on Bailey and his men, the court had believed him.

Bailey had hung. Matt had been offered a permanent job with the Pinkerton Agency. He'd gone back to Texas many times since then, but only to bust outlaws like Loring. And every time he returned, the memories assailed him, haunted him, and he couldn't wait to leave again.

He turned his head to look at Sky, who was still sleeping to the rhythmic rumble of the train. He gripped her hand a little tighter, but she didn't stir. She was so lovely, so innocent, so good. Exactly the opposite of Elizabeth. He wondered how he could have ever loved Elizabeth. He must have simply been starved for love, for attention, and so foolish as to take it in whatever form it was given and believe it could be right and true.

Nothing remained in his heart for Elizabeth Loring. Any feeling had died the day she had betrayed him. She had destroyed so much in him and taught him cynicism in a way that no other experience in his life ever had. But Sky McClellan had put new life in him. For that he was grateful, and for now he wouldn't think of tomorrow.

The train pulled into Cheyenne right on schedule. Red Sky stepped nervously into the aisle and

325

waited while Matt removed the parfleche and saddlebags from the overhead rack. They had to wait for the livestock car to be opened. When it was, Matt went inside to get the horses.

Red Sky waited near the train, feeling much too visible. But there were so many people coming and going that no one seemed to pay her any mind — for which she was thankful.

Matt finally led the horses out of the stock car and down the long, sloping ramp. Soldier was saddled; the other horse wore only a bridle and Matt had draped her parfleche over its back.

"Let's get the horses to the livery and find a room," he said.

"I can take care of that horse for you, mister."

They both turned at the sound of a young boy's voice.

Matt eyed the boy, scrutinizing him openly. Red Sky saw the hopeful expression in the boy's hazel eyes as he waited for Matt's approval. She also noticed his shabby clothes and hair that needed a comb and a cutting. She was glad when Matt dug into his vest pocket and extracted a fifty-cent piece. She sensed Matt had done it because he saw himself in that blond-haired boy and remembered the time when he, too, had been on his own doing whatever odd jobs he could to put food in his stomach.

He handed the horses' reins to the boy, and then the coin. "Take them to the livery and feed them. Give them some oats and they'll need a drink of water."

The boy glanced at the fifty-cent piece as if it were a twenty-dollar gold coin. He curled his grimy fingers tightly around it with gratefulness showing in his eyes, but his pride was too big for him to let too much of it show. He nodded in a businesslike manner. "I'll take good care of them, mister. Is there anything else I can do for you?"

"As a matter of fact. Can you run a message to the territorial governor for me?"

The boy's eyes rounded in surprise. "Cameron Welch? In the big building over yonder?" He pointed behind him.

"Yes, he's the one."

"Why sure I can, mister. Just tell me what it is."

Matt dug into his vest pocket again and pulled out a small black notebook and a stubby pencil. He scribbled down a message, folded the paper and handed it to the boy. "Give this to the governor and bring his answer back to me. We'll be at that hotel over there—the Cheyenne—if they have an empty room."

"Oh, they have plenty of rooms. Ain't full neither." The boy carefully put the message in his hip pocket. "I'll only be thirty minutes or so, mister."

"There's no hurry. Take your time with the horses and do a good job. I'll pay you fifty cents more when you get back from the governor's."

The boy's eyes lit up again and he gazed up at Matt with a look that fairly bordered on idolization, as if he thought he had met someone very important to have such money, someone who was kind, and who exchanged messages with the territorial governor.

He led the horses away and Matt and Sky walked across the street to the hotel. They weren't given any trouble by the desk clerk this time and were once again given a room on the second floor overlooking the street. Red Sky thought it odd that clothes could change the opinions and attitudes people held toward each other. Didn't she look as Shoshoni as she had yesterday morning in Rawlins?

Matt opened the window to get the stuffiness out of the room, then he turned to Sky. "Would you like to go into the dining room and get something to eat? I think we're far enough away from Long Moon Valley to feel relatively safe."

"I'm really not very hungry," she said. "That meal on the train was more than enough. Let's just wait for the governor's response to the message."

Matt removed his jacket and boots and stretched out on the bed. "Come here, Sky," he said, holding out a hand. "You're as tight as an Indian's war drum."

She laughed and stepped forward, laying her hand in his. Everything about him was warm and accommodating and made her want to melt into his arms and be loved, to forget about anything but the two of them, including the doubts she'd had about him. The troubled look she'd seen in his eyes on the train was gone now. He was no longer distant but fully receptive to her.

"Let me rub your neck and see if I can get you to relax a little," he offered with a seductive glow in his eyes. "Don't be so afraid of meeting the governor. He only wants to get this problem solved, the same as you and I do. After all, any illicit affairs in the state are a reflection on him."

She allowed him to undo the buttons on the suit's basque jacket and didn't mind how his hands rested lightly but provocatively against her bosom while he completed the task. He helped her slip it off over her shoulders, and as he did so, his warm gaze encompassed the lightweight fabric of her white blouse. He plainly appreciated the way it lay so softly against her bosom, revealing so much more of her curves than the shapeless buckskin had.

He turned her around and settled her in front of him on the edge of the bed with his long legs straddling her. As soon as his massaging fingers took command, she began to relax.

"It'll be over soon," he said.

"And then you will take me back home?" she asked quietly, turning her head to catch his gaze from over her shoulder.

Matt fell into the depths of her dark eyes which were framed by long, thick lashes. Oh, how she captivated him, controlled him! And with nothing more than a look and the nearness of her body.

"I said I would, and I'm a man of my word," he replied. "But is it so bad away from the mountains, Sky? Don't you think you would ever want to live anywhere else?"

She looked straight ahead again. After a moment of contemplation her shoulders drooped as if suddenly burdened by a great weight. "I'm not sure, Matt. You may not understand, but I . . . don't feel as if I really belong to the world anymore. Only to my own world."

He continued massaging her shoulders, trying to pretend her confessions didn't trouble him. "That's the way it is with all of us. We might run with the pack, but we're each a world inside ourselves. It's natural for you to want to avoid people right now. You've been alone for a long time. You don't need people to survive, and when a person is self-sufficient he becomes a loner. There's nothing wrong with that, Sky. It just means you're a strong person. No one will fault you for that." He paused. "I hope all this is over soon, but you know I can't take you home until those men are captured and in custody. I want them behind bars, or hung."

"Yes, but who will track them down?"

From the way she asked the question, he sensed she knew the answer already. His massaging fingers hesitated only a moment on her shoulders before continuing. "I will. If the governor asks me to."

"It's dangerous, Matt. Those men won't hesitate to kill you."

"I know, but I'll be ready for them. You must remember I track dangerous criminals all the time. It's my job."

He wondered if she really cared about his life, or if she might merely be afraid that with him dead she wouldn't get back to the mountains. He preferred to believe the former.

He leaned closer to her and kissed her neck, delighting in her soft inhalation of breath and the way she tilted her head back toward him. In only a few moments he had moved to the center of the bed and brought her with him. Simultaneously they began undressing each other. As they did so, the late evening sun reached a golden arm across the bed to warm their naked flesh. Red Sky, knowing now the nature and outcome of this game, boldly drew Matt into her arms.

He didn't have to move slowly or cautiously with her this time. She met his kisses fully and without shyness or fear. He took her yearning breasts tenderly in his hands and the nipples in his mouth. She arched her back toward him and toward the dazzling fires that his mouth drew from deep in her loins. She felt his extended manhood against her thighs and lifted her legs around him to pull his hips into the cradle of her own. He abandoned her breasts and his mouth took hers in a hungry, demanding kiss. Their tongues danced their own mating while their bodies moved in similar unison.

Sky felt it was as if they were together on the highest peak of the Wind River Range, climbing to its elevated greatness where clouds and eagles hover. Simultaneously, they cried out their pleasures. When the rush of the great tremor passed, Matt rolled to his back and brought Sky with him. Holding herself over him, she found the tension building again quite suddenly until she was riding him hard and soon crying out a second time with pleasure.

Fulfilled at last, she collapsed upon him and his arms closed around her in a fierce but loving embrace. She rested her head on his chest, listening to the pounding of his heart slow to a normal beat.

Matt pushed the silky strands of her fallen hair back away from her face, whispering against her parted lips. "You are the most wonderful creature I've ever known. My mountain lioness."

She felt him growing hard inside her again, and laughed softly. "I didn't know what I was missing before yesterday."

"And neither did I."

His mouth closed over hers hungrily and he rolled her to her back. He began to move inside her again when a knock sounded at the door.

"God, it must be the boy," he moaned.

He forced himself to leave her. He yanked on his pants and shirt, leaving the shirt unbuttoned. As always he took his Colt in hand, and moved toward the door, staying off to the side as if expecting gunfire or a break-in. Sky gathered her own garments and hurried behind the dressing screen.

"Who is it?" he asked, trying to force a casualness to his voice that he didn't feel.

"It's me, mister," came the boy's voice. "I got your message from the territorial governor."

Matt lowered his gun and pulled the door open. "That was fast, son," he said, smiling at the boy.

The boy's eyes were as large as platters. He was out of breath, apparently having run the whole way. "The governor wants to see you. Right now! He seemed awfully excited about the news that you were here."

Matt dug into his vest pocket and gave the boy

the fifty cents he'd promised. The boy stared at the big coin in his hand in unabashed awe. His face opened to a wide smile. "Thank you, mister. Do you need me to do anything else for you?"

"Not right now, son," Matt said, "but if I do I'll let you know. Where can I find you?"

Evasiveness entered the boy's eyes. "Oh . . . I hang around the rail depot . . . or the livery."

What the boy really meant to say was that he didn't have a home. Matt knew he probably slept in the livery at night, with or without the hostler's approval. He'd done it enough himself and he understood not to press the matter further.

"Well, don't worry. I'll be able to find you."

The boy nodded, thanked him again and trotted away down the hall, gripping the coins in his palm. Matt watched him until he disappeared down the stairs, then he turned to Sky. "Let's get cleaned up. It's time to go." With a half-grin, he added, "Tonight we'll pick up where we left off."

Thirty minutes later they stepped out onto the hot boardwalk. Red Sky wasn't sure if it was the black traveling suit, or simply the change in altitude, but it was so much hotter here than in the mountains. At least the sun would be going down soon.

Matt offered her his arm and she took it gratefully, feeling more secure when touching him and walking close by his side.

The walk to the territorial capitol building felt more like ten miles instead of a few blocks. The walking boots weren't nearly as comfortable as her

moccasins and she guessed she would have blisters
before they reached the impressive structure. As
they weaved their way along the crowded sidewalks,
she was overcome with a terrible attack of claustrophobia. Everything seemed so closed in: the buildings that lined the streets blocking the view and the
wind; the people bustling to and fro; the wagons
and horses traveling up and down the streets; the
incredible noise; the dust from hundreds of feet,
hooves, and wagon wheels filling her nostrils.

She wasn't sure if the claustrophobia was caused
by the people and the noise, or if their presence
merely crowded in on a mind that was already terrified. What if the governor said her testimony was
of no use and he saw no reason to offer her further
protective custody? Or what if they sent someone
back, like Matt, to Long Moon Valley but couldn't
find the killers, and then the killers came here looking for her? There was no place to hide in this city.
She felt vulnerable here, and she didn't like that
feeling. She was out of her element, and therefore
very much out of control. Suddenly she wanted to
run back to the mountains where it was safe.

The territorial capitol building was cool and
quiet inside, all gleaming polished wood, smelling
of furniture oil. The soothing atmosphere provided
a change from the busy streets and Red Sky relaxed
upon entering. The halls were wide and open, the
windows tall and without curtains. Peace and solitude prevailed.

Matt led her through the halls until they reached
Cameron Welch's office. His secretary — Mrs.

Leanore Johnson by her name plate—sat at a large oak desk outside the door that led to his private, inner office.

"Mr. Riordan," Mrs. Johnson greeted him with a smile. "What a pleasure to see you again. The governor said to tell you to go right in." Her gaze shifted to Red Sky and she perused her curiously but with kind eyes. "He said the young lady was to accompany you."

Matt thanked her and opened the door, allowing Sky to enter first. Her heart was thumping so hard she felt light-headed and her hands tingled.

She surveyed the surroundings in one quick glance. The governor had his high-backed leather chair swiveled toward the window. Only the top of his head could be seen. There were two other men in the room, and their presence made her uneasy. They were rough-looking, not the suit kind, and revolvers were strapped to their hips. The one near the window was pudgy and his face had a bloated appearance. The other one, by the door and to her left, was young and lean, perhaps just a year or two older than herself, and he was fairly handsome. He nodded to her in a polite, respectful way when their eyes met for a brief moment.

Matt closed the door behind them. At the clicking of the latch, the governor slowly swiveled his chair around to face them as if he had all the time in the world to do so.

It was odd how in that moment the bottom seemed to fall out from under Red Sky. The speed of her heart increased. Her knees began to buckle.

Her vision blurred, and she told herself this wasn't happening. But the raspy, mocking sound of the governor's voice was much too real, touching the raw chord of a memory that would never be forgotten.

"Aren't you feeling well, Miss McClellan?" he asked in that deeply derisive tone. "You look as pale as if you'd just seen a ghost."

A cold chill raced down her spine. She stared at the twisted smile, the head of prematurely gray hair, the pale blue eyes.

She had to escape. To run.

She started backing toward the door, but a hand closed around her wrist.

"What's the matter, Sky? Is something wrong?"

She dragged her eyes away from the governor and toward the man who'd spoken the question — the same man who held her wrist. When she saw Matt something inside her snapped. With no warning, she flung herself at him, kicking and clawing and screaming.

There is an hour in which they meet —
The Darkness and the Dawn.

Chapter Nineteen

"You bastard! I should never have trusted you! All your words were lies!"

It was all Matt could do to grab both of her wrists and protect himself from her savage attack. Her eyes blazed with a vicious hatred that sliced through his heart more painfully than any knife. He overpowered her purely out of necessity, and twisted her body around until her back was to him. Crossing her arms over her breasts, he held her as effectively as a strait-jacket could have done. She still tried to struggle, kicking back at him and bucking against his chest, but finally she had to give up, her energy spent.

"I shot him," she cried weakly, nearly sobbing. "I was sure he was dead."

Matt looked up then and saw that one of the governor's men had his gun drawn and leveled on both him and Sky. The other man had walked around to

Matt's back and now easily lifted Matt's gun from its holster.

Cameron Welch came around his desk and sat on the corner of it. He was a big man, over six foot, and broad in the shoulders, but overall rather thin. He smiled in a self-satisfied way. "You can't ever truly tame an Indian, can you, Riordan? They're like a wolf you've raised from a pup—you never know when they'll turn on you."

"What's going on here, Welch?" Matt demanded, feeling something very cold and sinister settling over him like a hunter's net.

"Why, exactly what you and I planned would happen, Riordan. You would go to the woman, pretend to be her friend, and then bring her to me."

Sky tried to break free again. "Damn you! You knew all along who Welch was!"

"I still don't know who he is," Matt ground out between clenched teeth as he continued to try to hold Sky to keep her from clawing out his eyes. "Except that he's supposed to be the governor of this damned territory! And he was supposed to give you protective custody in exchange for evidence."

"Come on, Riordan," Welch replied. "Don't play the innocent for the sake of Miss McClellan. I take it from her reaction to you that you and her have become . . . *intimate?* . . . and now she's found out that you were just using her."

"Welch, you've got some explaining to do."

"You knew all along my position in this case, Riordan, and that I was one of those who killed McClellan and his tribe of breeds."

Sky struggled harder and Matt denied it again.

"You lying son of a bitch! You told me nothing of the sort! Don't listen to him, Sky. He's only trying to pit you against me."

"You knew!" she insisted. Angry, scalding tears fell from her eyes, occasionally splashing onto his hands that still tried to hold her still.

"I didn't, Sky. He's the liar."

Welch chuckled, amused by their battle. Then he continued with the arrogance and ease of a victor. "You and I both know, Riordan, that McClellan nosed around a little too much and wouldn't let well enough alone. I had no choice but to kill him. I couldn't let him tell all and ruin my bid for territorial governor. As for Sky here"—his gaze raked her, barely concealing a level of cold lust and contempt—"she was just a bonus I tried to take. I didn't bargain for her being such a fighter. Her mother and sister surely weren't. They figured if they gave us what we wanted we wouldn't kill them."

His chilling burst of laughter brought a sudden spasm of nausea to Sky's stomach. She wanted to kill him, but all she could do was stand there with her hands curled into fists, her nails biting into her palms, and suffer being held captive in the arms of the man she had trusted and loved and who had so completely betrayed her. The dream of eagles had been a warning! Oh, why hadn't she listened?

Then Welch spoke directly to her. "I see seven years has brought you into full womanhood, Sky. I think you and I will have another chance to pick up where we left off. I'm glad you didn't forget me after all these years . . . just as I never forgot you.

339

Now, tell me, who else do you remember from that day?"

"No one," she replied defiantly, her back stiffening against Matt's chest.

Welch chuckled. "Now you don't expect me to believe that, do you? I believe you must have gotten a good look at the others."

Before she could respond, Matt cut in. "Why did you go on the wrong side of the law, Welch? What did you hope to gain? Why not just operate honestly, like McClellan? You would have gotten just as far—maybe farther. I expect you were—and are—rustling reservation cattle, too. Am I correct? It's no wonder the Indians can't get any action out of you."

Smiling smugly, Welch shook his head. "Still playing the innocent, aren't you, Riordan? You knew all that before you went on the case. As one of my hired men, you were told everything."

Matt suddenly released Sky and lunged for Welch, ready to kill him with his bare hands. "You lying bastard! I'm not one of your men!"

But before he could get his hands around Welch's throat he felt hard metal rammed into his chest. Welch had pulled a derringer from his vest pocket and now sat, still calmly where he was, smiling with maddening arrogance.

"Get back over there by the woman, Riordan," Welch commanded. "I see you're going to give us trouble on this. I don't know why, since we had a deal and all. But it doesn't matter because I had planned to have you killed right from the beginning. You see, you simply know too much and you're not a man I figured I could ever trust anyway.

"Now, you asked about the reservation cattle. Well, I'll explain it to Miss McClellan so she'll have no doubt as to why her father was killed and why she will soon be joining him.

"The reservation cattle are easy targets, Miss Mc-Clellan, and mostly unbranded. But I doubt a man of your father's high-minded nature, or even Riordan's for that matter, would understand the desire for power and wealth. I wanted both of those things, and I wanted control of Long Moon Valley—one of the best grazing lands in the territory. There were too many two-bit ranchers with a few head of cattle that were moving in, and I could see we were going to lose what was rightfully ours. I nearly have it all now—me and my financial partner, Rusty Glassman. And of course, to the world, it appears to belong to numerous small outfits, but we actually own them all. You see, people don't like their political leaders to own too much of what they're governing because naturally it creates a biased interest."

"I don't believe Rusty Glassman was involved in all this," Red Sky blurted angrily. "He was Monty's father. He was a friend of my father's. He wouldn't have condoned killing my family."

"I'm afraid you don't know Rusty very well. He not only condoned it—he orchestrated it."

"But Monty—"

"—was killed. Yes, I know. It was rather unfortunate. It was a case of the poor boy being in the wrong place at the wrong time."

341

"You're saying Glassman killed his own son?" Matt asked incredulously.

Welch made a clicking sound with his tongue. "Oh really, Riordan. Why do you persist in trying to make this woman believe you knew nothing about all this? What can it possibly matter now that you're both going to die anyway. So, to continue. . . .

"Glassman had no choice in the matter of his son. Of course *he* didn't kill the boy. I did it for him. The boy recognized him, even with the bandana over his face, and Monty was foolish enough to say he wouldn't go along with us. But enough of that. The two of you will be escorted back to Lander by me and my guards here, and when we get there Rusty can tell you the rest of the story himself."

The guards stepped forward and tied Matt and Sky's wrists with cotton rope.

"Take them out the back way," Welch instructed. "Keep them locked up in the woodshed until the next train leaves for Rawlins."

"Why take us all the way back to Lander, Welch?" Matt interjected with disdain. "Why not just kill us here?"

The pudgy guard shoved his Colt into Matt's back just beneath his shoulder blade, "Shut up and get movin', Riordan."

Matt kept his feet anchored to the floor. "Not until I have an answer."

Welch pulled a cigar from his inside suit pocket and went through the tedious and annoying motions of lighting it. At last he drew on it and released a puff of smoke to the ceiling, squinting against it. "Well, Riordan. Rusty says he wants to see you and Miss McClellan. Seems he's got something he wants to discuss with you."

"I have nothing to discuss with Rusty Glassman. I don't even know the man. Maybe you're just afraid to kill us here, Welch. Afraid somebody will find out what you're up to — like your secretary out there."

Welch shrugged as if it were all an annoying, petty problem he was growing weary of. "It *would* be much safer to have it done away from here. I don't like killings in my town. It gives the place a bad reputation, you know. Makes people not want to move into the area."

"Like the situation in Long Moon Valley?"

Welch remained mildly amused by their predicament and their questions. "As a matter of fact, yes. But Rusty and I have nearly succeeded in our objective. We've bought up a good portion of the land in Long Moon Valley. And of course Rusty came by McClellan's ten-thousand-acre spread for virtually nothing. The settlers remaining are minding their business and posing no threat for now. Most of them are so dirt poor they'll end up leaving before long anyway. Then we'll step in and do them a favor by buying their land."

"And I'm sure you're making sure they never get ahead either, by rustling their cattle and destroying or stealing their water supply, thus eliminating what small profit margin they have."

"Well, of course, Riordan. And we have a rebellious one killed now and then. It's a little slower

343

that way, but it's less conspicuous." He turned and spoke to his guards. "Okay, boys. Get these two out of here. I have some work to wrap up before we head for Lander in the morning."

There was no hope of escape. The guards shoved them into the woodshed and tied their feet and hands. "Open your mouths to holler," the dough-faced guard named Arnold said, "and I'll plug you full of lead. I'm right outside the door and I won't give you a second chance to be quiet."

"A gunshot will bring the law," Matt countered.

"Maybe so, but I'll be gone before they can get here. I have orders from Welch to kill you if I have to. He's keeping you alive only because he promised Glassman that he would. I'm sure he'd just as soon see you both dead and see his problem ended if it was left entirely up to him. My advice to you two is to get some sleep. You're going to need it before we get to the other side of this territory."

For the long hours that followed, the two men traded guard duty. They brought some food at suppertime, releasing Matt and Sky's hands long enough to allow them to eat. They both remained during this time, their guns drawn and ready to fire if either Matt or Sky made the slightest move to escape. After they ate, they were escorted in turn to the privy a short distance away, but trussed again tightly upon their return to the shed.

Matt and Sky sat a couple of feet apart, their backs against the shed wall. Sky refused to look at Matt. Refused to speak. After hours of silence he'd had all he could take. "I didn't know who Welch was, Sky. Granted, I should have gotten suspicious when your description of your attacker matched Welch perfectly. But for some reason I didn't put two and two together. I had no reason to suspect he was involved. All that crap he's feeding you about me being in on it is just his way of turning you against me so you won't try to escape with me."

Her eyes still gleamed murderously. "I'd rather die right now than to go anywhere with you. But at least you're getting your due. It's comforting to know there's *some* justice in the world."

Suddenly the door to the shed burst open. Arnold's rotund body filled the small doorway. "I hear you talking in here! You had better not be planning an escape. If you don't shut up I'm going to gag you. You won't get another warning."

"I thought you said you'd shoot us," Matt replied with a challenging sneer on his lips.

Arnold found himself faced with a decision that he couldn't seem to make. Whispering wasn't the same thing as shouting for help, and he was confused as to what to do.

"Get some sleep!" he finally snapped and yanked the door shut, once again leaving them alone.

Matt rested his head against the wall behind them, staring up at the black ceiling of the old building. Amazingly enough, he didn't feel hopeless. He'd been in worse situations than this one. But he was worried about Sky, regardless of the way she felt about him right now. He *would* be helpless to help her if Welch decided to expend his lust on her again. And since he couldn't convince her he was as much a victim as she was, he'd surely never be able to convince her to join in planning an escape.

In those miserable moments he cursed himself for allowing his senses to be dulled by love. He'd spent years honing his instincts for recognizing deception, or maybe he'd just learned never to trust anybody's motives. So why had he believed, without question, in Welch's honesty? Because Welch was a man in power? That alone was enough to attest to dishonesty. Many men in high political positions didn't get there without compromising their principles, or selling them entirely.

Finally, around midnight, Sky drifted to sleep. He slid closer to her, giving her his shoulder when her head began to droop. At first she rejected it, but soon fell too deeply asleep to make further objections.

In the hours to follow, he thought about all Welch had said. He puzzled over Glassman and wondered why he could possibly want to talk to him. He had the chilling feeling it was Sky he wanted more, if what Welch said was true about him being the brains behind the McClellans' murders.

He tried to think of the journey ahead and a good place to watch for an escape; it was truly their only hope because he saw no mercy in their captors. He would make Sky go with him even if he had to kidnap her. Somehow he would convince her that everything Welch had said about him was a lie.

She had turned inward again, a thing that pained him possibly more than their capture and impending death. He felt he had failed her. If he had spoken words of love, or marriage, would her faith in him have been so easily shattered? He knew all too well that oftentimes the key to survival was trusting no one but yourself, and Sky McClellan was a woman who had learned that lesson much too well.

It was still a long way to Lander, and he was not one to give in easily to death and especially to thugs like Welch. He might die before this was over, but he'd do his damnedest to take Welch down with him.

In the black hour of predawn the guards untied Matt and Sky's ankles and walked them to the train depot at gunpoint. No one was up and about yet, but they would be very soon. Their horses had already been put in the livestock car that would be coupled to the main train when it arrived. Matt and Sky were shoved in with the animals and put at the opposite end of the car. Welch joined them for a moment, just as the guards were re-tying their feet.

"When we reach Rawlins, we'll ride horseback to Lander," he said. "As you can see, we brought your horses and all your belongings. We didn't want any trace of the two of you left behind. Nobody in Cheyenne is going to miss you or wonder what happened. They'll just think you continued on with your journey."

After he left, the guards locked the door from the inside, barring it to anyone else.

At daybreak the train began its journey to Rawlins. Several hours into the trip, the young guard named Balkin uncorked his canteen. Arnold, the pudgy guard, seemed to think a drink was a good idea and followed suit.

At the sight of the water, Sky realized how thirsty she was. Her tongue felt dry and she had to keep swallowing to try to moisten it. It was terribly hot, stuffy, and smelly in the livestock car.

She eyed Balkin's canteen with longing. He wiped his mouth on his shirtsleeve, almost guiltily, and tried to avoid her gaze. At last he came to his feet and walked the short distance that separated them. "Would you like a drink, ma'am?" he asked softly, holding the canteen out to her.

Arnold nearly gagged on his water, sputtered, and lowered his canteen from his fat lips. "What in the hell do you think you're doing, Balkin?"

Balkin dropped his right hand to his gun and the kind expression he'd given Sky turned to a savage snarl. "I'm offering the lady a drink of water, you stupid sonofabitch. Are you going to make something of it?"

Arnold was nonplussed at Balkin's sharp tongue, but not for long. "Hell, she ain't no lady. She's just a half-breed tryin' to *be* a lady. You turn her loose and she'd have your scalp before you could blink your eyes."

Arnold put the canteen back to his lips and guzzled more of its contents, spilling a good portion out the corners of his thick lips and onto his dirty shirtfront. Balkin lowered himself to his haunches, putting himself sideways between Sky and Arnold so he could see them both.

He held the canteen out to Sky. Of course she couldn't take it because her hands were tied behind her, but he held it to her lips and tipped it slightly. Some of the contents dripped down the front of her black traveling suit and he apologized. When he figured she'd had enough he gingerly wiped the water from her chin with his finger, as if he felt it wasn't really right to be touching her.

Matt had sat quietly through the entire thing, watching, but boiling inside at the way Balkin eyed Sky and touched her so tenderly and the way she was kindly responding to him. An incredible pain burrowed into his chest, and he was fairly fuming when Balkin turned to him. "Want a drink, Riordan?"

Matt nodded and Balkin helped him as he had done Sky, except he didn't bother to wipe up the spilled water on his face. Matt used his shoulder to get the job done. Balkin recorked the canteen and shifted his position, but still remained balancing on the balls of his feet.

"I went to the Winds once, looking for her. Couldn't find nothing but a bunch of tight-lipped Indians. I don't know how you managed to track her, Riordan. It's a different country than what I'm used to. I'm up from Matagorda Bay . . . Texas."

"Hired gun?" Matt asked tightly, his blue eyes narrow and contemptuous.

He nodded. "Yeah—same as you."

"Not exactly, Balkin. We're on different sides of the law."

"Maybe so, Riordan. But we both kill for a living."

Matt gave him no answer, just a cold perusal, then Balkin continued. "That gun of yours has seen a lot of wear, Riordan. You either do a lot of target-shooting, or you spend a lot of time defending yourself. How many men have you killed anyway?"

"Balkin, get away from the prisoners," Arnold inserted again with a worried look in his small, close-set eyes. "Don't you remember what the governor told us?"

"Shut up," Balkin snapped. "I feel like talking to somebody besides you." He gave his attention back to Matt. "I imagine you're pretty fast on the draw?"

Matt's eyes bore into the young guard with disdainful impatience. "Quick doesn't count nearly as much as an accurate aim."

"I'd like to go up against you just the same. I think you're lying."

"Well, ask Welch. Maybe he'd let you give me my gun back so I can shoot you."

Balkin was silent for a time, refusing to let Matt's attitude upset him, as if he understood it well. He continued passing the time with small talk. "You don't seem too worried about dying, Riordan."

"Neither do you."

Balkin managed a chuckle. "You'll have a hard time killing me without a gun and all trussed up like a Thanksgiving turkey."

Matt's expression was void of humor. "I wasn't talking about me killing you, Balkin. I'm talking about Welch killing you when you've served your purpose and this is all over. You don't think he's going to let you live after what you know about him, do you? He can't risk turning you loose on the street where you might tell somebody all about him in a moment of drunken weakness."

Disturbed by the suggestion, Balkin stood up. "He can trust me."

"How long have you been with him? Years? Months? Weeks? Think about it. One way or the other you'd be foolish to think you're indispensable."

"Quit talkin' to the prisoners," Arnold warned again. "The governor told us not to."

Balkin went back to his position next to Arnold. He was intelligent — something Arnold wasn't. He was also experienced enough to know that Riordan was right. Riordan was probably only a year or two older than Balkin himself, but his eyes were wise with knowledge beyond his years. Riordan was a gunslinger in his own right even if he didn't like to own up to it, and he knew the nature of men like Welch. Whether Riordan really had been in on this with Welch he didn't know, but one way or the other, Welch's plan to kill Riordan was a sure example of how he treated people he no longer needed and who knew too much about him and his operations.

It made Balkin uneasy. He would be careful not to turn his back on Cameron Welch. He would be wise not to turn his back on Arnold either.

By the time they got to Rawlins, Matt and Sky's arms were cramped from being in the same position for so long, and their wrists were raw from the ropes. But they got no reprieve. They were put on their horses with their hands still tied behind their backs. Then Welch pushed them hard to get away from town.

That first night in camp, Matt and Sky leaned against a large boulder while the guards gathered sagebrush to build a fire. Welch unsaddled the horses and staked them so they could eat.

"There's not a stick of cover out here," Matt whispered to Sky. "We could never make a break for it."

She gave him a heartless glare. "Don't play any more games with me, Matt. Even if I could get away, I wouldn't go with you."

Welch glanced their way. "No talking unless you want a gag stuffed in your mouth."

"Talk is harmless, Welch," Matt countered sardonically.

"Then say it loud enough for everyone to hear."

"Very well, Governor," Sky said boldly, even in a tone more sarcastic than Matt's. "I was looking for some tall sagebrush to get behind. I'd like to change my clothes, and a woman has to have some privacy now and again."

Welch's cold gaze raked her. Matt feared that now would be the time that Welch would force himself on her, and Matt was powerless to stop it. But Sky, always rebellious, was now so full of hatred and venom that she seemed to be asking for trouble. At least the governor wasn't used to hard riding or much of any kind of exertion. He'd had an easy office job for too many years now, and he was pushing himself in order to push them. He was tired. It was clearly written in his eyes and in the haggard expression on his face. Maybe that alone would work to their advantage.

If Matt could only get the jump on him and get

Sky away. But any attempt he might make would be sheer suicide at this point. If by some stroke of luck they should manage to escape — and he doubted he would have Sky's cooperation — it would only be temporary. At daybreak they'd be spotted in this open country. Their only hope was to take all the horses or chase them off and leave their adversaries afoot. But he couldn't do anything with his hands tied behind his back. And the horses were bone tired tonight; they wouldn't be able to travel far enough to do any good.

Finally Welch said, "All right, Miss McClellan. I'll let you tend to your needs, but don't try to run. I'd just catch you anyway and I'm sure the boys can think of an appropriate punishment for you."

Sky glanced at the guards building the fire. Arnold gave her a leering grin, but Balkin glanced sharply at Welch with narrowed, disapproving eyes.

"I'll need my hands free," she said.

Welch wasn't happy about it, but he removed the ropes from her wrists. She immediately began to rub them to ease the sting of pain and to get the circulation flowing again.

"May I have my bag? I'd like to change into my buckskins."

Again Welch was apprehensive. He was positive she was up to something. He had personally checked her bag and had removed anything that could have been used as a weapon, but he didn't trust her. After all, she'd nearly killed him once. Plus, she'd been living like a savage for seven years and was sure to have picked up their sneaky, unpredictable habits. Her elusive, self-confident attitude unnerved him. She didn't seem afraid of him, or much of anything now. It was almost as if she dared death to come to her, and if it did, she would welcome it with open arms.

"All right," he said finally, not wanting her to see that unnerving, shameful fear he had of her. "But if you're not back in ten minutes I'll kill Riordan."

Sky's lips moved into a bitter smile. "Go ahead. He means no more to me than I do him."

"I don't believe you mean that, Sky. Your reaction to his betrayal is too strong for a person who claims not to care. He must have done an excellent job of seducing you, even to the point of making you fall in love with him."

His evil eyes slid over her bosom, set off to the best advantage in the tight-fitting basque jacket. "Ten minutes and I'll kill him. Then I'll come after you myself."

Sky needed no interpretation of his intentions, but all she did was sneer at him before turning into the darkness with clothes in hand.

When she was far enough from camp that they wouldn't see her, she quickly began to disrobe. She was all thumbs in her haste to get out of what seemed to be layers and layers of feminine garb. Her heart thumped violently, pounding out the seconds and the minutes. She expected any moment to hear a gun shot. This would be her chance to run and hide in the darkness, and she was sure she could elude them. But try as she might, she couldn't hate Matt enough to abandon him, knowing Welch would kill him if she didn't come back. No, she couldn't hate him enough to want to see him die. She was so confused. Could he possibly be telling the truth? She wanted to believe him, but how could she? She'd believed him once and look where it had gotten her!

Hurry. She had to hurry. She had to get the buckskins on. At least if she was wearing the buckskins and she had the opportunity to get away, she would be able to run. She would run with Matt if she had to, but only because he was a prisoner now, too. She found it a bittersweet irony that enemies could become friends, only to become enemies once again.

She stripped off everything but the minimum of underwear then slipped the doeskin blouse over her head. She was just pulling up the buckskin pants and tying the rawhide string at the waist when an arm snaked out of the darkness and closed tightly around her throat. The cold muzzle of a revolver made its impression in her back. A raspy chuckle sent cold chills snaking down her spine.

"Scream or call for help and Arnold has orders to put a bullet in Riordan's head—no questions asked. You and I are going to have a little get-together, so you might as well cooperate if you want to see Riordan again. I'm going to release you," he continued, whispering in her ear. "And you'd better not make a wrong move."

His arm on her throat loosened and she was free of him. She stepped clear and stole a glance to the distant campfire. She saw the dark, bulky figure of Arnold moving around in the orange glow, but she knew neither he nor Balkin could see her in the darkness. Even if they could, neither of them would come to her rescue. If anything, they would help Welch get what he wanted and then take their own turns.

She realized, in that moment, that she had at least experienced the love of a gentle man. Of Matt Riordan, her golden-haired stranger, her friend, her lover, her betrayer! Oh, dear God, how could she have been so wrong about him after having given him her body, her heart, and her soul! When he had made love to her she had been so positive that he'd had genuine feelings for her. So was she unjustly accusing him now?

"Riordan would like to help you," Welch said, "but I've got him tied to a cedar tree and he'd be hard-pressed to get loose. You know, I think he must care for you. He promised to kill me if I touched you."

Sky swallowed hard, the pain in her heart growing in leaps and bounds of confusion. If only she could talk to Matt in private, then maybe . . . but she'd had her chance the night in the shed and she had tossed it away. Second chances, she knew, were elusive things that came along very seldom.

She glanced away furtively to the darkness, wishing some avenue of escape would present itself.

"Thinking of running?" Welch inquired derisively. "Well, don't, because if you do I'll fire a shot, as I said, and Arnold will kill Riordan."

"You keep threatening me with Riordan's death." She curled her lips disdainfully, hoping to conceal her true feelings from him so that he couldn't use them against her any more than he already had. "Do you honestly think I would care if you killed him after he tricked me? Unless it's you that's lying and not him. Which is it, Welch?"

Welch's mocking smile hardened. He aimed the gun at her heart. "You'd really like to know, wouldn't you? Well, I'm just going to let you keep on guessing. Now, take the buckskins off. You and I have an old score that needs settling."

For some reason she had a feeling he wanted to kill her even more than he wanted to rape her. Would he let his lust cloud his vision and forget that Glassman wanted both her and Matt back in Long Moon Valley? Alive? Would she die here in these lonely hills so far from home?

She reached for the leather string at her waist. She was cornered and there was no way out. The pants fell easily to her ankles, revealing the length of her legs. An evil flame leaped into Welch's eyes.

"The top now," he said. "Take it off."

Her anger mounted. She wanted to fight. If it was only her life at stake, she *would* fight. And she would die fighting. But no matter how Matt had betrayed her, and for whatever reasons, she still loved him too much to want to see his life end because of her!

She took the buckskin blouse off and let it fall to the ground. Losing patience with her slowness, Welch grabbed her around the waist and dragged her down to the ground. With one hand he held both of her wrists in a painful vise over her head. In one swift movement with his free hand, he ripped her camisole off, baring her breasts to the cool night air and his demented intentions. Suddenly a voice boomed out of the night, and the click of a gun's hammer froze his movements.

"It can wait, Governor," Balkin said. "This isn't the time nor the place."

Welch didn't move from her. Ignoring Balkin, he roughly pawed her breasts. "Can't think of a better time — or place. Why don't you join me, Balkin? She's a wildcat and I could use you to help hold her down. You can get your share, too. I'll bet it's been a while since you had a woman. Think about it. It's here for the taking. Nice, too."

"I like my women willing, Governor. Besides, you'd be wise to wait until you're at Glassman's ranch. You try something like that out here and she's likely to get away, just like she did before."

"She won't, with you and Arnold helping me."

"Not necessarily. When you had me and Arnold over in the Winds looking for her, we heard some pretty scary stories. I guess I never did tell you what the Shoshoni say about her, did I? Well, they call her the Woman of the Wind. They think she's a ghost. Why, I wouldn't be surprised if she turns into a white vapor and just disappears. The Indians have witches, too, Governor. Did you know that? Those witches have great powers and they can change their forms. What if you got your cock in her and she turned into a panther? Personally, I wouldn't want to take the chance."

"Shut up, Balkin, and come and help me."

"I won't do it, Governor. It's not my sort of game."

Welch angrily got up from Sky and, still holding her wrists, yanked her to her feet. She was helpless to cover herself, but Balkin kept his eyes trained on

Welch, politely saving her any more humiliation.

"Get the hell out of here Balkin before I kill you," Welch commanded.

"You'd be wise not to kill me either, Governor. You need me to get these two back to Lander. Glassman wouldn't be happy if you showed up empty-handed again."

Welch remembered all too well how, seven years ago, Rusty Glassman had found him on the side of that mountain, shot in the side, and the McClellan girl gone. For a while Glassman had held a gun to Welch's head and threatened to finish him off for being so stupid as to let her get the jump on him. Finally, though, Rusty had relented and taken him to a doctor. Made up a lie about him having a hunting accident.

Rusty had since turned into an even harder and more bitter man than he'd been before. And it was all because of the McClellan bitch. No, Rusty wouldn't need an excuse to put a bullet in anybody that messed up his plans for her a second time. He had nothing to lose, one way or the other. Rusty didn't have dreams anymore, and it was because of what had happened that fateful day on the McClellan ranch. Rusty wanted his revenge, and he wouldn't be happy if he didn't get it. Maybe Balkin was right. Maybe it *could* wait. The bastard had come along and spoiled everything anyway. He couldn't have taken her now if he'd tried.

"All right, Balkin. Maybe you're right this time. Put away your gun and we'll go back to camp."

"If it's all the same to you, Governor, I'd rather you put your gun away first."

Welch chuckled, once again calm and in charge even slightly amused. He dropped his gun in his holster. "So you don't trust me? Well, I guess a man stays alive a lot longer if he doesn't trust anyone. Just remember who's putting money in your pockets, Balkin. Who's buying your whiskey and paying for your *willing* women."

Balkin lowered his gun but didn't holster it. "I won't forget, Governor. I've got a job to do here, and I intend to see it done. I think you're just not using good judgment on this matter. I can see why you'd like that woman. She's right pretty. But it can wait."

Welch conceded with a smile, as if he'd been mildly corrected over something that was totally inconsequential. Once again he had his smiling politician's face back in place. He turned to Sky. "Spend a few days in hopeful anticipation of what you and I are going to share, Miss McClellan. You might just find yourself looking forward to it."

He returned to camp, never looking back to see if they were following. When Welch was back by the fire, Balkin turned a grim, narrow gaze to Sky. She was by now clutching her buckskins to her exposed body.

"Thank you," she whispered, her heart still pounding so violently she could barely breathe.

"Don't thank me yet, Miss McClellan. I won't be able to stop him when he gets to Glassman's."

In forest shadows they bare their fangs,
Those crimson Wolves of Death.

Chapter Twenty

That night and the nights to follow, the guards took turns at duty. When they finally reached Lander, they bypassed the town and rode directly for Long Moon Valley. By the time they reached it, the sun had set.

In seven years the valley hadn't changed much except that Rusty Glassman's ranch was vacant and showing signs of neglect since he'd left it to live at the McClellan place.

"How can he live in my father's house after what he did there?" Sky demanded of Welch. "After he had Monty killed there?"

Welch's lips lifted in amusement. "Sentimentality doesn't control everyone, Miss McClellan. You see, Rusty was originally going to give his homestead to Monty when he moved onto your father's ranch. If anything, his own ranch reminds him too much of his son and what he lost."

"It sounds more like he chooses to live there because it feeds his hatred and his need for revenge," she remarked dryly.

It was almost too much for her to believe that Glassman had been hiding behind a facade all those years she had known him. She'd never really liked Rusty Glassman because he'd treated her rudely but she had never suspected him of being a rustler and a murderer. Never suspected he was plotting to kill her father.

They rode deeper into the valley, and darkness settled over them. A three-quarter moon lit the way, its white light stretching the length of the valley, unhindered by hill or tree. Silver ghost shadows flirted along the edges of the wooded valley, but deeper in the wooded area remained a darkly mysterious realm where neither moonlight nor starlight could penetrate.

They rode in silence now, their horses' hooves making the only sound in the grassy meadow. Sky noticed the guards and Welch, even Matt, appeared edgy. They kept their eyes vigilantly roaming the tree-lined perimeters of the valley as if they expected an attack from an unseen and unknown enemy.

Sky had seen the valley like this on many nights in her youth, and while it had always seemed mysterious and ghostly to a child with a vivid imagination, she had to admit reluctantly that tonight even she still felt that "something" watching from the shadows. It was much too easy to imagine movement in the play of light and dark. Perhaps it was the *NunumBi* scurrying along in the trees, following them. She had never believed in the *NunumBi,* the little people of Indian legend. It was said they were pygmies of evil disposition who dwelled in the mountains and brought destruction to men foolish enough to wander outside their tipis at night.

But something *was* here, if only in memory or imagination. Maybe ghosts truly did haunt Long Moon Valley, the spirits of those she had loved and lost here who still roamed aimlessly, looking for peace, possibly even looking for her. The Indian belief was that, if a person's body was mutilated upon death, his or her spirit would be unable to find the Star Road and would forever wander, troubled and lost, over Mother Earth. And Sky had no idea what Welsh and Glassman had done to the bodies of her family after she'd fled the scene.

The house she had grown up in finally came into view. Even with the kerosene lamps casting soft, warm light to the windows of the first floor, the log dwelling seemed strangely empty. It was much quieter than it had ever been in her youth with Jarod and Nathan, Bliss and herself, racing around it, playing games, laughing and singing or squabbling over silly things. Even at night in those bygone days, the ranch had always seemed alive with movement until the last person had turned out the last lamp and retired to bed. Tonight it looked as haunted as the valley that stretched eerily silver-white before it.

She had always wanted to return home, to find that nothing had changed and that she had dreamed all the sorrow. And she *had* returned once. She had brought Esup with her. He must have felt the pain she felt because he had laid his head on her lap and whined nearly the entire time. They had sat in the trees on the edge of the forest and watched the men at work and she had imagined that nothing had changed. But she had never returned a second time because to do so would have continued to erode the dream until she would have been forced to face the naked truth.

She felt tears burning the back of her eyes, and even though she felt as if she would choke, she forced them back inside. She had locked them inside all these years, not wanting to accept the fact that her family was gone. She made herself believe that if she never mourned for them then they weren't truly gone.

But they were. And she would weep for them now, except that she was too proud to do so in front of her captors.

As they drew nearer, voices from the bunkhouse reached their ears. The good memories faded and the horrible ones returned: the gunshots, the blood; the empty faces of her father and brothers and Monty; Bliss's dull eyes, Mama's last words.

Run, Sky! Run!

She had come full circle back to this house, back to death. She had delayed it, but only for a while. Might she not have been better off to have died then with her family? She could say she had gained something from those seven years she'd spent alone. She had acquired wisdom and maturity; she

364

had learned tolerance and survival. And she had known the uplifting hope of love even if it had dealt her an ugly hand in the end.

She glanced at Matt, riding by her side. He was watching the guards and Welch rather than the ghost shadows of Long Moon Valley. She knew he was looking for an opportunity to escape, but they were here now and the opportunity had never come. With all the men on the ranch, the chances were slimmer than ever before.

They rode into the yard and past the bunkhouse. The hired men were apparently so engrossed in their card game that they didn't hear the quiet approach of the horses. There were no dogs to bark and announce their arrival. They stopped at the hitching rail in front of the house. Arnold hauled them off their horses and prodded them up the wooden steps onto the porch at gun point. Matt hung back, and she wondered if he saw the house as the final trap, just as he had once envisioned the cave.

Welch stopped on the step next to him and without warning backhanded him across the face, a sound that cracked like a whip in the quiet night. "What's your problem, Riordan? Do you need a little nudging?"

Matt tasted blood in his mouth, but he spit it out, the glob landing on Welch's boot. "No, I was just enjoying the crisp night air. You lead the way and I'll follow."

Welch lifted a hand as if to strike him again, but suddenly changed his mind. He strode onto the porch and into the house, not bothering to knock. The captives and their guards obediently followed.

The first night Matt had come to Long Moon Valley while standing in the darkness of the house's porch, he'd been unnerved by Glassman's uncanny resemblance to Bailey Loring. And now, once again, the breath went out of his chest as if someone had landed a punch to his stomach. Sky had seen her ghosts in Cameron Welch, now Matt was seeing his in Rusty Glassman.

The rancher rose from his easy chair, setting aside the book he'd been reading. His hard, squinting eyes scanned the men and came to rest on Matt. "I see you've changed, Riordan. You look more the man now than you did when you raped my daughter."

Sky gasped, looking with disbelief from Matt to Glassman.

Matt remained outwardly calm, desperately trying to pull that calmness inward. But at the sight of Bailey Loring, Jr. all hope of an escape for him and Sky vanished.

"Elizabeth was a whore," he replied simply, hiding any telltale trace of shock or fear. "You didn't know that did you, Loring? Well, I didn't either back then. I was young and foolish and I thought she loved me. I thought that was why she sweet-talked me into her bed so many times."

Loring, alias Rusty Glassman, strode across the room and with no warning landed a fist to Matt's jaw, sending him staggering back against the wall. With his hands still tied, there was nothing Matt could do to avoid or block the blow. Sky instinctively tried to come to his aid but Balkin held her back. Loring grabbed him by the shirtfront and was ready to put another fist to his face when Welch pulled him off.

"I know how you feel, Rusty, but keep him coherent enough that he can ride."

Loring reluctantly obeyed his partner and reined in his rage. He released Matt with a vindictive shove. "I've waited a long time for this moment," he said to no one in particular but as way of explanation for his actions.

Matt got to his feet. He tasted blood on his lip from yet another, deeper cut, but he couldn't wipe it off. He saw Sky's concern, and a look in her eyes that he had seen there before when they had made love. Hope fluttered inside him. Maybe her heart would find the truth before their final moments.

"Where is Elizabeth anyway, *Red?*" His curling lip revealed his full contempt for the man.

"I go by the name of Rusty Glassman now," Loring snapped. "You'd be wise to remember that."

"It doesn't much matter," Matt replied. "I'll be dead soon, so I'll just call you Red. Elizabeth told me how much you hated it. You wanted to be called by your real name which, if I remember right, was Bailey, Jr. But you got stuck with your little nickname from the very day you were born and just couldn't seem to shake it."

"Don't mention Elizabeth's name again to me,

you bastard. I don't want to hear how you tricked her and then betrayed her."

Matt was aware of the confused emotions flying over Sky's face. All this talk of rape and betrayal would do nothing to improve her present opinion of him. If only he could take her in his arms and convince her not to believe Loring's accusations.

But those, coupled with Welch's . . . well, what chance would he ever have now of her believing in his innocence?

"Is that what she told you?" he replied. "What a little storyteller she was. I only thought she was that creative in bed. Where is she anyway? Did you kill her like you killed your son?"

Loring lunged for him, ready to tear him apart, but Welch pulled him back and held him. "Cool down, Rusty. Watch him. He's probably trying to cause a ruckus so he can make a break for it."

Loring was fighting to hold on to his temper. Through clenched teeth he said, "Elizabeth's back east in Pennsylvania. She's married to a decent man, not a worthless drifter like you were. And she has a family. Thankfully her husband never found out what you did to her."

"Yeah, me and a dozen others."

"Damn you!" Loring lunged at him again, but again Welch pulled him back.

Matt Riordan didn't care about Elizabeth anymore. What he really cared about was buying some time for him and Sky, and he needed to have some information. He needed to know if those boys in

368

the bunkhouse would help them or if they were part of Loring's gang.

"Why don't you tell me the rest of the story, Loring. I'd really like to know why you came to Wyoming and changed your name. Couldn't you hold your head up anymore in Texas? And who are those men roaming around the mountains? Are they still up there? Or are they out in the bunkhouse ready to come in at your signal and help you kill us?"

Loring finally shrugged Welch off and went to a sideboard. He poured shots of whiskey for himself and the governor. "The men in the mountains were hired to find the McClellan woman," he replied. "They could have had you on any number of occasions, Riordan, but I told them to hang back and maybe you'd lead them right to her. Then I'd have you both. But you vanished, too, and we figured you'd either given up or died. Until I got the telegram from Cameron I didn't know you'd slipped out of the mountains without my riders knowing."

"Are they still up there?"

"Why do you want to know, Riordan? You're dead one way or the other."

Matt shrugged. "I guess that's why I wanted to know. A dying man has a right to satisfy his curiosity and get all his questions answered."

Loring downed a whiskey and poured himself another. From the looks of his puffy, near-purple pallor he'd done a lot of drinking lately. "Yeah, they're still up there, Riordan. I just got the telegram from Cameron and didn't have time to call them back in, but we don't need them to kill you."

"Why did you leave Texas?"

"That's a stupid damn question and you know the answer to it! Your testimony not only destroyed my father but destroyed any hopes I had of keeping the ranch. People believed you when you claimed I was involved."

"You were."

"You couldn't prove it."

"Go on with your story, Loring. Let's not rehash old events."

Loring glared at him and downed another whiskey. He was rapidly losing control. "I was put out of business because people wouldn't buy my cattle or sell me theirs," he said bitterly. "I had no choice but to leave everything my father and I had built and drive my herd up here. I changed my name. We all changed our names. Except Elizabeth, and she had already married and gone."

Loring turned to Sky. His hatred for her filled him, clear to the marrow of his bones, and appeared to be slowly eating him alive. He took a step toward her and she took one back, only to be halted in her retreat by Balkin standing guard behind her.

"I'll bet you didn't know that Monty's real name was Samuel, did you?" Loring said to her.

Suddenly Matt remembered the red-haired Loring boy from Texas. He'd almost forgotten about Samuel, Elizabeth's little brother. He'd hung around the cowboys a lot, learning both the good and the bad from them, but he'd been a likeable

370

kid, a good kid. It was something Matt had found hard to believe since he'd come from such rotten stock. But Matt hadn't seen much of Loring's wife so maybe the kid's redeeming qualities had come from her.

"There were already quite a few people in the valley," Loring continued his story, "and McClellan had most of the land and all of the control. He'd been here the longest, you see. Cameron and I became financial partners and decided to do something about it. We wanted Long Moon Valley for ourselves. Cameron stayed in Cheyenne and made his plans to run the territory and thus help our success even further. He and McClellan only knew each other in passing. But I knew McClellan well, and I knew he would never throw in with us, regardless if it meant he could become richer and more powerful than he was. He was too ethical, and as straight as a damned arrow. He was a loner, too. He didn't want to work with anybody for any reason. But after a while he became suspicious of what was going on in the valley. He started doing his own investigating and he tried hard to hire Pinkerton detectives to come in and work undercover. We knew we were going to have to kill him."

"But why kill his entire family?" Matt asked. "What did you gain by that? I'm sure Mrs. McClellan would have sold the ranch to you for the right price."

Loring's lips thinned. His face became an even darker shade of purple. He paced the floor relentlessly now. "That halfbreed bitch would have bled us for more than this place could ever be worth. We figured she knew everything McClellan did anyway. But that wasn't all of it. No, McClellan wasn't the only one we wanted dead."

Loring's gaze shifted slowly to Sky. He sauntered over to her, lifted her chin roughly, and pressed her head back cruelly as far as it would go. She had no choice but to look at him.

"I wanted McClellan's daughter dead. *This* daughter."

"Leave her alone, Loring," Matt warned.

Loring was amused by Matt's attempt to protect her. "You don't have much to say about it, Riordan, not in your present situation."

"Why did you want her dead?" Matt asked, not only grasping for answers, but time for Sky. Loring appeared to be losing control.

"Why? Because Monty wanted to marry her. *Her*—a stinking breed! Monty wasn't content just to bed her, even though I told him that if he did it a few times he'd lose interest in her. No—he wanted to *marry* her. I tried everything I could to put some sense into his head, but he wouldn't look at another woman. I couldn't let that happen. Killing her was the only way to make sure it didn't happen."

Matt saw the color vanish from Sky's face. She staggered back a step before Balkin caught her. He was afraid she might faint from the cruel shock of the truth. His heart began to thud violently as Loring pulled his revolver. Welch leaped up, stalked across the short distance and grabbed Loring's gun

372

hand. "For Christ's sake, man, not here in the house. The men in the bunkhouse are only hired help. You don't want them to come running. Besides, we had a deal. I get her before she dies. She damned near killed me once and I want to make her pay for that."

Loring's jaw clenched and unclenched, as did his big fist that held the revolver to Sky's throat. "Yes, I had almost forgotten that you seem to have a penchant for her that's about as repulsive as what my son felt for her. There must be something about these breeds that make some men lose their better judgment."

At last he put the gun away and Matt was able to breathe again. Welch reluctantly returned to his chair, keeping his eye trained on his partner. Loring continued to stand directly in front of Sky, and his steely eyes remained on her during the entire recitation that followed.

"The day we got here everything would have gone fine," he said, "except that *she* wasn't here. We threatened all the others, but they wouldn't tell us where she was. Monty wouldn't even tell me. So I started killing them, one by one, and still they wouldn't tell me where this bitch was! I even had to let Cameron kill Monty because Monty said he'd turn me over to the law. He thought I'd gone insane."

He circled Sky's throat with his hand and backed her up against Balkin. "And all because of you," he said vehemently. "You stinking Shoshoni bitch! Did you know that because of Monty's death my wife left me? She didn't know who killed him, but she was beside herself with grief. Even though she wouldn't say it, I knew she blamed me and the ranch and us having to come to Wyoming. So she went back East to be with Elizabeth and she died there.

"I've lost everyone because of you," he said. "And you're going to pay dearly for it all before my men and I are through with you. What we did to your mother and sister is nothing compared to what we're going to do to you."

He let go of her with a shove that sent her sideways and almost to her knees, but Balkin caught her, breaking her fall. Matt saw the silent burden of truth and pain in her eyes and the denial that she was to blame for it all. He wanted to go to her, to comfort her, but Loring strode over to him, transferring his rage.

"I'm sure you're beginning to see how you got involved in all this, Riordan. I swore I'd get you someday for putting my dad away, and then we heard that this bitch had been seen in the mountains. Oh, the Indians claimed it was her ghost, but we sure as hell didn't believe that. Cameron and I decided we'd better find her and silence her, once and for all. I knew you had joined up with Pinkerton after you had my dad hung. I'm the one who requested you for this case, Riordan. I figured it would be a good way to kill two birds with one stone. And you were such an unsuspecting fool. You blundered right into the trap. You thought Cameron was on the up and up. You never suspected a thing."

He turned to the two guards. "Load him back up on his horse, boys. We'll head into the high country where nobody will see us. And Welch, while we're gone, have your fun with the breed, because when I come back, Miss Sky McClellan is finally going to die."

Is it Death?
Or only the Ghost of Death?

Chapter Twenty-one

Loring tried to shove Matt out the door, but Matt whirled on him and planted a booted foot to his knee. The rancher fell to the floor, writhing in pain. Arnold and Balkin rushed to restrain Matt but he fended them off for several seconds with his feet before they finally overpowered him. While Balkin held him, Arnold laid several hard punches to his stomach.

"Welch, call them off!" Sky demanded.

The governor seemed to enjoy the gruesome spectacle, but he finally responded to Sky's command in a dry, indifferent voice. "All right, boys. That's probably enough for now. You can take care of him later."

Matt shook free of Balkin's loosened grip and lifted his gaze to Sky. Fear was reflected sharply in the deep brown pools of her eyes. She reminded him of a doe bravely facing the hunter's rifle when

376

she has run as far as she can run. He regretted that they should both come to this vile end when they had left the mountains with so much hope.

"Don't believe what Welch told you," he said softly. "I would never betray you, Red Sky."

Perhaps Sky merely wanted to believe, but she looked for sincerity in his eyes and saw it. She saw love there, too. Love that lifted her heart from the dark place it had fallen and into the sunlight where, for a few splendid moments, it sang like a little golden finch.

She went to him, wishing she could put her arms around him, and feel his lips on hers one last time, wishing she could take back the hurtful things she had said on the journey here. But all she managed to say was, "I'm sorry," and yet he seemed to understand it all in those two words.

"Don't be troubled, *nehaynzeh*," she murmured. "We'll meet again . . . in the shadow of the eagles."

Loring came to his feet, grimacing with pain. His eyes were filled with murderous intent. "The only place you two are going to meet is in the grave. Arnold, get Riordan on his horse. We're taking him to the mountains where we'll have our privacy and no interference. And when we're done with him the wolves can have him and nobody will be able to connect us to his death. Balkin, you stay here to help Welch with the McClellan woman."

They shoved Matt out the door. Silence descended on the room. The only sound was the clock over the mantel, ticking away her life and Matt's. Welch didn't move a muscle, just stared at her with evil building in his light blue eyes. He continued to do so until the sound of galloping hooves faded away and Loring, Matt, and Arnold were gone.

He then drew his revolver and pressed the muzzle of it between her breasts. To say she was not afraid would be a lie, but her fear for Matt and what they would do to him was even greater. She gave Welch only quiet insolence as he grabbed her arm and shoved her forward, ahead of him up the stairs. From over his shoulder he said to Balkin. "I'll need you to tie her up. Come on. And no excuses this time or I'll kill you."

Welch picked up a hurricane lamp from off a small table near the sofa to light the dark staircase. Sky walked the distance of the room and started her journey's end to the second floor.

In a way, it was like the last time she had climbed these stairs. She was walking toward death, only this time it would be her own. She did not know what to expect of death, even though she had come close to it on several occasions. She wondered if she would endure a great deal of Welch's torture, or if she would die quickly. But she was a strong woman in both body and spirit. Therefore she feared death even more because she knew it would be slow in coming.

Loring didn't leave the ranch without first riding over to the barn to pick up a branding iron, which he tied to his saddle horn.

He swung into the saddle and adjusted the reins in his big hands. In those moments, he looked so much like his father that they could have stepped back in time and traded places. But he'd had a bit too much whiskey, a mistake Bailey would never have made. Matt suspected Loring had been drinking even before they'd arrived. Maybe he would slip up. Once was all it would take for Matt to make his break.

"Dad and I might not have succeeded in killing you in Texas, Riordan," Loring said, giving him a hard, calculated stare. "But you won't survive this time. I made a promise a long time ago to myself that someday you'd die for what you did to us."

"Yeah, I believe you said that before, Loring."

Loring ignored Matt's cockiness and led the way into the mountains on a lope. He seemed to be in an incredible hurry to get on with the business at hand. It was only minutes before they were away from the ranch, out of the valley, and traversing the first lift of the mountains. Loring slowed his horse to a trot, and finally to a walk when the path narrowed and became increasingly treacherous. The trail they took was partially hidden by trees, partially lit by the moon. Matt rode with his hands still behind his back. Loring led Soldier, and Arnold brought up the rear. The climb became progressively steeper and harder on the horses as they wound their way deeper into the pines where the darkness became more complete.

Matt considered his situation, but was more worried about Sky than himself. Time was running out for her, if it hadn't already. It all depended on Welch and how much he wanted to toy with her before he killed her. Perhaps it was that part that enraged him the most, knowing that at this very moment Welch was taking his pleasure with her, wounding her in a way that no amount of love or understanding could ever fully heal.

As for himself, he'd rather die by a bullet than face the heat of that iron again. Loring was sadistic and always had been. He had years and years of accumulated anger that could now be avenged, and he certainly wouldn't fall short of his promise to do it. Matt knew that nothing he could possibly say would make any difference either. Loring felt that he and his father had never done anything wrong. He felt that *they* were the victims simply because they'd been caught in their lawlessness. All of his misfortune, even the death of his son and the abandonment of his wife, he would blame on someone else.

In the faint moonlight filtering through the heavy timber, Matt was able to make out a steep, rocky embankment to his left that dropped off into another stand of thick pines which were old and big. If he could escape to the darkness of the timber, he might be able to elude his captors.

"You headed any place special, Red?" Matt asked sardonically, knowing how Loring hated the sobriquet. "Or are you just out to show me a tour of the mountain?"

"You don't think I'd tell you, do you, Riordan? You might try to make a break."

"Wouldn't do me much good now, would it?"

"Shut your goddamned mouth, Riordan."

"Might as well shoot it off as much as I can. After all, it's going to be my last chance."

Their conversation was temporarily interrupted

by the distant, mournful howl of a timber wolf. The sound split the peace of the night, but it was only one wolf and no answering call came.

"Sounds like a mighty lonesome bastard, doesn't he?" Matt commented. Then without warning, he threw his head back and released an ear-splitting imitation of the wolf's howl. Both men were so startled they yanked their guns from their holsters and whirled toward him. Loring trotted his mount back to Matt and stopped alongside him. He backhanded Matt across the face, but luckily it wasn't with the revolver.

"Shut your goddamned mouth, Riordan. I already warned you once. I won't again."

Matt's lips curled derisively. "I was just answering the poor bastard. He sounded like he'd lost his best friend. Thought I'd let him know he isn't alone."

"Do it again and I'll kill you."

"What? And deprive yourself of the fun you're going to have seeing me suffer at the end of that branding iron? Come on, Loring. I don't think you'll shoot me. That's too damn easy and not nearly satisfying enough for a crazy bastard such as yourself."

Just for the hell of it, Matt let out another long-throated howl. He saw Loring's fist coming at him but he dodged it, and it barely clipped his chin.

He let out another burst of short, little howls, more like coyote yips this time, mocking Loring, amused by the big man's discomfiture. "Why don't you just gag me, Loring. I'm feeling the call of the wild and I can't seem to stop myself."

The real wolf howled again, as if in reply, and it sounded closer, much closer. But sound could be elusive in the night and in these mountains. It could travel far, or it could be lost completely.

He looked up into Loring's threatening eyes and challenged him to take action.

Loring dropped his gun back into his holster. "Gag the bastard, Arnold. I've heard enough out of him."

Arnold hoisted his bulk from the saddle with obvious effort and then fumbled with the knot on his bandana.

Matt continued to talk, so blithely that one would almost think they were on a Sunday afternoon pleasure ride with a picnic waiting at the end. "Old Arnold here and Balkin must have been in on that raid at the McClellan ranch with you — and all the other murders, too," he said. "Where are the rest of the boys who so bravely helped you kill the women and children?"

Matt hoped if he talked incessantly he'd distract Loring from other things — namely a plan of escape he'd been working on since they'd left the ranch.

Loring didn't look at him; he was more interested in the distance they still had to travel. He turned his head enough so his voice would carry over his shoulder. "Arnold and Balkin weren't with me and Welch back then. As for the others, they're all dead, Riordan. They got to where they couldn't be trusted. Course that half-breed bitch back at the house killed one of them. Buried a hunting knife in his back clear up to the hilt."

"Yeah, you've got to watch out for those Indians," Matt said flippantly. "You just never know when they might be sneaking up on you. You should have seen the hard time I had finding that woman. She was like a ghost. I swear, I thought she *was* one at first, and even after all this time, I still have my doubts. Why, I wouldn't be surprised if she up and appeared right here in the path before us.

"And she's got friends, too. Indian friends. One is an old medicine man who seems to have a sixth sense when she gets into trouble. He shot me from ambush and then left me to die. And then there's the young buck that's sweet on her. He has a knife sharper than a straight-edge razor. Carved my chest all to hell with it. I had to sneak her out of the mountains so they wouldn't find out what I'd done."

"Shut up, Riordan."

Matt shrugged. "Just thought you ought to know that those two might be out here somewhere . . . waiting."

Loring shifted uneasily in the saddle, his head moved from side to side as he suddenly became interested in the dark terrain on either side of him and not just on the path ahead. "Hurry up, Arnold. For Christ's sake, am I going to have to gag him myself?"

Arnold finally got the bandana off his fat neck. He stepped up to Matt. "You're gonna have to get down, Riordan, so I can put this gag on you."

Matt glanced at Loring one more time. He was still searching the darkness — more intently now. Was he afraid of Indians — or ghosts?

He grinned down at Arnold. "Why certainly, Arnold, old boy. Anything you say. Wouldn't want to inconvenience you and make you have to lift those heavy arms of yours up over your head. It might put undue stress on you."

Matt swung his right leg over the saddle horn, easily clearing the horse's neck. But in that same movement, throwing Arnold completely off guard, he drew both feet back swift and deadly and kicked the obese man squarely in the face. Blood shot from Arnold's nose. He stumbled backward, crying out in surprise and pain.

Matt leaped the rest of the way off the horse, landing on both feet. He took one jump from the path and disappeared down the rocky incline into the darkness before Loring caught a glimpse of him.

Sky entered the room on the outstretched arm of frail lantern light. She had expected to see and hear the same things that she had seen and heard the last time she had been here. But this time there were no birds singing outside the open window. No golden streams of sunlight coming in through the white curtains and creating a false illusion of peace.

All the secrets of this room were tucked away, unseen. A stranger would have no way of knowing, simply by looking at this room, of the horrors that had once taken place here. A stranger could sleep in this room and never know that people had been viciously murdered here.

Sky's mind worked frantically as she thought of

how she could make an escape. Balkin closed the door behind them and locked it. Welch went to the bed and set the kerosene lamp on the small round pedestal table that was covered with a white, lacy cloth. All the furniture in the room was new. None of it had belonged to her parents. Nothing was the same anymore. All she had were her memories.

A slight breeze lifted the edges of the curtains, revealing the darkness beyond. Welch saw her interest in the open window. He stalked to it, slammed it shut, latched it, and pulled down the shade. Then he came toward her. She tried to step away from him, but there was no place to go. Balkin stood by the locked door, blocking any hope of escape. Would he help her a second time? Nothing in his eyes gave her a clue to his thoughts, but she saw the rigid set to his jaw and knew he didn't approve of what Welch was doing.

Welch backed her up against the wall and leaned into her with the full length of his big, suffocating body. He slid his hand beneath the doeskin blouse and fondled her breasts. She wanted to fight him, to scream and shove him away, but there was nothing she could do with her hands tied. She tried to kick at him, but he only laughed and side-stepped her attempt.

He turned her around abruptly and pushed her face against the wall. "Balkin, untie her."

Balkin searched for his pocket knife, found it, cut through the rope, then stoically returned to his post by the door.

Welch grabbed her by the shoulder, yanked her around, and pushed her hard. Stumbling, she fell across the bed. He licked his lips as his gaze slid over her ripe, young body. "Take the buckskins off," he demanded. "Make it snappy, and don't try anything funny."

She wished for a savior, a miracle. But the end had come and she couldn't stop it. "You won't get away with this," she said fiercely. "Some day you'll get caught and you'll hang."

"I've gotten away with a lot over the last decade, Miss McClellan. I'm the power in this territory, in case you've forgotten. I own a lot of people. Those I don't own, I buy—or kill."

"If Matt gets away, he'll kill you himself."

"Riordan won't get away. And neither will you." He waved the gun at her, pressing her for action. "Now, do as I told you."

Sky was suddenly thankful for small things. Thankful she'd spent the years with her family and had known their love. Thankful even for the years in the cave and her association with Many Claws, Esup, and with the creatures of the mountains. Most of all, she was thankful that Matt Riordan had showed her what love was all about, because somehow it made it easier to face what was ahead, knowing Welch's perversity was the exception and not the rule. But what else would he do to her? What cruel and demented tortures would he invent to make her suffer? Wasn't it enough of a torture to know she was to blame for her family's being murdered?

"I can't let you do this, Governor. Drop your gun or I'll shoot you."

Balkin's gruff words and the click of a gun hammer, snapped Sky from her reverie. He was still by the door but his revolver was pointed at Welch's heart.

"It's no way for a woman to be treated," he continued, "and I can't stand by and be part of it."

Welch's upper lip lifted into a sneer. "What do you mean, you can't be part of it? Are you some saint, Balkin? Surely you're not going to be squeamish about a little woman sport? But I guess I should have suspected as much after you came to her defense the first time. I should have killed you right then."

"She doesn't deserve what you're planning—no woman does," Balkin said levelly.

"I've noticed how you look at her. I know you want her, Balkin, but you'll never have her if you don't do it now. She'll never go to your bed willingly, or even out of gratitude for saving her life. All you'll ever get is a thank you."

"Then that's enough, Governor."

"This is incredible, Balkin. You're a hired gun. A man who *kills* for money."

"Call it a moral limitation. Now, drop your gun, Governor. I'm turning you over to the law."

"No, Balkin," Welch said. "I won't surrender to you."

In a split second and with no warning whatsoever, Welch fired at Balkin. The bullet hit its mark and Balkin staggered back against the door. By reflex alone, Balkin returned fire and his aim was as true as Welch's had been. His shot was followed by another and another in rapid succession.

The impact of the bullets threw Welch backward

into the pedestal nightstand, bringing it down on top of him as he hit the floor, dead. The lamp shattered on the hardwood floor and the kerosene spilled out. Fire swelled up, engulfing the cloth table cover, then springing to the trailing edge of the bedspread. The flames reached out for Welch's clothing and caught.

Balkin crumpled to his knees, then fell to his back, clutching the wound in his chest. Sky rushed to his side. The fire was spreading rapidly, leaping up the curtains and spreading out onto the wallpaper, dancing over Welch's body and consuming it.

She tried to lift Balkin and get her shoulder beneath his. "Come on, I'll get you out of here."

"No. Get out . . . help . . . Riordan. You can't . . . help me."

"No, come on, you can make it."

He stared at her for a minute but she saw the light rapidly fading from his eyes and a distant look entering. "Go . . . ," he rasped. "Just go. There's . . . no hope. . . ."

His body went limp in her arms. His eyes stared sightless at the ceiling. She laid him gently to the floor and rose to her feet. The flames were too far out of control now for her to try and fight them. The men from the bunkhouse were already clambering up the porch stairs and would soon find her and the bodies. They might detain her, ask questions, demand explanations, and perhaps not even believe her. She couldn't afford to take that chance. She needed to get to Matt.

She took Balkin's gun and quickly unbuckled his gun belt for the cartridges she might need. With a tug she pulled it out from under him. She hated to treat him with such a lack of respect after he'd saved her life, but she had little choice.

The men from the bunkhouse were downstairs now, shouting their confusion and flinging questions back and forth. The first one started up the stairs.

Sky hurried into the next bedroom, the one that used to be her own. She closed the door swiftly but quietly behind her and went directly to the open window. She slipped through, as easily as a shadow, and jumped, landing like a cat on the porch roof some distance below. From there she jumped to the ground.

She darted up the dark hill behind the burning house. It was the way she had gone the last time she had fled her home. At least this time, no one was following.

Matt heard shouts. Soon gunshots were fired into the ravine behind him. He dodged behind a large pine for cover. He had to wait only a few seconds before he heard dislodged rocks tumbling down the embankment and the two men skidding down after him.

The wolf howled again. This time it was so close it seemed to be in the same canyon with them. It seemed odd that the gunshots hadn't put the animal on the run.

The moonlight couldn't filter through the big, heavy boughs of the ancient pines and it was almost pitch black in the ravine. Loring and Arnold probably wouldn't see him if he stayed put, but they might accidentally stumble onto him in their blind search. He needed more distance to prevent that from happening.

He moved from pine to pine, fading into one dark shadow after another. He felt awkwardly off balance with his hands tied behind his back.

"Hey, boss," came Arnold's voice. "I'll bet he heads straight back to the ranch to help the woman. Why don't we just go back there and wait for him?"

The guard sounded very close, but Matt knew at least a hundred feet separated them.

"I'll get the bastard," Loring declared. "He can't have gone far."

"But I don't like it here," Arnold whined. "You can't see a darn thing."

"What's the matter with you? Did you let Riordan's ghost story scare you?"

"Well . . . I've heard that story about the soul of some Indian woman walking around these mountains. Been going on for seven years, I hear. Who knows, maybe it belongs to McClellan's wife that you killed. The Indians sure believe in it."

"Christ, Arnold. What can a ghost do to you besides scare the piss out of you?"

"Balkin told me those Indians can change into things—animals."

"And do you believe that crap?"

"Well, who knows what those Indians can do. They're just likely to be able to do anything. I don't like it here, boss. It gives me a real bad feeling."

While they talked, Matt moved farther away,

hoping their voices would cushion the sound of his footsteps. He stepped lightly but still cracked several twigs. He knew they were moving again, too, because Arnold sounded like a bull moose coming through the trees on a charge. More than once Loring cussed him and told him to be quiet.

Matt could see them easily enough. He had the advantage of having seen them come down the ridge, but they hadn't been able to see which direction he'd gone. He moved when they moved, always staying to the shadows. He found to his relief that they were going the opposite direction.

While they worked their way deeper into the ravine he worked his way back out, finding that the rocky embankment he'd made his escape on was only an outcropping. Farther on, the ground was once again covered with a thick bed of tall summer grass and could be ascended with very little noise.

Crouching, he worked his way back up the slope to the trail where the horses stood, quietly grazing, making no sound but the occasional pop of a joint or the clink of a bridle ring.

He crept back to the edge of the rocky embankment, knowing he would be silhouetted to those below if he wasn't careful. If he could get back to the ranch, maybe he could get the hired men to help him.

With Soldier's reins in hand, he hurried back down the trail. He wanted to get a distance away before trying to remount, which wouldn't be easy with his hands tied behind his back.

Suddenly a dark form loomed up in the path, blocking his way. Almost simultaneously something hard came down on his head from behind. His horse wheeled away, and he stood for a second, fighting a wave of darkness. But in the end he sank to the ground, unconscious.

Sky stayed on the bluff only long enough to see the hired hands start a bucket brigade to the burning house. But since the fire was in the upper story she knew they would never be able to fight it without more manpower. The destruction of the house was the loss of the last link to her past.

With tears suddenly scalding her face, she turned away and took the trail Loring and Arnold would most likely have taken into the mountains. The trail was used often by the cowboys in their cattle forays and hunting expeditions into the high country. It was also used by game and wild horses, and it had once been beaten down as hard as clay by the busy, happy feet of the McClellan children.

She forced her mind away from the burning house and the memories of her family that had come so vividly alive again. She also forced herself not to dwell on the fact that because of her they had all died. It was a burden too great to bear right now. She would think of it later.

She stopped to listen. She had to allow her breathing to slow and her heart to quit thumping so violently so she could differentiate the small noises of the forest from those made by the interlopers. Not far away, possibly the distance of one or two canyons, she heard the howl of a wolf. Then she heard a second howl, but it sounded more like a human's emulation. It was puzzling, but she hurried on.

As time rushed on and she saw no sign of Matt and Loring, she fearfully began to wonder if they had taken another trail. She'd seen what appeared to be fresh tracks, but she was in such a hurry, and without sufficient light to read them by, she might have been mistaken.

But finally, up ahead, beneath the overhanging boughs of some heavy pines, she caught a glimpse of the flickering flames of a campfire. Cautiously she moved closer until the glow became more distinct and she recognized Loring and Arnold moving about the fire and heard them conversing in low tones.

She moved within thirty feet of the fire and saw Matt staked out on the ground, face-up and spread-eagled. He stirred slightly, as if just coming awake. Arnold was twisting and turning a branding iron in the fire. Loring stood by, pacing and talking.

"He's coming to. Is the iron hot?"

"Ain't quite red hot, boss. Give it a little longer."

"That's just as well. We've got all night. By morning there won't be anything left to his body but burned flesh."

Arnold glanced over at Matt; his tone was clearly apprehensive. "Why not just put a bullet in his head, boss? Would be just as effective. I'd kinda like to get back to the ranch and have a shot at that woman before Welch and Balkin have her all used up or dead."

"Shut up, Arnold. You're with me and you're going to stay with me until I'm finished with Riordan."

"Well, personally, I think branding a man is . . . well . . . kinda sick. Makes my stomach turn. A man's hide ain't nowhere near as thick and tough as a cow's. And to do it all over his body, well . . ."

"I didn't ask for your opinion, Arnold, so keep it to yourself."

Sky's pulse pounded in fear and dread of what Loring had planned for Matt. She had to stop it. But how?

Suddenly she heard something in the brush behind her. A noise so faint it might be a figment of the imagination or nothing more than a breath of wind. She turned. In the pale moonlight barely filtering down through the heavy pines, she thought she saw movement — something white, billowy, ghostlike. The feeling of a presence became stronger and very disturbing. She wasn't sure why, but she thought of her mother, and she felt an odd comforting sensation. But as quickly as the feeling had come, it was gone.

She decided she'd merely imagined it. She turned back to the scene before her, but then to the right of her she heard something more distinct, a definite movement this time. Another white object took shape, but this one had bulk. Her breath caught in her throat as the big wolf moved on silent feet directly toward her. The animal knew no fear. Closer it came without hesitation.

Esup?

Suddenly she sighed with relief. The wolf padded

up to her and licked her face, faintly whining in his delight to see her.

"Sh-h-h-," she hissed, closing her hand around his mouth. He obeyed because she had taught him the command from the time he had been a pup. She wondered why he was so far from the cave. Surely he hadn't followed her and Matt's trail down off the mountain, and then stayed near Long Moon Valley where she had brought him once before? Had instinct possibly told him that a part of her still remained in this place and that she would return here?

Whatever had brought him here, she was glad to see him. With him by her side, she crept closer to the fire. It reminded her of the many times she had done this same thing when Matt had first come to the mountains and she had watched him those many nights out of pure fascination and from a need she hadn't understood then. But those days were over and if she didn't move quickly, the man she loved would die.

The wolf lifted his nose to pick up the scents of the men around the fire. His ears perked forward at the sight of Matt. He seemed to sense the threat to Matt's life and his lips curled back in a silent snarl of disapproval. Red Sky whispered the command to stay for she feared he would bound forward, and she didn't want him to—not yet.

Arnold moved the branding iron around in the fire, stirring up sparks that filtered up through the trees into the star-filled sky.

"I think it's about ready, boss."

Sky lifted Balkin's revolver and cocked the hammer at the same time Arnold broke a stick over his knee to toss on the fire.

Loring removed his hat to wipe away sweat that had collected on his brow. In the reflection of the flickering flames, his hair looked the same color as the fire. He lifted the branding iron up to inspect the intensity of its heat. The brand wasn't the one she had grown up recognizing as Rusty Glassman's. It was the same one that was already imprinted on Matt's back, and it burned white hot against the backdrop of darkness.

He sauntered over to Matt and stared down at him, gloating. Sky's heart began to pound fiercely. She had only one choice. She could not take them both as prisoners. Sure of her decision, and amazingly calm in that moment of action, she rose soundlessly and purposefully to her feet. She aimed her gun at Arnold and barely lifted her voice, pointing to Loring with her other hand.

"Paika, Esup. *Paika."*

The men heard the sound of her voice and whirled toward it. Arnold went for his revolver and Sky pulled the trigger of Balkin's gun. Arnold clutched his chest and fell face forward, barely missing the fire. At the same time, Esup hurtled his great body into the air and came down on Loring. Loring screamed and dropped the iron, automatically trying to protect his face and throat from the wolf's deadly fangs.

Sky gave Esup the command to stop but to remain on guard. The wolf stayed straddle of Loring, his fangs bared and mere inches from the man's throat. Sky then hurried forward, removed

Arnold's hunting knife from his belt scabbard, and sliced through Matt's bonds.

As soon as he was able, Matt pulled her into his arms. "Sky! Thank God you're alive." He buried his face in her long flowing hair and held her tightly. "I was so afraid for you. I wanted to get back to you. I tried. I'm sorry I failed."

She held him tightly, realizing again how wonderful it felt to have him in her arms. "I knew you would try. I never doubted it. Welch is dead, Matt. Balkin tried to help me and they killed each other."

Matt glanced at Esup still guarding his quarry. "I'm glad to see that wolf. But I wonder how he found us."

"I don't know, but he's apparently been searching for me."

"A loyal friend indeed."

"Yes, the best."

"Call the wolf off," Loring said cautiously, never taking his eyes from the animal dripping saliva into his face.

"I'm afraid I can't," Matt replied unsympathetically. "He doesn't obey anybody but Sky."

"Then tell *her* to call him off."

Matt took the gun from Sky and came to his feet. They had beat him up pretty bad after he'd attempted to escape, and he had some difficulty standing upright. His face was bloody and battered; one eye was almost swollen shut.

He moved the few feet to Loring. "Go ahead, Sky. Call the wolf off."

"Wenr, Esup. *Wenr."*

The wolf reluctantly left Loring and went back to

Sky's side, but he didn't take his eyes off Loring. He was ready to attack again at the first sign of aggression.

"Stand up, Loring," Matt commanded.

"You son of a bitch, Riordan."

"That I am, Loring."

Loring glowered at Matt while he picked up the cotton rope that had been around his wrists and tied enough pieces of it together in square knots to make a length about three feet long.

"Did you hear that Welch and Balkin are dead?" Matt asked. "It doesn't look as if anybody's left to come to your rescue, Loring." He turned to Sky. "Get the lariats from Loring's and Arnold's saddles, would you? And tell Esup to stay here."

She obeyed and quickly returned. The wolf sat on his haunches next to Matt, still watching Loring with alert, gleaming eyes.

Matt handed the gun to Sky. "If he tries anything, shoot him."

Even in captivity Loring maintained his arrogance. "Going to turn me over to the law, Riordan? I own Wyoming. Remember that."

"Your dad thought he owned Texas, too, but we found out he didn't. Okay, hands behind your back."

Loring reluctantly obeyed again and Matt tied his hands behind his back with the small cord rope. He then secured one of the lariats over the limb of a large pine tree. It was crude, but it looked an awful lot like a hangman's noose. Loring watched with new fear entering his eyes while Matt walked back to Sky and took the gun.

"What are you doing, Riordan? Every man deserves a trial."

Matt cocked a brow at Loring. "Well, I'll be damned, Loring. I don't believe I got one in Texas when you accused me of raping Elizabeth. I don't believe I got one here in Wyoming either. It doesn't seem to me that trials are in order."

Loring's jaw set harder than usual.

Matt pointed to Loring's horse with his gun. "Get on your horse. I'll help you."

"You can't hang me."

"I can do it as easy as you and your father branded me and left me in the desert to die. I can do it as easy as you and your father rustled thousands of head of cattle and killed more people than you can probably even keep a tally of. Yes, I can do it, Loring, probably easier than you think. Because you're not the only one with a score to settle. Now, get on the horse. My trigger finger is getting heavy."

Loring obeyed, and once in the saddle, Matt led the horse over to the noose and slipped it over Loring's head, tightening it enough to make Loring twist uneasily in the saddle.

"Now, Loring," Matt said, pulling out his little black notebook from his inside pocket. "There might just be a way for you to keep from swinging. You tell me what I want to know and I'll let you go. I'll take you to town and let you face a jury. I'm going to write down your confession and you're going to sign it. It's going to include all your rustling deeds, all the people you've murdered — if you can remember them all — and all your accomplices."

399

Loring's top lip curled contemptuously while Matt scribbled down a testimony on the paper and read it back. Then he lifted the pencil from the paper and said, "Okay, start by telling me everybody that was ever involved with you and Welch's little power play — even the dead ones."

"That slip of paper won't hold water, Riordan. Especially if I tell a jury you made me do it under duress. The law will be on my side and so will the people."

Matt considered his words for a few moments. Finally, he closed the notebook and placed it back in his pocket. "You know, I guess you're absolutely right. Sometimes justice just has to be served without the help of a judge and a jury. The way you tried to serve justice down in Texas, and the way you tried to serve it here. So I'm going to leave you on that horse, and just see how long it will stand there before it gets tired, or thirsty, or hungry."

He took Sky by the arm and they started to walk away.

"Damn you, Riordan. Come back here and let's talk. I'm sure we can work something out. Maybe agree on something — some cattle or a big chunk of Long Moon Valley for the Indian woman."

Matt sauntered back. "You're talking a plea bargain?"

Loring nodded.

"Actually, I'm not in favor of that sort of thing. I was thinking, though, that it's a shame Elizabeth is going to find out just what sort of person you are. She's the only one you have left, isn't she? You know if you fight this, there's going to be a big trial

400

and she'll probably come out to Wyoming to be with you. Then when she and her husband learn the truth, it might appall this good husband of hers so much that he divorces her and kicks her out without anything—even her children. She'll hate you then, and you'll truly be alone. But if you sign a confession, it'll be over, quick and quiet, and maybe she won't have to hear all the sordid details. You could even tell her you'd been railroaded and she'd probably believe you."

Matt reached in his pocket again to extract the notebook and pencil. "Want to reconsider?"

"To hell with you, Riordan," Loring snarled. "I won't sign your stinking confession."

Suddenly the outlaw rancher spurred his horse hard in the flanks. The horse squealed and bolted forward. The rope tightened around the old pine bough, held, and yanked Loring from the saddle.

Matt hurried forward to catch the dangling body, but saw right away that Loring's neck had snapped. He was already dead. Matt took a deep breath and reached out to stop the pendulumlike movement of the body and the eerie squeal of the rope rubbing the limb. He cut the rope and eased the body to the ground.

It wasn't the way he would have preferred it, but justice had been served. And maybe in the end, it had been the best way.

In the Shadow of the Eagles,
So shall we meet.

Chapter Twenty-two

Matt pulled Red Sky into his arms and turned her away from Loring's body. They clung to each other for several moments, giving the comfort each so desperately needed. She placed her head against his chest, and Matt sensed her strength was gone. It was not surprising, considering what they had been through. Now that the danger was over, they would both need some rest. He sat her on a log and joined her, bringing her snugly into his embrace again. Esup collapsed at their feet, head on paws, adjusting his behavior according to theirs. Matt, and he supposed even Esup, listened while she told in greater detail what happened after they'd been separated.

"It's over now, Matt," she whispered at the conclusion of the explanation. "Everything is over."

Matt suddenly felt uneasy. Maybe it was the lifeless tone of her voice or the lack of fire in her body, but it was as if something in her had died along with their tormentors. Whatever it was, a depression was settling over her that went deeper than mere physical and mental exhaustion.

He lifted her chin and made her look at him. He would have felt better to see tears, for that was an emotion, but he saw only a troubling emptiness in the wells of her dark eyes.

"What is it, Sky? What's wrong, *nehaynzeh?*"

He saw a flicker of life at the use of the word they had adopted as their own term of endearment, but then darkness clouded those brown eyes once again, making him think of the dark empty spaces in the night sky that held no stars or light of any kind. And he couldn't help but fear, despite what she'd told him, that Welch had finally had his way with her.

She continued in that voice that was almost monotone. "I'm the only one left," she said.

Long moments passed and she placed her head back against his chest. His heart pumped hard beneath her head, laden with this new concern. He tried to soothe her, stroking her hair and her back, scattering kisses to her forehead. It was natural that she would feel the loss of her family all over again.

Then suddenly she sobbed. "The memories are hard to bear!"

Before he could stop her she had sprung up and sprinted away toward the shelter of the forest that would hide her grief from him and prevent him from doing anything to help ease her pain.

"Come back, Sky!" He started after her. "Talk to me."

She halted in the dark shadows of a big pine. He could barely see her through the covering of night, let alone her expression. But he saw her put out her hand toward him, in a movement that held him back. "I must go now, Matt. Please don't follow."

"Damn it, Sky! You're not still believing that I was in on that with Welch, are you?"

"No. I believe you were innocent, just as I was. But I must go back to the mountains and live alone. To seek my peace. It's the only way for me."

He took another step toward her, but she held out her hand again for him to keep his distance, and he obeyed her wishes. "I don't understand, Sky. Why? I thought you would come with me. I'll get this mess straightened up in town with the sheriff and help him round up the rest of the riders out there still searching for you, and then we can be together. I'll come back to the mountains with you."

"No, I . . . don't want you to. I need to be alone after . . . all that has happened."

"Sky, what happened here was beyond your control or mine. We fought for our lives. There was nothing else we could do. As for Loring being hung—he would have faced the noose sooner or later and he knew it. He preferred to save himself the humiliation."

"You don't see, do you, Matt? I've been the cause of all this death, and all that went before it. From the very beginning, all that has happened was because of *me*. My family *died* because of me.

404

Monty died because of me. Even this" — she indicated the dead bodies — "was because of me. Mama and Daddy's house is burning to the ground right now. Balkin and Welch are dead. All because of me."

"And me," Matt said, angry at her self-reproach. "What happened then, and now, wasn't your fault, any more than what happened in Texas — and now here — was mine. It happened because Loring thought he could control everybody and everything, and he went too far in trying to control his son's life. He even went too far in trying to control Elizabeth's life ten years ago. It happened because of Welch's greed and lust. He was no better, or less to blame, than Loring. You have to live with it, Sky. You can't run away from it. You can't cease to exist because you don't want to face it. You were strong and you survived."

"No, I survived because I ran," she said. "I should have stayed and helped my mother. What is my life worth now, knowing that they all died when it was really me who should have died! God, I wish it *would* have been me!"

"Stop it! Don't talk like that. You saved my life — twice. I love you," he added in a softer tone. "I'll be with you to help you through the hard times. We'll start over together. We'll marry and have children."

Now that he had bared his soul and his intent, even though he had done so with an outward air of confidence, he feared her rejection.

Tears streamed down her face now but her stance warned him — begged him — not to come any closer, not to touch her again, but to leave her alone to deal with her pain the best way she could. She seemed determined not to forgive herself and refused to yield her stubborn stand of self-persecution.

"Oh, Matt," she cried helplessly. "Don't you see? I'm not worthy of your love!"

"That's nonsense, Sky. Don't do this. Don't run away when we need each other the most. It's dangerous for you to go back out there. As far as those men know they're still supposed to kill you. Come back to town with me. I'll get you a room at a hotel and get somebody to watch over you until I get all this straightened out."

"No, I can't return to the town."

"But it's the only safe place."

"I'm safer here in the mountains. In the cave."

"Then I'll join you in a few days."

"No. You must leave forever."

"I won't."

"You must go on with your life. It's the only way for us. You've been a good friend, Matt Riordan. Now, I must tell you good-bye."

She turned on her heel and ran into the woods, vanishing into the darkness. Esup followed. Matt considered following her, too, but he didn't.

A friend? Was that all? Just a friend?

The crisis was over, or would be when he had those riders behind bars. What had gotten into her? They could be together now. After all they'd been through, he was losing her *now*, and because of something he couldn't fully understand. Didn't she know that if she shared her grief with him, that his love would help her conquer it? Her wounds would heal. He knew that, even if she did not believe it, and he would bide his time until she *was* healed.

He had taken the chance from the very beginning that she might never want to return to civilization, let alone return there with him. He had also taken the chance that in the end she would go to Gray Bear when she was out of danger. Who was to say that she still might not, and that this wasn't just her way of telling him she did not love him enough to stay with him? Whatever it was, he had no choice but to let her go if he ever hoped to get her back.

He returned to the bodies of Loring and Arnold. As usual, he had work to do.

Many Claws awoke suddenly. An inner sense told him he wasn't alone in his tipi. His heart began to thud as it always did when he felt the presence of Chilsipee. After seven years it still unnerved him, even though he knew the ghost meant him no harm. Chilsipee was in great anguish and couldn't find peace until she knew Red Sky was not in danger. Many Claws didn't know how he knew all these things, but it was as if Chilsipee could communicate with him and make him understand. He had once told Riordan the ghost belonged to Red Sky, but he had done it only to frighten the detective. Little did Riordan know that the spirit was real and was that of Red Sky's mother.

Slowly, he turned over on his pallet toward the small fire in the center of the tipi. The fire was nearly gone and barely lit the dark enclosure. The ghostly apparition, without a true shape or form, was still visible.

They are dead, she seemed to say.

Who is dead, Chilsipee? He asked without speaking.

The men who killed us are dead.

What of Red Sky, your daughter?

She has returned to the mountains. She is safe.

And Riordan?

He lives.

Then it is over?

Yes, it is over.

The apparition began to fade.

Where are you going, Chilsipee?

I am going home, my friend. Good-bye.

The apparition vanished.

Many Claws sat up and placed a few more sticks of wood on the fire. The flames lifted and pushed back the dark shadows in his lonely dwelling. He stared at the empty spot where Chilsipee had been and he knew she would not return. Justice had been served to the men who had terrorized Long Moon Valley, and Chilsipee would now rest in peace at last.

He rolled to his side and tried to go back to sleep, but found the pleasant dreams he'd been having would not return. He was anxious for dawn to light the mountains of the Sun Father. There was much to be done tomorrow. He must go to Red Sky and plot a course for her future. Surely she would want to leave the mountains now and make a life for herself with Gray Bear.

Yes, first thing in the morning, he would tell Gray Bear the good news.

The bushy-faced telegraph operator named P.T. Jackson swung around in his chair when Matt walked through the door. His perpetually cheerful, chubby face lit up even more than usual. "Ah, Riordan! I have Mrs. Frazer's response to your telegram. It came in the day after you and the posse headed into the mountains. I see you caught that bunch of renegades. Surrender, did they?"

Matt nodded. "Yeah, they didn't have much of a choice. We surrounded their camp while they were asleep and they were taken by surprise."

Jackson rummaged around on his cluttered desk for the message from Elizabeth. Matt's nervousness increased when it looked like he might not find it, but the telegraph operator didn't seem concerned.

Jackson kept talking because it was something he liked to do. "We were sure surprised to hear about old Rusty Glassman and the governor himself being behind those killings and all the rustling going on around here. Of course, it shouldn't have surprised us about Glassman. I don't know of anybody that really liked the conniving SOB. Constantly tried to throw his weight around and, near as I know, he didn't have any genuine friends. But the governor—now that's something else entirely. Makes me wonder what the world is coming to. Ah, here it is! Mrs. Frazer's telegram. At least she didn't take long in answering you. Apparent-

409

ly it wasn't much of a decision for her to make."

Matt didn't comment, just took the slip of paper and read the choppy message. Jackson watched him, waiting for his reaction. Matt kept a straight face through it and when he was finished he folded it in half and tucked it in his vest pocket.

"Would you mind not saying anything about this, Jackson?"

"I'm sworn to secrecy, Riordan. Wouldn't have this job if I couldn't keep my mouth shut. You don't have to worry about anything. I'm just glad to hear that the McClellan girl is still alive."

Matt paused at the door out of politeness, wondering if Jackson would ever let him get away. As for the man being able to keep his mouth shut, Matt truly had his doubts. He liked to talk—a little too much.

"We all just figured she'd died in those mountains," Jackson was saying now. "She must be a hell of a woman to have survived."

"Yes, she is certainly that," Matt said quietly.

For five days he'd done nothing but wonder and worry about her and hope she was all right. He didn't even like to think that she would never want to see him again, so he kept that thought from his mind as much as possible.

"Figure she'll come down out of there now?" Jackson asked.

Matt pulled the door open. "I don't know, but I'll be going up to see."

"Well, I'm sure it'll be an adjustment for her. You'll be back for the trial of those five you brought in?"

"Yes, I have to be."

"Well, good day to you, Riordan. Be seeing you around."

Matt got away before Jackson thought of something else to say. He swung into the saddle and headed on a lope toward the setting sun. He was anxious to see Sky. He'd never been more anxious over anything in his life. But first he had one more piece of unfinished business. If he was lucky, it wouldn't take long.

The sun dropped behind the jagged peaks of the Wind River Mountains, leaving the sagebrush-covered foothills awash in a pink afterglow. Matt slowed Soldier to a walk when they reached the outskirts of the Shoshoni Indian village. Wary of the laughing children and barking dogs, the big gelding obeyed but pranced nervously with his small ears perked forward.

The women of the village worked methodically, engaged in the perpetual chore of preparing what food the government supplied them with. Men lounged about, talking and drinking whiskey, gambling, and growing old and out of shape. Now that they had been relegated to the reservation there was little else for them to do.

Matt pulled rein in front of Many Claws' colorful tipi and stepped to the ground. The tent flap was up, which indicated he could go in without asking permission. He left Soldier's reins trailing, knowing the horse wouldn't wander.

Many Claws was inside, sitting cross-legged in

front of his small fire. His eyes were closed and his weathered old hands rested on his skinny knees.

At the sound of Matt ducking beneath the leather flap, he opened his eyes, but they remained somnolent. He didn't seem surprised by Matt's visit. He lifted a hand and pointed to the spot on the opposite side of the fire. Matt had the odd feeling that he had somehow been summoned by the Indian's thoughts.

"So you have come again, Matt Riordan. Are you once again searching for the Woman of the Wind?"

"No, Many Claws. I know where Red Sky is. I came to tell you the men who killed her family are all dead or in jail. It's over."

"Oos. Red Sky's mother, Chilspiee, came to me last night, and she told me these things. Red Sky can now continue her life in peace. *Tsande.* That is good. And you, Riordan—what do you plan to do?"

Matt stared dubiously at Many Claws, thinking perhaps the old man had lost his mind. "The ghost of Chilspiee?"

The faintest of smiles touched the old man's weathered lips. A vague twinkle lit his black eyes. "It was always her ghost that came to me at night, Riordan. I only told you it was Red Sky to frighten you away. I am happy now, though, that you were not a man to be easily frightened. Now Red Sky can continue her life without fear. I must thank you for that."

Matt decided not to argue with the old man on whether he'd been in communication with a ghost.

412

He had other more important things on his mind. Sky had told him to get on with his life, but he had no intention of doing that without trying one more time to make her understand just how much he loved her.

"The reason I'm here, Many Claws, is to discuss Red Sky's future. Because you are her closest living relative, I've come to tell you that I intend to return to the mountains to claim her as my wife."

Many Claws' face darkened and he shifted uneasily where he sat, as if his old bones might be objecting to the hard earth beneath them. Soon his gnarled fingers lifted and fell on his knees as if moving to a rhythm only he could hear. "Are you confident that Red Sky will consent?"

Matt hesitated, meeting the wise, black eyes that oftentimes seemed to see to the very soul of a person. "No, I'm not sure."

Many Claws considered the response, and his gaze continued to probe Matt's. He had many questions, but voiced none of them. "You should know that I am honored that you have come to me to tell me of your love for Chilsipee's daughter. But you should know that Gray Bear, too, has gone to her dwelling place to take her as his wife. He left this morning. If Red Sky has a choice to make, she must be aware of it before she gives herself to Gray Bear. You should go, Riordan. Before it is too late."

Matt's heart began to thud so violently he suddenly felt short of breath. It was quickly followed by a rush of anger and fear moving over him so swiftly that he felt as if it might consume him all in one painful gulp.

"You must have told him about your 'discussion' with Chilsipee," he said sarcastically, trying to conceal his pain.

Many Claws smiled with slight amusement. "Yes, I told him."

Matt rose to his feet, anxious to be gone, but hesitated at the tipi entrance. "I hope for Gray Bear's sake she hasn't chosen him."

"And why is that, Riordan?"

"Because I have already made Sky my woman and she could be carrying my child. If Gray Bear insists on claiming her, I will have no choice but to fight him to the death."

Matt left the tent and swung into the saddle, not waiting for Many Claws' reaction. His emotion drove him as viciously as a teamster cracking his whip over the backs of his mules. He glanced upward at the peaks of the Wind River Mountains. He had to get to Sky before it was too late, but never had those high mountain meadows seemed so far away.

Matt heard the mournful, haunting chant long before he reached its source. It echoed eerily through the canyons and over the mountain peaks, and the sound sent cold chills rippling down his spine. The chant was sung in Shoshoni, and the female voice so full of anguish and pain clearly belonged to Red Sky.

He had heard of the Indians' death songs and he

knew she grieved at last for the loss of her family, a sorrow she had held in silence for seven years. He sensed, however, that her pain went even deeper, to a personal level. Red Sky McClellan was in the process of finding herself, her peace, and her path to the future. It was a path that, in the beginning, might be as hazy as an early morning mist in the mountains. But the way would clear with the heat and the light of the sun, and Matt intended to be the force that brought clarity.

It disturbed him that she had chosen the Shoshoni way of mourning, though. He feared it was an indication that she had turned away completely from the white ways, and that in the end she would turn away from him, as she had during those distraught moments after Welch's death, giving him no second chance to prove his love.

He rode on, wishing the plaintive wailing would stop, but it penetrated the mountains, his mind, and his soul.

When he reached the high, lonesome lake, he saw her sitting on the rocks at the top of the cliff beneath the eagle's nest. She sat like royalty in her most exquisite beaded and fringed costume of white buckskin. With head high and shoulders squared, she faced the panorama of her world below her in all its splendor and solitude. The land lay hushed and silent, seemingly waiting patiently for her to purge her heart of all sorrow and pain.

He realized in that moment that the great mountains truly belonged to Red Sky, and she to them. He had told Many Claws he would fight for her — and he would — but if he won the battle, would the outcome be what *she* wanted? And if he won, would he be wrong to try to persuade her to leave here? It might be selfish on his part. The decision should be hers. After all, a bird in a gilded cage might be lovely, but it could bring no joy to itself or the world if it had no song in its heart.

As he gazed at her exquisite form up on the cliff, and had his second doubts about what should become of her, a prickly feeling crawled down his spine.

Something was wrong.

He reached for his binoculars in his saddlebags and pulled them up to his eyes. In a snap they brought her image close enough to touch, and, in so doing, made his heart leap and cry out in astonishment and fear.

From the distance he had first thought that the black, silk length of her hair had been merely drawn back and neatly braided, but he saw now that the mesmerizing cascade had been cut off nearly as short as a man's. That initial jolt was not the worst of it, however. It was the bright streams of her blood staining her arms and the white fringes of her doeskin shift that caused him to swear and leap from the saddle. He headed toward the cliff in a near-run but had gone only a few yards when he was halted by the familiar sight of his rival stepping from the trees and into his path.

"I see you have returned, White Eyes."

Matt's hand went to his gun, even though the brave wielded no weapon. "Get out of my way, Gray Bear. I've got to get to Sky. She's going to bleed to death."

Gray Bear took a casual position against a tree that hugged a bend in the path. He folded his arms across his hairless brown chest. "No, Riordan. It is not her wrists she has slit. You could see that if you would take the time. She will not die. It is the way of the People when in mourning to slash their arms, but unless they cut too deeply, they will not die. It is their way of releasing all the grief they hold inside at the death of someone they love. And Red Sky grieves not for just one person, but for six — her family and her white friend, Monty Glassman."

Matt wouldn't be pacified. He tried to get past Gray Bear, but the Indian put a hand to his chest to hold him back. "She will be all right, Riordan. The bleeding is not great and will soon stop. Leave her to this thing she must do."

Matt's gaze locked with Gray Bear's and he saw the calm assurance in the depths of the black eyes. At last he took a calming breath, but his eyes lifted to Sky. "You'd damned well better be right."

Gray Bear scrutinized him another moment before finally removing his hand from his chest. "I am."

There were several moments of uncomfortable silence as Matt tried to contain himself. He still wanted more than anything to go to her. How the Indian could sit here and watch her hurt herself was beyond him.

"I did not think you would return, White Eyes," Gray Bear said casually. "Your purpose with her is over. All that waits for you here is death."

Matt's gaze slid to Gray Bear's sheathed knife.

Gray Bear was almost amiable, almost likeable—arrogant, but likeable. "If we fight, Gray Bear, it's you who will die."

A faint smile touched the Indian's straight lips. "In this you are mistaken, White Eyes. My love for her is great."

"Perhaps. But the love of the victor will be the greater."

Matt saw no indication that the brave wished to commence the fight immediately and sensed it would be something that would wait until Sky had completed her mourning. To take his mind from the heart-piercing tone of her voice echoing over the land, and to make the slow seconds more rapidly disappear, Matt turned his back on the brave, returned to his horse, and retrieved his horse brush and curry comb from his saddlebags. He'd ridden Soldier hard and long and the animal needed a good brushing to remove the dirt-caked sweat that had accumulated beneath the saddle blanket. He set to work while Gray Bear watched.

"Did it ever occur to you that she might not want you even if you win the battle?" Matt asked. "She might not want either one of us. She told me as much the last time we parted."

Gray Bear lifted his eyes to Red Sky's lonely figure. Her plaintive wail had gone on for hours since he'd been here, and he didn't know how long it had gone on before that. Her voice was weakening. She would not be able to continue much longer. He sadly wondered if all her pain would ever be released. His black brows drew together.

"She cannot stay here—alone."

"Why not? She's done it for seven years. Maybe it's what she wants. Maybe we should let her decide. I want her as much as you do, but I don't want her unhappy. Let it be *her* decision, Gray Bear. I'm man enough to face her answer. Are you?"

He had made it sound simple, but his heart felt as if an Indian's lance had penetrated it. If he had to ride away from this place without Sky, he knew he would ride alone for the rest of his life. He would never find another woman like her. There could be no other woman more perfectly matched to him. He'd wandered for years, working, living in loneliness. But living without her would be a loneliness deeper than even the depths of hell. If she chose Gray Bear . . . well, he didn't know how he would deal with life at all, except to convince himself that it was her happiness that was most important.

He scrutinized Gray Bear for a sign that would indicate whether he and Red Sky might have made love. But he knew the only way he would know for sure was to ask, and he couldn't bring himself to do that. He didn't want to know, for the knowledge of it would be too great a burden.

Gray Bear turned his attention back to Matt. "I think you are a coward, Riordan. You fear for your life. That is why you say what you say."

"I could have killed you once, Gray Bear, and you know it. I spared you because Sky asked it. Think about that. What if I kill you this time we do battle, and it was you she wanted all along?"

Gray Bear considered the gamble he might be

taking, the winning or losing of this woman they both loved. Matt could tell there was a great battle inside his mind. But finally he spoke with absolute assurance. "There can only be one man in Red Sky's life, Riordan. One of us must die."

From out of the Silence
Comes the beating of my Heart.

Chapter Twenty-three

The silence brought Matt from his bedroll and Gray Bear from his blanket. Red Sky's mournful wail had kept them from sleep, but it had ended so abruptly it was almost frightening.

The moon was hiding behind a strand of ghostly clouds, making it difficult to see her. But soon the clouds passed over and silvery light reflected off her white doeskins. They saw her slump, her chin nearly touching her chest. Her wrists were turned upward and were resting on her knees; her palms lay open to the sky as if waiting for something to fill their emptiness.

Matt started toward her but Gray Bear caught his arm and held him back. "She is not yet done, Riordan. She has mourned the loss of her family, but now she will seek her own path to peace from the Great Mystery."

Matt was growing impatient with the entire ritual. "My God, she's been up there for hours! Without food or water!"

"It is the way of our people. She may be there for days longer."

Matt watched her there above him. So like a goddess — or a ghost — but once again the mysterious woman who could not be touched and whose thoughts could not be fathomed. These rituals were of the Shoshoni, probably learned from her mother and Many Claws. She did them with utter dedication. The longer she stayed there in the private, spiritual realm, the farther she seemed to travel from him.

With increasing uneasiness, he lay back on his bedroll to wait.

Red Sky pulled all her awareness inward. The darkness isolated her until she felt not of the world, but of a sphere somewhere high above it. She reached out with her mind, farther and farther toward the sky, toward God, above where the eagles fly, above where the clouds roam, above where the moon floats on its invisible tether to the earth. She reached out even beyond the stars to the infinite blackness that enveloped her like a great, comforting cocoon, insulating her from everything but what was deep inside herself and deep inside the black sphere of knowledge and spiritual healing. She had never before felt such a great calm and wonderful inner peace. Nothing from the outside world could enter her mind.

Early on the third day, Red Sky collapsed. Matt grabbed his canteen and led the way up the rock slide with Gray Bear following, offering no resistance this time. They both knew if she stayed longer in her personal quest for peace, she might very well die.

They dropped to their knees on either side of her. Her breathing was shallow and the hot sun had burned her face and lips. Her hair, even though cropped off, was still as shiny and beautiful as the coat of a black cat.

Matt reached her first and lifted her head and upper body carefully to his lap, cradling her head. He touched the canteen to her lips, but the water slid from the corners of her mouth.

"Come on, Sky," he coaxed. "Drink some of it."

There was no indication that she had heard him. He and Gray Bear exchanged worried glances, afraid they might have let her go too long.

"Let me try, Riordan," Gray Bear insisted anxiously, apparently thinking he could succeed where his rival had failed.

Matt wouldn't relinquish Sky and repeatedly tried to get her to swallow the water. At last some went down her throat. She choked and began to cough, but even when the coughing subsided she couldn't seem to come back from that distant place to whence she had traveled.

"Red Sky, wake up," Gray Bear said. "Come back to us. We await you."

423

She stirred and her eyelids moved as if she were trying desperately to pull herself from a deep, drugging sleep.

"Matt?" she mumbled weakly through dry lips. "Matt? Is that you?"

"Yes, Sky, I'm here. Right here." He squeezed her hand tightly and glanced at Gray Bear. The brave sat back on his heels, a peculiar expression on his dark face. Sky turned toward Matt and he pulled her up into his arms, holding her close to his heart. Without opening her eyes she melded her body to his, not needing to see him to know it was he who held her. Matt, too, closed his eyes, and returned her fervent embrace. He said a silent prayer of thanks that she was all right. When he opened his eyes moments later, Gray Bear was gone.

He visually searched the cliff and the small meadow below and finally saw the brave sprinting across the rock slide. He watched him gather his belongings and swing onto his pony. Gray Bear looked up at him, lifted his arm in a sign of fare-well — and friendship — then rode away into the trees.

Matt didn't know why the brave had chosen not to fight, but he sensed Gray Bear would not chal-lenge him again. Had the Shoshoni considered Matt's words and decided that, ultimately, Sky's happiness preceded their own? If that was so, then Matt easily imagined the pain Gray Bear was surely feeling, and he held a degree of sympathy for his rival. But his own heart did not yet soar. He was a man of caution, and he had long ago learned never to take anything for granted. Least of all, love. Sky had only spoken his name. She had made no promises.

He lifted the canteen to her lips again. "Here, Sky," he said. "Drink some more water."

She accepted the offer this time. When she'd had a few swallows, she looked up at him with a certain wonder in her eyes that he could not recall having seen there before. It was as if a gauzy curtain had hindered her view of the world and now it had been lifted, leaving everything clearly before her for the first time. It was a look that gave his heart cause to leap with hope.

"I should have known you would not obey me, *nehaynzeh*," she whispered weakly, lifting a hand to his face. "And I am very glad you didn't because I have so much to tell you."

"I have some things to tell you, too. But they can wait. First, let's get you back to the cave. You need to rest and eat and I need to attend to your wounds."

He lifted her into his arms and she held tightly to his neck. Smiling contentedly she closed her eyes again and rested her head against his chest. Before he had reached the cave she had fallen asleep.

Red Sky came awake eight hours later to the smell of a pine hen cooking over the fire. Her vision cleared to the pleasant sight of Matt balanc-

425

ing on his haunches, jabbing at the grouse with the tines of a fork, as if by those nervous little movements alone he could make the bird cook faster.

She sat up, aware of the bandages on her arms and the smell of the yarrow Matt had used for healing. While she had slept, he had tended to her wounds just as she had once tended his.

"It smells good," she said in whispery, hoarse voice. "I'm starved."

He appeared both surprised and relieved to see her awake. He rose to his full height, unwinding his tall, lean body in such a fashion as to arouse a stirring of desire deep inside her. He had been much in her thoughts during her search for solace on the mountain. As her mind had whirled away to great reaches of the universe, it had always come back to earth and to him, and always he was there, waiting for her with open arms.

What is it you search for, Sky? he had asked over and over during her spiritual journey, calling her back repeatedly from that distant place deep in her soul where for a time she had longed to stay forever. *I'm here. I'm all you need. Don't you understand?*

"Come and join me, Sky," he said, interrupting her thoughts. "We'll eat and then we'll talk."

She laid aside the fur robe, left the pallet, and settled near the fire. He sat across from her and forked out two pieces of grouse onto a tin plate.

"It's hot," he warned needlessly, handing it to her.

She found herself slipping into the depths of his

426

blue eyes in almost the same way she had transcended earth and entered that magnificent realm beyond, where all the answers to life were awaiting those with the courage and the forbearance to seek them.

"Where's Esup?" she asked, suddenly remembering the wolf and glancing about the cave for him.

"He seemed restless. I told him to go hunt."

"And he obeyed?" she asked with mock surprise.

Matt returned her wry smile with one of his own. Happiness thrummed in his heart, almost too good to be true, but wherever that secret road she had traveled had taken her, it had brought her back to him.

"I'm second in command," he replied. "He had no choice. Now, eat, before it gets cold."

She obeyed with an impish grin. Where once she had thought her life would be shrouded in doubts and fears, she now felt as if the darkness had at last relinquished its power to the sun.

They ate in near silence, but in high awareness of each other. Red Sky was painfully conscious of how she must look and her self-consciousness was made worse by Matt's constant thoughtful perusal. She lifted a hand to the close-cropped locks to try to smooth them, but he reached across the distance, his hand closing over hers.

"It's still beautiful, Sky," he whispered, and then a smile crept into his eyes even though he tried to keep a straight face. He shrugged. "Well, maybe a little trimming here and there . . ."

His smile was contagious and she looked away, grinning shyly. "I didn't do a very good job, I guess."

"What can you expect? It was your first try."

She went back to her food, happy in the knowledge that he did not find her appearance repulsive. He continued to watch her in a sensual, hypnotizing way; watched her lips, her hands, and captured her eyes with his. She ate with practically no awareness of what she ate, so much control did his presence have over her mind. His thoughts were indiscernible, all except for one. She knew he wanted to make love to her.

He finished first and set his plate aside. Much had changed since he had come to the mountains. The past was in its proper place and she was no longer held its prisoner. Matt's job here in the mountains was done and yet he remained. Yes, for all she had said, for all she had done, he remained.

"We caught the riders," he said. "They're all in jail awaiting trial."

"Then my enemies are gone?" Her voice was soft and hopeful.

"Yes, your enemies are gone."

"I had forgotten how it felt to be free. You've made it happen, Matt, and I am grateful."

Solemnity darkened his blue eyes, making them more thoughtful than before. "What will you do now, Sky?"

It was not what she had hoped he would say, but there was an intensity in the set of his face while he awaited her answer that made her believe his love hadn't altered since he had last professed it. Once upon a time, not too long ago, she had feared his love had only been intended to keep her willing until his job had been accomplished. But he had professed it freely after Loring's death. He would have had no reason to do that if he hadn't truly meant it. She wanted him to make some overture to it now, but he remained silent on the subject. He seemed to be leaving the decision of their future up to her, and for good reason, since a few days ago she had foolishly rejected his.

Tension was strung across the distance between them like a bow taut with an arrow. Even though they'd made love, they seemed to have momentarily regressed. It was as if they would have to start over from the beginning. Now, it was not he who would try to gain her trust and seduce her. He had handed that role to her.

"What will I do?" she repeated, contemplating the question for several moments. Thoughtfully, she stood up and set her plate aside. "I'm going to do something I've wanted to do for seven years, Matt. I'm going to bathe in the lake in broad daylight without fear of becoming someone's target."

She flashed him a smile, knowing her answer was not what he had wanted to hear any more than his question was what she had wanted to hear. Still, she proceeded, because for as cold as the mountain lake was, she sensed it would be just the thing to break the ice between them. Even though they had made love, a barrier had come up when she had run away from him.

429

She went to the corner that contained her clothing. In a basket she placed some soap, a towel, a hairbrush, and a plain suit of buckskins to replace the white doeskins she wore. She moved to the cave's narrow doorway. At the entrance she glanced over her shoulder at him, affecting an innocent expression. "I may need some help washing my back. Would you be willing?"

He rose to his feet slowly, likewise affecting the reluctant movement of one who is asked to do a most unpleasant chore. But a lambent glow in his eyes told her he easily read her suggestive message and was truly more than willing to comply. "I think I could give you a hand," he replied nonchalantly.

She ran lightly from the cave and down over the rock slide, unable to completely cast aside the feeling of wariness she had lived with for so long. It was ingrained in her to glance over the cirque of the mountains, checking for predator movement of any kind. Maybe in time she would be able to forget. . . .

At the lake she set her things on a rock and lifted her hands to the rawhide strings that held her garment closed up the front. She heard Matt's boots crunch on the small pebbles behind her. When he ran his hands up her arms to her shoulders she couldn't stop the glorious thrill that cascaded over her body. How could she have been so foolish as to tell him to leave her life? What would she have done if he had obeyed?

"Let me do it for you, Sky."

She turned to him slowly, not wanting to appear too eager for the pleasures he could give her. She lifted her eyes to his sultry, mesmerizing gaze. She stood as stately as the forest's greatest pine and waited in breathless anticipation while his hands lingered alongside her face; waited while they glided down along her neck and over her collarbone; waited until they found the rawhide strings. Oh, the sweet agony of his slowness!

Only when he loosened the doeskin blouse and laid it open did his gaze drift away from her eyes and settle on the swell of her breasts and the dark shadow of her cleavage. He cast his hat into the grass and bent his blond head. Sky breathed in sharply as his lips found the soft fullness of her breasts even though the leather ties crisscrossed her bosom and caused an inconvenient obstruction. His hands followed his kisses and moved lower to cup her breasts, one in each palm. She gripped his shoulders for support because she suddenly felt too weak to stand.

"You are beautiful, Sky," he murmured against her flesh. "The most beautiful woman I have ever known."

Had he said the words before? It didn't matter because she wanted to hear them again and again for the rest of her life. And she would have told him this, but she couldn't speak. She could only need and want and yearn for his kisses to continue. The heat in her loins grew in sweet, pulsing intensity. At last she managed some words. "I don't know if I'm beautiful, Matt, but you make me feel as if I am. You make me feel very much like a desirable woman."

He straightened and she lifted her hands to his chest, urgently undoing the buttons on his vest and shirt. She forced herself to slow her movements, to prolong the anticipation of their joining. She slid the shirt and vest off his shoulders, down his arms, and finally over his wrists until the clothing lay discarded on the summer grass near his hat, and he stood before her seminaked.

She leaned into him, laying kisses to the thick mat of hair on his brawny chest. His hands encircled her waist, slipping beneath the tunic to find the heat of naked flesh.

Slowly and purposefully, they continued removing each other's clothing until they stood before each other completely naked. The sunlight warmed their skin to each other's caresses, then Matt took her hand and led her into the water, not knowing or caring if anyone besides the forest animals watched.

The cold water momentarily chased away the heat of their passion.

"Damn, I'd forgotten how cold this friggin' lake was!" he exclaimed.

Red Sky's laughter bubbled forth as freely and as lovely as a song. "You've never liked my lake, have you?"

He suddenly forgot the cold and felt only her body against his, warming it. Her arm encircled his waist in the way of a woman who is comfortable with her possession.

Indeed, it *was* her lake. Just as the mountains were hers—and the trees and the rivers and the sky. It was all hers and a part of her. It was that wild, untamed aura surrounding her that had made her so intriguing to him from the very beginning. How could he possibly take her away from here, or even ask her to go? How could he risk changing her and losing the sweet and innocent Red Sky he had come to love with a passion he had never dreamed he could be capable of feeling? Maybe he should never tell her what was in the telegram, but just toss it away and stay here in this paradise with her forever.

He found the soap and slowly began to lather her back and buttocks, enjoying the sleek, sensual smoothness of her skin. "I like your lake fine, Sky McClellan," he finally said in response to her question. "I just wish it was heated."

Her laughter was sweet music to his ears again, but she soon became lost in his touch, just as he became lost by touching her. He moved behind her and pressed his body to hers, felt her firm buttocks against his hard male flesh. He put his arms around her and she closed her eyes while he massaged her breasts and stomach with his soapy hands. She tilted her head back until it rested against his chest, and to steady herself she gripped his thighs behind her and held on to him. He saw her lips part and her breathing become more intense and erratic. He felt the fire she felt, all the way to his toes.

"Oh, you are a *pohagande,*" she murmured with a smile.

433

He kissed her temple. "My Shoshoni fails me. I hope a *pohagande* is a good thing."

She laughed lightly. "I said you are a shaman."

"And why would you call me a shaman? Surely I don't remind you of Many Claws?"

"I called you a shaman because your hands are filled with magic."

His laughter was as light as his heart. "You've paid me the ultimate compliment. Does that mean you want me to continue my magic?"

"Oh, yes, Great One." She turned her head and kissed his throat. "Yes, indeed."

He explored her body in an erotic, leisurely fashion. She took the same path of knowledge in learning his until they no were longer aware of the icy waters of the mountain lake, but only the heat of desire for each other.

She led him from the water and to the grass, but he lifted her into his arms. "Not here, Sky," he murmured. "From the very beginning I have wanted to make love to you next to the fire, on the furs, in that wild and seductive dwelling. Come with me to the cave."

Red Sky studied this man who had so miraculously come into her life and who had so thoroughly changed both it and her. Her heart swelled with love. Tenderly she kissed him, touched him, felt she could not get enough of him.

"I didn't know you found the cave seductive."

"It was only that way when you were there."

"Then let's go to the cave."

Carrying their clothes, they hurried to the rock

434

slide and clambered up over the rocks, laughing like small children in play. At the cave's entrance, Matt twirled her toward him, handed her his bundle of clothing, then lifted her into his arms. He carried her through the cave's narrow doorway to the cool, semidarkness within and to the pallet she had given to him. It had been hers before he had come, but now it would be theirs, together.

Matt lowered her to the furs. He left her just long enough to place sticks on the fire. The flames leaped up onto the dry wood, crackling and bringing more light to the interior.

Matt returned to the pallet and stood before Sky, who was now kneeling on the bed of furs. She lifted her hands to his bare legs. While their gazes held, she ran her hands up his naked thighs to the flat of his stomach and finally to the bulk of his manhood. He inhaled sharply at her exquisite caress. She pulled him toward her and her kisses followed in the wake of her hands.

He held on to her shoulders, burying his hands in the black thickness of her short hair. She took his hands in hers and drew him down onto the furs next to her. He lay on his back and she rose above him, giving to him the unselfish love he had given to her. They became flesh against flesh, heated by the fire, the furs, and felicity. There was no greater, no more glorious splendor than that of the unselfish giving and taking of two people in love.

When he knew he was nearly lost to the fulfillment of his desire, he rolled her to her back. She moved like a panther, slow and sensual, lifting her softness to his hardness, claiming him as her fervor grew. He was lost to the silky touch of her fingers on his body, drawing him deeper into the velvety vortex of her being.

As they built the flames higher with need and with love, their shadows rose and fell against the ancient rock wall of their dwelling, twining and separating in rhythmic lyricism, like the words to a song. They gave, they took, they shared, and at last they became one.

Red Sky cried out her pleasure, cleaving Matt to her in body and soul, in heart and mind. She understood clearly in that instant the true meaning of the dream of the eagles. It had haunted her in her dreams and again in her quest for spiritual peace on the mountain. It was none of the things she had originally thought it to be.

The tumultuous clouds racing overhead had merely been the symbol of her indecision about the future and about who she was. It had been the symbol of the conclusion of previously unfinished business. With the deaths of Welch and Loring, she had been able to at last close the door on the past and choose the path for her future. The joining of the eagles was not the death of one, nor the deceit and betrayal by the other. It meant that she would become one with her mate, Matt Riordan, in ways that far transcended physical communion.

She had found her peace with God and with herself during her lonely and painful sojourn on the cliff. She had decided then that she had no choice but to leave the mountains. Now the fear and apprehension that still lingered with that decision was gone. Just as the eagle had vanished, so had her fear. The eagle had not really vanished, it had merely become stronger because it had joined with the other. Their two strengths together would enable them to weather all storms of life.

She understood the way of things now; the way of love, the way of life, the way of fire. And if this man still wanted her, she would go with him wherever he chose, and to whatever ends.

She propped herself up on her elbow and studied his rugged face, touching her lips to his. "You are my life, Matt Riordan," she whispered. "You are everything to me."

The wonder she had felt at her union with him seemed reflected in his eyes. He touched her as she did him, neither having enough of the touching.

"I hoped to hear you say that, Sky, but I feared I never would. I thought I would have to walk away from these mountains without you. I was afraid you'd go to Gray Bear."

A look of surprise crossed her face. "After what we've shared? Matt, don't you know Gray Bear could never be more than a friend to me?"

"He wanted you for his wife. He was here while you were alone on the cliff."

She became alarmed. "Did you fight again?"

"No." He told her what had transpired between them.

Her alarm changed to a look of sadness. "I wish only the best for Gray Bear," she said. "It hurts me that I have hurt him. But I can't change the way I feel about you. I want to be your wife, Matt. That is, if you still want me to be."

He took her hand in his and pulled her into his arms. "If I didn't want you, I wouldn't be here now, Sky. My love for you will never change except to grow stronger."

"I was afraid to accept your love. I hope you can understand that. I was afraid of so many things, and after Loring told me it was because of me that my family died, I couldn't accept the idea that anyone could—or should—love me. Beyond accepting that burden of guilt, one of my greatest fears was leaving these mountains where I had found a sanctuary. I knew I would have to if I was to marry you. In Rawlins and in Cheyenne, and again in Lander, I truly wondered if I could ever return to the white man's world. I felt I didn't belong there anymore. I felt that the white people would always treat me as an outcast. I'm still not sure that they won't, but I'll make a world of my own, wherever we go, just as I have here. My destiny lies with you, Matt, and I'll follow you wherever you go."

"But we don't have to leave here, Sky. I'm willing to stay here with you as long as you want to."

"No. This is not the place to raise our children. It's only a place for you and me to return to now and again, to remember these wonderful moments, and to relive them."

A smile curved his lips. "I like that idea. This will be our secret place. Just yours and mine."

"But before we go," she said earnestly. "I have one request to make."

Matt took her hand in his and gave it a reassuring squeeze. "I'll do whatever you ask, honey. You know that."

She took a deep breath and plunged on. "Then, will you take me back to Long Moon Valley? I must see it one last time. I must see it in peace and without fear in my heart — the way I did when I was a child."

Take my hand to journey's end,
And we shall sing our song.

Chapter Twenty-four

Tiny spirals of smoke rose from the huge mound of burned and charred timbers that had once been the house that Charles McClellan built.

Red Sky brought her horse to a stop to gaze at the scene before her. Not just the house was gone but that entire portion of her life associated with it. She supposed it was that aspect alone that was the hardest thing for her to accept. In the mountains, time had stopped and had seemingly remained constant. The seasons had changed but nothing else had, at least not to the degree that one would actually recognize the change. She had clung to the idea that when the time was right she could turn around, go back home, and find everything as she had left it. And, as long as she did that, the past and her family and Long Moon Valley would remain the same. Now she knew it had been only a dream that had given her false hope. At least it had been a dream that had sustained her.

She nudged the horse and rode into the yard. Matt followed, as did Esup, who had returned from his hunt and had been allowed to join them this time. As they advanced toward the house, there was only the movement of the three of them and no sound but the clip-clop of the horses' hooves on the packed soil.

"The hired men must have left," Sky said, glancing at the quiet bunkhouse and empty corrals.

Matt nodded. "Yes, I guess with their boss dead they didn't see much point in staying to see what would happen to the place."

"Oh, Matt," she sighed, looking at it all wistfully. "Mama and Daddy worked so hard and put so much into this place. I wonder what's going to happen to it now."

They drew their horses to a halt again. Matt rested his forearms on the saddle horn. "I guess that depends on you, Sky. You see, after I turned those riders over to the law, I sent a telegram to Elizabeth to tell her that her father was dead. I asked her what she wanted to do about the McClellan place since she was her father's closest heir that I knew of. The ranch, luckily, wasn't in Welch's name."

Sky's straight back stiffened even more. "You contacted Elizabeth?"

"Yes, I did. And she answered me."

Matt reached into his vest pocket and removed a folded slip of paper. "I would have told you sooner, but the time didn't seem right."

He handed the slip of paper to her. She looked

441

away, struck with a sudden stab of jealousy. She didn't want to touch the telegram. Even though Elizabeth hadn't written it herself, the words on it were hers. This was a woman Matt had loved once. A woman he had made love to more times than he had made love to her. It was hard to think of him in someone else's arms, doing the passionate things he had done with her. He had asked her to marry him, but why had he contacted Elizabeth?

With shaking hands and a painful fear in her heart she finally pulled the telegram from between his fingers and opened it. Her heart pounded so viciously, she felt light-headed. She began to read:

"Matt Riordan STOP I'm sorry to hear of my father's death STOP I cannot come to Wyoming STOP Yes, I will sell you the McClellan property for the price you offered STOP I don't want it STOP I will send a letter of written guarantee STOP My lawyers will handle everything STOP It is the least I can do for hurting you STOP Best Wishes STOP Elizabeth Frazer STOP"

Red Sky's hands were shaking worse now than before. Tears pooled in her eyes and spilled onto her face. The words on the telegram blurred.

"It's yours, Sky," Matt said. *"Ours*—if you want it to be. We'll make our life here. Raise our children here."

She carefully refolded the telegram and wiped at the tears. She looked out across the valley, feeling the old love for this place return and lighten her heart. She slid from her horse's back and lifted her hand to Matt. He stepped to the ground and she went into his arms, weeping against his chest.

"Oh, Matt! You did this for me!"

"Yes, Sky. I took the chance you'd marry me."

"But what of your work with the agency?" She looked up at him with concerned eyes. "You can't just walk away, can you?"

He smiled and pressed the tears from her cheeks with his thumbs. "It was always just a job for me, Sky. Staying here with you in Long Moon Valley would be my life. I never dreamed Elizabeth would sell it to me, I could only hope, especially on such short notice. But as you can see by the telegram, she didn't want it. She didn't even want to come out here to settle the estate. It should have been yours all along. We could have taken it to court and tried to get your legal claim back, but I didn't want to take the chance of your losing it a second time.

"I've always wanted a place like this," he continued with the longing very evident in his eyes and his voice. "A place where I could take root and raise children. I need children, Sky. It's as if I need to make up for something I lost, or maybe something I never had when I was a kid. I want to love a child the way my mother never loved me. When I met you, I knew you were the woman to have my children and share my life. But you've got to be honest with me. If it's going to be too difficult for you to live here—after what happened—I'll understand. We'll go to another place. I have the money. I've never had much to spend it on so I've just invested it over the years."

More tears of joy spilled out onto her cheeks, but she didn't bother to wipe them away. "Oh, Matt. Both of our pasts lie in this place. I have learned

443

from living in the mountains that no matter where a person goes, he goes with his memories. We can't run from the past, you and I. So we will make new memories here. Good memories."

She drew his head down to hers and kissed him slowly, ardently, starting yearnings inside them both. She reveled in the feel and taste of him, and in the knowledge that he loved her and understood her — possibly better than she understood herself. She reveled, too, in the knowledge that her love was secure with him. They would love each other with a passion that would never die. She had reached the stars and beyond, and now she knew their love was written in the stars, truly meant to be.

She lifted her lips from his. "I love you, Matt Riordan. So very much. Many years ago I dreamed of a tall, handsome stranger with golden hair, riding into Long Moon Valley. He was there because he had come for me. You were that man, *nehaynzeh*."

"Then our time has come."

"Yes, it has come."

Suddenly her face took on the light of a child's who is eager to begin a new game. "Run with me to the top of that hill!" she insisted playfully, tugging at his hand. "We'll decide where our new house will be! I'll race you!"

Laughing, she ran away from him on feet as fleet as those of a deer. Esup merrily followed her, not wanting to miss out on the fun.

Matt caught the spirit and put speed to his own feet, but he knew full well he could never catch her. He knew also that it didn't matter because sooner or later she would let him. He preferred to stay behind her anyway so he could watch her, so he could keep her in his vision all the while and enjoy the wonder of her beauty, and witness the happiness and delight that was finally hers. There was a great satisfaction, too, in knowing that he had helped her find that happiness.

Halfway up the hill she turned and called down, "Come on, slowpoke! Come on! I'll have to make you some moccasins for running!"

Grinning, he halted to catch his breath and watch her run the remainder of the way. At the top, she stretched her arms to the sky, seemingly claiming all the world as her own. Soon the sweet strains of joyous song filtered down over the valley in a voice pure and crystal clear, just as it had been years ago.

Beautiful, reckless, and carefree — Sky McClellan had returned home. It was a good feeling to know he was the one who had brought her here and who had helped put the song back in her heart.

But he had come home, too. Little could he have known when he set out in search of Red Sky that he would not only find her, but he would find himself as well. It had been a hard journey of many miles, many years, and many heartaches. But he would gladly do it all over again — and again — for the love of Red Sky McClellan.

Author's Note

The Shoshoni words used in this book come mainly from the "Shoshone Thesaurus" compiled by Malinda Tidzump of the Wind River Shoshone, and published at The Summer Institute of Linguistics, University of North Dakota, in 1971. Other Shoshoni words come from "The Shoshone Language" by George W. Hill, 1877, and "Vocabulary of the Utah and Shoshone or Snake Dialects," by D. B. Huntington, Indian interpreter, 1872.

The verses at the beginning of each chapter are my own, composed in the spirit of authentic Native American poetry.

LS

PASSION BLAZES IN A ZEBRA HEARTFIRE!

COLORADO MOONFIRE (3730, $4.25/$5.50)
by Charlotte Hubbard

Lila O'Riley left Ireland, determined to make her own way in America. Finding work and saving pennies presented no problem for the independent lass; locating love was another story. Then one hot night, Lila meets Marshal Barry Thompson. Sparks fly between the fiery beauty and the lawman. Lila learns that America is the promised land, indeed!

MIDNIGHT LOVESTORM (3705, $4.25/$5.50)
by Linda Windsor

Dr. Catalina McCulloch was eager to begin her practice in Los Reyes, California. On her trip from East Texas, the train is robbed by the notorious masked bandit known as Archangel. Before making his escape, the thief grabs Cat, kisses her fervently, and steals her heart. Even at the risk of losing her standing in the community, Cat must find her mysterious lover once again. No matter what the future might bring . . .

MOUNTAIN ECSTASY (3729, $4.25/$5.50)
by Linda Sandifer

As a divorced woman, Hattie Longmore knew that she faced prejudice. Hoping to escape wagging tongues, she traveled to her brother's Idaho ranch, only to learn of his murder from long, lean Jim Rider. Hattie seeks comfort in Rider's powerful arms, but she soon discovers that this strong cowboy has one weakness . . . marriage. Trying to lasso this wandering man's heart is a challenge that Hattie enthusiastically undertakes.

RENEGADE BRIDE (3813, $4.25/$5.50)
by Barbara Ankrum

In her heart, Mariah Parsons always believed that she would marry the man who had given her her first kiss at age sixteen. Four years later, she is actually on her way West to begin her life with him . . . and she meets Creed Deveraux. Creed is a rough-and-tumble bounty hunter with a masculine swagger and a powerful magnetism. Mariah finds herself drawn to this bold wilderness man, and their passion is as unbridled as the Montana landscape.

ROYAL ECSTASY (3861, $4.25/$5.50)
by Robin Gideon

The name Princess Jade Crosse has become hated throughout the kingdom. After her husband's death, her "advisors" have punished and taxed the commoners with relentless glee. Sir Lyon Beauchane has sworn to top this evil tyrant and her cruel ways. Scaling the castle wall, he meets this "wicked" woman face to face . . . and is overpowered by love. Beauchane learns the truth behind Jade's imprisonment. Together they struggle to free Jade from her jailors and from her inhibitions.

Available wherever paperbacks are sold, or order direct from the Publisher. Send cover price plus 50¢ per copy for mailing and handling to Zebra Books, Dept. 4127, 475 Park Avenue South, New York, N.Y. 10016. Residents of New York and Tennessee must include sales tax. DO NOT SEND CASH. For a free Zebra/Pinnacle catalog please write to the above address.